Bella Zilfa Spencer

Right and Wrong

Or, She told the truth at last. With other stories.

Bella Zilfa Spencer

Right and Wrong
Or, She told the truth at last. With other stories.

ISBN/EAN: 9783744747967

Printed in Europe, USA, Canada, Australia, Japan

Cover: Foto ©Andreas Hilbeck / pixelio.de

More available books at **www.hansebooks.com**

Right and Wrong;

OR,

SHE TOLD THE TRUTH AT LAST.

WITH OTHER STORIES.

By BELLA Z. SPENCER,

AUTHOR OF "TRIED AND TRUE;" "ORA, THE LOST WIFE,"
ETC., ETC.

SPRINGFIELD, MASS.:
W. J. HOLLAND & CO.
1871.

INDEX TO CONTENTS.

RIGHT AND WRONG.

1*

WOMAN IN THE WAR.

THE PRISONER'S CHILD.

PRESENTIMENTS.

THE COQUETTE'S FATE.

Right and Wrong.

CHAPTER I.

MUCH IN LITTLE.

There was a stir, followed by profound silence in the village school-room. The new master, notwithstanding a most kind and good-natured face, was about to prove himself master, indeed, of that little world where the small people had hitherto governed themselves according to their inclinations, and decidedly mischief-loving propensities. There was something terrible, now, in the dark flashing eyes and upraised hand of the master—that slender hand, grasping a rod yielding as willow, but strong as steel. The little sinner under the threatening instrument, looked up with flinching eyes, and flesh that crept, in momentary dread of the blow.

"I give you one last chance of saving yourself from a severe punishment," said the man, in deep, suppressed tones. "You understand me, John Truslow, and must learn this day that I mean precisely what I say. Are you sorry for being disrespectful and disobedient?"

One moment the boy hesitated and shrank more visibly under the rod; then he answered with a brave, clear ring in his voice:

"No, sir, I am not."

That was enough. Blows, thick and fast, fell upon the shoulders, covered only by a light linen, for he had been commanded to remove his coat, and stood in his shirt-sleeves. Some of the children covered their eyes and sobbed; others set their teeth and looked on horror-stricken, while a few sprang to their feet, too excited to remain in their places. Then there was a sharp, sudden cry, accompanied by an action which electrified both teacher and scholars. A very slight girl, of ten years, darted into the middle of the room, and stamping her foot, imperiously shouted:

"Stop, sir! You are cruel, cruel!"

Mr. Garton dropped his hand and looked at the girl, then back at the boy, writhing in pain, and drenched with the crimson tide freely flowing from his lacerated shoulders. This it was which had caused such horror among the scholars, and made one of them utterly to forget herself. He understood it at a glance, but knew too well the value of power to risk it now by yielding an inch, though his own heart was tender, in defiance of his anger; and his eye shrank from contemplating what he had done. It had not been his wish to be quite so severe. Passion had betrayed him into it. Yet he would turn this to use.

"Miss Prince will resume her seat, and await punishment for rebellious and unbecoming conduct."

The passion of the child sank under his severe, freezing tone, and she returned to her desk, awed into silence. Her excitement had reached a turning-point when she gave utterance to those words, and his commanding manner did the rest. Humiliated, and filled with apprehension for what was to come, she bowed her head upon the desk and sat still.

"John Truslow, resume your coat," continued Mr. Garton, "and stand beside me until school is dismissed."

John obeyed readily, but managed to make an ugly grimace while his back was turned from the master, which action failed to produce the desired effect. No one was disposed to laugh, then, before the pallor had left their faces, or the tears could dry upon their cheeks. So he stood up behind Mr. Garton and dropped his eyes gravely.

"Before I dismiss the school, I desire to say to my pupils that I am sorry to have been forced to use such severe measures with any one placed under my care. But this must be fully understood—I will have obedience and respect. I have come here to do you good, and require only that the rules laid down shall be strictly observed. I am still more sorry that John Truslow should have been the first to force me into so painful a position, because he had been represented to me as the worst boy in town, and I had made up my mind, when I looked into his face, that my informers must have been mistaken."

John sent a glance of surprise to Mr. Garton's face, and a peculiar expression came into his eyes.

The gentleman met it with a calm, steady gaze, but continued :

"My rules are simple and plain; and I took the greatest care to impress upon every one present my intention of having them strictly observed at the beginning. John has chosen to break two of them, and you have seen the consequence. Let this be the last time I shall have anything to do so painful. I do not want to rule you by fear, however. If you do what is required of you, no friend will be so kind, or love you so dearly as myself."

The words, spoken in an earnest and sorrowful voice, made a visible impression upon the school. Mr. Garton deliberately scanned each little face, and concluded his wisest course would be to say no more. As he took his seat, the boy who had just been punished, stepped out before him, and asked respectfully:

"Please, sir, may I speak ? "

" Yes."

" Well, sir, I want to say that I am now sorry for being disrespectful to you. But it was not the whipping that made me sorry."

" What then ? "

" What you have just said, sir. I was wrong to disobey you ; but it was fun to do it, and I would not say I was sorry for it, when I wasn't."

" Not even to escape a whipping?" asked the master, curiously.

" No, sir ; I never told a lie in my life, and I am not a coward. Besides, I've got used to being whipped, both for my own faults, and for what other boys do."

"Very well. You can stand aside now. I accept your apology, hoping that in future we may understand each other better."

John bowed, and without glancing around the school as usual, became occupied with his book. During the remainder of the afternoon the most perfect order reigned, though the child at the desk never lifted her head, nor was John permitted to sit down. At four o'clock the little band was set free, and evidently escaped with much joy, casting sly glances at their companion, as they went. John departed with the others, and was the center of attraction as they turned their steps homeward.

"I say, John, ain't he a stunner?" began one of the older boys, eagerly. "He made all my hair rise on my head, when he got up there! Such eyes as he has, when he is mad! And then, don't he lay it on to a fellow, heavy?"

John took out his knife and deliberately cut a stick, which he whittled as he walked along. The children waited to hear what he had to say.

"He's a regular brick!" came out at last, rather stunningly, from the boy. "I like him, and I don't mean to be half so bad as I have been. He suits me."

The children laughed, and the first speaker continued:

"You don't mean to be so bad, 'cause you don't dare to. He would whip every drop of blood from your body before he'd give in. I saw that in quick time."

John's lips curled.

"You know I ain't afraid of being whipped. I've taken many a one for other boys, and two or three for you, Charley Turner. But I like him because he means what he says, and won't fool with us. We never had a teacher that we couldn't badger into anything. Remember how many we have driven from the place. Mr. Garton won't stand trifling."

"He beat you like a dog," said Charley. "If he was to do so to me, my father would not let me go to school to him."

"Well, if you don't mind him, he *will* do it; so look out, if you want to get any good out of him. For my part, I think we ought to set to and try and learn all we can. He knows a great deal, Mr. Prince says, and I don't see the use in spending so much time and money without getting something for it. We can't have fun as we have had with other teachers, so we had better make up our minds to get knowledge, and be men, not muffs, all our lives."

"Hurrah! here's a go!" shouted Richard May, swinging his cap. "John Truslow, the worst boy in Princeton, has turned preacher. I expect we'll all be turned into regular saints in short order, now that John has found his master."

"I say he's a trump," put in Charley again, in his defense. "If John is bad, he is never mean. He don't tell lies, and he ain't no coward; neither does he abuse littler boys than he is. He stands up fair and square, and when he is wrong, he ain't afraid to say so. You have no right to badger him."

A warm discussion now rose between the two boys, and John left them abruptly, to argue his cause to their hearts' content. Whistling softly, still at work upon his stick, he took a little by-street and soon disappeared. The other children separated singly and in pairs, till the crowd was dispersed.

In the meantime the teacher and his erring pupil who still awaited punishment, were alone in the school-room. Mr. Garton patiently allowed every child to get beyond hearing, and a profound silence to fall upon the place. He watched the sunbeams receding from the oaken floor; she sat still, her face hidden by her heavy black hair.

"Geraldine," he said at length, and softly.

"Sir," without rising.

"Come to me."

She got up slowly, put back her hair, and confronted him with a pallid face. His hand caught hers, and drew the little figure to his knee, where he placed her gravely.

"I threatened to punish you," he began, "and I must do it; not as I punished John Truslow, for open and deliberate defiance of my authority, but in a manner befitting your offense."

"Indeed, sir, I am very, very sorry, and deserve to be punished. Yet it seemed so dreadful, and made me so wild with pain, I forgot myself. If it had been to save my life, I could not have helped it."

"It is more than possible that you mistake yourself, I think. You did not take one moment to reflect that it was not your place to chide a grown-up person, and your teacher. I am grieved, mortified and disappointed in you. Above all others I had depended upon you to help me keep harmony and peace in the school, and here I am forced to punish you amongst the first offenders, and before the first week has ended."

Tears which had refused to come through all the pain of the afternoon, now rose and flowed freely. Bowing her face upon her hands, she sobbed as if her little heart would break.

"Do you think, child, I have not tried to understand you, for your own welfare? For one month I have been in your father's house, and in this time I have made you a study. I know that you are high-tempered and impulsive; that you are sensitive to a high degree; also, that you are truthful, honest and kind. What I did not know of you was that you could be capable of doing as you did to-day—springing up like a little fury, stamping your foot at me, and commanding me to stop! More than that, you took it upon yourself to judge me by calling me cruel before the whole school."

"Oh, sir, you hurt me!" sobbed the child, "a great deal worse than you hurt John. I could not help it, then; it seemed as if every blow fell upon me ; but it was the sight of the blood that made me forget myself."

For awhile both were silent, Mr. Garton's thoughts were complicated. Geraldine evidently had something else upon her mind besides her own fate, which finally came out, much to the gentleman's surprise.

"I am sorry for John Truslow, always."

"And why, pray?"

"Because people have made him bad by charging him with every bad thing that is done and punishing him for it. Mamma used to say they would harden him into a villain, and all because he was naturally a bold, merry, mischief-loving fellow, who only needed proper treatment to make him superior to any other in town. His father drinks and abuses him, and his mother never had any control over anybody. It began by making these people despise and ill-treat their child, and he would always be even with those who abused him. Then they took to getting him punished, till finally there was not a bad thing done in Princeton that was not laid to his charge, whether he did it or not. Mamma used to cry about it, and say it was enough to make any boy utterly reckless."

Mr. Garton sat still, allowing her to talk on as long as she would; and from her words he gleaned a whole volume of meaning. They decided him to look more closely into the character of the little "scape-goat," against whom everybody had warned him. If Mrs. Prince had defended him, there was reason for it beyond what he had yet seen. She was a lady of remarkably clear judgment and justice of disposition, a part of which had descended to her daughter. Geraldine had loved her mother with an idolizing devotion, and seemed never to forget one word of what she had heard her utter, quoting her actions and opinions as the highest and holiest authority by which her life was guided.

"Doubtless your mother was right," said Mr. Garton, at length, "and I will try in future to correct some of the many errors existing here. But I want you to tell me what she would have thought of her daughter, could she have seen her actions to-day?"

"O, she would have been overwhelmed with grief! Pray, pray don't speak of it any more! Whip me as you did John, if you like, but don't talk about it any more."

"Get your hat and we will go home."

She obeyed him, and yet lingered in going out.

"What is it, Geraldine?"

"I am so ashamed, so sorry for what I have done! Won't you say you forgive me, before we go?"

"No, dear; not yet. I have not punished you sufficiently."

She stepped out and he followed, closing and locking the door. He did not put out his hand to her as usual, and though she walked close at his side, the loving familiarity that had existed between them since his coming appeared to have been suddenly lost. Her eyes brimmed, and her little throat swelled achingly with sobs pride could not let her give vent to.

The school-house stood upon the border of a beautiful woodland, and a broad field lay between it and the village. They crossed this silently, passed up the straight main street to a large stone house on the hill at the opposite end, and entered. By this time a new terror had restored Geraldine's courage. She caught Mr. Garton's hand imploringly.

"Please do not tell papa of me!"

"I must," he answered, gently, but with an inflexible purpose in his tone. "The faults of children should never be concealed from their parents. We shall find him in the library. Come."

Mr. Prince was seated before a bright fire, a favorite book in his hand, when the young man entered, leading Geraldine. He looked up, and seeing that something unusual had occurred, asked what was the matter. Mr. Garton deliberately stated that he had found it necessary to punish very severely one of his scholars, and that Miss Prince had flown into a passion, ordered him to desist, and constituted herself his judge. Mr. Prince looked shocked, and the child ready to drop with shame and distress.

" The offense being against me, her teacher, I presume you will deem it best to leave her wholly in my hands," he concluded.

" By all means!" was the grave response.

Mr. Garton bowed and led Geraldine from the room and across the hall to the foot of the broad staircase. There he paused.

"You must go to your room, and not think of joining us as usual this evening. Your supper will be sent up to you. The only thing I shall give you to do is the task of examining yourself and reflecting upon the talk we had last Sunday about self-government. I told you then that it was the imperative law controlling the wise and good."

Without another word he left her then, and she crept sobbing up the stairway, entered her own room and threw herself prostrate upon the floor.

Poor child! Her punishment was more terrible for her than all the blows that had fallen upon him for whose sake she suffered. Mr. Garton knew it, and for this reason chose to leave her for a little while entirely to herself. Still he was not wholly wise in his course, since it was not possible for him to comprehend the character of his little pupil under all circumstances, and he might not gain the desired result from this rigid and cruel course of action. Cruel it was, but not intentionally so. Between the firm, strong man and this child had sprung up a strangely tenacious and peculiar friendship—because, perhaps, he had many childlike qualities, and she many that might be called womanly. Yet it was not in the nature of things that there should be a perfect sympathy between them. Without this sympathy, how was it possible for him to judge the effect upon her of his hard code of government. He meant it for the best, having at heart her earnest good; and in seeking to establish it through his own judgment, overreached himself!

It was not natural that the two gentlemen could forget the child through all that long evening, as they sat chatting in the library, for her accustomed chair was empty, and they missed the fair little face and intelligent eyes. But they purposely avoided speaking of her—the teacher reluctant to allude to her punishment, the parent throwing into his young friend's hands the whole responsibility of his charge, with a determination not to interfere. Mr. Garton's wholesome rule was greatly needed in Princeton; Mr. Prince had been the first to propose and induce his coming, and he would not be the first to put himself in the way of his chances to do good by questioning the wisdom or justice of his course. So it happened that while Geraldine wept, and writhed upon the floor in her disgrace and wretchedness, her name was not once mentioned below, except by the servants, who secretly murmured against the "hard young master," of whom they stood in awe while they liked him.

Mr. Garton's room, for the sake of convenience, had been appointed him in conjunction with the library, so that he had only to throw open a side door and enter it after bidding good-night to his friend and patron. Then he sat down, leaning his head upon his hand, when the glow of a pleasant little fire flashed across his features. The nights at Princeton were nearly always chilly, even in summer time, and the young man had a great love for the little sparkle and glow upon the hearth which made the room so cheerful. He sighed now, thinking of his pupil, who dearly loved to be allowed to sit beside him and talk in their strangely familiar way, after study hours. Geraldine was in nothing like other girls of her age, and never retired until she chose to go of her own free will. Many things were more singular at Prince Hill than this, as we shall see in time. It was not so very odd, however, that an only daughter, made motherless in her sixth year, should have had her own way in everything all her life; and this thought gave a more serious import to the punishment he had inflicted upon her, when Mr. Garton had time for more quiet reflection.

Suddenly the young man withdrew his glance from the tiny heap of ruddy coals, and looked up to see the object of his thoughts only a little way from him, standing with her hands upon the back of a high chair, and her burning glance fixed with a strange, fierce glitter upon his face.

"Geraldine! is it possible that you are here!—and at ten o'clock—nay, it is almost eleven! I thought you asleep."

She did not seem to heed his surprise, and was intent only upon giving expression to her own feelings. Her words, uttered in a clear, bitter tone, startled him.

"I felt ashamed and sorry to have been rude to you, and I begged you to forgive me. If it had been my mother, she would have drawn me to her bosom, and kissed me; and then I should have felt glad and happy, and would have resolved never again to pain her. I would have been able to lie down in my little bed and sleep, like a good child. But you refuse to forgive me! You shut me up in my room with my miserable shame and angry thoughts, and think to subdue me. You cannot do it! You are cruel and unkind, and you make me feel too wicked to think of anything good. If you treat me this way when I feel so badly, I shall hate you, for I do not deserve to be treated so. I spoke the truth!"

"Geraldine, what is the matter with you?" he cried in amazement. "This cannot be my gentle little friend, with whom I have been so happy. Come here and let me talk seriously with you."

"No," she answered stubbornly, "I am not gentle—I cannot be, when you are unjust. I did speak the truth—you were cruel to whip poor John Truslow so dreadfully, because he was honest enough to speak out and say he was not sorry when he was not. If he had lied and said he was, you would have let him go, and he'd have done the same thing again. But he told the truth like a brave boy, and took a beating for it. Then when I spoke you punished me too. I *couldn't* help it, and I *was* sorry to have been disrespectful to you, and you might have forgiven me."

Mr. Garton was not angered by this freak of his little favorite. On the contrary, something in her voice and manner showed him that she suffered keenly, and made him question earnestly within himself. With one stride he caught the little burning hands, drew her to his knee resistingly, and sat down, holding her fast.

"My child, have I indeed been cruel to you? Have I almost broken your little heart?" (He felt that it throbbed painfully against his arm.) "Let us be patient for awhile. I think we have not quite learned to understand each other fully. Now I see by this hot cheek and blazing eye, what I had not intended to excite. Take my forgiveness, Geraldine, and let us be better friends."

She laid her head wearily against his shoulder, but though the strained expression passed from her face, she did not look satisfied. Thoughtfully watching her, he asked:

"What is it, child?"

"I cannot understand it at all—things are so deep. You have so often told me the importance of self-control—always."

"Well?"

"And you lost yours to-day—you forgot yourself, and beat John until the blood ran in a stream! Oh, it was awful!"

It seemed as if she could not banish that picture from her mind, and shuddered violently, hiding her eyes. He was very grave, feeling an uncomfortable justice in her rebuke.

"And have you disobeyed me a second time—come out of your room to me here close upon midnight to impress upon me the necessity of casting the beam from my own eye before plucking the mote from my brother's?"

Mr. Garton hid a smile behind her heavy black hair.

"I felt as if I should go mad up there. If I had not come, I should have been very ill, and I would rather be punished for both at once, than to stay there. Besides, I want to know why every one—even you, tells me that things are wrong, then does them in spite of their being so. I cannot understand it."

"Things that are wrong for you might not be for me."

She looked up into his face with her clear, searching eyes.

"My mother told me that those things which involved great principles, were the same in child or man. She never told me anything that was not true."

This staggered him—so strange and positive, coming from such childish lips. There was no real cowardice in the action, but he did feel the need of thinking deeply before coping with so exacting a mind as Geraldine's. So he put her off his knee gently, and said, looking steadily into her face:

"Sometime I may be able to make you understand

.why there cannot be discussions of this nature between us. Wait until you are in a calmer state, and I able to explain these things to you better. I am weary now, and you ought to be asleep. Come, I will take you to bed."

She suffered him to take her hand, but sighed heavily as he led her out.

"It is always the way! If I cannot understand, and want to, I am always told to wait."

"Because it is best for you. Child, you are too impatient, and are trying to live ahead of your time. I promise you to try to help you the better to understand people and things in the future. Now promise me to go to bed—will you!"

"Yes, sir."

"There! That is like my Geraldine—as I thought her. Good-night."

He put her gently through the door, drew her back again to kiss her, then shut her out.

She went to bed, and soon fell asleep. He, in very singular mood, paced his room nearly all night.

3

CHAPTER II.

A RARE BIRD.

"Authors are often accused of exaggeration in their descriptions of children. I wish the cavilers could see your daughter at this moment."

Mr. Prince who had just entered the library, while waiting for the breakfast bell to ring, came smilingly to Mr. Garton's side, as he stood at the window, overlooking the large rear yard.

"Few will stop to think that those prodigies are selected from the rare ones," he answered. "Yet I scarcely blame them, since it needs the personal interest of parent, kindred or dearest friends to invest them with wonderful charms. Geraldine is odd, and has interested her teacher, for which I am thankful; but to most people she is a wilful, saucy child, exciting more anger than love, I fear." And he sighed.

"How can you say it?" said the young man in warm deprecation. "In all my life I have never seen her equal. She puzzles, perplexes and makes me love her, but I cannot be vexed in the least degree. Her powers of thought amaze me, and her decision of character is quite as remarkable. Such a memory is rarely bestowed upon any one, while the use she makes of the knowledge she gains, is not only odd, but amusing. For the last quarter of an hour, I have been watching and listening without her knowledge, and I have made a new discovery."

"What is it?"

"That this strange little daughter of yours has a reason for everything she does, and attaches some especial meaning to everything around her. It was but a day or two ago, that I came in here, and found her with a large Bible upon her knee. Not seeming to notice her, I passed curiously around where I could see the portion she had chosen, when all at once she shut the book with a snap, exclaiming: 'There! I have a name at last for my speckled hen!' and ran out of the room. This morning, the mystery has been solved. Having my attention drawn by her manœuvres, to a very wicked little hen, I observed that she was speckled, and heard the little lady call her Jezebel!"

Both gentlemen laughed.

"Did she ever ask you for your christian name?" inquired Mr. Prince.

"Yes—the first day of my arrival here. Perhaps I owe to that fact, her sudden and almost perfect confidence in me. It is decidedly flattering."

"Nathaniel—'the good.' Rather, I confess; but I must say that your face and manner probably had a good deal to do with it. I have been surprised to find at times how acutely she analyzes character. In nearly everything, my child is like her mother."

Instantly Mr. Garton was interested, it was so seldom his friend allowed himself to speak of his dead wife. To draw him out more fully, he remarked with all sincerity:

"Mrs. Prince must have been a very rare woman."

"I have never seen—never can see her like on earth. If mortals can be purely faultless, she was so. Yet she was strong in every trait of character—not merely mild, insipidly good. She could meet the world, mingle with it, combat its evils, root out a few, soften many down, and yet receive no stain. Geraldine inherits her peculiar beauty of form and feature, her deeply searching nature and her lovingness of disposition. Probably when she grows older she may have her clear strength of judgment and self-control. Yet I fear not, at times."

"I have often wondered where the child could have gained all her peculiar traits, since there is not one in the house who is like her. That which would at once attract the attention of a stranger, is her precision of language. I have scarcely been able to detect in her a single error in her choice of words and construction of sentences, while she seems to have a particular aversion to abbreviations. With all this precision, her language, while it is odd, is never stiff."

"All from her mother. While she lived, Geraldine had no other constant companion, and it is not surprising that she should have grown into her habits. Besides, the poor little thing worshiped her; you have noticed that?"

"Yes—new proof every day. I think Geraldine possesses an unusually impressible and tenacious nature, especially where her affections are engaged. And I have been thinking this morning how fearful it would have been, had she been brought under different influences in her earliest years. Now the greatest danger is past, for she is no tame, yielding thing, even where she loves, as I have discovered."

Mr. Prince looked inquiringly at him, and the young man explained what had happened the night previous.

"I can trust you to be careful, Garton," said the father gravely. "Do not lose your mastery over her, or I may sometime have reason to be very sorry. You will do her good, if you can only manage her."

"Thank you, my friend; and believe that I am grateful for your confidence and good opinion. As my life, I will faithfully guard the welfare of your young daughter."

Just then the subject of conversation looked up and discovered the two pairs of eyes bent upon her, smiled brightly, nodded, and resumed her occupation with her pets, which were many and varied. From the beautiful young horse straining vainly at his halter in the stable, down to a lame puppy in the kennel, she had won love, abundant and faithful, which she returned with fervor. For every one according to its recognized disposition and value, she had a name that was significant, obtained no one knew how, but when analyzed, always found to mean just what she intended.

"Seeing her surrounded by that brood of chickens, reminds me of something that greatly amused us at the time," said Mr. Prince, still regarding her with his fond smile. "When she was about three years old, her greatest delight was to be carried into the poultry-yard, and to count, in her baby fashion, the new ones added to the lot.   But one day she was taken ill, and we soon found that she had a light attack of that unpleasant disease, the chicken-pox. For some time she was kept in the house, but the first thing she asked for on recovering, was the ''ittle chittens.'   Accordingly, she was carried out, and looked long, and with earnest purpose, amongst the swarms of little chirpers.   Finally, with most amusing gravity, she pointed at one poor, stunted thing, that had been pecked half to death by the stronger ones of the brood, and said, solemnly :

'You are the chitten that gave me the chitten-pox.' "

"Just like her," laughed Mr. Garton ; and then, as the bell rang, turned with his patron to the breakfast-room.   Geraldine was there as quickly, looking fresh as a rose.   First kissing her father, she ran to Mr. Garton, and after a like salutation, whispered in his ear :

" I want you, please, to let me stay at home from school to-day.   May I ? "

" What for ?   I must have a good reason."

" Oh, please, trust me this time.   I will study to make up the time lost, at home.   I want very much to do something here."

" Shall we consult your papa about it ? "

" If you please to do so."

" What is it ? " asked Mr. Prince, overhearing.

" Miss Prince desires a holiday for some reason of her own, which she declines to give.   Do you think I may indulge her ? "

"Act precisely as you think best, as it is a matter that comes under your direction alone."

"Then I will grant it, provided she gives me explanations at a more convenient season."

"If it is to be a conditional permission, I will withdraw my request," she answered, taking her place at the table; and during the meal she was grave and silent.

In the interval between breakfast and school-time Geraldine disappeared. But when the young master stepped from his room into the hall, she was there awaiting him. For a moment he was tempted to bid her remain, if she wished it, but reconsidered the matter, and they went out together. No sign of rebellion appeared in their quiet walk to the school-house; she was quite docile and obedient by will and manner—that was plain. He made a few remarks which she answered simply, and so they entered the school-room, where the whole school had gathered in confusion. Loud disputing had been perceptible before they reached it, which subsided at once on the master's approach; but his keen eyes saw that something was amiss. Geraldine glided to her place through the crowd, while the master stood up in their midst and demanded the cause of such confusion. Pretty soon he learned that some injudicious persons had chosen to take exception to his rules, and their heedless discussions before the children had sown the seeds for an incipient rebellion. There were signs of a necessity for his abdication, or preparing himself for open war. Some one said that John Truslow's father had flown into a rage and had beaten his son again for having allowed the school-master to flog him; and under its smart the desperate boy had threatened to kill Mr. Garton. Others said their parents had declared no man should whip their children so, and the master must take a different course, or leave the town. Under all this, Mr. Garton remained perfectly calm, and in the midst of the growing clamor, called the school to order.

As usual, the roll was called. John Truslow, being the eldest, was first upon the list, but did not respond. A moment afterwards, however, he stepped in, took off his hat and bowed respectfully, then assumed his proper place. One quick, keen glance showed Mr. Garton that the boy was very pale and looked weary; but there was nothing evil or vindictive in his face.

As the names were called, responses at first came, promptly and respectfully. When it reached the middle class of boys, neither large nor small, there was a general stir, anxious and expectant; then one saucy little fellow cried out boldly:

"On hand, like a burnt boot."

Mr. Garton did not seem to heed. The next name was pronounced, to which a like answer came: "On hand, like a sick kitten."

"Thomas Carlisle," said the master, still oblivious.

"All right, like a squirrel with head and tail up."

At this there was an explosion, and Mr. Garton stopped short.

"Young gentlemen, I am confident that you have been incited to this by other parties. Stand out here and tell me instantly, who prompted you to such acts of insolence and disrespect."

His manner was too positive and terrible for dis-/
obedience, yet they seemed half inclined to rebel
against the command.   When they stood before him,
he repeated the question.

" We won't tell," said the first boy, sturdily.

" You will tell me this: ·Was it John Truslow ?"

" No," simultaneously.

" I knew it was not. Go to your seats. I will
deal with you another time. John Truslow, I want
to say to you that I am glad to find you had nothing
to do with this shameful matter. But it has been
said to me this morning, that you threatened to kill
me. What answer do you make to the charge ?"

" That it is not true." And Mr. Garton knew he
spoke the truth.

" Is it true that your father punished you a second
time ?—and for allowing yourself to be punished by
me ?"

John hesitated, then answered with ashen lips and
eyes that glared,

" Yes, sir, it is true."

" How is it that I find you here so promptly this
morning, after such hard usage ? You are reported
to me as one who attends school when it pleases you
—not otherwise."

" My father did forbid my coming, sir, but I preferred to come. My schooling is paid by the county,
and as I work nights and mornings in paying for
what I eat and wear, I do not consider he has a right
to command me when his commands are against my
best interests. I have made up my mind to study
and try to become a useful man."

The clear, honest tone in which the boy uttered the words, caused Mr. Garton's blood to tingle along his veins pleasantly. He looked into his eyes and said with sincerity:

"I believe you will, John, and I do also believe, in spite of your waywardness and bad reputation, that at heart you are a noble and generous boy."

"Thank you, sir. I will never forget your words while I live; and you will see, sir, that I can be good, though I have been very bad."

"Very well. Now young gentlemen, you are to take your hats and leave this room in order, and with perfect respect. The boy who dares to infringe upon one rule of politeness in the slightest degree, shall be made to feel my displeasure quite as severely as John has felt both mine and his father's. For this day go; you have a holiday. To-morrow I shall expect every one of you back, and that you will come prepared to act as pupils guided by a master—not as rebels against his authority."

Greatly astonished, the boys obeyed. This was an entirely new method of dealing with their daring, and they could not guess what was to come. As they trooped off in various directions, some sadly frightened, others bent upon a merry day, Mr. Garton took Geraldine and walked rapidly back to Prince Hill. On the way he never spoke once, but looked very pale and stern. In the hall, however, he stooped to her tenderly, kissing her troubled brow with a brother's fondness.

"Do not be troubled, my child; all this will end to-day. Take the holiday you asked, which I must

now give you perforce, and let no thought of what
has happened mar your happiness."

"Only tell me you will not go away," she begged,
with an anxious voice.

"I will not."

He was confident, and she was satisfied. While
he went to seek Mr. Prince, she flitted away, intent
upon some project of her own.

For a time the two gentlemen gravely discussed
the occurrence of the morning, after which, horses
were ordered out, and they mounted for a tour
through the district of which the school was composed. What arguments were used to convince
people that Mr. Garton was not an ogre, and that his
judgment might be fully trusted, are not known.
But it is certain that the tide of popular opinion
changed, and that the young man resumed his duties
with the certainty of their co-operation. For the
first time in years, the teacher was suffered to remain in the school unmolested, after that first onset,
and not only gave satisfaction, but was induced to
remain when the trial term expired.

CHAPTER III.

A BODY WITHOUT A SOUL.

No sooner had Mr. Prince and his friend ridden from the house than Geraldine, with her usual freedom of manner, slipped through a side gate into a lane and ran down the hill, from the foot of which she turned off into a miserable street leading to Mrs. Truslow's cottage. She found the woman sullen and gloomy, dolefully sitting over her neglected work, whilst John tried to comfort her. The child was no stranger to this abode, evidently, and glided in like one who had a right to expect a welcome. She had it, John rising hastily to place his own stool for her, which his mother as hastily brushed off with her apron.

"You have been crying again," said Geraldine, compassionately.

"Tears ain't no new thing to me, you know, miss. I was born into sorrow, and I shall die of it at last. For my part I can't see no use in such miserable critters comin' into the world."

"Mother's fretting because she thinks the school's broke up and I shall get no more learning."

Geraldine's face flushed all over with a sudden joyful light.

"John, I bring you good news. Papa and Mr. Garton have gone out, I think, to visit the people, and as he started, Mr. Garton promised me he would not leave; so I know he will arrange matters some way."

John looked at her earnestly.

"If he promised you to stay, he'll do it, and I am glad. He makes me feel like trying to be something, and I like him. If it's a whipping he promises, why a fellow is sure to get it; and if it's a good word he says, there is some comfort in believing he means it."

"Yes, indeed," cried Geraldine, warmly, pleased with John's confidence in her friend, "and I do think, John, that he means to be good to you. I talked to him about what mamma used to say of you, and he seemed very much interested."

"What did she say of me?" and a faint glow began to rise on John's brown cheeks.

"Kind things, you may be assured; when was my mother ever unkind to mortal?"

"She *was* good," averred Mrs. Truslow, who had resumed her doleful posture and her pipe, a black thing whose odor made her visitor shudder with disgust. "You'll never get such another mother as she was. Indeed I do pity you when I think what you may have to go through in the future. Step-mothers is nearly always bad."

"What do you mean?" asked the child, with wondering tone and eyes. "I do not understand you."

"Oh, well, never mind! Time enough to meet

trouble when it comes. I never have to go far to find mine, but it's different with you."

"I must know what you mean," cried Geraldine, now roused and fearful, seeing how vainly John's warning glances strove to check his mother.

" Is it possible you do not know your father's going to get married again? I thought he'd 'a told you—his only child."

" Oh, mother, it's only the town gossip, and who's going to believe that—unless it be some new evil against me; then everybody will believe it, of course. Now I come to think of it, do you know, Miss Prince, who told Mr. Garton I had threatened to kill him?"

" No. It was one of the boys up at the school-house; but in the confusion I cannot say which one."

" I wish I could find out."

" What for ? "

" To teach the fellow that truth is better than falsehood—sometimes. How I hate liars! I had rather be skinned alive than tell a lie!"

" Never mind the others then. If you try to find out, perhaps it will get you into some foolish trouble, which is useless, since Mr. Garton believes your assertion that you did not make the threat."

" But you know John couldn't live if he wasn't always gettin' into somethin' or other," snapped Mrs. Truslow. "He's got the name of bein' bad, and goes on to worse day after day. He gets into fights, then gets whipped at school for fightin', then he comes home and gets whipped for bein' whipped at school. The boy'd better been born dead than live the dog's life he's livin'!"

"It will not last always, mother. Only wait until I get enough education to make a showing, and I will find some kind of work to do that will pay better than the little father gets. Then we will live in a nice house, and you shall have good clothes."

At this Geraldine, who had remained very thoughtful for some moments, looked up and smiled, as she took a small roll of something from her pocket.

"I brought something for you to make John some nice collars and a bosom," she said, and I had intended to ask you to cut them out and let me help you to make them to-day, so he could look nice at school, you know. Now I think I do not feel like staying; but I will help you some other time. It is very odd!"

"What is odd?" asked John.

"Why, that the things we wish most to do should be done through difficulties. 'I asked for a holiday to-day, just to come here. But Mr. Garton refused me because I would not tell him what I wanted to do. When he dismissed the school, I thought then that I was free any way; and now, I am here, I do not want to do the work."

"Mother has troubled you with all that nonsense!" cried John, regretfully. "Don't mind it, Miss Geraldine."

"I cannot help it, until I ask my father if it is true."

She uttered this in a low voice, as if it was an effort. Then after a few more words she ran off saying as she went out:

"Do not forget Saturday, John. You will come and help the gardener."

"Yes, I'll be sure to come."

That was the way John was to pay for the new collars. This odd little lady was not chary of giving aid to those around her, but she always found something for them to do in return, that they might not be gifts so much as payment for labor. She had early learned the lesson of inculcating ˈprinciples noble and worthy; and this, too, from that matchless mother sleeping in the distant church-yard, whose white shafts and glaring monuments shot up dazzlingly in the bright sunlight of this lovely morning.

That was a wretched day for poor Geraldine. She wandered through the house aimlessly; from the house to the garden, and all through the shrubbery. She gathered flowers and filled all the vases in parlor, library and chamber; then she tried to read, and finding she could not sought her pets, where the great absorbing interest of her heavy little heart made it impossible to enjoy being with them.

At length the gentlemen rode, laughing and chatting, under the archway and dismounted. Geraldine was down stairs in a moment, and flew to meet them. But it was Mr. Garton's hand she caught first.

"Is all the trouble over?"

"I think so, my anxious little pupil. At any rate, I shall not go away yet awhile. Look at her cheeks and eyes, Mr. Prince. Are they not flattering testimony of pleasing interest in my welfare?"

"Very. Well, daughter, what is it?"

Geraldine had slipped from her teacher's clasp, and had hold of his hand. She was trembling like a leaf:

"Papa, if you please, I want to speak with you alone for a few moments," she faltered.

"Heyday! what important subject·demands consultation now. Has Jezebel met her fate, and been eaten by the dogs?"

"Oh, papa, please! Do not laugh at me. I want you very much."

"Very well, child; but wait until I have had my dinner. Be useful; run and tell the housekeeper to order it served at once; we have fasted ·since breakfast."

She loosed his hand and sped away swiftly; and then waited with throbbing heart and burning cheeks for the wished-for hour to arrive, when she might know the truth. During dinner the gentlemen seemed in high spirits, recounting the adventures of the day with much relish. But though she was keenly alive to all that concerned Mr. Garton, the little creature ate in silence, putting no question to either, answering them only when necessary.

This excitement and pre-occupation did not escape the observing eyes of Mr. Garton, and he tried to aid her by going at once to his own room the moment they left the table, wondering meanwhile, if she would tell him likewise, what had so much disturbed her.

Mr. Prince went whistling into the library, a youthful habit which had returned to him quite recently, and had forgotten the child's eagerness for a private interview, when her troubled face appeared before him, as he sat down by the window.

"So, so! I had forgotten you, pussy. Well, now, let us have the secret."

"Oh, papa, answer me quickly, please; 'yes' or 'no.' Am I going to have a step-mother?"

He started as if a pistol had gone off near him; but her slender hands caught his and held them fast.

"Where on the earth did you get such an idea?" he asked when he could command himself, thrilled by her intense, burning gaze.

"Only tell me if it is true?"

"But there are some things little girls cannot question their elders about, and preserve a proper delicacy in handling sacred matters."

"Papa, papa, you torture me! Only in this, do tell me!"

"I believe you have lost your senses, child! Still I will tell you, what you must know sooner or later. I shall bring a new mistress to Prince Hill, this autumn—a beautiful, grand new mamma, my Geraldine."

White as death she sank upon a stool and covered her face with trembling fingers. To her this blow was awful, and he could not see how he had hurt her, though an undefined dread had sealed his lips upon a hint of the coming change in his home. Perhaps he had thought it best to bring home the new wife, and trust to her powers of fascination over this little worshiper of the dead.

"Papa," she gasped, "how can you? No one!

Oh, there is no one so good, or that can be so beautiful, as my own mother!"

"Why, darling, as to that, I think you are not a judge," he answered, touched by her overwhelming distress, and feeling the old tenderness of his first love sweeping full upon him as he stooped to draw her up to his bosom: "You will learn as you grow older, that the world is filled with beautiful women, many of whom are good and true. You know I would not bring any other, knowingly, to reign where *she* has reigned. See, Geraldine, how lovely she is."

He lifted her drooping brow with his hand and gently placed under her gaze a miniature. She seized it with a gesture almost fierce, and gazed with eager eyes and parted lips, her breath coming fast and thick. Startled at this phase in her character, not a little awed by the force of her passion which he was made to feel, rather than see, the young father regarded his child while she scanned the picture hungrily. He hoped to see the dark eyes soften, the parted lips close contentedly under the spell of beauty. But she dropped it slowly, and, leaving the golden case lying in his hand, sank once more upon the stool at his feet. Her action had been that of a child thirsting for a draft from a cup suddenly revealed. She had stretched her hands too quickly for denial, drank with avidity, and found the taste too bitter for her childish philosophy.

"Geraldine, my daughter, how strangely you act! What have you to say of her whom you will one day know, as next dearest to you, with myself?"

To his profound astonishment, she answered him with a single terse sentence, rendered still more startling by the manner in which she uttered it:

"*Corpus sine pectore!*"

With that, she fled, and he heard her swift feet pattering upon the hall floor until the sounds were lost on the carpet stairway. A great heaviness settled upon his heart. This child was very dear to him, and he was going to render her miserable, perhaps. And yet, as he sadly pondered, distress gave place to hope. He trusted so wholly in the power of his new love, it seemed impossible that any one ever could be unhappy under her influence. When did man's philosophy ever fail to gather strength from the tender passions? He wished that this thing might be, and his own infatuation told him that it was easy of accomplishment. So he dismissed troublous thoughts, and took his cigar out upon the piazza where he was soon joined by Mr. Garton.

They sat talking quietly for an hour; but often through the lulls of the conversation, the father seemed to hear that passionate reply to his question, which sounded so strangely from the lips of such a child. At length he said, as if seeking some relief from the thoughts it called up:

"I see you have been teaching Dine Latin."

"I? No. I have frequently observed that she used Latin phrases, but do not know where she acquired them, if you did not teach her."

"I am not fond of teaching children, and by no means apt to teach them dead languages. She has picked this up, I suppose, as she does everything."

Nothing more was said on the subject, and shortly afterward the gentlemen returned to the library, their usual evening haunt. Each took a book and was soon absorbed in the contents, so when Geraldine crept slyly in, her face pale and tear-stained, neither noticed her presence for some time. She managed to slip a chair along the book-case where she could reach the volume she desired, and taking it to a low seat just back of where Mr. Garton sat, became as much absorbed as he.

Thus the three sat for nearly half an hour, until the silence was disturbed by Geraldine, who glided to her father's side and placed her open book upon his knee. Her finger pointed to an engraving, representing Catherine de Medicis, the features so startlingly like those of the miniature, that Mr. Prince turned pale and trembled. There was the large dark eye, the delicate yet pouting lips, the straight nose and oval cheeks, with the chin so indicative of subtle and deadly power. As he looked into the child's sad eyes fixed upon his full and steadfastly, he felt that she had gained a singular power over him.

"What am I to understand by this?" he asked, more disposed to question and argue, than to command.

"This history says the engraving is from a picture painted from life and very like. I have studied it a great deal, and whenever I saw people who had any features like hers, I tried to study them also; to see if they had any traits of character like hers. At first the coloring of miniature made me forget whom it resembled, and it was so beautiful I did want to love her.   But all at once I saw the same features, and I thought of the description I had seen of her hair and eyes.   Then I knew that she was 'a body without a soul.'"

"Suppose I grant the wondrous resemblance? You will admit that I ought to know the vast difference in real character?"

"Nature does not lie," answered the child firmly. "Besides, *you* could not see it, perhaps; because, as mamma used to say, it is so hard to see evil in those we love.   Catherine de Medicis was noted for her fascinating manners, which, together with her beauty, gave her unexampled power over various minds.   Her youth was a deception, her middle age unnatural and shocking.   She lured her own children into debaucheries that she might by weakening their minds the more easily control them as she pleased.   Then came the murder of the Calvinists, in which it is said forty thousand souls were sent to their Creator through her instrumentality.   Oh, it was awful!   Yet how many, how very many really good people loved her."

Mr. Prince would not have been willing to acknowledge that she made him nervous by this dissection of character for his benefit.   But when he tried to laugh it off her grave eyes checked him, changing the uneasy feeling into decided anger. More harshly than he had ever spoken to the petted child, as he shut the book he bade her go to her room and have done with nonsense.   When he needed her assistance or advice, he would call upon her.

The angry words and tone did not cause her to flush, as was usual with her. On the contrary she grew paler, and her lips quivered as she turned to obey. Before reaching the door, she came back and laid her arm up over his shoulder, pleadingly:

"Papa, if I am naughty and annoy you, for my dead mother's sake forgive me."

The tone and action went to his heart. With a sudden impulse he caught her tightly in his arms, and kissed her several times with fervor, his anger swallowed up in self-reproach.

"There! go, dear—you strange, strange child." But instead of letting her go, he held her still, looking into her sad, dry eyes. When he freed her at length, he followed her to the door, sent her off, and stood as if in deep thought until she had time to reach her own room. Mr. Garton, who had heard a little, and witnessed the closing scene, waited with a good deal of interest for the explanation Mr. Prince should give; but after a short deliberation that gentleman went out, and did not come back again before the school-master retired.

Even after Mr. Garton had entered his room, he saw Mr. Prince in the garden, pacing slowly up and down, smoking his cigar, sufficiently restless to show that he was troubled. He longed to go out and with the privilege of a friend seek a share of that which had come in to disturb the harmony of the two lives dearest to him. But Nathaniel Garton was too truly delicate and unobtrusive to ask to be admitted to family secrets.

"He will tell me in his own good time, I suppose,"

was his self-consolation, "and if my little pet recovers her spirits and happiness I can wait without impatience."

How little either of them dreamed of the changes that were soon to come. Geraldine, with her passionate heart-protest against what seemed to her the desecration of her mother's memory, had no conception of a real sorrow. Alas! she had to learn all too soon.

CHAPTER IV.

LOVE CONQUERS ALL THINGS.

ALTHOUGH Mr. Prince dismissed at the time any uneasy feeling called up in his mind by the distress of his child, a few days served to fix it with pertinacious influence in his thoughts. She uttered no word after that night which could lead him to believe she retained a painful memory of their interview on the subject; but he knew well that it haunted her continually. With most scrupulous care she avoided the mention of it; and he saw with much distress that she rather avoided him, as if fearful he would renew the conversation which he felt had been so hateful to her. Consequently he preserved a silence as profound as if no thoughts of so important a change had ever entered his brain, and as she avoided him, sought her with more demonstrative tenderness, striving mutely to establish a perfect confidence between them.

The silent struggle had an interested spectator in the person of the young teacher, who observed, wondered and made no sign. But it surprised him greatly that his friend should drop no hint concerning the nature of his growing uneasiness, or that

Geraldine, so frank and free always with him, should have no word to say.   And day by day she grew more thoughtful, more reserved ; while her step was slow and her eyelids drooped heavily over burning orbs, which seemed striving to shrink from betraying what was in her heart.

As a natural consequence, the freedom and harmony of life at Prince Hill gradually faded away. While the three important characters of the household followed without interruption their usual occupations, a perceptible restraint had fallen upon all, that rendered one moody, another thoughtful, and the last morbidly unhappy.

So it continued until the first tints of the autumn painted forests about Princeton in rich and varied pictures.   The time was drawing near when the secret would be a secret no longer, and the burthen that had grown upon the mind of the master might be removed.

It happened one day that the mail which should have come in the early morning, did not arrive until late in the afternoon, just after Mr. Garton reached home from school.   Mr. Prince, with a pile of letters before him, sat at a table by the south window, leaving Mr. Garton to peruse one from a widowed mother, whose faithful hand penned a long epistle weekly to her only son.   Geraldine sat down before Mr. Garton with a weary sigh, which made him glance from the beloved page to her delicate face, where his gaze lingered sadly.   Unconscious of his regards, she sat still for a moment, watching her father as he broke the seals and glanced rapidly through his correspondence. Suddenly he saw her eyes dilate and gleam with a wild, eager stare. Her lips dropped apart, and her steadfast look never quitted her father's face until he slowly broke the seal of a small white envelope, which he had been examining with a lingering tenderness of manner unlike that called forth by any other letter in the heap. Mr. Garton, alternately observing the two, saw a happy smile creeping about his friend's mouth, while his eyes softened and grew inexpressibly tender. The child's lips became white and shut close, her bosom heaving as if she had to struggle hard to keep back sobs. The white forehead wrinkled heavily with the brows drawn down in a frown over the flashing eyes. And while her teacher gazed in astonishment at the sudden transformation, she rose and glided stealthily from the room, her hands wrung together and held tightly over her bosom.

A half audible exclamation from Mr. Garton caused Mr. Prince to look up and meet his friend's questioning eyes. For a moment the smile lingered still about his lips, but a flush spread over his face as a second look showed him Geraldine's empty seat. In much confusion he flung the letter upon the table, and, rising, paced the room several times before speaking.

"Garton, I suppose you are wondering what it all means?" he said at length, but without pausing in his hasty walk.

"Yes, and I have wondered for some time; but you need not tell me until entirely disposed to do so. I would not force your confidence."

"I know it, and I have been wrong to withhold from you that which you should have known. No lack of trust kept me silent, you may be assured. The reason lay in my cowardice. I was reluctant to speak of those things nearest my heart, and sacred, the more especially as they have been the cause of visible unhappiness to your little friend and pupil. You have seen it, Garton?"

"Yes, with a heavy heart."

The young man's answer produced an unexpected effect. Mr. Prince shrank and caught his breath quickly, after which he recovered himself and came with hasty abruptness to the point.

"You will be surprised, but the trouble has risen wholly from one simple fact. I am about to bring a new mistress to Prince Hill."

Mr. Garton was surprised. He had not dreamed of this as the cause of their trouble.

"Is it not a sudden determination?" he asked.

"No, I have been engaged nearly a year, but preferred to wait, for several reasons. In this time I have made few visits to Eastbrook, where my affianced resides; but our correspondence has been uninterrupted. Only for some officious gossips, Dine would have known nothing about it until my own good time; but some rumor got afloat in the village, I know not how, and came to her ears. From that time she seemed to have grieved silently, but will not talk about it, and of course it disturbs me. I cannot wish to purchase happiness at the price of my child's, you know."

His tone was questioning at the close of the

sentence, and, as he paused, he regarded his friend earnestly.

"You should know best whether in such a step there is any real danger. The character of the lady would determine the effect of her presence upon your child. After the experience you have had in association with so noble a woman as Geraldine's mother, I should not think it likely you might be easily pleased with another."

"True! One year of life with her was enough to make me fastidious for the remainder of my existence. To tell you the truth, Garton, I do not know my own mind just now. When I had that talk with Geraldine about it first, I was wholly confident that it might all be right in the end. The lady is a very superior one in every respect, and has a most wonderful influence upon all with whom she comes in contact. But I am ashamed to say the child's foolishness has affected me. I showed her the miniature I have kept since our engagement, and she startled me by pronouncing it a body without a soul. Furthermore, she brought out an engraving of Catherine de Medicis, and pointed out features that were like hers, indicative of certain treacherous and subtle traits of character."

Mr. Garton burst into a fit of merry laughter, in which Mr. Prince joined. When he proceeded, it was in a lighter tone.

"Since then I have been silly enough to compare the two, and find a great resemblance so far as personal appearance goes. But the frank, pure tone of her letters is too eloquent of goodness for a thought

5*

of distrust to come in while I am reading them. I wish from my soul the subject had never risen, for I am afraid my over-sensitiveness with regard to the child of my dead wife may make me unjustly suspicious of the living one that is to be."

"I hope not. You should think more of the influence a good woman may exercise over a character like Geraldine's, and nurture confidence. To begin by distrust would be certain death to your happiness."

"I know it, for suspicion once engrafted in the nature of a Prince is hard to root out. When I am with her it is as if a spell chained me to her side. I live only in her. She fascinates, entrances, bewilders and intoxicates me with a delirium of happiness. All the sensuous emotions of my nature are kindled to vivid life, but held in absolute check by intellectual powers which grow stronger and stronger under her influence. I am enslaved, heart and brain, and would not free myself from my chains. Yet I know myself so well, were any positive sign of change in her to show me a phase of character like that which I hate in others, it would subject her from that time forth to a cruel and jealous regard from me, which would feed upon the merest trifles. What shall I do, knowing this, Garton? Is it safe to go on?"

"*Can* you withdraw honorably? It seems to me you have gone too far for that; and furthermore, you may be foolishly sensitive in questioning the safety of the step. So delicate a matter cannot be advised upon well by a third party, however.

Since your passion does not enthrall your judgment, it were better to act for yourself without interference."

"Perhaps I claim too much for myself, in assert-
ing freedom of judgment. All my heart and soul
and mind and strength lean to this union. I am
afraid, not for myself, but for my child, should I be
mistaken. How can I tell that my love for her has
not so swayed my judgment in her favor as to render
it impossible for me to feel the truth in connection
with her?"

He spoke with passionate excitement.

"If you doubt the wisdom of the venture, there is
but one course for you," answered Mr. Garton
quietly. "It would be better to break off at once,
than to take the step which would doom your peaceful household to helpless misery."

"But as you said, I cannot do it with honor,"
declared Mr. Prince, hastily; and Mr. Garton smiled
at the justice of his friend's self-judgment. He was
not fit to take a stand against his own happiness.

"Then why torture yourself with the doubts and
fears, which may be—doubtless are—wholly ground
less?"

"Certainly! why should I? The reason lies in
the fact that love makes fools of us, my friend; and
my wayward, spoilt child, has helped me on to render myself ridiculous!"

"One word more: will the change render it necessary to alter my plans?"

"By no means. Go on just as you are until after
the wedding, which will take place in November.

We shall make a short tour before coming home, about which time you will probably feel like visiting your mother, during the children's vacation. By the time we shall have been settled a week or two, you can return to your duties and the home to which you will always be welcome."

Mr. Garton extended a hand in silent response to the warm words his host had uttered, which was clasped and wrung hard. For a moment Mr. Prince's arm rested on his shoulder, and his eyes filled. Both gentlemen were strongly moved by some secret emotion which seldom came to the surface in more than general ways of kindness and esteem. When Mr. Garton did venture to speak, his voice was broken and husky:

"Dear old fellow! May God be with you always, and grant that you may be as happy as I wish you from my soul!"

"Thank you. I hope I may never grow more unworthy of your friendship, Nathaniel."

"Nor I of yours."

A few moments later as Mr. Prince stood by the window, looking afar off to the purpling hills, he said wistfully:

"Garton, may I trust you to help me to root out Geraldine's prejudice against her new mother?"

"I will do all I can, assuredly."

Still he stood dreamily gazing, while his hand glided within his bosom and rested upon the miniature lying warm above his heart. A foolish pride caused him to disregard the impulse to draw forth that beautiful face and show it to his friend. Had he done so, his entire after life would probably have been changed. And not his only. The history of the three persons most dear to him would have been differently written, if indeed it had been written at all. But he let the momentary desire pass away, and his fate was sealed.

Truly, "love conquers all things."

3*

CHAPTER V.

HOME AND A SMILING WIFE.

PRINCE HILL awoke from its sleepy quiet to undergo a change, the master presiding with fastidious care. He had left it until the last, that everything might appear fresh and attractive to the bride who was to leave a gayer home for this plodding little town of Princeton. So the rich old tapestries were removed, that richer and brighter might replace them; and carpets laid that a queen might have trodden with a sense of fitness in their magnificence. From top to base, the grand old house which had sheltered his mother in her youth, in which he had been born and to which he had brought his first bride with proud delight, must be renovated and adorned with livelier hues to suit the peerless beauty of one yet to come.

Teacher and pupil saw little of the work—only the changes as they were completed. Mr. Prince liked to have things done without confusion, and managed that they should be accomplished without interference with any family comforts habitual to the little circle. On those days when there was no school, Mr. Garton would take Geraldine away to the mount-

ains botanizing, or gathering specimens for her cabinet from rock, tree and river. She passionately loved
nature, and when wandering thus with him, forgot
the haunting misery of her young life, seeing which,
he sought oftener for opportunities to get abroad into
the grand old woods.

Brief and few as they were, those last days before
the coming of the bride were merry ones. Mr. Garton reveling in the freedom of action after close con-
finement, his young life stirred and quickened by the
pure, bracing air of the mountains—the spicy fragrance of the pines and cedars—became a most delightful companion. He would climb a tree like a
squirrel, to pluck a tuft of moss from its branches,
or peer into the deserted nest of some little bird, to
see if there might be left an egg, perchance, to grace
his little pupil's cabinet. Ravines were traversed,
caves explored, pebbles gathered from the river side,
ferns plucked and classed and pressed with the
most scrupulous care. Rocks were turned up for
snails, bark peeled from trees in search of bugs, bats
and beetles routed from their nooks in caverns—
until the room which Mr. Prince had appointed for
her use at the top of the house, fitted up with
shelves and cases, presented a strange and interesting appearance.

While thus engaged one day near the river, Mr.
Garton, who was seated upon a huge stone with Geraldine at his feet, watching the arrangements of some
autumn leaves with pebbles and shells, was surprised
to see floating down the stream, a skiff painted in
glaring red colors, in which sat a man of singular

and striking exterior. His dress was a suit of black, with a flashy neck-tie and a large pin flaming in his bosom. Over his brow was carelessly thrust a slouched hat, tipped just enough to one side to give it a jaunty air, and allow the gleam of a dazzling white forehead.

Seeing people on shore, he gave a stroke with his oars that turned his little bark in their direction, and coolly stepped to the ground with a familiar nod, when he had brought it close enough:

"Fine day this, for the season, stranger," he remarked.

"Rather," answered Mr. Garton, with some reserve, yet looking steadily into the sunny face of the man before him.

"May I ask what occupies you so pleasantly? That seems to be rather a curious affair," indicating the leaves and pebbles with a careless gesture.

"It would be difficult to give a name to it, since it is merely the working out of a fancy of my own. I have chosen these leaves of various colors, as you see, and am trying to match them with pebbles of like colors. I class the leaves and the stones, and find some interest in tracing something of a relation between them."

"Humph! Stuff!"

Geraldine's eyes flashed at this rude response to her teacher's remarks. She looked up quickly:

"Sir, you were not invited to land, that I am aware of; and if you can find no better amusement than to be insolent to those who treat you civilly, we can dispense with your society without delay."

The stranger burst into a merry laugh, and sat down upon a stone opposite them with a free and easy air, amusing, while it nettled the young gentleman who had become the subject of a threatened dispute between them.   In order to prevent further words, he began to gather up his treasures.

"Pray do not let me drive you away. I do not mean to be offensive, I assure you. In answer to my little lady here, I would ask her if God's free earth is not open to all. What better right have you here than I have, eh?"

"I have a much better right, since this land belongs to my father, and I am on my own rightful dominion," she answered disdainfully.

"Ah, indeed? That alters the case, and I must apologize. I suppose that is your house, then, just discernible beyond this hill, on the rising ground?"

"Yes, that is Prince Hill."

"Prince Hill! So, so! Mr. Prince, I have heard, is a very wealthy gentleman, and much respected in these parts. Let me see! He's lately married, is he not?"

The question was addressed to Mr. Garton, who answered very coldly, displeased with the man's manner.

· "No, he lost his wife some years ago."

"But I heard he was to take another," said the stranger, in no way disconcerted. Geraldine became white as marble.

"Let us go home," she whispered. "This man makes me feel wicked. Why does he ask these questions?"

Mr. Garton rose and took her hand, nodded slightly to the inquisitor and turned with deliberate coolness toward home, without deigning to reply to the last remark.

The sunny face clouded, and the eyes burned angrily, but without uttering a word he got up, and beginning to whistle, stepped into his skiff and floated out into the river.

The incident, small in itself, made an impression upon Mr. Garton's mind that was not pleasant. Strangers were few in Princeton, and the manner of his approach was singular. Geraldine's remark as they proceeded onward seemed very near the truth.

" He acted just as if he wanted to find out something without letting you know it," she said wonderingly. " Why should he care to know if—if—"

" If your papa was going to marry again," supplied Mr. Garton boldly. " I cannot guess, I am sure. My child, why do you so dread this marriage? Your father is far too young a man to condemn himself to a life of loneliness."

" I do not know, but the thought of it makes me sick. I can never, never bear to see any other woman sit where my mother sat, and be treated as she was treated by my father. It will kill me?"

" Foolish child! Why, Geraldine, do you not know that you are acting very selfishly."

" No, I am not selfish! How can my father forget my sweet mother, and let another take her place? It is not right, and I shall never, never love her. I believe I shall *hate* her, and it makes me afraid, because my mother told me never to hate any one!

Oh, I live such a torturing life! If my father would only pity me!"

Mr. Garton, much disturbed by this passionate mood, sat down upon a fallen log and drew her to his side. From the depths of his heart he pitied this poor child, struggling with her jealousy and tortured by fear lest she should hate where she ought to love. As was his habit, he began to reason with her as he would have done with an older person.

"Your mother was right; you should hate no one, and you are correct in your efforts to overcome such a sentiment. But I think you are wrong to construe your father's actions into a lack of respect for your mother's memory. Had she been a coarse, cruel or evil woman who rendered his life unhappy, do you think he would dare to venture again into such a relation? On the contrary, he might have learned to dislike and doubt all womankind. As it is, he furnishes the highest proof that man can give of his appreciation of truth and virtue in your sex."

Geraldine laughed disagreeably, plucking at the crimson leaves of a gum tree over her head.

"I am a child, but you cannot cheat me with sophistry!"

"Sophistry! Heaven forbid!" cried Mr. Garton, surprised out of his self-complacency. "Do you think I would try to influence you with that? Come, you are unkind to me, now, as well as your father."

"How am I unkind to my father?" she asked quickly.

"You want to cut him off from the sweetest associations that make man's life beautiful and good.

His house must be dreary always—no light step to meet him when he comes, no sweet voice to bid him welcome, no tender hand to smooth his brow when weary, or his pillow, if ill. I do not know what could be more selfishly unkind."

Geraldine bent her head against his shoulder, a crimson stain upon her cheeks and brow.

" If this is unkind, I deserve all you have said, for it is truth. I think of it often, and I know how I shall feel to see her and hear her when she meets him and talks to him and caresses him! Do not talk any more about it, for these are the thoughts that drive me crazy with hate and fear. I wish I could die without ever seeing her ! "

" Geraldine, hush ! You do not know what you are saying, child."

" Yes, I do. It is you who will not understand me—nobody ever can or will as long as I live, and I wish I had died and been buried with my mother."

How to deal with her now was something of a puzzle to the young man. After sitting silently awhile, however, a bright thought came into his head.

" I am going soon to visit my mother, Geraldine. How would you like to go with me and remain through vacation ?"

" Oh, very, very much ! Then I need not see her come, you know. Where does your mother live ?"

" A long way from here; but it is a beautiful country, and you would see lovely scenes. Then my home, though not a fine one like Prince Hill, is very dear to me, and my mother an angel—much like what your own mother was, I fancy. You would love her."

"Has papa ever seen her?"

"Yes, many times. He used to go home with me from college, and have rare hunting times in our belt of woods."

"I have never heard you say so before. How nice it was to know him then—was it not? For he was so bright and handsome. Papa was always bright till mamma went away to the angels; but he is handsome still. I never saw any other gentleman so much so, till you came."

Mr. Garton laughingly acknowledged the compliment, adding :

"Being older than he, I had not hoped for the favorable impression I have made upon his daughter."

"You older than papa! It seems impossible! Why did you never marry?"

A sudden faintness swept the color from Mr. Garton's face, and his brow drooped to his hand, involuntarily hiding its pallor. He seemed not to have heard her until she repeated the question.

"Why? I could not well explain to you, Geraldine. So many things come into the lives of men of which they cannot speak, of which they would never think if they could control thought as they do speech. When your father married we were both young, and his was the fulfillment of an engagement entered into long before, whilst I had no attachments outside of my home. Soon after my collegiate course ended, my father died; then misfortunes began to flow in upon us. Nearly all our property had been involved

6*

in some way, and ere I could get hold of the end of the snarled affairs pertaining, all was swept hopelessly away. Can you imagine what I had to do then, little friend? My dear mother was widowed and homeless. I must set about my work with earnest vigor, and redeem the shelter endeared to her by life-long associations. Of course such a life could furnish me little time for society, and sentimentality were best left out of the bargain."

He did not say that it had been left out. Only that "it were best left out!" Geraldine took it up quickly, thinking she saw a deeper meaning now than his light tone, half playful in closing, conveyed.

"But you have had a good deal of trouble, have you not?" she asked, pursuing the subject.

"Why do you think so?"

"I do not know, quite. Probably because you seem to understand everybody so well and have sympathy for them. If you had not known trouble you would be careless and easy, and never stop to think if other people suffer. I have noticed that those who have been most afflicted are always the kindest and best."

"Or the worst. Trouble either softens or embitters. Yes, I had trouble, as you will understand, naturally. How could it be otherwise?"

"Of course, I know! You grieved for your father, and loss of property must have vexed and annoyed you. But I feel something else—I do not know what. You appear to have been *tried*, and act as if you always want to control yourself—to suppress something. The need of it makes you think of it, and try to impress it upon me as very important. You must have some particular reason?"

She turned her eyes full upon him in questioning, and he met her gaze too much disconcerted to answer at once.   Why must this child forever make direct applications of principles he strove to impart in general forms? With her searching mind and extraordinary powers of analysis, coupled with her precision of speech, she was often too much for him. When brought thus closely in contact, his wish was always to escape, and he did it as people are apt to do anything without proper meditation—abruptly, and with a touch of impatience.

"Do you know this habit you have is very embarrassing, Geraldine? One cannot feel like disclaiming such applications as you make, and it would be infinitely more unpleasant to admit them. If you go on always in such a searchingly personal way, it will cause you innumerable entanglements and annoyances. The world will not bear it. Be content to take people and events as they come, and if you must study them, reserve your thoughts more carefully until facts develop themselves, and prove to your own satisfaction whether your impressions are true or otherwise."

"How can I accept your teachings in all things when they are inconsistent?" she again asked, though evidently pained by his tone.

"Inconsistent? How do you find me so?"

"If I understand you, the present lesson is to teach me reserve; and many times as an attribute

of truth, you urge me to entire frankness. How can
I act as you wish me, understanding as I do?"

"My child, we are not necessarily lacking in
frankness because we happen to deem it wisest to
remain silent. I might let you talk to me always
with perfect freedom of your thoughts and feelings;
but if I let all occasions pass without cautioning you,
you may some time speak in a like manner to others,
when it would be wrong, and result in trouble. Are
you satisfied?"

"Yes—better, though it seems as if you said most
of this because you did not want to answer my
question."

He drew a quick breath and his teeth closed
tightly over his lip. As he rose up, he felt his brow
to be flushed, and the blood tingling through his
veins with impatience. She was unwittingly pressing upon unhealed wounds, and it angered him to
feel the smart, and know that his mightiest will, his
deepest self-respect, could not banish the lingering
tenderness that made him shrink from an unwonted
touch.

"Have I vexed you?" cried the child, in peni-
tence, seeking to read his averted face. "Do forgive
me, dear Mr. Garton."

"Forgive you? My child, I have nothing to forgive; but you do try my patience sorely at times.
And let me say to you now what I wish you to remember. If you would avoid giving me pain, do
not try to get beyond what you see, or take more
than I give you. I have weak points of which you
can know nothing, and when you blindly assail

these, you not only pierce me, but wear out my strength."

How pityingly she gazed at him now—he so seemingly strong, owning a weakness, and pleading with her, a child, to spare him! Both little hands closed over the one by which he led her, and with her tender heart on her lips, she bent them to his fingers, there to press a silent, tremulous kiss. As if an adder had stung him, he snatched his hand away:

"Geraldine! What are you doing, child? Has some sprite taken possession of you that you should do as—dear heaven! I have frightened the poor child to death!"

Remorsefully he stooped to gather the little one in his arms from the ground, where she had fallen in a sudden swoon. She was too delicate for such handling, and his violence had smitten her down as with a blow. In a moment he had lifted her, and run to a little brook where he dashed water over her face until she was restored to consciousness, all the time reproaching himself.

"What did I do to you?" she murmured, struggling to sit up. He held her firmly, pressing her slight figure in his arms.

"Listen to me one moment, dear. I alone was to blame, and I am very sorry. Your caressing action, which was intended to convey a sweet and assuring love, had the effect of recalling something that happened to me once—something that I cannot remember without pain. I did not mean to startle you so much; but was surprised out of my self-control. Can you forgive me, little friend?—for I fear I have made all this afternoon miserable for you."

"Do not mind me; it is over now. I am so sorry I made trouble for *you*. Please let me go home."

She was so weak, however, that she staggered as she attempted to walk, and he took her up in his arms like an infant, carrying her until they reached the lawn gate. Here she insisted upon walking into the house, for fear "papa should be frightened."

That night Mr. Garton begged to take his pupil home with him for a visit; and after a good deal of hesitation and argument, Mr. Prince consented.

A few days later, they departed for his home in another county, two hundred miles distant.

It was an auspicious day for the coming home of the bride in the fading glory of an autumn sun. Servants with horses met them at the station six miles above the town, and they rode down through the spicy woods, now flaunting their royal hues before gladdened and admiring eyes. The bridal trip had been very brief, and in returning, Mrs. Prince had invited a choice party of friends to meet and accompany her home. So it happened that a gay train swept into the pretty main street of Princeton, at which many a bright pair of eyes peered from the shelter of their windows as it passed. At its head rode Mr. Prince, looking handsome and happy, while the stately figure at his side became more gracefully beautiful as a consciousness of her position dawned in the lustrous eyes of the bride. A dark blue velvet riding habit set off the loveliness of her form, and the glossy black plumes drooped low against a flushing cheek. Many a young man exclaimed at her beauty; many a young girl heaved a gently envious sigh, as with curious gaze they watched the train sweep into the drive and wind more slowly up to the hill.

Before the great front entrance they halted, and the master sprang lightly to the ground, ready to lift from her horse the woman upon whom he looked with proud and glistening eyes. ·The other gentlemen followed his example, and amid a gay and musical little ripple of words and laughter, the ladies were safely placed upon the ground. Broad streams of crimson sunlight poured over the hill and flowed down upon them; and in this sunny glare, Mr. Prince led his wife up the steps into the hall where the servants were gathered, and with loving grace, bade her welcome home. One quick glance from the brilliant eyes took in the scene, and she seemed pleased. Her lips smiled—her glance rested tenderly on his face, and her kindly nod to the servants made them welcome her presence there with less of fear and more of joy than had shone upon their faces at first. But as the bride's foot pressed the threshold of her own chamber, the sun sank behind the distant hill, and a cold, gray light wrapped the hitherto happy homestead. All at once the pretty room looked cheerless, and she shivered, but turned to her husband with a smile.

"God grant that you may be happy here, my darling," he murmured, touching her brow with his lips.

"I must be since *you* are here," was her answer,

low murmured and thrilling, as she fixed her eyes upon his face, bent so devotedly toward her. And in his intoxication he stood there looking into her eyes, feeling her warm, fragrant breath upon his cheek, the witchery of her influence penetrating his whole being—forgetful of the feet that had trodden that floor, the eyes that had beamed upon him, the holier love that had passed out with the dead. God help him!

CHAPTER VI.

THE EXPERIMENT OF THE CROSS—THE DECISIVE TEST.

THE Truslow cottage looked less dismal than usual. It was about a week after the arrival of the bride at Prince Hill, and John, who had been lucky enough to win favor there in several quarters, had come home laden with delicious freight. Mrs. Prince had given a grand party to which all Princeton was invited, and from the rich store her kitchen afforded, all the poor were made glad.

A crackling fire blazed upon the hearth, for the night was chill; and before this genial blaze sat John, Mrs. Truslow and little Dick, perched upon his small stool in one corner, raised to the seventh heaven of enjoyment by the possession of various riches hitherto unknown in his childish catalogue. In truth, Dick's appearance is worthy of description, as he sat there upon his stool, greedily devouring sundry delicious morsels rare in that humble household.

First, he had John's sunny blue eyes, but deeper set and amusingly cunning in their quick and eager rovings about all objects which came within their range. His hair was a bright yellow, curling tightly about his little round head, and the tiny face was piquant and pretty, in spite of its pallor and thinness. In truth, the child's mouth was beautiful—a pair of exquisite lips parting over a row of pearls rarely displayed, but fascinating when revealed in a smile. His tiny hands were white and dimpled, now crammed with pieces of cake, slices of bread laden with salad, nuts, candies and other dainties. As he sat there with one small leg thrown up over his knee and his tight nankeen pants showing their slender proportions, he presented a grotesque figure to those unused to the sight. A body of the same material, fitting close to the skin, was a decided auxiliary to the grotesque picture, which was finished off by a pair of boots three sizes too large and coming up over the tight nankeen pants, giving a singular finish to the simply ridiculous costume.

John sat near his mother, and watched the little creature with unbounded delight.

"Is the cake good, Dick?" he asked, regarding him amusedly.

"Yeth," lisped the little one. "Bring me thome more every day, won't you?"

"I wish I could," said John, and then he turned to his mother.

"Oh, if you could have seen the beautiful lady, mother! She came out into the dining-room where they were laying the table. I was helping Jim to carry in the silver that made the table glitter, and when she saw me she asked if I was the boy that helped the gardener; and when he said I was, she said: 'Give him all he can carry home of the very best the house affords. And see that all the other poor people in the town have something nice. I could not be happy if I thought they were contrasting our plenty with their own wretchedness.' Oh, mother, you can't think how sweet it sounded! I could have gone on my knees to her—dear, beautiful lady!"

"What a pity Miss Geraldine ain't at home! I wish she was."

"So do I, for I think she would feel better. Did you notice how pale and thin she had grown before she went away?"

"Yes, indeed! I knowed she'd fret her life away. Do you think the new lady will be good to her, John?"

"Good! Why, bless you, mother, she couldn't be anything else than good to everybody!"

"I'm glad, for the poor little thing deserves to be well treated. She is her mother's own child for goodness."

"Mother," said John, mysteriously, "do you know I think Geraldine won't live long? I have heard the housekeeper talking and worrying about her a great deal of late. She says that the slightest shock makes her faint away, and she looks littler every day. Besides, she says the girl is too sweet for this world."

At this moment a knock came upon the door, much to John's annoyance. But he admitted a stranger who accompanied his father home, with as good grace as he could muster, and politely invited him to be seated, while he put his inebriated parent to bed. Such incidents were no novelties at the Truslow cottage.

Accepting the invitation, the man sat down before the fire, and after winning the wife to him by a few judicious remarks, completed the conquest by turning his attention to little Dick.

"Hallo! my young friend, you seem to be doing finely over there. Pray where did you get those splendid boots?"

"Clinthem Peter made 'em," answered small Dick, greedily munching a candy bishop.

"He means Peter Clinchem," graciously explained Mrs. Truslow. "He's the shoe-maker just over the way."

"An' Docty Colt cut off his leg to pay 'im for 'em," volunteered Dick, steadily gazing into the fire, with his mouth very full.

"Indeed! A most delightful way to meet obligations, truly—especially for men of the Esculapian profession. I must be allowed to say, however, that I'd much prefer paying small debts in some other way than by the sacrifice of so important a member of my physical system. What do *you* think about it, hey?"

"Jus' tho," nodded Dick, so knowingly that the visitor seemed exceedingly to relish it as a rich joke.

"Rather a smart young 'un," he said to Mrs. Truslow, who looked delighted and prepared to entertain him with the prodigy's tricks.

"I reckon you'd think him smart if you could see him at some of his pranks. I do get scared half to death sometimes, but I can't help laughin' at him neither. Why, it was only last Sunday that I went

out for a few minutes, and, when I came back, there
sat Dick upon his pap's stool before the lookin'-
glass, with a razor open in his hand! I could 'a'
screamed, I was so put about. When I did get my
breath to ask him what he was doin', he turned to
me as innocent like, an' said kind of surprised: 'I'm
only thavin' mythelf!' You bet your life he got a
good spankin' fur the scare he'd give me. But
•when I'd set him down on his little stool an' told
him not to dare to stir till I told him to, he kept still
as a mouse for ten minutes. Then he looked up at
me and says, quite like: 'Dot over yer bad feelin's,
mammy? Feel any better now?' Oh, he'll be the
death of me some day, I know," at which delightful
prophecy the mother laughed until the tears came
into her eyes, joined heartily in her mirth by the
stranger.

"Well, but you haven't told me how it happened
that Dr. Colt came to pay for your boots?" again
addressing the child. Dick's round eyes winked
gravely for a moment, after which he concluded that
he could not express himself with sufficient clearness, therefore had better save his credit by remain-
ing silent. Having come to this decision, he rather
deliberately changed his position by taking down
one leg and putting up the other across his small
knee. This done, he discovered some very attractive
qualities in some nuts and raisins. Mrs. Truslow
was less cautious, and became the brilliant medium
through which information might be conveyed without too much risk to the happy possessor of the
boots.

7*

"You see, sir, Dick was named for Doctor Colt, an' he's such a cute child, the Doctor likes to make him a present now an' then."

"I s'pose the Doctor must be rich, isn't he?" asked the stranger, seemingly much interested in Dick's welfare.

"Oh no, not to speak of. He's got a house of his own, an' a horse an' gig, besides mod'rate practice."

"Ah, well, out of that he can afford to do something handsome for his namesake. Now, if he'd been named for *me*, I won't say what I'd done for such a bright and promising bairn. Pity I could not have made your acquaintance sooner."

"Oh, that don't make no difference—not the least in the world! His name's never been set down in the family Bible, an' it'ud be easy enough to just put any name you like before the Richard, you know."

The visitor had heedlessly given the proud mother an opportunity for an admirable effort at *finesse*, and she was not slow to use it. Before he was aware, he found himself very neatly trapped, a fact which he rather enjoyed than otherwise, as one might have seen by the smile that crept about his lips.

"Much obliged to you, I'm sure," he said, good-humoredly. "But you see he knows one name already, and it would not be easy for you to get into the habit of calling him by any other. I like to hear my namesakes called by my own name."

"An' pray what is that, sir—may I be so bold as to ask?"

"Not a very pretty cognomen, I am compelled to own. Knight—Rufus Knight."

"Why, that wouldn't be a bad name at all—Rufus Richard Truslow!   Indeed I think it's real nice. Here's the Bible, sir, an' if you like, you may just write it yourself.   I'm sure it would be for good luck."

She brought the Bible, dusty, and covered with cobwebs, from an old book-shelf, not forgetting a quill pen and old-fashioned inkhorn.   The pen was found to be in need of mending, for which service the gentleman took out a bright, new knife, and leisurely trimmed the point to his liking.   John, who by this time had quietly resumed a seat near the fire, looked on the process with all a boy's genuine admiration for glittering steel, a fact which did not escape the stranger's notice.   Indeed, he seemed to see and understand everything without effort.   If he asked questions, it appeared that his inquisitiveness arose out of a desire to talk more than to gain information—so easily did he pass from one subject to another.

"Now, my young hero," he said, addressing Dick without looking at him, "in less than ten minutes you will have taken upon your shoulders a weighty responsibility.   If I give you a grand name, you must bear in mind that it is your bounden duty to do it honor equal to that it does you.   I am sure you will, however.   Dick Sheridan's boy was nothing to what you will be, particularly after the acquisition you are about to add to your already brilliant pretensions.   He thought the sun must hide his face in shame when Master Tom condescended to open his eyes of mornings ; but not sun, nor moon, nor

stars, will ever shine again with undimmed luster!
You will pale their puny lights by contrast, my infant Phœbus! Thou shalt go forth to create wonder, admiration and delight; but let the powers
beware, or the huge Cyclops of the world may grow
blind, and give up the ghost at thy hand! There, it
is done. Rufus Richard Truslow, henceforth my
blessings shall attend you; and as an evidence of
good intentions—see! here is something to buy
goodies with when the gracious lady upon the Hill
grows weary of benevolence."

He carelessly tossed a bright gold piece, which
fell into Dick's boot, and occasioned him some scram-
bling before he could bring it up to regale his delighted eyes, and the eyes of the mother, who was
half beside herself with his good fortune. As carelessly he tossed the pretty new knife to John.

"It's against all rules to give sharp things away,
so I lend it to you, if it will be of any use. If you
forget to return it—why, I suppose I can buy another. The old gentleman appears to be in a happy
state."

This last was occasioned by the sound of a deep
snore escaping from the little chamber adjoining.

"He always sleeps well when he drinks," answered John, stoically. "Where did you find him?"

"At the public house, where he seemed to be disposed to get into a row; so, as nobody else was round
to care for his welfare, I inquired where he lived and
brought him home."

John thanked him, while turning over in his
brown hands the knife, to him the most exquisite

piece of workmanship in the world, with its fine silver mountings.

"I seem—all of us seem to be in luck," he remarked. "How long will it last, I wonder!"

"I trust, until you are rich and prosperous; because I think, if I am any judge of faces, you've got the stuff in you to become a great man. Since I have been in town, a good deal has been said about you to me, and you will find me a friend that never will forsake you, if you will try your best to see what you can do for yourself."

"Thank you, sir—I mean to. The lady up at Prince Hill has been very kind to me, too, and it makes me feel like trying very hard."

"Right. I doubt not she is a munificent lady, and may help you a great deal, if you will only manage to keep in her good graces. You must show an appreciation of all she does, though, in a delicate and unassuming way."

"I don't know much about fine ways, sir—a poor boy like me can't. But I'll serve her willingly, whenever I can."

"Right again. I like your spirit, and I will make it a point to give you a hint sometimes, as I may be around here for some months. Think some of going into land speculations. But I am making a visitation. Drop round to my rooms at the hotel, sometimes, my boy, and if you should want a helping hand, don't be afraid to signify it. Master Rufus Richard Truslow, I have the honor to bid you goodnight," he said, rising. "Mrs. Truslow, if I see your husband again trying to walk on both sides of the pavement at the same time, I shall consider it my pleasurable duty to convince him of the impossibility of such an achievement, and bring him safely to you. John, take care of yourself, and keep *le couteau* until I call for it. Good-night."

And with the easy, half-swaggering air of a good-natured, generous and indolent man, he sauntered out and walked down the street, whistling. Mrs. Truslow launched forth a small torrent of praises, in which John joined more temperately, but in hearty sincerity, while small "Rufus Richard":

"Dest he was a whopper!"

If Mr. Knight had set out to win the hearts of these humble people, he was eminently successful.

CHAPTER VII.

PERHAPS A LITTLE SPARK IS CONCEALED.

THE guests had dispersed to their own rooms to dress for dinner, and the great drawing-room had but one occupant when the carriage drove up under the archway, and Garton sprang out to place Geraldine in her father's arms. A few cheerful words were exchanged between the friends as they mounted the steps, and then Mr. Garton hastened to his own apartment, while Mr. Prince took charge of his daughter. He turned toward the drawing-room.

"Come in here, love. You are cold, and there is a splendid fire. Besides, we shall find mamma here, and alone."

She did not hesitate, though he felt a sudden tremor run through the slight frame. Advancing to where Mrs. Prince reclined in an easy chair, the child held out her hand.

"Oh, you are come!" said Mrs. Prince, starting up and taking the slender fingers within her own. "I did not hear the carriage. And you are shivering with cold. Sit here, dear, and let me take off your wrappings so you can get thawed a little."

Geraldine suffered herself to be placed in the chair Mrs. Prince had vacated, and sat passively, while the white fingers undid her wrappings. Cloak and hood were removed and laid aside, then the lady looked closely into the little pale face and smoothed back the silky black hair from the forehead. Seemingly satisfied with the scrutiny, she bent to press a soft kiss upon Geraldine's lips, murmuring:

"I am glad the journey is over, and to have you where we can make you comfortable, my child. Are you not tired?"

"Not at all; but I got very cold."

"Yet you traveled all day?"

"Yes, since dawn this morning."

"And not weary? Why, I should have been terribly fatigued. Are you warm now? Will you go and have some dinner immediately? I am sure you must need it."

Geraldine rose and gave her father her hand, signifying that she desired him to go with her. As she was about to leave the room, she turned and lifted her solemn eyes to the lady's face.

"You are very beautiful," she said, "and if you will make my dear father happy, I will try with all my soul to love you. Good-night."

"Then you will not come down again?"

"I had rather not this evening, thank you."

"Be it so. Let me see you looking a little more rosy in the morning. I do not like pale cheeks on childish faces."

"I never have color except when much excited, or angry. It is not natural to me."

"We will see if we cannot make it so. I shall take you in hand for this purpose at once."

Geraldine only bowed and retreated, anxious to escape to her own room. Evidently the husband and wife ·had come to an amicable understanding about her, judging by the glance that was exchanged as he went out. When the door closed upon father and child, she sank back in her chair, a very peculiar expression upon her fair face.

"Has made up her mind to be magnanimous, and love me *conditionally*, *if she can*," she murmured with a soft little laugh. "I wonder if I have not gotten my hands full since I volunteered to put her in training? We shall see!"

Sitting still, the ruddy glow of fire-light falling all around her, softly and slowly folding over the shining silk of her crimson dress, with pearly white fingers on which blazed costly jewels, the lady pondered long. It would be half an hour before the last bell would ring, and she enjoyed the luxurious loneliness of the great room, where dusky shadows played at hide and seek with flashes of light from the coals in the grate. Opposite her chair, a large mirror reflected the elegant figure, to which she lifted her eyes languidly now and then, admiring in a passive way her own peerless beauty. To-night she wore a changeful crimson silk with heavy black shadows playing over it as she moved, bringing out the pearly whiteness of her skin in strong relief. A narrow lace collar, rich and fine, was fastened at the throat by a large opal brooch bordered with diamonds. Slender pendants to match graced her ears;

and a diamond clasp fastened a snowy camelia with a faint blush of red in its heart, upon her lustrous hair. The silent voice of the flower told the story in a sentence—"Perfected loveliness." In her attitude of easy grace, shrined in the rich beauty of her surroundings, she formed a picture that would have delighted the eye of a Paul Veronese, though here no incongruities were seen. Everything was in perfect harmony or in splendid contrast. Perhaps she owed to her exquisite taste in dress much of the charm her beauty cast about her. Few women know how to adorn themselves as best becomes them at all times; but Mrs. Prince was one of these few.

Mr. Garton coming in unheard and unheeded, thought of the "burning eastern lilies" of which Aldrich passionately sung, with the first glance. But that first glance had only revealed a portion of her side face, turned from him in a study of the lighted marble hearth. When he had gained a more advanced position, his arm sunk upon the mantle-piece, where he stood with whitening lips, supporting his brow and looking at the royal face with sickening pain at his heart. Probably if she felt a presence near her, she thought it one of the guests, and was not disposed at once to rob him of a quiet contemplation of her charms.

The sound of a quick-drawn, quivering breath reached her ear as a glimmering smile began to dawn upon her lips, and then, as if surprised, she looked up. In an instant she was upon her feet, staring at him as at a specter. The soft smile was frozen—the warm glow dashed from her cheeks.

"My God! my God!" came in a stifled voice from her cold lips.

And so they stood, face to face, both white as Parian marble—both stricken mute by the painful force of an unexpected meeting. He was first to break the dreadful silence that followed.

"Then it is you whom my friend has married?" with an indescribable tone, and a dash of unspeakable bitterness.

"Yes! and you are the *school-master* of whom I heard my husband speak. I knew the name was the same, but oh, I did not know that it was in truth yourself who bore it."

"And you never suspected it?"

"Never once! Good heavens, no! God forbid that I should have crossed this threshold knowing it! *I* should never have come, or *you* had never returned."

"I believe you," he answered, very bitterly. "Oh, you would not have dared! But it is fate, you see. Pity one of the fatal Three had not led me to a knowledge of this truth ere my poor friend was sacrificed. In stabbing him, I shall as fearfully wound myself; and you know better than any one, perhaps, how selfish is human nature."

"Oh, Nathaniel, you cannot—you will not be so ungenerous as to tell him!" she cried, imploringly. "He knows nothing, and he is so—happy! You would not kill his peace to gratify a selfish and unworthy revenge!"

"Revenge! I revenge myself upon you! It could never come to that, you well know. Men do not cast women aside, then turn and talk of vengeance. No. I do my duty through different motives. My friend has been duped, and I reveal the treachery of which he has been made a victim—that is all."

The expression that passed over her beautiful face was terrible—hate, fear and anguish, mingled with passionate love. She struggled for composure to speak, but could not for several moments. By this time there was the sound of passing feet in the hall, and rustling silks on the stairs. The guests would soon be in the drawing-room.

"Only promise me one thing!" she gasped, hurriedly; "promise me that you will not say aught to my husband until I see you once more."

"You expect to charm me from my purpose?" he sneered.

"No," she said, haughtily, "I expect to speak a word to Mr. Garton's reason which will have the effect to make him pause before he brings irreparable ruin to a household like this."

"When shall this word be spoken? As soon as possible, I hope."

"Yes; as soon as possible."

"I will wait to hear it."

She waited for no more, but glided through a side door, leaving him alone. A moment later, two ladies entered, followed by as many gentlemen. One of the latter, a slight man with a frank, open face and manner, walked up to Mr. Garton and held out his hand.

"I should know George Garton's son by his resemblance to his noble father. Allow me to introduce myself—Frank Bruce—son of Edward Bruce."

Mr. Garton warmly grasped the offered hand.

"Son of my dead father's dearest earthly friend! Indeed I am glad to meet you. When I came home after a long absence once, I heard of little else than Frank Bruce, Midshipman in the U. S. Navy. What is his present rank?"

"*Was* a Lieutenant—have resigned, and am nothing now in consequence."

"How was that?"

"Got tired of the service, and preferred living on a snug little income left me by a maiden aunt, to 'sailing the seas over,' Enoch Arden like. But pardon me—allow me to present you to my friends, Mrs. Darby—Miss Eldridge—Mr. Garton, Mr. Darby."

The ladies bowed graciously; the gentleman cordially offered his hand, after which the party were seated and entered into general conversation. During this interval, Mr. Garton had time to observe that Miss Eldridge was a slight and graceful blonde with a dreamy, half sad countenance, while Mrs. Darby was a sprightly little brunette, with a sunny, saucy face, set off by a wealth of very short, clustering curls. They were dressed alike, in flowing white cashmere, but trimmed differently—Miss Eldridge affecting blue, while Mrs. Darby wore red. The husband of the latter was a young man, very tall and slender, at whose side his wife would have looked like a child in anything but a sweeping dress.

Pretty soon he discovered that the little lady was not only witty but daring, as she proved by a remark she managed to edge in when a short pause occurred in the conversation.

"You cannot think how glad I am that you are come at last, Mr. Garton. I am dying for somebody to flirt with, having grown tired of all the gentlemen here."

Such a remark from any other might have embarrassed him greatly; but seeing the amusement of all the party, he joined in the general laugh and answered in the same tone:

"I owe you thanks both for the compliment and the warning. Forewarned, forearmed, you know."

"Oh, I don't mean to say that there is the slightest danger where you are concerned. But I have known all the gentlemen here so long, there is not the slightest amusement to be got out of them. They are like the tasteless pulps of oranges long since drained of their sweetness."

"You acknowledge, then, that there was sweetness —once upon a time!" put in Mr. Bruce. "Thanks for this much, at least. I had not flattered myself that I had ever been more than a mere 'pulp' in your estimation. Doubtless the other gentlemen will join me in a vote of thanks as soon as they hear of this concession."

"Do not be in too great a hurry, Mr. Bruce. You must remember that politeness forbids us to speak of the qualities of persons in their presence, therefore you could not have been included."

"I am no less indebted, fair lady, since in that case I must be excluded also from the pulpy characteristic which excites your disgust, so strongly."

"Oh the vanity of man!" cried Mrs. Darby. "But I will not add fuel to yours, sir, by talking with you all the time. Mr. Garton, why did you not come sooner to attend the party here, last evening?"

" I did not like to leave my mother sooner than was positively necessary. Besides, I think my partiality for parties has passed away with the need to grasp life in more earnest ways. You must know that I am not a man of ample means and leisure, like our friend Bruce. Only a poor village schoolteacher."

" That's a comfort," answered the lady quickly. " Because a school-master may still be a gentleman, while his work forces him to dispense with a vast deal of nonsense inflicted upon us by those beperfumed and becurled gentlemen of leisure we too often find in society."

She cast a sly glance at Mr. Bruce, who only laughed good-naturedly, while her husband pinched her check, and advised her to take care that she did not become too personal in her remarks.

" No fear of that. No one is called upon even to try if the cap fits him. Therefore, there can be nothing personal about it. To return to the party, Mr. Garton—I enjoyed it mightily—the only one I have enjoyed in an age. Your young Princetonians are so very droll."

" In what respect, may I ask?"

" Oh, a number of respects! In the first place, they are as numerous as the Danaides, and almost as ferocious as the little warriors who sprang from the Dragon's teeth. I judge that young ladies must be very scarce in Princeton."

" They are! Probably that will account for their

ferocity. They have learned it through rivalry for the attention of the few their native place affords."

"Just so, precisely—that is my idea. You ought to have seen them. If one young Apollo led out a blushing nymph, and another dared to look at her while under his care, the eyes of the successful one shot daggers through him mercilessly. If it was not for the stupidity of the race of beaux, one might have royal fun exciting their jealousy of each other. But once get them started, and they'd never know where to stop—and I, for one, would not like to have blood on my hands!"

"What dreadful things are you saying, Mrs. Darby?" asked Mrs. Prince, coming in with a number of the other guests at this moment, followed by her husband, who presented her to Mr. Garton as to a stranger. She bowed with a changeless cheek, and again turned with easy grace to hear Mrs. Darby's answer.

"Sensible things, *ma petite cherie*, not dreadful! What a talent you have for misnomers."

"But you were talking about blood upon one's hands with a shudder?"

"Oh, I was only saying what fun it would be to excite the jealousy of the Princeton youths against each other, if they were not so stupid as to render it dangerous. I dearly love to get people into a 'muss' where there is no danger of duels and murders, and such little amusements."

"Amusements! Horrible! You ought to have lived in the reign of Robespierre when women sent men of gentle blood to the guillotine and from their windows amused themselves with counting the seconds, and calculating when their heads would fall."

"Oh, now you are unkind. I said were it not for the danger, and now you would make the danger my real amusement. Bah! I'll talk about my nice little foibles to my husband after this. He'll understand me—won't you, Pert?"

"Dare say I shall understand the foibles—but whether they are nice, is another question."

"There, now! Even Hubs is going to turn against me. I declare it's too stupid. Mr. Prince, do you think the dinner will be announced soon!"

"Doubtless—for there is the boy bowing in the door at this moment, which he has thrown open, inviting your exit. I am glad to find our mountain air gives you an appetite!"

"On the contrary, I am absolutely pining away; but my philosophy points me to the table, where, if sharp things must be dealt with, it may as well be a knife as any other destructive weapon."

Mr. Prince glanced at Mr. Garton as he offered his arm to Mrs. Darby, requesting Mr. Darby to conduct one of the other ladies out. There was no escape, therefore, and Mrs. Prince was thus forced upon his escort. A great repugnance to the duty was in his heart, but he could not refuse this act of courtesy to his friend's wife.

Once as they proceeded he glanced at her features, marble-like, save where a touch of carmine took the pallor from her cheeks. Her face was not unlike the camellia in her hair, snowily fair, with its faint blush of red. He felt her hand tremble, light as was its touch upon his arm, and knew that she struggled beneath that icy calm even as he was struggling within himself. But women are better at acting than men, and while his voice faltered slightly in answering the questions she put about his journey and visit, hers was clear and sweet.

Dinner was served under a fire of wit and repartee from all parties, after which, according to the English custom, the ladies rose to withdraw and leave the gentlemen over their wine. At the same moment a servant entered, and, before Mrs. Prince could leave her place, presented her with a bouquet of flowers.

"How queer!" she exclaimed, taking them from his hand, "where did they come from?"

"John Truslow left them, madam, and begged that you would accept them as a very small tribute from a poor boy you'd been very kind to. He has nothing else to offer."

"How very, very funny!" said Mrs. Darby, coming closer to examine them. "Your rustic admirer exhibits strange taste. Pray who is he?"

"Only a very poor boy, as you have just heard, who helps the gardener sometimes. I ordered something to be given him from the table last night, and he takes this mode of thanking me! Shall we adjourn to the drawing-room?"

She led the way, holding the flowers carelessly, with a somewhat imperious and haughty step and manner. Mr. Garton alone had noted a quick movement of a hand that was pressed tightly over her heart, and the pallor of the lips no longer protected by carmine. Her agitation could not have risen from the simple act of the humble boy. She was not likely thus visibly to betray an emotion of such a nature; consequently he remained quiet after the ladies withdrew, pondering the incident and puzzling himself as to its meaning. Something beyond his power of comprehension was enshrined in this homely offering—an unseen spark whose flame she dreaded perhaps. And his mental resolve was, for his friend's sake to seek for the key to all mysteries wherein she might be concerned, and thus gain a controlling power over her.

CHAPTER VIII.

AN EMPIRE WITHIN AN EMPIRE.

"I'm delighted that this is Saturday instead of Monday, Mr. Garton."

Mrs. Darby looked up from a trifle of embroidery that occupied her fingers as that gentleman came in with his pupil from a long walk.

"Thank you ; but you have a reason for honoring me with so pleasing a compliment ?".

"Certainly. Being Saturday, you have no school, and I am selfish enough to wish to be amused, especially as Celia is too indisposed to come down. My husband has gone off with Mr. Prince for a ride, Mrs. and Mr. Goodman are driving, and the others are luxuriating in their rooms. Consequently I am thrown upon Mr. Bruce entirely, and he has grown too stupid to be longer endurable."

The gentleman alluded to bowed lowly, laughed and resigned his seat, taking another near by. But a glance showed Miss Eldridge sitting alone in a distant window, and as soon as he could disengage himself without rudeness, he left the sprightly little lady for her more quiet friend. She was seated upon an ottoman, her cheek pressed upon her hand, looking off at the distant mountains. She did not look up as he approached, but spoke quietly:

"I have just been wondering whether I should envy, or, following the example of our darling little friend yonder, take liberties and scold you."

"You alarm me. What have I done to deserve the latter?"

"Nothing terrible," now lifting her blue eyes with a smile, to his face. "Only it is such a grand morning for a scamper over the hills, and I saw you going out with your pupil. I could not help envying you."

"If I had only known it! But I really thought you still asleep when we went out, and I could not know that you loved the woods. There is a keen frost, moreover, that might have bitten your fingers rather more than would be pleasant to a delicate lady."

She laughed.

"I see you judge me by the general standard. But I can assure you, though I am pale and slight, I am not at all delicate. Nor do I ever sleep later than seven; while I dearly love the keen air, and the biting frost which stings the cheeks of Nature to such glorious blushing."

"Can it be possible that you rise so early? I confess myself interested to hear how you can amuse yourself so long before the others are up."

"I wonder at your implied question, since you have tasted the excellencies of Mr. Prince's library. The companionship of books is an unfailing source of pleasure to me."

Something in her tone and expression charmed and set him at ease. He took a chair to which she pointed invitingly, and sat down near her. A volume lay closed upon her lap, and as his eyes glanced toward it she handed it to him laughingly.

"Do not imagine that my choice of reading, I pray you. A mere incident made me take it up this morning."

"Ghost stories! Certainly I should not charge any lady with a choice of such things as these," he said, elevating his brows. "I believe the whole race too universally timid."

"Allow me to say that you are much mistaken, sir. To most ladies there is a fascination about the alleged supernatural which makes them read while they quake. I am not complimented by being included in the timid class, however."

"Then you are not superstitious?"

"Not in the least. At the same time, I like to read about mysterious things. At one time in my life, the terrible old legends from the German were my favorite books, I like now to read such things as 'Owen's Footfalls on the boundaries of another world.'"

He looked at her curiously.

"Do you ever read 'Swedenborg?'"

"Yes—'Heaven and Hell!' is a favorite book."

"Why?—because of its Spiritualism?"

"No. I like the wonderful and original beauty of his ideas. That our friends can come back to us after death, I have never believed for an instant. But the idea of eternal progression is very fascinating. Robert Browning has grasped it, and embodied it most beautifully in his 'Evelyn Hope.'"

"You believe, then, that to each is assigned a position in heaven, higher or lower as the case may be, according to their merits? How is your faith in Biblical history?"

"Almost perfect. Many things I cannot understand; and I am perplexed by the frequent contradictions that meet me in my reading. But so far as it bears upon the coming of Christ and the redemption of the world by His death, I have no doubts or fears of its truth."

"With this faith, how do you reconcile Swedenborg's idea with the Savior's parable of the laborers in the vineyard—the last of whom were paid as much as the first who had wrought all day in the burning sun?"

"I have often thought of that, and I do not know that I can give you a satisfactory answer. Justice is doubtless one of the greatest of the Divine attributes, and if the husbandman deemed it just to pay the last equally with the first, it must have been that the *capacity* of the last was greater, and consequently they in a short time were enabled to do what the others had accomplished in a day."

"You have no authority for such a conclusion. The husbandman answered the murmurers that it was lawful and just to do as he willed with his own, and that they had agreed with him for a penny a day; therefore they had no reason to expect more. He did not plead their superior abilities, or say that, though hired at the latest hour, they had wrought as much as the first."

"I know it, and you are right in reminding me that we can overreach our authority to satisfy a fancy of our own. To me it seems incredible that the low, plodding, half-besotted intellect can rise equally high with'the brilliant soul that God has touched with sparks of His own glorious light. Can I reconcile it with my idea of His justice to believe that the soul who has through a whole mortal career trampled upon His laws, and insulted God by sin, profanity and negligence, can stand side by side with the pure and humble worker that lived only for the glory of the Father? Oh, no, that is impossible."

"But His mercy is farther reaching than His justice. For that reason He sent His Son, by whose death the door was opened for every sinner that could believe and repent."

"Do you think there can be any repentance when the flame of life has burned to its socket? I have no faith in death-bed repentances. If we would hope to have paid to us the penny for our labor, we must go into the vineyard while there is yet time to *work*. It is so far from my idea of a great and true God, I am revolted by the pretensions of some who claim that the soul growing sin-sick from terror in the last moment of his life, cries out his repentance, and is placed at the right hand of the Father with the Son who died for such as he."

"If the world could look upon it as you do, fewer would be so tardy in entering the vineyard," answered Mr. Garton, thoughtfully. "But to lay aside these prolific questions for theological handling—you have not told me what incident made you choose this book for your morning's reading."

Now she did not smile, but said gravely, looking out upon the fiery dahlias:

"I am reluctant to mention it, for I am satisfied that a practical solution might easily be deduced from what I choose to characterize as a mystery."

She paused, and he waited for her to proceed.

"Yet I dare say I ought to tell you, as an inmate of this house, and one likely to be interested in what concerns it. To be brief, I was sitting by my window last night, enjoying the moonlight on the beautiful mountains, when I saw a man's figure stealing through the shrubbery toward the garden. There another figure met him, whether man or woman I could not tell, for it was slender and enveloped from head to foot in a long cloak. I might have thought it a romantic tryst from the lower circles, the kitchen, had it not terminated so soon. The man seemed to stop but a moment, then glided hastily away while the other disappeared in an unknown direction. Of course I choose to look upon it in its most irresponsible light; but if you will take the trouble to warn Mr. Prince without making my testimony a necessity in the matter, it may be that he will save his favorite horse, or that the contents of the silver closet may remain intact."

For a moment he regarded her searchingly.

"You imagine it to be thieves?" he asked, at length.

"More probably they than anybody else," she replied; and her face showed no other suspicion.

"I will do better than to warn my friend, by taking pains to look into the matter myself. Allow me to thank you for your kindness in telling me this."

"There is nothing in it to thank me for. Had I told Mr. Prince, he would have told Celia, and she is timid enough to feel worried. To have recounted the affair to any other gentleman in the house would have been folly. An unpleasant stir would have been the inevitable consequence, and I dislike any such excitements—especially if I would be in any way connected with them."

"How did you know I would not plunge you into one, eyes deep?"

She looked at his smiling face, and their eyes met.

"I knew you would not from a brief study of your face last night. There is Geraldine looking at us shyly from the door. Does she want you?"

Seeing herself noticed by them, the child came up to Mr. Garton and delivered a message from John Truslow. He was anxious to see him as soon as convenient.

"Where is he now?" asked Mr. Garton.

"I told him he might wait in the library till you could come to him. He seems troubled and anxious about something."

"I will see what it is at once, if Miss Eldridge will excuse me, and you will entertain her until I return."

"A good arrangement, for I want to get acquainted with your little friend," said Miss Eldridge, pleasantly, taking the child's hand. And as he rose to go out, he was pleased to see Geraldine settle down with a confiding air at the lady's side, though her manner was marked with a shyness and reserve which he knew would rapidly pass away.

Crossing the hall, he passed down the corridor and entered the library where he expected to find John, but he was not there. The door of his own sitting-room stood slightly ajar; so, thinking still to find the boy, he pushed it open and went in. There, instead of the one he sought, he found the wife of his friend. She was standing before the lighted grate, the warm gleams flashing over her white cheeks and rounded, polished arms, from which the flowing sleeves of the dark blue wrapper fell away. As his look of surprise fell on her face, she crimsoned deeply.

"Pardon this unseemly intrusion, but necessity hath no law, you know, and I could not rest until I could see you. I came down the back stairway and to the library, when I found John Truslow waiting to speak with you. So, as he said Geraldine had gone to fetch you, I sent him down to the kitchen for half an hour, then slipped in here, believing it to be safer."

"And now that I am here, what have you to say that can convince me it is my duty to hold my peace?"

"God knows whether I can say anything that will move you, Nathaniel. But you will listen to me, at least?" she answered, passionately, turning with a half-imploring expression to face him fully.

"Go on. Who knows but you may be able to

rule me still—even now? I find that you have not lost much of your old power over the objects you make up your mind to charm. Geraldine told me, with a burst of penitential tears, not two hours ago, how she had wakened last night and found you sitting by her bed, with her hands pressed softly in yours, and pearly drops on your fair cheeks. You are a quick-sighted woman, to see your shortest route to her heart so soon. But I am not surprised at that."

"Curl your lip as you will, and show me as you will, how utterly you despise me! I know my own heart, and that my motive for winning the love of my husband's poor little sorrowful daughter, is pure. Has my life been so happy, think you, that I can afford to trample all chances for the future beneath my feet? Do—"

He put out his hand imperiously.

"Celia, no more of this! Your real motive I cannot fathom yet; but I will in time. I know you too well to be made to believe for one instant that you are capable of an unselfish action. Let the child alone, or I warn you that the day will come when you will repent it in sackcloth and ashes."

She let her cheek droop to the corner of the mantel-piece, her lips quivering, her bosom heaving with suppressed sobs.

"You are cruel, cruel. You would force me back from all hope of earthly happiness, and crush me down beyond the possibility of rising. Have you no pity in your heart for a miserable woman, who sees only wretchedness before her?"

"Pray, why should you be miserable and wretched? You have won a husband who not only idolizes you, but has all your heart desires of wealth and luxury to lay at your feet. I should say that having reached this triumphant end to your aim, you have no reason to complain."

"No reason to complain—with you here to impute to me the unworthiest motives, and betray my past misery to my present destruction. It would have been dreadful enough to meet you here, after what has passed; but to have you array yourself vengefully against me, is maddening. Oh, Nathaniel, hear me this once, and spare me, as you hope for mercy in your own extremity."

He stood before her, looking at her beautiful face, while she poured forth a torrent of eloquent entreaties. All that she said we will not repeat now, but he listened with a mixture of incredulity, pity and scorn. When she had done, and tremblingly waited his answer, he said, solemnly:

"I give due weight to all you have said, and I am willing to offer you a fair chance to redeem the past. What is done now cannot be helped, and I would spare your husband's peace, while I feel myself bound to guard his honor. But if I forbear, you are to prove to me by your daily actions, that you are sincere in the professions you have made to me. Be kind to my little Geraldine, but no more. Let her affections alone. And see that every action shall be so open and pure, I shall have no cause to doubt you. Otherwise, so help me heaven, I will reveal to him all that you implore me to suppress. God forgive me if evil to him or his should arise out of this concession to you. I warn you that I put no faith in your promises, while I give you fair trial. From my heart I believe the child was right when she declared that yours was 'a body without soul'—a fair and beautiful cheat."

CHAPTER IX.

THE ART IS TO CONCEAL ART.

"You are disposed to be complimentary," she answered in proud bitterness. He saw that his words stung deeply, and that she chafed restively under his powerful hold. By her beauty, her wit, and intelligence, she had been used to rule at will; but here her power had a limit and the queen found her master in one she had sought to make her subject. The thought was very bitter, but womanlike, she submitted to present necessity, that the end might recrown her victorious.

"I am in a fine mood for compliments," he said coolly. "To deny your charms would be folly, for I think I never saw a fairer type of human loveliness than you are at this moment. I call you a cheat, because I have been cheated by you, affording me good proof upon which to base my assertion. You are a living embodiment of a heartless woman, using your beauty as a snare for unwary men whom you choose to play with, as a lioness plays with a kid before tearing it to pieces."

She raised her eyes and fixed them upon his face in a steady gaze, and her lip curled while ber bosom rose and fell with the force of an inward struggle.

"At least be just to yourself, if you will not be just to me. Do not utter things you know to be false."

"You know I utter only truth."

"You do not! I never was the heartless thing you paint me, and never took pleasure in giving pain to mortal—man or woman. I have been truer than you have!—and I would not stoop to the meanness of torturing a creature held in my power, as I am in yours. Is it nobler for the lion to goad his helpless victim, or less cruel than the play of the lioness? Truly men are noble creatures, and marvelously generous with themselves! For the sins that fall to the lot of humanity, they can pat their own shoulders and complacently cry 'good boy!' But woe to the luckless woman who chances to be at their mercy! They will plant a foot upon her neck, and with a sword's point against the breaking heart, coolly tell her of her sins and exult in her helplessness—oh, noble and generous man! How dearly we should love them, should we not? How we ought to glory in the power they have to break our hearts?"

He had grown very pale under the scornful passion her words expressed. A troubled and doubtful expression swept over his features.

"Celia, answer me truly. What was your object in marrying Mr. Prince?"

"You have done me the honor to answer your own question. He is young and handsome, and rich. He loves me. Perhaps I love him!—why

not, as a dutiful wife should? It surely is not impossible for a woman to love twice. Her affections,
for the sake of her own peace, should be as con-
veniently flexible as the men at whose mercy she is
placed, that being her only protection."

"You trifle with my question; but listen: If I
could be assured that you loved him, that you would
be to him a good and true wife, you could ask no
friendly help that I would not give you. It is the
fear that you will cause him to drink of the cup
which I have tasted, that makes me harsh and stern
with you."

Again she looked into his eyes, throwing back her
head proudly.

"I will not try to win your leniency by professing
that which I do not feel. Whatever you may choose
to think, I did not marry him for his money; neither
did I marry him for love. It would be equally unjust to him and myself, were I to profess such a
sentiment. But I do honor and esteem him above
all other men. If I gave him no heart, it is because
I had none to give. That was buried with my best
hopes long ago. It is a weary while since life looked
bright to me. Darkness deeper than Egyptian blackness fell upon me years ago, and left me groping
hopelessly after the light that can never come. He
found me and loved me. I thought that in trying to
make his happiness, and in caring for his child, I
might learn peace and contentment at least. Judge,
then, how bitterly I meet my disappointments, and
how hard to see my one last little hope drifting away
from me!"

"Celia, are you speaking the truth—the whole truth?"

He snatched her hand and wrung it hard in his clasp.

"If I had chosen to lie, I would have told you I loved him."

"Oh, I would to God that I could trust you, woman!"

The hand was flung back to her side, and he paced the floor several times in excitement and uncertainty. Her softened voice recalled him.

"You may trust me, Nathaniel. I have no earthly thing to live for now outside my husband's home. Scan my actions as you will, and you will never find a fault henceforth. Only, let the past lie in the grave; looking at the corpses of my dead, sickens me, while I learn too sadly to know that my heart, though buried too, has retained its trick of aching."

"I do not comprehend you. That it must be disagreeable to have the past recalled, I can imagine, but why it can pain you, is beyond my power to conceive."

"You too say this! But this is not a subject to discuss longer. If you have no more to say to me, I will go."

"You are right," he answered, with a sudden coldness, "and I will not encourage you to imply things you could not speak, or I hear, without dishonor to my friend, were they even strong enough to shake my unbelief, which they never could be. One thing more before you go. After what you have said, you cannot refuse to tell me why the receipt of a homely bunch of flowers should affect you as you were affected last night."

Without any visible surprise, she answered, quietly:

"You warn me to remember that you have taken Ascalaphus for your model, and I may expect to be called to account if I am red or pale! There was something in that little bouquet that reminded me of days gone by—something that I banished long ago from my sight as too suggestive of hours once happy and precious."

He pressed her mercilessly.

"What was it?"

"Arbor Vitæ."

He recalled the time when he had placed a fragrant sprig in her hand and asked her if she could read its language; and her only answer was a vivid blush, as she pointed to a ring on her third finger. His lip trembled.

"Will you let me see that bouquet, Celia?"

"Certainly, if you desire. Test me as you will, I shall not murmur, though you heap insults upon me to the very last extremity."

"I do not want to insult you, but to learn faith. Go bring them to me."

She obeyed him with a queenly step and patient air. While she was gone, he stood leaning his brow upon his hand, his handsome face overspread with deep sadness. In dealing with her the whole of his kindly nature seemed changed, and he realized it with a heavy sigh.

"Can we, when once wronged, ever be just to those who wronged us? It may be that she speaks the truth, and deserves for her patient forbearance more than I. If I could believe what she would have me understand, I should not wonder at her agitation—poor heart! But I cannot, cannot trust her."

She came back soon, the withered offering in her hand, and gave it to him.

"There it is—the poor little boy's honest tribute of gratitude for a broken heap of luxuries from my table."

"Celia, if I had thought it an honest offering, prompted alone by that boy's grateful impulse, no suspicion had ever been expressed."

"Why, what could you think?" she asked, wonderingly. Nathaniel Garton found it hard to resist the fair face lifted openly to his gaze, to all appearance innocent as a babe's.

"Will you look me in the face and tell me that this seemingly harmless thing has no deeper meaning than you claim the boy has given?" he asked, turning and scanning the flowers. His face was gradually hardening.

"I do not know what you would have; but I do know that the martyrdom of endurance is worse than the martyrdom of action! God pity the woman whose life is wrecked by a worthless love—who carries a cross on her heart to which the iron spiked cross of the devotee were rest and ease—and yet must go out into the world with a smile upon her lips, lest it should see and mock her shame! I

promised too much when I said that I would not
murmur. You make my burden too heavy by con-
verting trifles like that into objects for analysis."

"Wait! You may say too much before I have
done. Whom did you meet in the garden last
night?"

It was a random shot, but it went home with telling force. The quick start and telling look of terror
cast at him involuntarily, betrayed what she thought
she had concealed from all eyes.

"Ah, I see how it is! And you had a double motive for your tender vigil by the bedside of the hap-
less child who is bound to look upon you as a
mother. My God, to what lengths will not headstrong women run!"

"Your system of espionage must be complete indeed, if you succeeded in discovering me in the garden last night."

There was a strangely taunting, scornful look in
her eyes now, as she rallied from the effects of the
blow. It stung him into exposing himself, and he
answered, imprudently:

"I have organized no system of espionage, and
did not claim to see you. Others did, however, and
it ought to prove to you that nothing imprudent can
be done without danger of exposure."

"Who under my roof dares to say he saw me."

"No one claims to have seen you, but some one
was seen. I could not be far wrong in fixing upon
you as the only one likely to indulge in such mysterious trysts. All your actions tend to prove it no
other than yourself."

10*

"You cannot point to a single proof."

"Not even the vigil by Geraldine—where if you should be missed by Mr. Prince and occasion inquiry or search, a touching and telling explanation might ensue?"

"That is no proof, but the coloring given to a simple action by an unkind and suspicious mind."

"But I have yet another."

"Name it."

He went to a table, and taking up a piece of paper, began to turn the bouquet in his hand, and make notes. Watching him intently, she became still paler, but made no sign. Presently he returned to her side, and held up the paper before her eyes.

"Here is the story told by this trifle. I begin from the point where the ribbon is tied, and read around the first circle. By supplying a few words, the result is:

"You are the queen of coquettes. Constant and devoted, I am forsaken. I am slighted—you are treacherous. Have I not suffered enough? Pity me—give me some encouragement. Meet me in the garden. I have a message for you."

He waited for her to speak, but she was silent, and he continued.

"Your correspondent has shown marvelous tact, for where autumn will not supply a June flower to do his bidding, he slips in a good imitation from the milliner's shop which passes muster exceedingly well until the others fade and the rainbow hues of the Iris refuse to grow dim. What have you to say to my solution of this little mystery, or the proof it gives?"

" Here is the story told by this trifle."—*Page* 114.

"Nothing, for I might waste words until doomsday without one atom of faith as the reward of my words. Your confidence in your own sagacity is too great to be overturned by a denial from my lips."

"Dare you deny it."

"I do, most emphatically. You have read a meaning in that paltry thing of which I never even dreamed ; and I can take my oath that I did not once put my foot beyond the door after sunset."

She turned haughtily, and swept from the room without another word, leaving him perplexed and doubtful.

"It cannot be possible that I am mistaken," he mused. "I know her old passion for the language of flowers, and how perfectly she could read a message through my beautiful offerings. And yet— perhaps—I may have been too hasty. She betrayed no uneasiness when I asked for them. As she said, my lack of faith may make me unjust in everything. Yet how shall I explain her agitation when I asked her whom she met in the garden ? This bouquet asks for a meeting in the garden, and is the plea of a slighted lover that she will relent and pity him. I will get to the bottom of this thing ! Artful as she is, she shall not conceal her art from me to my friend's destruction. My God! to think that I should be brought to wrestle with such a demon in human shape ! Heaven grant it may not terminate disastrously to one or both."

He threw the flowers in a drawer, locked it and went to seek John Truslow.

CHAPTER X.

ARMED WITH TRIFLES.

In the hall Mr. Garton met his friend, who had only a few moments before returned from the ride. The latter stopped him.

"Have you seen Mrs. Prince lately? I cannot find her."

"I think I heard one of the ladies say she kept her room with headache this morning," he answered evasively, feeling a weight upon his heart that would grow heavier from day to day, as he was forced to deceive the trusting husband. He longed to link his arm within that of Mr. Prince, and openly tell him all he had reason to fear. But his judgment bade him wait—spare his friend and give the woman a chance to redeem herself, if indeed there was an atom of good in her nature. So he stifled the impulse and stood for several moments talking to him.

"I have not had time to get a word with you since your return. Tell me what you think of her?"

"Your wife?—that she is beautiful as woman can be," he answered with a smile.

"Ah, yes, I know, but it is not that exactly,

Nathaniel. Everybody will acknowledge her beauty; but I want to know how she impresses you."

Mr. Garton regarded the happy, fearless face of his friend, and knew that there was no room for distrust in his fond heart, now. The thought of it seemed cruel.

" You forget that I have not had time to pass judgment safely," was his guarded reply.

" When you come to know her, I am assured of what the verdict will be :—that she is as good as she is lovely. You will spend this evening with us in the drawing-room ?"

" I would rather be excused."

" Oh, no; be social. We shall have the old quiet again ere long."

" I will come if you wish it."

" Then you will be with us," and Mr. Prince sprang lightly up the stairs, suffering Mr. Garton to proceed in search of John. Evidently John had grown weary of waiting, for the cook said he had loitered about the door for some time, and then he went off, she could not tell where.

Still intent upon the talk he desired with the boy, Mr. Garton gave a look round the premises to see that he was not there before strolling down to the cottage to find him. But he was equally unsuccessful when he arrived there. Mrs. Truslow said he had not been home, and she was quite certain he must be up at the Hill, as he seemed anxious to see Mr. Garton.

" Do you know what he wanted with me?" he asked, declining the stool she offered with a wave of the hand.

"No, sir.   I tried to find out, but he wouldn't tell me.   You know he is a headstrong boy."

"Perhaps he will be the better as a man for that, though I certainly would rather see him respectful to the wishes of his parents."

"He's been good to me, sir, but he never could be respectful to sich as us—never! a drunkard, an' a poor ailin' critter that can't do much but scold."

"Look at my new clo'es!" cried little Dick, thrusting himself into sight to display a new suit of bright blue which made him look exceedingly smart.   "Ain't they nice?   Stranger man give 'em to me."

"Indeed!   And who is this liberal 'stranger man' who can afford to dress you out so trimly?" asked Mr. Garton, kindly, stooping with a pleasant smile to stroke the yellow curls.

"He's a stranger man 'at's dot lots o' shiners. He gi' me ten dollars.   Mammy hid it to keep pap from gittin' it to buy whisky."

"It's a kind gentleman, sir, as took a fancy to the young un, an' promised me to be a good friend to him ef I'd change his name an' give him a part. We call him Dick when nobody's by, 'cause you see it comes so handy.   But when the gentleman's about, we call him Rufus—that's his new name."

"Well, Rufus, or Dick, are you coming to school shortly?"

"No."

"Why not?   You are getting large enough to learn to read."

"Don't want to; want to stay home an' wear new

breeches an' eat goodies from the big house up yonder. John's going to bring me some more."

At this Mr. Garton turned away; and whatever the thoughts the child's allusion called up might have been, they were not agreeable. His brow clouded, and he sighed heavily. With another pat upon Dick's curly pate, and a nod for the mother, he walked away and took the road back to Prince Hill. Half-way up the lane he met the boy, who, seeing him, crimsoned, and looked as if the meeting was anything but agreeable.

"Why, John, I have been looking for you. Where have you been?"

"Up at the Hill, sir. I hope you had a pleasant visit, sir."

"Yes, thank you. Have you been a good boy in my absence, John?"

"Not very, I'm afraid, sir; but as good as I could. It isn't easy for a boy like me to try to reform. You know everybody's bound to put me down."

"I know it, my poor little fellow. But you will persevere, won't you? Show them what you can become in spite of their opposition. I have not thought of any other of my pupils with such anxious interest as of you."

John colored with pleasure, and assured him that he would always try to be better, to deserve his interest.

"I heard that you wanted to see me particularly. What is it?" asked Mr. Garton, curiously watching the boy's face change to its first confused and troubled expression.

"Oh, nothing much, sir! I wanted to see you after being away so long, and I took the liberty of going up."

"But there was some other reason, I am sure. You waited in the library until Mrs. Prince came and sent you away. Where did you go then?"

"To the kitchen, sir."

"When I came out to find you there, you had gone. Where were you then?"

"I took a little walk out to the stable to see the lady's new pony. She's ordered one for Geraldine, and is going to teach her to ride."

But John could not hide his uneasiness, and Mr. Garton pressed him cautiously, suspecting that there was more behind than his worst suspicions could fathom without difficulty. After a short, thoughtful pause, he remarked, in a casual way:

"You seem to be getting on remarkably well with Mrs. Prince, John. How did you manage to get so entirely into her good graces?"

"I'm sure I don't know, sir. She has been very kind to me."

"How came you to send her those flowers last night? It was a bold, odd thing for a boy like you to do, and I cannot help thinking it was at some-body else's suggestion. Am I not right?"

John's confusion was so painful now, Mr. Garton pitied him; but he could not recede from his purpose.

"You know, sir, a poor boy like me has not much to offer in exchange for kindness. I did not intend to be bold," he stammered, shuffling his feet clumsily, and looking down.

"That is not a satisfactory answer. Who told you that it would be right and proper for you to send flowers to a strange lady so far above you?"

"Who should tell me, sir? If it was wrong, I must bear all the blame. I'm used to being blamed for what I do."

John concluded his answer with a mixture of trouble and defiance. Looking steadily at him, Mr. Garton felt assured that while the boy would not tell an absolute falsehood, he had made up his mind not to explain further than he had done already. It vexed the young man exceedingly, and his fine face clouded with deep displeasure.

"John," he began in a hard, sharp tone, "whatever your reasons may be for declining to answer my questions, I feel constrained to tell you that you are wrong. Already I am pretty well convinced of the truth, and your refusal to enlighten me will not make much difference. There is a stranger in the place, who has been making presents to your little brother. It was that man who either gave you the flowers, or advised you what to get. Do not deny it, but answer me this; what do you know of him?"

"Nothing sir, except that he is a pleasant gentleman, and says he is going to buy land somewhere round."

"That may be, but I have reason to doubt it. John, will you listen to me and take my advice? Keep as much aloof as you can from this stranger, and do not let him make a tool of you. Otherwise the time may come when you may be made to suffer for your indiscretion."

"I think you are wrong sir, for I'm sure Mr. Knight wouldn't hurt a kitten. He's one of your easy-going, good-natured sort of fellows. Everybody likes him."

"Allow me to say that you can scarcely be a competent judge of his character on such a short acquaintance."

"But you judge him without having seen him at all," answered the boy, quickly. Mr. Garton's severe expression softened involuntarily.

"True; but I do not like the idea of his taking such liberties. It seems to me he is trying to place you under obligations to him, and win your confidence for some purpose you cannot now understand. Do be careful how you make the acquaintance of strangers and suffer them to control your actions."

The warning made no visible impression on the boy. He evinced a desire to escape Mr. Garton's presence, and that only. The confusion so visible at first, had evidently given way to wilful self-confidence, and, convinced that he would be wasting time to tarry longer, Mr. Garton dismissed him, and proceeded slowly up the hill.

The more he thought of what had passed, the more he became vexed and worried, being convinced that John was acting under influences that might prove ruinous to more than one. He had little doubt of Mrs. Prince's movement in the matter. When she went out for the flowers, it was more than probable she had used some means of persuasion to induce the boy to keep her secret; and having become her sworn ally, he was sure to prove faithful.   Accepting this explanation, he must assume that he had been correct in all his surmises; and being correct, what duty lay plainest to his view?   That was the most perplexing point of all. He might step between his friend and the blessedness which had flowed into his solitary life, and check the warm current forever.   But the result? He knew Mr. Prince would not doubt him, though his words should blast every hope of his existence. Man's love is often paramount to honor, in its first intoxicating sweetness, and he will barter his all on earth for the one bright object of his passion.   Mr. Garton knew that his friend, while capable of an intense love, was not cast in such a mould, however; and for the sake of his honor, and his daughter's future, he might be changed from the fond husband into the jealous tyrant.   He had but to go to him with a history of the past in which he had been too sorrowfully mixed, and all responsibility would pass from his shoulders forever.   But, in easing himself of the burden, he would crush his friend hopelessly, strike from his lips every drop of earthly joy his present brimming cup contained.

"I cannot do it," he said mentally, as he crossed the threshold and heard Mr. Prince's light, happy laugh from the parlor.   "I must be patient and silent, and whatever comes, may God help me."

Mr. Garton did not leave his room again that day. Locking the door on the inside, he sat down with his face hidden in his folded arms as they rested upon a table.   A more bitter, miserable and unhappy day he had never known, and he was unwilling to cast the sombre shadows of his own spirit over others. Once Geraldine tapped softly at the door; but he let her go away without answer. Later he heard the gentlemen. passing to and fro, talking cheerfully. Still later the sweep and rustle of silks betrayed the presence of a lady in the library. A delicate, yet subtle perfume crept through the crevices and floated about him. Was it Miss Eldridge? He felt tempted to go to her, hoping to grow better under her gentle influence. But the next moment Mrs. Darby's voice challenged the inmate of the library from the door, and Mrs. Prince's clear, sweet tones replied lightly. Hearing it, a bitterer wave swept through his soul, and bore away tender plants growing there, leaving it more waste and desolate than before. He got up, grinding his set teeth with a fierce self-denunciation, muttering under his breath :

"Shall I let that woman embitter my whole life? Oh, if I could escape from the torture she brings to me wherever we meet—and I will do it!"

He lit the gas, and saw the reflection in the glass of a deathly face, which, by its fierce and direful expression, startled him. Then he took a decanter from a closet, poured for himself a glass of wine, and drank it; after which he made his toilette carefully and went to dinner.

CHAPTER XI.

IT INCREASES AS IT TRAVELS.

THE ladies were gathered together in the drawing-room. The gentlemen had not yet left the table. Miss Eldridge sat apart as usual. Two fair, good-natured young matrons occupied the sofa in quiet conversation, and on the opposite side of the hearth Mrs. Prince reclined in a luxurious chair, with Geraldine on a low stool at her side. One hand toyed with her silky black hair, the other was surrendered to the child's close clasp. The little girl's head had dropped against the lady's lap, and her eyes were lifted in rapt admiration to her beautiful face. Mrs. Darby, who was tormenting a pretty lap-dog at a short distance from them, looked up to say, pertly:

"I declare, Celia, it seems as if you must be a regular sorceress! Cannot you trace your lineage directly to Circe? That child looks as if she was bewildered. Take care, Geraldine! I think I see bristles and hoofs growing, and my ears ache in anticipation of the sound I expect to hear; and I never could abide the squealing of pigs!"

"Oh, please do not talk so!"

Geraldine put out her little hand deprecatingly.

11*

"Ah, it hurts you, does it? I see you are familiar with the story, so if you run into danger with your eyes open, I shall not feel myself at all responsible."

"I think you must have been one of the things which Epimetheus let out of the box sent to his brother, containing Pandora."

"What! a plague? Upon my word, Celia, she deserves to have her ears boxed for being so saucy."

Mrs. Prince's clear, sweet laugh rippled out in answer; then she took Geraldine's face between her two hands, and bent to press a lingering kiss upon the delicate lips. Mrs. Darby exclaimed against such punishment, but her bright, laughing face was much at variance with her assumed severity of tone.

"Self-defense is a first law of nature, you know," returned Mrs. Prince, at length. "My little daughter is only striving to protect herself from your teasing propensities."

"Doubtless—just as we probe an aching tooth, to give it something to ache for. I assure you, Geraldine, that it is very dangerous to play at tit for tat with me. Be wise and let me alone."

"I am willing to declare 'quits' whenever you please. But I am not afraid of you. I had much rather you would let *me* alone and not tease me, however, for it makes me unhappy."

"Oh, poor little baby! It sha'n't be made unhappy, so it sha'n't," mocked the little lady, willfully. "Bless me! don't I wish I had such a little darling to take care of! Only touch it, and like the delicate sensitive-plant, it curls all up."

"The simile is inapt," said Mrs. Prince, "for the

sensitive-plant appeals mutely for pity, while my pet, though as tender, throws out defenses with which nature has provided her. Were she only as plain and uncouth, I would sooner liken her to the 'fretful porcupine.' Her quills fly when she is attacked, and they prove barbed and stinging."

"I hope you do not speak from personal experience, my urbane and bewildering young stepmother?"

"No; I judge only from the few passages it has been my lot to note between yourself and others who chanced to attack her."

By this time Geraldine's cheeks were hot and crimsoned. The lady bent again over her, and whispered, tenderly:

"What is the matter, dearie? Do we annoy you."

"It is not annoyance, but I cannot bear to be talked about in my own hearing. Please do not notice me."

At this moment Mrs. Darby's attention was called from the two by the entrance of the gentlemen. She turned immediately to them and commenced a vigorous attack upon Mr. Goodman, while the others disposed of themselves according to taste. Pretty soon a whist party was made up, and Mr. Bruce challenged Miss Eldridge to a game of chess. She declined to accept it, and Mrs. Darby consented to be gracious. Mr. Garton, therefore, assumed a seat near the young lady, and began to point out certain places in the drawings she had been turning over idly.

"This is your home?" she said, taking one up from the heap.

"Yes. It was sketched a good many years ago. Since my father's death I have been compelled to spend much of my time from home, and it is not so beautiful in consequence. I am pained to think I have so sadly neglected to keep it up."

"Geraldine speaks glowingly of it still."

"Yes, the little one liked it. All these scenes were familiar to me as a boy, and have been under lock and key until to-day. She succeeded in persuading me that you wanted to look at them."

"It has been a source of pleasure to be allowed to do so. You sketch well."

"Scarcely so well as I once hoped. At one time I cherished glowing dreams of an artist's career; but misfortunes sent me from pallet and pencil to the rod and ferrule. Truly it may be said, in this case, that there is but a step from the sublime to the ridiculous."

"I hope you do not deem it 'ridiculous' to teach, as your words would seem to imply."

"Certainly not. But from the artist's easel to the master's birch we must admit there is a broad space. The contrast is striking. I would not have you imagine for one moment, however, that I am discontented. The necessity was imperative, and I could not wait for the fruits of toil which, too often, come tardily. My mother's present comfort must supersede all other aims or wishes, and I deem it an honor to labor for her in the humblest station, if I cannot enhance the honor by a higher walk in life."

Miss Eldridge glanced at him quickly, her dreamy, blue eyes lighting with sympathy and respect.

"The time will come, I hope, when you may find your reward. Such devotion is ennobling, and worthy of praise."

"Oh, no. No man deserves praise for doing his duty, when his happiness and his honor are involved in that duty. As for reward—I have it every day beyond my deserts."

She smiled, thinking how happy the mother must be who was blessed with such a son. But her face became serious as a shade crossed her mind, bringing up a vision of that gentle mother in loneliness and desolation.

"How she must miss you," she said, feelingly. "I was thinking about it to-day while Geraldine was talking, and wishing I lived near to cheer her."

"That would be delightful for her, indeed."

"And for me, having no mother myself."

"Then you are an orphan?"

"No. My father is living; but he is never much at home, and I have no one to care for particularly, which is unfortunate, since a woman only half fulfills her destiny without some one to be dependent upon her for happiness."

"Yours has scarcely begun, and the time has not yet come for the development of your capabilities in that line."

His meaning glance brought a faint rose to her cheek.

".I doubt if it ever will. There is such a thing as being choice in the subjects upon which to expend what is best in us, if nature denies us those who have a lawful claim."

"True. I wish I had it in my power to recommend a worthy candidate for your care. Were it not for the presumption of the suggestion, I might—"

Here an exclamation interrupted him, and his eyes fell upon a drawing she had just turned over. Instantly his face became white, and his lips closed on a curse against his folly in allowing the drawings to leave his possession without previous examination. He put forth his hand and she gave it to him in silence—the head and bust of a woman. For a moment his heart had been warmer and lighter in her presence. He had it on his lips to say things which might have awakened sympathy, perhaps in time a deeper feeling—when fate seemed to check him. All the past with its stinging pain and hideous mockery of truth and goodness rushed back instantly, freezing him to silence. But she had recognized the features, and he was in honor bound to explain away the seeming mystery, that she might not mistake him in her judgment to the ill of others.

"I was not aware this still existed," he said constrainedly, and in a cold measured tone. "Years ago it was drawn when the original and I were friends. We ceased to consider ourselves in such a relation, and I thought to bury the remembrance until a short time since, when I unexpectedly found her—here."

"Then you did not know it before?"

"No; and I shall endeavor to forget it in future."

She thought she understood him, and was silent. Now things but dimly seen before with a woman's keenly penetrating glance, seemed clear to her.

From the fair face of Mrs. Prince she glanced at the pale, stern face of the young man, and pitied him as women pity those whom they believe to love hopelessly.

He folded the paper and put it in a side pocket, intending to destroy it on reaching his room. The restraint which had fallen upon both did not pass away, however, and she was glad when he asked her to play for him. After leaving the piano, she sought Geraldine whom Mrs. Prince had abandoned for a time to take part in a game of whist, and coaxed her from the room. Mr. Garton was thus relieved of a painful *tête á tête*.

"Where are you going?" asked Mrs. Prince glancing from her cards, as the pair was leaving the room.

"To see Geraldine's famous cabinet which she to-day promised to show me."

"Oh, horrors! It is at the top of the house, and full of bugs, beetles, bats and snakes! Better put it off until next week and take daylight for it, if you do not wish to enact a scene in Inferno while sleeping to-night."

"I will risk it, I think," replied the young lady, and they disappeared. Holding by Miss Eldridge's hand, the child led her up flight after flight of stairs until they reached the top of the house. Here they paused upon the landing until Geraldine could light a taper lying ready upon a shelf beside the door. With this they entered, and Geraldine applied the taper to a wide-spreading chandelier which depended from the ceiling in the center. In a moment the cabinet was brilliantly lighted, and the visitor uttered an exclamation of delight and astonishment.

"Why not call it a museum? You have everything rare and beautiful here."

Geraldine's face lighted with pride and pleasure.

"Is it not nice? My mother put the idea into my head, and ever since I was a tiny little girl I have been collecting these things. When Mr. Garton came he asked papa to help me, and all these cases were made under his superintendence. See how beautiful they are, and how perfectly he has arranged all the specimens they contain."

Miss Eldridge passed from case to case, admiring the corals, geological specimens, mosses, insects, and birds. At the upper end of the room a beautiful stag threw up his head, with his wide-branching antlers, and seemed ready to dart off in affright. At the other crouched a tiger, in the attitude of preparation for a spring toward the stag. At her feet coiled snakes of every species the country affords, with stuffed toads, terrapins, turtles, and tortoises. Branches were cunningly arranged about the room, with the nests of birds just as they had been built, and adorned with their proper eggs. And beside their nests perched the birds, looking life-like and natural. The entire room gave evidence of great care and rare taste, and the young lady thought the more kindly of the man who had spared so much time to gratify the peculiar tastes of his interesting pupil.

"I think you must bring me here every day while I stay, that I may study these things," she said, kindly. "They are invaluable, and unlike any collection I have ever seen in the possession of so young a naturalist."

"You cannot give me that title with justice, for I am much too deficient in knowledge of natural history. But I will ask Mr. Garton to come with us. He understands so well, and makes things appear so very interesting and beautiful."

"Where did you get so many snakes? Are there many in these mountains?"

"Yes, quite a variety. If you will come and visit us next summer, I will show you a place where they come down from the cliffs to the river, and have worn a hard, smooth path. Sometimes I have seen fifty or more lying in the sun near the water, and stretched out upon the rocks."

"Were you not afraid to get so near them?"

"Oh, no. You see, snakes never hurt anybody unless they are disturbed, or you happen to step too close to them by accident. Usually they run away the moment anybody approaches. I killed that great black snake by the other—that large rattlesnake."

"You? How was it possible?"

"Easy enough. One day we were fishing, and I heard the rattle of that old fellow a short distance from where I sat. I knew something had made him angry, so I slipped over the rocks in the direction of the sound, and saw those two close together. You cannot imagine how splendidly they looked—the one with his shining black skin, and his body all in wavy curves; the other with his beautiful spotted sides and erect head. I was careful to keep out of their

reach, and watched them. After a moment's threatening they darted upon each other, and the struggle
was fearful. They writhed, and twisted, and bit, and
the rattle sung a perfect song while it lasted. But
the black snake was the strongest, and in less time
than I thought it possible, he had slain the other.
Then he seemed exhausted, and stretched himself out
in the sun to rest. While he lay there, I took up a
stone as heavy as I could throw with force, and
struck him on the head. It pinned him down, and I
then left him there until quite dead. By this means
I got the skins of both perfect and unbroken. John
Truslow took them off and stuffed them for me."

They lingered awhile after this recital, and then
put out the lights and went down stairs. Geraldine
would not again enter the drawing-room.

"It is late for me to be up," she said; "I must
retire."

"Well, kiss me good-night, and remember that I
depend chiefly upon you for the pleasure of my visit.
I like to see odd and pretty things, and you have
not shown me the pictures yet, which we were talking about this morning."

"If you like, we will look at them to-morrow."

"Very well. Good-night, dear little Geraldine."

The young girl took the little creature in her arms
and held her there closely, kissing her many times.
Geraldine returned the caresses impulsively, and
Miss Eldridge resolved to use her entire influence in
keeping her beside her as much as possible. She
had noted the expression of pain that flitted over
Mr. Garton's face when he saw how absorbed his

little friend appeared on entering the room after dinner, and imagined that she could now understand
why the idea of her devotion might be disagreable
to him.   Without knowing it, Mr. Garton was gain-
ing to his cause a strong and faithful ally.

"Here, Katie, take my place, will you not?   I am
weary of being beaten, and think you may change
the tide of luck in my partner's favor," cried Mrs.
Prince, as she entered.   Without demur, she com-
plied, and Mrs. Prince resumed her former seat,
sinking into its luxurious depths languidly.   Mr.
Garton followed, and drew a chair near her.

"I presume you have come to lecture me," she
said in a low voice.   His face was from the others,
and she alone saw its stern, unhappy expression.
But though bitterness rankled in her heart, the
placid face was smiling and quiet.   The perfection
of her acting galled him, for he was incapable of deception without a deep sense of self-loathing as the
result, and she was forcing him every hour to hate
himself.

"No, I come only to warn you.   By an accident
Miss Eldridge has discovered that we are not strangers to each other, and knowing it, she must understand necessarily that we are not friends.   It is ad-
visable, therefore, that you should guard yourself
well, as I shall endeavor to do, lest she should think
that which would be disagreeable to us all."

"I presume this fact will account for the young
lady's sudden interest in Geraldine," she said sus-
piciously, and with a slight tremor that betrayed
uneasiness.

"By no means. I hope she has not detected in me the repugnance I feel toward the course you are taking with the child. And here I must say again, that if you are not wholly lost to all sense of goodness, you will desist, and leave her in peace. Once win her love as she is capable of bestowing it, and in your fall you crush her hopelessly."

"Really, you are kind to anticipate so confidently such an event."

"It is inevitable, sooner or later. As Sampson in his wilfulness and blindness pulled the walls of the temple about his own ears, so will you destroy yourself."

"There will be one great consolation when I think of the catastrophe beforehand. My enemies must perish with me."

There was a strange glitter in her eyes. He looked at her and shuddered, believing her capable of desperate deeds, and feeling vaguely that he might yet be the victim. Her words confirmed the half-formed thought.

"Leave me in peace, Nathaniel, and allow me to deal with my own as it pleases me. Otherwise I may forget my late submission, and rebel. If you tread upon the worm, it is bound to sting you!"

Strange words to fall from such proud, imperious lips. Even he had not power to subdue her wilful spirit to her fate. Her words roused all the opposition that was within him, and he answered positively:

"I will let you alone on condition that you deal with me according to promise. But if you step one inch beyond the limits I have marked, the crash will

come—and so the end rests with you entirely. This
is my final warning."

"Be it so. Let the future take care of itself!
We shall each see in time who wins the stakes for
which you are playing so high a hand."

At this moment the whist party broke up, and
after a short desultory conversation, they separated
for the night. Mr. Prince was last to leave the
room, and as he did so, a folded paper rustled under
his feet. He picked it up, and saw penciled upon it
a little verse of Byron's, rendered into Spanish. The
initials below were Mr. Garton's, and as he read the
lines he smiled meaningly.

" So my good fellow," was his mental comment,
" you have not escaped after all. Sly old boy, not
to tell me a word about it."

He thrust the paper into his pocket and would
soon have forgotten it, had not Mr. Garton unexpectedly reappeared looking anxious and embarrassed.

" What's the matter, Nat? Lost anything."

" A paper. Did you see it?"

The expression of his voice was so peculiar, Mr.
Prince laughed outright.

" Come, this is too good. I have half a mind to
punish you for being so close in *les affaires du cœur.*
Listen :

> 'Hay un labio que el mio ha comprimido,
> Y que antes otro labio no estrecho.
> Luro hacerme feliz, y envanecido,
> Mi labio lo comprime y otro no !'

" You must pardon me, Garton, for the liberty I
12*

took in reading, but I really could not avoid it.   Besides, being only a quotation, however expressive, renders it a pardonable action.   Who is the fair lady, whose lip has been hallowed to your touch alone !   Come, I must know."

He held the paper in his hand, his merry face kindled and glowing with mischief.   Through the mind of the tortured man before him ran a remembrance of what he had once said with regard to the nature of a Prince when once suspicion was aroused, and cold drops rose like dew upon his forehead.

"You do not know—you have not examined the paper ?" he faltered.

"No.   What is it? shall I look?" and he was about to open it.

"For heaven's sake—no, my friend!   Give it to me," and he almost snatched it from his hand to hide it instantly in his bosom.   The merry face clouded, whilst an expression of surprise and wounded feeling dawned there instead.

"Nathaniel, is this the way to treat a friend? You looked as if you feared I should look into your secrets in spite of you, which does not betray a friendly trust.   If I thought to amuse myself at your expense, I disclaim any dishonorable intentions of taking further advantage of your carelessness, if there is in truth need for a disclaimer."

"Indeed there is none!" Mr. Garton hastened to say, much hurt and troubled at the changed tone. "Forgive me for my impatience, and be indulgent still if I decline to explain anything about this unfortunate paper.   It has reference to a miserable passage in my life, and could give you only pain without bringing me relief. Will you try to be satisfied with this?"

"Yes—but trust me, Nathaniel, and do not fear to share your troubles with me, whatever they may be. I do not say this to compel your confidence, but to assure you of my sympathy and my aid wherever human love and service may be welcome."

A keener pang never convulsed the heart of man than that which wrung Mr. Garton's at that moment. He surrendered his hand to the pressure of his friend's, but his voice was too husky for the advent of intelligible words. Looking into his eyes, Mr. Prince saw womanly tears had dimmed them, and his lip trembled. Never before had he known him so moved.

"It must be a sad passage indeed, whose memory can so disturb you now. Is there no help, no relief in the world?"

"None in the world. If I could wipe it out by a sacrifice of one-half my future, I would gladly do it. But that cannot be, and this talk is foolish. Only tell me I am wholly forgiven for having pained you, and that you will not withdraw your regard and confidence because I am forced to appear reticent?"

"Certainly, and since it distresses you so, think no more about it."

"You know there are things which cannot be confided to the dearest of our earthly friends; and yet it is not for lack of trust that we withhold them."

"True. Pray do not consider further protest necessary. Rest in peace, and for whatever pain you suffer, may heaven grant a balm, and speedily. Good-night."

For a moment they looked into each other's eyes, then separated, Mr. Garton hastening back to his own room in an agony of distress which he longed to indulge without the witness of that gentle, noble eye. Once there, safely locked in, he dropped into a chair, and covered his face with his hands. The escape had been so narrow—the danger had been so fearful, he stood appalled in remembrance. Without dreaming of ill, Mr. Prince had held in his hand the instrument of destruction. It had lain near his loving, trusting heart, and wakened no fear. One glance inside the paper, and how different had been the scene! The thought of it sent his blood chillingly through every vein.

Hour after hour he sat there, struggling with himself for the mastery over feelings that would arise in defiance of his will. Once he took out the drawing and was going to burn it, but a spell seemed upon him. He could not see it wither and curl up in the flames—the fair semblance of what he once loved with all his soul! Instead, he laid it away in a secret drawer with a few other things sacredly kept, and locked it securely. Then he took out a journal and added many pages to the history there penned, after which he paced the floor until daylight. He could not rest, and what he did seemed a necessity, as if in preparation for some great change. He wrote minutely and clearly, though without dreaming that the words would meet other eyes than his own, and thus bring to light the hidden facts of a history which even he had imperfectly read. But to mortal eyes the future is impenetrable. Not the faintest gleam of light reaches beyond the hour in which we live; nor can we know, in closing our eyes for a brief rest, if they may ever open again upon earth.

CHAPTER XII.

FORESHADOWINGS.

THE Sabbath rose bright and clear.   Down from the gorgeous hills swept a gentle breeze laden with spicy autumn odors, and swaying softly the stately dahlias and snowy chrysanthemums.   Overhead the sky hung spotlessly pure, with not even a fleecy cloud floating against the pale azure.   Blue mists curled over the mountains, and the quiet was so profound, the roar and rush of the river as the waters dashed through the shoals far below Princeton, could be distinctly heard.

Miss Eldridge stepped out upon the terrace, around which a few hardy vines still clung, laden with crimson flowers—and looked abroad with a calm, yet intense worship of the beautiful in her heart, and serenely shining through her gentle eyes. Here were no rude rush and jar—no glaring inconsistencies to pain the sight.   Mansion and cottage were wrapped in the same holy hush of Sabbath loveliness, and the streets were free from all objects that could break the silence with a sound of discord. A row of rustic seats were ranged upon the terrace, and, brushing the leaves from one, she sat down, leaning against the arm dreamingly gazing over the landscape with soulful eyes.

While she sat thus the door opened, and a light step sounded upon the stone floor. She did not look around, but a faint tint, like the delicate flush of a sea-shell, mantled her cheek. The moment afterward, a shade of disappointment crossed her features, as Mr. Bruce bade her good-morning in a genial tone.

"I do not wonder to find you out in the enjoyment of such bewildering beauty. One falls hopelessly in love with the country, having it presented from such a stand-point as this. How beautifully these hills rise and fall in abrupt and picturesque views; and how lovely the gleam of the river skirting the town. Of what does it remind you?"

"A description in Aldrich's poem, Castlenoire:

'Here the land in grassy swells gently broke; there sunk in
        dells,
With mosses green and purple, and prongs of rock and peat,
Here, in statue-like repose, an old wrinkled mountain rose,'"

—pointing to a large mountain rising north. "But the likeness there ceases, for his head is crowned with hues as gorgeous as the 'tiger lilies' of which my poet sings. I can imagine those trees stripped bare, and snows lying whitely upon the summit of the hills. The glitter of ice-drops on the boughs in a winter day, and the sullen murmur of waters locked under the frozen crystal of the river, would make this place no less attractive than now."

Mr. Bruce shrugged his shoulders and made a grimace.

"Beautiful it certainly would be, but cold! I love warmth and vivid coloring too well to long for a glimpse of winter's handiwork in these fair mountains. Here it would be like a Chinese community in mourning. His white robes would too painfully remind me of the dead summer—the passed autumn; and when he shakes his snowy locks over my rainbow tints, and sweeps from the woods their odors of spice with his icy breath, I shall rejoice in being cosily shut up in my bachelor quarters, with the rush and turmoil of the metropolis around me."

"Tastes differ, and it is well, I suppose, for the sake of variety. I have accepted an invitation to remain for some weeks, and I expect to enjoy the scenes you dread, ere I return to the city."

Mr. Bruce appeared surprised and not a little disappointed:

"I am sorry to hear this. We shall miss you in our circle sadly, and while I cannot feel it otherwise than selfish to urge it, I am still disposed to express a strong desire that you may reconsider your decision."

"Why should I? No one will miss me, and I shall be far happier here."

She regretted her speech the moment it was uttered, for it gave him an opportunity to say what she did not wish to hear.

"Is it kind to say this? You know that all will miss you, and I especially. Oh, Miss Eldridge, if I could hope to produce any impression upon you by the avowal, I would tell you how constantly you are in my thoughts, and how happy I should be to know that you do not wholly dislike me."

"I have no reason to dislike you, Mr. Bruce; but it is worse than vain to waste thoughts upon me. I am ungrateful enough to feel no pleasure in your avowal, and too selfish to forego my visit here for the sake of pleasing others."

Her reply was purposely cold and ungracious, but in her heart she felt the pain his face plainly .expressed. He sighed, and said, regretfully :

"I know, at least, that you avoid me, and more especially since we came here. Once I hoped it might be different. Am I never to cherish that hope again ?".

"No, Mr. Bruce," she said, rising and assuming a serious tone that was honest and positive without being cold. "By my manner I have endeavored to spare both myself and you. Finding now that I cannot, I am forced to speak plainly, and beg that you will seek elsewhere the interest which it is not in my power to give in return for that you have expressed toward me."

"And which you have probably given elsewhere," he replied, with some bitterness, his brow flushing.

"I do not know what you mean."

"Then you are less discerning than most ladies. Prince Hill appears to possess various attractions, and while I cannot be expected to appreciate them, I am assured that you will not be at a loss to find sympathy in your pleasures."

Neck and brow crimsoned angrily at this ungenerous attack. She turned her eyes full upon him, now scornful and fathomless in their depths of outraged feeling. He quailed under them, and en-

deavored to stammer an apology. She did not
deign a further reproof, but turned and walked
proudly to the other end of the terrace. He hesitated and looked penitent and mortified at his own
folly. In another moment he would have followed,
humbly to plead forgiveness for the offense of which
he had been guilty, but his intention was frustrated
by the appearance of Mr. Garton, whom he had begun to look upon as a rival. Mr. Bruce answered his
salutation as graciously as he could, and beat a hasty
retreat, leaving the open field to Mr. Garton. That
gentleman saw at a glance something had gone
wrong, and thought his coming inopportune. It
was too late to retreat, however, and he made his
way to her side. Her greeting was cold and constrained to a degree that was surprising, and his
fears instantly pointed to a different cause. Was
she thinking of that drawing? And had she, after
a night's reflection, concluded that it was best to re-
pel what she must have considered a dawning interest, as his words were intended to prove? The
position for both was embarrassing in the extreme.

"I fear my coming must be unwelcome, Miss
Eldridge. If so, do not hesitate to send me away."

"No one can be quite so welcome as Mr. Garton,"
she answered, frankly, her manner changing at once
on perceiving the absence of Mr. Bruce. The tone
was so sincere, the expression of her face so sweet,
he felt himself soothed and comforted in the wretchedness that had overtaken him. Very gratefully he
thanked her, and accepted the temporary respite her
presence gave to his gnawing pain.

"How pale and weary you look," she exclaimed, suddenly, observing his haggard face. "I hope you are not one of those 'midnight students o'er the dream of sages,' who consume the proper hours of rest by improper labor."

"No; but I sometimes pass sleepless nights, nevertheless; and I had that disagreeable experience last night."

"Horrible!—to lie and coax the somnolent god in vain! If Young conceived all his 'Night Thoughts' in the night time, truly, he must have been a miserable man, and purchased his fame at heavy cost to mind and body."

"Doubtless he did, and we are gainers by his loss. But I?—who shall be the better for my night watches? I am sometimes tempted to think life a very miserable farce, indeed, where some people are concerned—so little are they of consequence in the world."

"Oh, you have risen with a pair of 'discontented spectacles' on this morning."

"By no means—I did not rise at all, not having lain down. But I have no doubt my mood is less gracious than usual, which is not saying much for myself. Possibly a good breakfast and a substantial sermon may have the effect of taking off the discontented spectacles which you just now thought you had discovered. Are you going to church?"

"Yes. It is a glorious day for church-going. One feels reverent and desirous to be good beforehand; therefore the good seed may not fall in stony places altogether."

"Let me have the pleasure of accompanying you. Who knows but a germ may be planted in my stony nature, to spring up and bear fruit to my everlasting good?"

"That may rest largely with yourself. Is it not in our power to clear away the stones and till the soil for the reception of divine truths, sown by the laborers He has called to His work?"

"I do not know. My personal experience has not led me to believe so comforting a doctrine. I want to give root to the seed, and feel its strength a support when I am weak; but I cannot do it any more than Pharaoh could relent when God had hardened his heart."

. "Do we, in this day, need proof of God's greatness, and goodness, and power? If He hardened the hearts of the Egyptians, it was only to show to the oppressors and the ignorant how infinitely beyond them His power extended. Since that age, a living truth was sent to us through a glorious medium, and He no longer hardens the hearts of men against Himself and His commandments. These are the words He lovingly utters to every soul now: 'Come unto me, all ye that labor and are heavy laden, and I will give you rest.'"

"Rest," he repeated, with a deep inspiration. "The word has a sweet sound but is impossible in realization. There is not a heart on earth which knows its full meaning—or can, till the—end. How near or how far that may be from us, who can say? 'We see through a glass, darkly,' and my eyes are weary striving for the light. Do you often think of death?"

" Yes. I was thinking of it when I came out here
this morning, and wondering as I looked at the beautiful world, whether we could gather from it any real
idea of what is to come."

" How can we *know* that there is anything to
come ? "

He searched her face earnestly, a wistful questioning in his eyes.

" You do not doubt it," she returned, smiling up
at him confidently.

" No, but there are moments when such thoughts
take possession of us all, I presume. If we indulge
them, the result is a perplexity that drives us hither
and thither, like fragments of a wreck upon a tem-
pest-tossed ocean."

" Then why indulge in them? A season of doubt
is a season of torture. My faith is like a child's, and
I would not give it up for all the glories of this
world. I feel that I was not created for this little
span of life alone, where we are too often fretted and
vexed through a miserable existence. That within
me, which I cannot understand, is still potent enough
in power to make me feel its greatness above simple
clay. It points to the all-enduring work of God,
showing me how all things die to live again in fairer
and in different forms. And I am assured that I
shall rise from my sleep in the grave to a grander
life, as the butterfly escapes from its shell to spread
golden spotted wings to the sun."

" But the after life ? What is that ? If we could
but know ! All histories are faulty ; and who shall
prove those things on which we base our faith and
13*

hope, wholly true? Bright are the dreams we dream, colored by this faith and shaped by this hope. But from the invisible world no disembodied soul has ever returned to tell us of its after fate."

"We cannot know this. Often it would seem as if invisible agencies must control our actions when we are forced to do things wholly at variance with judgment and inclination, and which result in our own good. I imagine better influences around me always, but I have no faith in their ability to hold communion directly with the material world."

"Could that be possible, doubts would no longer exist. No. If the spirits of the departed could return, surely it would be to those struggling ones who long for a clear knowledge of the truth, and not to the ignorant, careless, thoughtless class claiming to hold converse with angels! Bah! I am so sick of trickery and deception where the purity of truth alone should exist. How shall I escape it? You are not driven restlessly to and fro by uncertainties. Can you teach me a part of your cheering philosophy, that I may be able to accept whatever may come contentedly?"

"I fear not, for you would not accept my teaching. A woman's faith is all she has, no matter how she comes by it. If we tell you, a thousand arguments are launched against us. What we receive as simple truth, you seek to undermine, laughing the while at the ignorance which leaves us in bliss. Were we to seek for flaws in our priceless jewels, contentment might flee us also."

"Well, if the flaws were not in your jewels, you

could not find them by the most minute search," he smilingly argued.

"Those who want to find them may do so.   There are such things as optical illusions, and tricks of the imagination, to say nothing of the self-conceit which may lead us to declare against the established truth of ages.   If, as some seem anxious to prove, the life of man ceases with this world, why should all the beings of the earth cherish the same vain dream? Why did the Greeks worship their gods, or the Hindoos set up their gaudy idols?   Why should the Indian talk of the ' happy hunting grounds,' or the Kirghis bury with their dead the best dress, hunting-knife and rifle, and the faithful horse and dog, to render him presentable in the new land to which he is traveling?   Throughout the earth some mode of worship proclaims man the possessor of the inherent belief that something within him must live after death.   The Japanese deify their great men, and pray to them, as the Catholics pray to their saints; only the heroes are themselves the controlling powers, while the Catholics own a God and Saviour."

"And these things are proofs to you of the immortality of the soul?"

"Yes, as satisfactory as I can ask, in conjunction with the Book which has been given us.   And they all teach the one lesson which Tennyson expresses in a verse of his Introduction to In Memoriam.   He says:

' We have but faith, we cannot know,
       For knowledge is of things we see;
   And yet we trust it comes from Thee—
       A beam in darkness—let it grow.'

Take this 'beam in darkness,' Mr. Garton, and let it grow in your heart. There is no other comfort in the world, apart from faith."

"Is yours strong enough to sustain you under all difficulties?"

"Perhaps I cannot answer positively as to that. I have not been very seriously tried. But I *believe* that I can bear any blow that may come to me, and feel resigned."

"Even were you to find yourself stripped of all you held dearest in life, and had no reason to hope that joy could ever again come to you?"

"It is a hard question," she said, her ardor dampened, her face serious. "I know how the human heart rebels against trials, and I should have to struggle. But I should conquer at last, and be happier in the belief that God knows what is best for me."

"You cannot think that He takes cognizance of all earth's miserable creatures, and controls them to certain ends? In that case, do you suppose a loving and just God could create and lead us on to the destruction we have held up, a crying terror before the eyes of sinners?"

"If the hairs of the head are numbered, and no sparrow is allowed to fall to the ground unheeded by Him, there is no reason in doubting that He will control those who give themselves to Him and His work. All of us are born in sin; but He has provided a means for our salvation, and leaves us to choose. If we come to Him, we are guided by Him; if we go from Him, dare we say He leads us to our own destruction, after having created us?"

"You should have gone into the ministry, Miss Eldridge. I could more easily be converted under you than by one of the long-faced priests who take pleasure in assuring me that I have an immortal soul, doomed to eternal punishment."

Something in his expression made her feel vexed and uneasy. She thought he had been forcing her to talk for his entertainment, and was no more a skeptic than herself.

"Now you do me injustice," he said, reading her face. "I acknowledge myself in an unfair mood this morning; but I have not tested you without purpose. What you have said has done me good, and I shall remember your words gratefully. While I have not lost the faith my mother taught me, I am often sadly tossed by doubts and fears. For some reason they have taken stronger hold upon me now than usual, and I want to get rid of them."

The church-going party gathered in the hall at the appointed hour, and walked down the Hill together. But at its base they separated. Princeton boasted of four churches, and each was destined to the honor of hearers from Prince Hill. Mrs. Darby and her husband accompanied their host and hostess to the Presbyterian, by far the most handsome and stately edifice in town, of its kind. The others went to the Methodist and to the Baptist, while Mr. Garton and his fair companion quietly walked into the little white building whose stained glass windows and cross-crowned spire proclaimed its denomination.

During the services, he sat at her side, knelt by her, turned the leaves of her prayer-book, and joined in the responses with a clear, precise voice. Her ear detected the mechanical tones, utterly devoid of feeling, and her warm heart ached. She went to church with a pleasurable. sense of duty, a longing to be taught—a desire for more devout and direct communion with God. Could it be possible that any soul was so shut out from the warmth and light of His love as to be unable to feel an interest in acting and hearing that which constitutes the laws of the Father? In darkness and blindness he was groping hopelessly, and her soul was moved to compassion. An intense longing entered her heart; all her silent prayers were for him, this stranger whom she had known but a little while, yet whose salvation had become a dear and first wish. The thoughts that crowded upon her forced tears to her eyes, that brimmed over the white lids and dropped down upon the leaves of her prayer-book. Her hand trembled and her bosom heaved with silent sobs, which Mr. Garton could not but observe with wonder. What was there in the services to move her so? Nothing that she was not accustomed to see every Sabbath. The minister who ascended the pulpit was neither learned nor interesting. On the contrary, his oratory lacked force, and his reasoning lacked power, and not a word he uttered was calculated to stir the fountain of tears. Still her tears fell, as he saw by occasional sly glances at her flushed face, which the thin veil refused to conceal. Both were glad when they were able to pass out from the eager, curious glances bent painfully upon them, and breathe the calming spicy air.

As they descended the steps, he took the book, and they walked away silently, moving with slow steps to the brow of the hill. There he paused where a by-path led off through a line of stately oaks and pines skirting the lawn, and for the first time spoke to her.

"It will be some time before luncheon. Will you walk through this path with me? I will take you through the shrubbery and garden as we go back, and the walk will do you good."

She threw back her veil and looked up gratefully in thanks for his consideration. They turned into the path and proceeded onward to a huge, moss-covered stone, and there sat down in the sunshine.

"Now tell me," he begged, "what has occurred to disturb you so much? Of course I do not wish to be impertinent, but you cannot wonder at my desire to know."

A burning blush stained her cheeks, but she answered candidly:

"I was thinking of all you said to me, and was pitying you, Mr. Garton."

"And were those blessed tears shed for me?" he asked, a surprised and eager expression spreading over his face, as he reverently unclosed the book and looked at the blistered leaves still damp with them.

"Yes; I could not help it."

He turned away his head, and his lips moved. Underneath the calm she did not try to penetrate. The heart of the man was beating fast. Every fiber of his being thrilled to a sense of delight, a revelry of silent joy at being so cared for. He saw the pure sincerity of her nature, and knew that no art prompted the action he had witnessed. She had tried to conceal her emotion, and being unable to do so, she had confessed its cause frankly. Her truth and goodness inspired him with respect. Her simplicity shaped a hope he had not dared before to cherish. He caught it joyously, and enshrined it in his heart, with a murmur of thanks that reached no human ear.

What he thought and felt she could not divine, until she caught a glimpse of his radiant face. But without looking at her, he tore a tear-wet leaf from its place, and hid it in his bosom.

"This shall go with me—my priceless amulet—the first tears ever shed for my unhappy soul, and consecrating the words to me that shall henceforth be mine. What good angel sent you across my path, at this, of all times? If ever the tears of repentance moisten my eyes, they shall fall where yours of compassion have fallen."

Her lips quivered, but she dared not trust herself to speak, and he took her little gloved hand and pressed it gently.

"Just now all my heart and soul are stirred," he said, retaining the hand he had taken. "From the depths of my nature, I desire to be all that God intended the men He created to be and to accomplish. Yet I know myself so well, I am assured that all this will pass, unless I have some one to help me keep these wishes alive. Will you do it? With your aid I may yet be a happier and a better man."

What tender-hearted woman, thrilled with sympathy for an unhappy man, could resist such an appeal?   Her eyes filled again, and her voice trembled in answering :

"If aid of mine can accomplish such a work, you shall not strive in vain for the peace that 'passeth understanding.'"

He thanked her only with his eyes, but his joy was great, and surpassingly sweet.

"For this day, at least, I will be happy," was his mental resolve, and he was so.   He talked much and well, betraying the current of his feelings so plainly, that her heart was kept in a continually pleasant flutter.

When they returned to the house, his mood did not pass.   It lasted throughout the day, and extended charitably to all.   Even Mrs. Prince, between whom and him only the most formal courtesies had passed, felt the change gratefully.   He was now courteous and kind, and woke in her a hope that was refreshing.   Womanlike, she could not forbear to question him, as he stood at her side for a moment by the window, ostensibly looking out at the shrubbery, lighted by the splendor of the autumn sun.

"What has put you into such gracious spirits?" she asked ; and his unexpected answer amazed her. Taking the torn leaf from his pocket, he read in a low, exultant tone from the Litany :

"That it may please Thee to give us true repentance ; to forgive us all our sins, negligences, ignorances ; and to endue us with the grace of Thy Holy Spirit, to amend our lives according to Thy Holy Word."

"You speak in riddles—a sphinx. Explain," she demanded, seeing that he meant to give her no other answer. But he smiled, carefully returned the leaf to its hiding-place, and walked away.

"Ah," she murmured, with a low laugh, "I see what it is now. My quondam lover is in love once more. Be it so! I may hope then to find some peace; for what man in love ever troubled himself about anybody else?"

Accordingly her spirits rose also, and she was delightful all the evening.

When Miss Eldridge went up to her room for the night, she found an elegant prayer-book lying upon the toilette-table. The fly-leaf bore her name, written in a bold, manly hand. A little note accompanied it, begging that she would accept it in the place of the one he had despoiled of a treasure. The message was simple and earnest, and closed with a hope that the angels might guard her innocent slumbers.

And she?—she knelt in her spotless robes and angelic beauty, praying for him, as those pray only whose hearts are wrapped in their petition. With a beautiful blush at her own action, she took the note up and kissed it, after which she turned out the light and lay thinking of him until she fell asleep—the missive pressed against her soft cheek.

CHAPTER XIII.

WARMING A SNAKE IN ONE'S BOSOM.

ONE little week brought a variety of changes to the people on the Hill. All the guests, with the exception of Miss Eldridge, had departed, and Mr. Garton had resumed the routine of duties which brought him to Princeton. In the quiet that succeeded, Mr. Prince found more time to look into the workings of his own household, and had seen things that were not calculated to render him at ease.

This came about by a more acute observance of Mr. Garton's conduct toward Mrs. Prince. He was naturally anxious that they should be friends, and was not a little puzzled to understand the peculiarity of the gentleman's manner. Always when Mr. Prince was near, he was polite and respectful, but rather reserved. On several occasions, however, he had come upon them in the parlor or library, engaged in more earnest conversation, which dropped invariably into studied formality, at his approach. He one day questioned her concerning it, and elicited nothing satisfactory in reply.

"I have observed that you seem to treat Nathaniel

oddly," he said. "What is it about him that causes you to be so different with him from all others?"

They were in their own apartment, and she leaned her head confidingly against his shoulder, as she answered:

"I believe there is a natural antipathy between us. We can never agree on the subjects that happen to rise in our conversations, and I am too impulsive to hide my feelings; consequently we sometimes argue them till they nearly amount to *casus belli*."

"And does it vex you, my dear wife? If so, I could sooner dispense with him than to allow you to be made unhappy."

"What, your Pythias! False Damon, even to hint at a separation!"

"Now you are laughing at me. Be candid, Celia, and let me know your whole heart in all things," he urged tenderly. "While I should regret to see him go from my house, I could do it, and be none the less his friend."

"There is no need, for he will not cause me any unhappiness.   Besides, it would spoil everything."

"Of what are you speaking?"

"Have you not seen what a pretty little drama is being enacted in the house? He likes nothing better than to question me about his lady love—her antecedents, her goodness, her amiableness, merely for the sake of talking about her."

"You mean Katie Eldridge?"

"Certainly; who else could I mean. Perhaps you may be called upon to supply his place ere long, and he will go without being sent."

"It would be a good thing for him, as she is rich enough to place him above the necessity of drudgery. I hope it may turn out so."

"So do I," and this time she spoke truly. To draw the breath of freedom once mofe had become a passionate longing that she dared not gratify by accepting her husband's generous offer. There was a risk in sending him away, which might be avoided by allowing things to take their course; and she was forced to curb her impatience.

No more was said at this time, but he was not satisfied. Thoughts returned to him again and again, until suspicion was fixed in his mind she never could root out by all her loving arts. It was on Monday evening, precisely a week from the departure of their friends, and on going into the conservatory to cut some flowers to be laid in the coffin of a neighbor's dead child, he found them standing at the far end, her face flushed, his passionate. He did not catch a tone of either voice, and the evident confusion they betrayed on seeing him fired his heart with the keenest anguish. Instantly she bent down and began to clip off some flowers with the scissors she held in her hand. But he stood still, battling with the feelings that surged hotly within his bosom. Mr. Prince came up and regarded them keenly.

"I fear you have been quarreling," he said, in a husky, constrained voice. "May I ask the cause of your evident disagreement?"

"It is all my fault," she exclaimed, rising quickly. "I have taken it into my head that he shall change his treatment of a pupil of his to whom I have
14*

taken a fancy—John Truslow. He refuses, and I have said hard things to him."

"Has any new trouble risen with him?" asked Mr. Prince of the school-master.

"Nothing very unusual. Lately John has been very negligent about his studies, and two days chose to absent himself from school altogether. He has fallen into bad company besides, and answers me insolently when I advise or chide him. It seems as if all the good I hoped to do him has passed entirely beyond my power."

The look which Mr. Prince now turned upon his wife asked plainly, "What have you to do with the boy?"

"Geraldine is his sworn ally, as you know, and there is something about the child I like. His fate has been a hard one, and I pity him. Gentler measures were better than the harsh course Mr. Garton has chosen to take, and I have taken the liberty of saying as much."

"I think we may give Mr. Garton credit for understanding what is best for a bad boy like John, rather than you who are a stranger; therefore you had better allow him to pursue his own course," said Mr. Prince in a lighter tone.

She turned pale at the rebuke and lifted her head haughtily. The next moment she was sweeping away toward the glass doors, whither her husband followed her. But by the time he reached them she had disappeared, and he turned a look backward to Mr. Garton, who stood leaning his brow against a marble vase, his face deathly pale.

With steps as rapid he returned and grasped his arm :

"For God's sake, Nathaniel, tell me what all this . means?" he cried, shaking the arm in an agony of apprehension. "I have been blind, but I cannot be blinded longer. Remember that your are my friend, and she—my wife!"

"I never can forget that," was returned in a voice of such utter wretchedness as he had never heard issue from mortal lips. The young man seemed so racked and shaken by the violence of his feelings as to be unable to stand without support. One hand clung to the marble rigidly; the other was thrust into his bosom.

"This is not the result of a mere quarrel about a bad boy," continued the husband striving for self-possession. "And what am I to understand by your present agitation? For some days I have been forced to notice your formality to her in my presence, and a greater intimacy when you thought yourselves alone. But I have not till now conceived one suspicion against you or her. It is insupportable, and I must know the truth."

Mr. Garton groaned and murmured too low for Mr. Prince to catch his words:

"My God, my God! it has come at last!"

"What are you saying?" demanded Mr. Prince, his self-control fast giving way.

The other lifted his head and looked at him mournfully, his lips tremulous and white.

"Then you do doubt me?"

"I must doubt you or her, or both—unless you

can so clearly explain away this mystery as to set my mind at rest forever."

"She is your wife, and I conjure you to spare yourself and her. Let no suspicion against her mar your love. Remember you are bound to her, and sworn to cherish her for life."

"And do I not love her? My God, how I have loved and do love her! But least of all on earth, will I tolerate deception in those I love."

"Spare her from your wrath; and since I have become an element of discord, let me depart. The man is accursed who comes between a man and his wife. I will go."

"By this you acknowledge yourself unworthy the place I have given you. I have nourished a serpent where I thought a dove reposed, and it has stung me to death?"

He staggered back and sat down upon a bench, panting heavily; and a pair of dark eyes saw him through the plate glass door. But the white face was screened by the curtains within, and neither discovered it. Mr. Garton took a hasty step toward his friend and lifted his hand.

"I swear to you, before high heaven, that I have never in my life done you an injury! In every thought and action I have tried to be the honest, faithful friend whom you honored, and sought only for your happiness."

Struggling once more for self-command, Mr. Prince rose and confronted him.

"I have warned you of my nature, and in justice to her you must prove every word you utter. Horrible thoughts have come to me. You have acted strangely, and all brings me to the verge of an awful gulf. Whose picture was that you refused to let me see a few nights since?"

"You must allow that I have a right to decline answering such a question."

"What, under such circumstances? Oh, man, beware! You know not what you are doing! I must and will know!"

"You have no right to demand it, and you never will know from me."

"Then by heaven—"

What he would have said cannot be recorded. Aware that he was beside himself with excitement, he used all the power he had left to check the words, and turned abruptly away. When half way to the door, he turned and said huskily:

"When we are both calmer, this matter must be settled between us. Now it must drop."

"It is well. A blinding flash of lightning may serve to show us a danger at our feet; and it were best to think before you cast off on such unreasonable grounds the truest friend you ever had on earth."

With this they parted. Mr. Garton went to his room, but soon came out again in search of Miss Eldridge. He found her alone in the drawing-room, trying to read.

"Come out upon the terrace with me a little while, won't you?"

"It is bitterly cold. See how the hoar frost whitens the panes."

"No matter. Let me thus mantle thee."

He took a warm shawl belonging to Mrs. Prince from a sofa, and wrapped it around her. His face wore an expression that was startling.

"What is the matter? Something has happened," she cried in alarm.

"Come!" was his only answer. Silently they went out, and the cold moonbeams lay whitely upon the stone floor of the terrace. The frost glittered there, and the wind blew cuttingly from the river. He did not seem to feel it, and bared his head, as if seeking to cool its fevered throbbings.

"Katie?" he began, "there are times in the lives of men, when a great calamity crashing out from some hidden nook, treads down all forms, all rules of conventionality. Such a time has come to me. Something has happened which will force me to leave Prince Hill, and—you! There is not one moment to lose. What I can say now I may not have an opportunity to say at another time before this anticipated change, and I must say it. Look up into my eyes and listen."

He paused at the end of the terrace, where the moonbeams fell full upon his face; and she raised her eyes anxiously.

"In one little week I have learned to love you as I thought never to love again. Once I poured out my heart's best treasure on a woman who proved unworthy. But the time came when I despised where I had loved, and I thought the sentiment strangled forever within me. Lately I came and found you here—good, pure and artless. My maturer judgment told me on reflection, that I was not deceived this time and I gave myself up to the joy of loving a good woman. Oh, how happy I have been in my thoughts of you, even in the midst of misery. I have hoped, for you let me do it, that you would put your hand in mine and promise to be my wife. I have a home to offer you with my mother, and a name that has never known dishonor. I will love you as a strong man alone can love, and you can make me what you will. Give me your answer quickly, Katie. If I go from this house, as I must, some one will soon take my place in the school, and then I shall be free to claim you."

All this was so sudden and overwhelming, she stood trembling, without a word of response. He bent to her, whispering:

"Oh, Katie, do not tell me that I have been mistaken? Can you love me?"

For reply, she dropped her burning face upon his arm.

"And will you be my wife?—share my humble lot contentedly?"

"I could ask no happier future," she murmured and he drew her to his breast, folding his arms closely about her. She felt her brow lifted up gently and a kiss pressed upon her lips—a lingering, burning kiss that she never forgot. For a few minutes they stood thus oblivious to all the world apart from themselves, and deliriously happy in each other.

"And now, darling," he said at length, "now that

I feel safe, and am assured of your love, I must let you go into the house. I could not tell you there what was in my heart; the same air breathed by others should not bear one thought of mine to you through the medium of sound. Here I have spoken with God's pure heavens above us, and only the stars to look with mine into your sweet eyes! Come, dearest one!"

He led her tenderly to the door, saw her inside, then turned back. As he ran down the steps to the graveled walk, a figure stole away under the shadow of the shrubbery, and was swallowed up in the darkness beyond. He did not see it, but walked briskly up and down the garden paths, till weary. It was late when he went to the window opening into his room and tried its fastenings. They were not secured on the inside, so he threw up the sash and stepped in. Here the air seemed hot, for a great fire still smouldered in the grate, and he left the window wide open when he sat down, and, shading the small lamp that stood upon his desk, took up a pen to write.

The varied scenes he had passed through in so brief a space of time had left his nerves unstrung too completely for that exercise. After vain efforts to compose himself for the task, he gave it up and leaned his arms upon the desk. Gradually his head sank upon them. He was not conscious of drowsiness, but a faint and peculiar perfume seemed to rise about him. Soon it wrapped his senses in a delicious languor. He forgot his troubles; he thought only of his love. Dreamily his hand scarched for a pencil; languidly he wrote in faint and uncertain characters the endearing words that went floating through his brain. And then he slept—

" Slept the evil sleep that from the future tore the curtain off."

15

CHAPTER XIV.

REST IN HEAVEN.

IN the cold gray of a chill morning Miss Eldridge
was awakened by the touch of a little icy hand.
From her sweet and innocent dreams of a first pure
love she started in affright to see beside her bed the
white-robed figure of Geraldine Prince, standing
there with chattering teeth and livid lips. Her first
thought was that the child had been dreaming, and
too frightened for rest had come to her, and involuntarily she put out her hand to draw her into her own
warm bed. Geraldine drew back.

"What is it, little one? What brings you out of
your nest at such an hour?"

"He is dead!" gasped the child in an almost in-
audible voice.

"Who is dead? I think you are not awake yet."

"It is you who are not awake! I heard a strange
stir in the house, and got up to listen. At the head
of the stairs I stopped and heard them say somebody
had murdered Mr. Garton! How could anybody
kill him?"

"Dead! dead! murdered! Oh, my God, it cannot be possible!"

She sat up in bed appalled, and wrung her slender hands frantically. Geraldine stood still and tearless, looking at her with dilated eyes.

"Child, child! are you sure you know what you are saying? Who could murder him—my—my—promised husband?"

"Did you promise to marry him?" asked Geraldine, drawing nearer.

"Did I promise him what? To marry him? Yes, only last night. Oh, heavens, this is too awful for belief! I will not believe it. Nathaniel, Nathaniel!"

Too much beside herself to know what she was saying, one thought uppermost in her mind, she sprang from the couch and rushed out. Her white robes streamed about her, and her feet gleamed pearly white on the dark carpet. Down over her shoulders streamed her long, fair hair, and her hands were clasped over her bosom. Thus she glided swiftly to the foot of the stairs, her face pallid—her eyes staring. Mr. Prince, who at that moment came into the hall, saw her making for the library, and caught her in his arms.

"Katie, what would you?—where are you going?"

"To see if it is true! Let me go! I must see, or my heart will break."

She struggled like a wild bird, and he could scarcely hold her.

"Indeed you cannot go! To look upon such a sight would kill you. Oh, heavens, what misery has fallen upon this house! Whence comes this curse so black and bitter! My child, be still. It is too late! We can do nothing."

"Dead—murdered!" she murmured, sinking passively in his arms. Then her eyes closed and she was as pale and still as the dead lover whose warm lips last night had kissed her. With a groan he lifted the slight form and bore her back to her chamber, where in a few moments several servants were summoned to apply restoratives. Seeing her well cared for, Mr. Prince hastened away the moment signs of life appeared. The household was in confusion, and his own wife lay in hysterical convulsions in her room. As he went springing down the steps, his daughter suddenly appeared before him. She had slipped a wrapper over her night-dress, and put her feet into slippers, while all this was going on around her.

"You, too, my dear?" he cried. "I shall be driven frantic!"

"No, papa; I will not give you any trouble. I want to help you if I can."

"To help me?—you! What could you do? Go back to your little bed, my darling, and lie still awhile."

"Oh, I cannot. Tell me who did it. I want to know everything."

"Nobody can tell. Like a thief, the destroyer came in the night, and he is gone—our friend! My sweet one, you look white and sick. Here! lay your little head on papa's heavy heart and cry. Come!"

He sat down on the stairs and drew her to his bosom; but she still resisted sympathy.

"No. I cannot, I am too cold to cry. I feel as if my heart had turned all to ice. Let me go and see him, papa."

"Not for the world!—such a horrible, horrible sight. The coroner has been summoned and will soon be here; and until all this dreadful business is over you can best aid me by trying to keep things quiet. Can you not do something for poor Katie?"

"I will try. He loved her best of all."

"How do you know that?" he asked quickly.

"She told me that she had promised to be his wife."

"When?"

"This morning when I told her he had been murdered. It came out in spite of herself, and it was only last night she made the promise. Do you think it will break her heart?"

"Oh, hearts do not break easily, or mine would be shattered to atoms. Go to her, little one, and try to bear this thing as well as you can."

She obeyed him, and went at once up the stairs; but it was with a step as heavy as lead, and a face so ashen, his throat swelled with a sob of anguish, dry and bitter, as he watched her. Then he wandered all over the house, finding something to do everywhere except in the room where his wife lay sobbing, moaning and wringing her hands, with her frightened maids around her. He could hear her cries, but kept as far off as he could, until the dismal sounds ceased, and the confusion became less confounding.

Before sunrise, the coroner came, and an inquest

was held on the body. The facts brought out were few, but tended to fasten suspicion upon the boy, John Truslow, whose knife still remained in the deadly wound, inflicted as the sleeping man sat bowed over his desk. The aim had been sure and true, the keen, slender knife passing under the left shoulder-blade to the region of the heart, and allowed to remain. The cook who had risen very early, seeing the window of Mr. Garton's room open, had ventured to peep in, and discovered him in the attitude described, the handle of the knife contrasting with the black coat he wore, and stained with his blood. Her first action was to call up Mr. Prince's servant, who after a peep into the room through the window to be assured of the horrible truth, rushed up to his master's room to arouse him. To his first knock, no answer was made; to the second Mr. Prince responded, demanding to know the cause of the disturbance. In telling him, Mrs. Prince shrieked out, having overheard the news, and from that the confusion spread. When Mr. Prince reached Mr. Garton's room, the servants were gathered about the door and windows, but no one dared to touch him. He rushed forward and lifted the dead man's head. Icy cold, and rigid in every limb! He must have been dead some hours. Seeing this, he bade them all keep away from the body, and dispatched a man to fetch the doctor and the coroner. In the investigation, it was proved that the knife found in the body belonged to John Truslow, and furthermore, that he had threatened to kill Mr. Garton at the time of his severe punishment; and this

"He rushed forward and lifted the dead man's head."

Page 174.

was deemed sufficient for his apprehension.   A warrant was made out for his arrest.   The officers found him sleeping soundly in his bed, and dragged him out to prison, feeling that he was the most hardened little sinner it had ever been their fortune to deal with.

No wonder, for the poor boy, who was used to being roughly handled, believed it all a joke, and could not credit what they said until the faces of the people proved the truth of what had been said to him.   Then he became so frightened as to lose for a time his presence of mind, and confuse everybody. Finally, by dint of a little tact on the part of Mr. Prince, who kindly addressed him for the purpose, he became calmer and answered more composedly the questions that were put to him, before the magistrate.

"Where were you last night between the hours of ten o'clock, and three in the morning?"

"At home in bed."

"Where before ten o'clock in the evening?"

John was confused and hesitated.

"I can't tell," he said at last.

"Boy, remember that your life depends upon your truth, and do not trifle now," demanded the examiner solemnly.   "If this murder can be proved as the work of your hand, you will be hung for it."

"Oh, I swear I never did it!   I never threatened to kill him?   It was all a lie, and I would not have hurt him to save my own life.   Oh, Mr. Prince, you will not let them hang me," turning appealingly to him.

"Try to prove your innocence—speak out honestly, my poor boy," was the reply.

"Well, then, this much. I went to carry a note from a gentleman to a lady; but I promised not to tell who it was, or to say anything about it."

"Was the errand performed in the vicinity of Prince Hill?"

John hung his head, and still refused to answer. When the question was repeated sternly, he said:

"I was not to tell."

"It may cost you your life to refuse."

"No matter," now said the boy, his spirit roused, "I promised not to tell, and I won't. I did not kill Mr. Garton, who has been kind and good to me, even when I vexed and troubled him; and that is all I have to say."

Further than this they could not get out of him. To all questions he was dumb, and stubbornly refused to answer.

The interest which Mr. Prince manifested in the examination of John Truslow, was peculiar, being intense, but apparently free from suspicion. He had carefully taken notes of the points made out against him; and when the evidence seemed so strong as to justify his committal for trial, and the boy began to sob and tremble in his terror, the gentleman bent forward and said distinctly:

"Do not be afraid, John. If you are innocent, you shall be saved from injustice. I will find the murderer of my friend, if it requires every dollar of money I possess to accomplish it; so, if you are free from the black sin of this deed, you have nothing to fear."

John's glad, grateful eyes were lifted to his face, with a beam of hopefulness in them that was in itself a proof of innocence. Nevertheless, he was taken away in a violent paroxysm of weeping, bemoaning his fate, compassionating his mother, and wondering what now would become of poor little Dick, with no one to take care of him.

Mr. Prince returned home, with the boy's lamentations and the details of the examination painfully prominent in his mind. There no comfort came into his heavy heart. The surroundings were all calculated more fully to bow his head in grief and perplexity. Gloomy and desolate seemed the lately bright and happy household. The servants crept about solemnly, or talked in hushed tones at times, gathered in groups about hall, piazza and kitchen. Above it was no better. Miss Eldridge reclined upon a sofa in her sitting-room, pale and silent, attended by Geraldine, and would notice nothing. When he approached and spoke kindly to her, she turned her face into the pillow, and moaned ; and he left her with tearful eyes, knowing that silence was kindest. But on the threshold he paused and brushed the mists from his eyes to look back, and take in the dreary picture without flinching. The utter abandonment of the woman to her sorrow, and the stoical strength of the no less loving child, furnished a curious and striking contrast. Geraldine's face had assumed a strange stoniness, like chiseled marble, lighted by burning eyes, still dry and moving only with slow, deliberate glances. All the restless fiery impulses were smothered by the magnitude

of her woe. No complaints escaped her. She was
the embodiment of tearless despair—of calm, self-
possessed misery, looking past herself to others without hope or interest. Even the tender feelings of
the morning seemed to have been paralyzed, and
what she now did was mechanical, slow and mean-
ingless.

Once more a groan passed the man's lips as he
turned again to depart. Reaching the hall, he took
a few steps toward Mrs. Prince's apartments, but
hesitated, and leaned his brow against the post of
the balustrade at the head of the stairs. Over his
face swept an expression of anguish too deep for
portrayal. His eyes closed, his brow contracted, and
his teeth were set over his nether lip as if to crush
back words that sought advent—bitter, anguished
words that might ease the tortured heart.

"Not now! not now!" he muttered. "I could
not bear her eyes. Oh, my God, can the *innocent*
produce results like this? I *must* know!"

The remainder of the day was passed in an obscure apartment, little used, in a wing of the building. Once or twice servants sought him there for
instructions, which he gave shortly, without altering
his position. He sat with his arms resting on a table, and his head bowed upon them. No message
could induce him to move; all refreshments were
refused, and the intruders were bidden to let him
alone.

"How strange he does look!" said one of the
servants to another coming out of the room to join
his companion who had waited curiously to see if he

would answer a message from Mrs. Prince to come
to her. "If you'd only seen him!"

"Well, how does he look strange?"

"White and fierce. He just lifted his face for a
second, and his eyes flashed at me as he said: 'Tell
Mrs. Prince to wait!' He must feel awful to send
such an answer as that to *her*. I know'd that he
loved Mr. Garton, but I didn't know how much
before."

"Do you suppose it's all grief for the school-master that cuts him up so?"

"To be sure—that and the shame of having him
murdered in his own house. Who wouldn't feel cut
up, I'd like to know?"

"You're right. It is awful. But I don't believe
John Truslow killed him. He's a bad boy, but I
don't believe he has pluck enough to kill a man."

"Pshaw! he had pluck enough to kill a hundred
if they gave him a chance."

"No, he hasn't. I'd be willing to bet you anything you like on it."

"And why?"

"Because he believes in ghosts; and superstitious
hags are the worst cowards in the world when it
comes to blood-sheddin'."

"May be so."

This conversation, though carried on in a low
tone, was heard by Geraldine as she stood watching
them. She knew that her step-mother had sent to
him, and she had cautiously followed to discover
why her father chose to remain alone. She was in
hopes that she might enter and talk to him, having

grown too weary to keep her silent vigil by Miss
Eldridge. But, as she stood in the gloomy corridor
and heard his sharp answer, she crept quietly after
them, and could not help hearing what the servants
said. In a moment they separated, one proceeding
below stairs, the other to his mistress's room; and
the child, pondering deeply, stole with soft steps
back to the sofa where the young girl lay, and again
sat down beside her, mute and tearless.

Shadows deepened throughout the dwelling, while
the murmurous sounds of the outer world gradually
died away. Princeton gathered around firesides and
in bar-rooms to discuss the event most prominent in
all minds, and exchange opinions freely. Both Mr.
Prince and his beautiful young wife were objects of
commiseration with all, while the mystery of the
school-master's death furnished food for warm discussions. A few were inclined to give the boy
credit for better feeling; some thought him too
cowardly at heart, but the majority fixed the crime
upon him without the benefit of a doubt. Who
was there to do it, if not he? Mr. Garton was
not known to have an enemy beside. All had
liked him; none seemed to think badly of him;
and John Truslow was the only being who had
fared so ill at his hands as to give grounds for
suspicions through a motive for revenge. Men had
seen him talking to the master, evidently vexed and
ill at ease. Boys declared to many threats having
been uttered in their hearing; and, as is ever the
case in a thing so exciting, each story gathered force
as it went, until no hardened villain, no abandoned,

world-defying man, old in sin and crime, could have been painted in blacker colors than the poor boy who lay shivering and tearless on his hard prison bed, too miserable to give even this natural vent to grief and fear.

In the meantime Mr. Prince roused himself from his severe and rigid self-examination, and cast from him all the weakness that for a few hours had battled mightily with his resolves. The mobile features became like granite, stern and unbending now. The purpose he meditated had taken root in his heart, too deep for uprooting, though the strained chords of life might snap in pursuing it.

He raised himself from his bowed and abandoned position, and looked out into the corridor. All was still and dark. He shut the door behind him, walked with deliberate steps through the gloom, and descended to the main hall. There he found the hall chandelier burning brightly, but the library door was closed, and on entering the room a few dim tapers alone showed him that the place was untenanted. Surprised at this, he stepped hastily to the bell, intending to ask why the watchers had not taken their place in the discharge of a duty imposed upon them. But while his hand was on the cord, a figure glided from Mr. Garton's chamber and confronted him.

"You here, madame!" he demanded, sternly. "It is no place for you."

"I know it," she faltered, leaning for support against the pedestal of a bust near the door.

"Then why are you here?" still more sternly.

"Speak, for now I will know all you are striving to conceal."

"Don't look so! Don't speak in that way! I could not help it, indeed. Oh, my husband, do not be so cruel to me. No drop of traitorous blood ever beat in that heart, now so cold! Why should you so bitterly condemn him?"

"He would not prove himself loyal. If you can prove what he declined, it must be at the expense of all faith in you. I warn you to beware."

"Alas! what can I say? You will not hear reason. If I defend him, your curse will fall upon me. And to let him suffer—no! he cannot suffer more! poor——! Oh, I cannot, will not let you wrong him! You never had a better friend!"

"How do you know that?" he asked, grimly, his eyes mercilessly searching hers.

"You have said it yourself," she answered, rallying under his look. "And I have seen it—I have heard him speak tenderly of you."

"That goes for nothing. It is the love that we take deepest within our hearts, that can turn to bitterest gall. But I will know the truth yet—wholly, entirely. Even the grave shall not shut it from me!"

She met his look now with one of trembling terror. He seized her hand and drew her to the door.

"What would you do?" she gasped, struggling to free herself. "Not there! Oh, not there again! It will kill me!"

"Hush!" was the colder, sterner command, uttered in a low voice. And as he spoke, he drew her inside the door of the dead man's chamber, and turned the key to keep out intruders. Still holding her hand in an unyielding grasp, he drew her to the couch where the dead reposed, and put back the curtains.

"Look!" he whispered. "See in what an icy sleep cold death has laid him. But I will make him the instrument of knowledge to me yet. Cold and rigid as he is, he yet has power to speak to me."

"My God, he is mad!" she breathed, turning more deadly pale with fear.

"No I am not mad. But I bid you look into this dead face, and swear to me, by all your hopes of the future, that you never loved him."

The question paralyzed her. Against her will she seemed constrained to speak, yet had not the power. With a shivering sigh she sank down by the couch, and hid her face in her hands.

"Oh, you dare not speak! You cannot deny it. And while you have lain upon my bosom, while your arms have encircled my neck! while your red lips pressed their sweet kisses upon mine, in your false heart you have cherished another image. Rise, traitress! You shall not insult my sight with this lingering virtue, shame! Such feeble good must die like the rest, and leave you a fit object for loathing and contempt, without a shade of pity."

All the sense of justice—all the chivalric delicacy that man extends to woman by force of habit and inherent refinement, were swallowed up in his jealous passion. He looked down at her with withering scorn, cowering upon the floor, stricken and abased.

Hard and cruel thoughts took entire possession of his mind.   And as the drowning man is said to see a panorama of his past life in a moment's time, now he seemed to see how all her course had tended to prove her the personification of falsehood and deception.   Had he loved her less, he might have been charitable, and sought excuses from his harsher judgment.   As it was, standing in the midst of a desert, with the scorching, withering, unshaded rays of a merciless sun upon him, he could feel only his hopeless thirst, and the cruelty of the wrong which led him here to die in worse than loneliness. Jealousy founded on a love like this, becomes insanity; and in this insanity he felt a cruel pleasure in nursing the thought of destroying her.   To see her lying in her matchless beauty, cold and still as the treacherous man who had stolen her heart from him, would have yielded at that moment a sense of ecstatic delight.   Involuntarily he looked around as if in search of some instrument by which to accomplish the mad desire; but seeing nothing, contented himself with drawing her roughly to her feet, and bending the full force of furious glances on her face, more terrible in their silent concentration than more cruel violence could have been.   She quailed and trembled, her heart throbbing with quick, irregular bound in her breast, until the evidence of her deathly fear wreathed his pale lips with a scornful smile.

"Traitress, sorceress, unworthy woman, false-hearted wife!" he hissed.   "Well may you tremble and quake before the man whom you have wronged

as never man was wronged. Oh, it is easy for a
woman to blind a man who loves her. Wrapped in
the veil of your peerless beauty, you could hide the
arts that killed my honor, like a beautiful, slender
serpent creeping noiselessly through flowers to sting
the happy idler, basking voluptuously in the shade
of fragrant trees. You could woo me into confidence by your voice of music, your honeyed words,
and your enthralling smiles—by the cursed art with
which woman appeals to the self-love of man, and
pleases him with the bewitching thought that he is
loved above all others! But it is past. I have rent
the veil asunder. Hideous in all your beauty, you
stand revealed before me, and I can curse you, as we
have a right to curse the murderess who slays men
without pity and glories in the number of victims
lain upon the sacrificial altar of her selfishness and
her vanity. You are true neither to the one nor the
other, but loving him deceive me, and when I find
you creeping like a thief from his chamber, where
you have stolen to caress, perchance, the dead, you
would appeal to me by lying looks, themselves a
mockery to the fear and agony in your heart. A
faint protest you made in his favor, it is true. But
an animal is nobler than you ; for what animal will
not strive to defend her dead mate from the de-
spoiler? You would creep away, and were I still
blind, nestle in my bosom to grieve for him! Ah,
the farce is played out and the laugh that woke con-
tagion on the stage sounds hollow and mirthless behind the curtains. The queen is uncrowned—the
faithless, false, dishonored woman grovels at her
16*

husband's feet in fruitless prayers for pity! What if he should dash into tragedy and kill her, in justice to his wrongs? He has a right to do it."

All this burning tirade she had received without attempt to answer. But her pale cheek kindled, and her drooping eyelids hid the smouldering fires his fierce words wakened. By the time he reached the close, pride and passion steadied the quivering nerves. Her head rose proudly, and her eyes flashing under her veiling lashes, rebuked him as scornfully as his had accused her.

"Kill me if you will!" she cried in a low, clear, thrilling tone. "It were better to die than live with one who can so wrong me on such slight grounds—who can condemn me unheard. But before you do the kindly deed, it is my right to clear myself from so base a charge, and I swear before high heaven, in the presence of the dead, that you wrong me bitterly. No love brought me to this place to-night. I hated him living, and pitied him dead. My sense of justice would not let me rest, and as a sort of atonement for my unreasonable dislike, I came here and nerved myself to look upon him—the man you loved, and of whom I, your wife, was madly jealous. You praised him, confided in him. He stood between us, and divided your heart. That, my nature rebelled against, and I hated him. I could not help showing it. Whatever he did, I found occasion to criticise; I chided him, I vexed him; I tormented him as much as was in a jealous woman's power. But love him I did not! And now that my remorse is gone, you may think of him as meanly as you will. Woman will bear much, but outraged honor endures a certain limit only."

She turned from him proudly, and passed through a side door leading to a private stairway. Before he realized it, she had gone, and he lifted his head with a gesture of bewilderment. Like a man rousing from a nightmare to meet the smiling assurance of Nature, it was but hideous dreams that peopled his night with horror, he felt the revolution within him. The cruel light died out of his eyes, and the scornful lip was as soft and quivering in a moment. Over his whole face the sudden joy spread like a radiance. He panted, he trembled until he could scarcely stand. Then he darted after her, and went with swift, springing steps to her chamber.

CHAPTER XV.

TRUTH IS MIGHTY, AND WILL PREVAIL.

ON reaching her own room, Mrs. Prince hastily took a small key from her bosom, and locked it within her jewel-case, the first receptacle that presented itself in her excitement. The unnatural tension of the nerves was giving way, and a moment after securing the treasure she threw herself upon a couch and burst into tears.

Soon the sound of steps on the floor reached her, and she felt herself lifted up within her husband's arms. A passionate, broken voice was in her ears; hot, passionate kisses showered upon her face. This storm of remorse was almost as violent as his anger, so wild are the extremes of strong and excitable natures.

"Oh, my wife, my darling, can you forgive me for the wrong I have done you? It was my boundless love, my jealous selfishness, that made me so unjust. Had I loved you less, I could not have broken your heart so cruelly. But I was beside myself. I have left you to grieve alone; I have insulted you; I have wronged you shamefully, but I have nothing to plead beyond this love. Speak to

me! say that you will forgive me, or I shall go mad
in my utter grief and shame!"

She drew herself from his passionate embrace,
only to take his brow between her hands and kiss
it tenderly, a mute seal of forgiveness upon all the
past. Overpowered by the magnanimous goodness,
the nobility of the action, thrilled by the entrancing
proof of her love, that could look past such bitter,
burning words as he had lately uttered, the husband
dropped his face against her bosom and wept—
great, hot, happy, yet remorseful tears, that rained
swiftly upon the little hands imprisoned within his
own.   Many a time the tender eyes had filled; but
these were the first tears that had fallen from them
since Geraldine's mother had been laid in the
church-yard.   They relieved—they softened, they
purified him, as swollen waters will sweep obstruc-
tions from the bed of the stream.   He let them flow
unshamed by the childish indulgence, until her
drooping frame refused him longer support, and he
raised himself to find that she had fainted.

Quickly and tenderly, he applied himself to the
work of restoration; but he would call no help.   He
bathed her face and hands with cologne; he chafed
them, calling her name with passionate love, reproaching himself in humiliation until she recovered
consciousness and again smiled confidingly up at his
anxious face.   Transported, he cradled her in his
arms, and the reconciliation was complete.   Never
had he loved her as now.   Never had she seemed so
good and beautiful as when she lay like a flower
crushed by his hand upon his breast.   At such mo-

ments it would be well to die. The human heart, rising from pain, to feel the thrilling tides of happiness pulsing through, were better stilled in the very height of bliss, than to grow cold under following blows ; or lie, like a mountain whose center has been drained of its molten seas, crusted over by the frozen lava no more pervious to heat, and covered by ashes of the things consumed.

He remained, wrapt in the sweet oblivion that clouded all things but one, until her gentle voice begged him to take some rest.

"I cannot, sweet love," bending murmuringly to her ear. "I am too happy for a thought of sleep. But rest yourself, and I will watch you."

Resistance was vain. She longed to escape the searching glances of his loving eyes; but he would not be sent away longer than to suffer her maid to attend her. Smothering the hot impatience of her irritated nature from his sight, she allowed him to sit beside her pillow, holding her hand and breathing fond endearments, until fatigue stole insensibly away, giving place to sleep.

He was happy then—happier, he thought, than he had ever been, after the terrible ordeal that had snatched from and restored to him his love. The silken masses of her shining hair lay scattered over the lace pillow. Fair and soft as an infant's were the rounded cheek and arm supporting it. On her brow the peacefulness of rest was supreme, and the dark eyes hidden by the sealed lids left the face without a trace of will—a sign of opposition. Abandoned to his love, helplessly confiding in slumber, she made him adore her with a wilder passion. With her breath upon his face, he closed his eyes and wished then that death would seal this reunion of their hearts beyond the possibility of severance. The very fullness of his joy made him cowardly for the future. He was afraid to look beyond this hour, lest the sweetness of his cup should receive from some demon hand a drop of gall.

Can we tell by what process the mind passes from the dizzy heights of delirium down to the cold plains of reason? We wake from our fervid dreams to find gentle, friendly faces around us; but we miss the fiery beauty of the tropical lands, remembered but vaguely, perchance, yet never to be forgotten. So this man gradually came out of his insanity to meet facts as friends, and be guided by them to a sure foundation of strength. He thought so, at least, as he moved softly away from the side of his wife, a smile upon his lips, unspeakable tenderness in his eyes.

"My darling, I will place doubt beyond a possibility in the future," he said, whisperingly, while he lingered regarding her. "If I have wronged both the living and the dead, I must atone; but it will make my happiness and yours, my wife, my idol! Oh, love, thou blissful tyrant, to whose power we alone bow proudly! how wholly hast thou made me thy slave!"

He came back and bent over her; and, half waking, she felt the soft pressure of his lips upon her own. He saw her smile and heard her indistinct murmur, as if responding to his caress; then he glided away and was lost in the gloom of the corridors, until the pale light of the tapers round the dead man's couch, showed whither his steps had tended.

A moment since, the silent man had stood over the living image of beauty. Here the mystery of death disclosed only the door through which the soul had passed—nothing beyond. With subdued eyes he contemplated the marble features, marking the contrast, and wondering if any part of him lived to see what was passing around the clay, so calm and peaceful now. There was a thought of the mother, who would come on the morrow to receive the remains of her only son, and the heart already softened grew still more sensitive to pity. He was her all on earth, and the assassin's hand had left her desolate. Who was that assassin? A thousand times this question came up, but he could not accept public opinion. Sealed in a mystery, as impenetrable as death, was the name of the murderer. Would he ever know the truth? Hope whispered that the time might, nay, must come; but when?

There is something subduing in the contemplation of death. Unless too utterly wrapped in our own feelings to take cognizance of the lesson it teaches, we are drawn to reflect with an awful sense of certainty upon the end of all earthly aspirations. Into the mind of Mr. Prince's thoughts peculiarly solemn came now, when the silence was most profound, and the deep night added impressiveness to the scene. This calmer moment led him more firmly to feel his late desire for the endless rest his friend had found, and his answer was less positive. No! He did not want to die now. The momentary passion was gone. Dearer than ever was the life beating in his veins. He put his hands on that icy one, and recoiled, appalled at the touch. So lately that hand had grasped his! So lately those sealed eyes had looked into his own! and this thought led him to the last scene in the conservatory. Every look and tone rushed back overwhelmingly, bending him as a sapling is bent before the blast.

"Oh, Nathaniel, Nathaniel!" he groaned, "death has parted me and you, and my last words to you were words of anger. But, if to the enfranchised soul all the things that are dark here become known, you must understand now, and I shall be forgiven."

The longing desire for truth, that is in every human heart, sometimes finds comfort in coincidences. Skeptics will call it chance; Christians say it is Providence. But who shall say *what* it is, since we can live only by faith and not by knowledge? Mr. Prince rose from his knees, where had rested his head against the icy shoulder of the corpse, and after covering the face with the sheet, sat down by the desk on which lay the prayer-book, from which a leaf had been torn, and a little Bible. The latter he lifted, and the leaves parted as if by a hand, revealing a verse enclosed in pencil marks, and deeply underscored.

"And I say unto you, ask, and it shall be given you; seek, and ye shall find; knock, and it shall be opened unto you."

"If this be true, then I shall know that this dead man's heart never did me wrong—or I shall know his treachery so well as to lose all pity. Surely, where so much may be at stake for me and mine, I shall not be doomed to darkness and doubt—if God hears and answers the prayers of His creatures."

His purpose had not been defined until now. That he came to satisfy any lingering doubt, seemed the strongest idea, but how to do it had not yet presented a conclusion to his mind. He looked about him carefully, but saw only those books, and the scrawled lines upon the paper which had been the last thoughts of the young lover.

Why had he not examined them more closely before? They bore evidence of an absorbing passion, and there was a name written there which he did not notice when the paper was pointed out to him in the morning. Faintly that name was traced, and in a smaller hand. But he recognized it and sighed, thinking of the young girl above, lying crushed under the blast that had swept away her first sweet dreams of love—poor Katie Eldridge.

Carefully folding the paper, he put it in his pocket, murmuring:

"I will give it to her, and she will prize it as an evidence of how he loved her. And now shall I leave the place, or seek for other proofs? What has come over me, that I cannot stifle the promptings of my jealous heart?"

Once more he rose and wandered searchingly through the room. Finally he opened the drawers of the bureau, and took out a little box bearing a silver plate upon the lid with the words "Nathaniel Garton"—and below it a card labeled "Private Papers." His heart beat fast. One look into that box would set his mind at rest forever. Had he any right to open it? Yes, for Nathaniel Garton had been his dearest friend, and he had distrusted him. His actions had caused suspicion, his property must effectually clear him; so he looked for the key, but could not find it. The keys of his own private drawers were in his pocket and he tried them. One fitted and turned the lock. Opening it, he saw several loose papers, and the diary which Mr. Garton had kept so faithfully, so sacredly; and with the box in his hand, he sat down by his desk to look at those sad relics.

First of all, he took out the folded paper which had caused the first sense of pain that had ever risen out of Mr. Garton's actions. The lines of poetry were now so nearly effaced as to be illegible, as if a rain of tears had washed them away. Unable to forget the impatient eagerness with which this paper had been snatched from his hand, he hesitated before opening it; and once his fingers moved to put it back; but a second impulse conquered the compunctions of conscience or honor, and he looked at the drawing.

Had the head of a Medusa been suddenly held up before him, his face could not have expressed more horror or assumed a more terrible change. Smiling eyes and mouth, and flowing silken hair, were life-like as the breathing ones lately touched by his impassioned lips. The blood leaped to his forehead, and his bosom heaved with a return of the jealous storm just quelled. Now there could be no more dallying with his fate! Now the truth must be *wholly* revealed; and with bitter murmurs on his lips he crushed the miniature in his hand, and turned determinedly to the perusal of the dead man's diary.

In the cold gray of the morning, Mr. Prince came out into the hall. A servant who had all night watched outside the chamber door, started at seeing him, but said nothing. Something in his face never seen there before, and rendered more forbidding by the dreary light, made words, had they been desired, impossible. He drew aside to be farther out of the way, and his master passed him without even seeming to see that he was there. He had reached the main entrance, and had his hand upon the door, when another servant came and touched his arm.

"I have been looking for you, sir, to go to Miss Geraldine."

"Is anything the matter?"

"She has been taken ill in the night and we found her lying upon the floor of the room where Miss Eldridge lay yesterday. The doctor is with her now, and Mrs. Prince has taken care of her since we discovered that anything was the matter!"

"How long ago did you find her?"

"A little while after midnight. Mrs. Prince sent at once for the doctor."

"Why did you not summon me at once?"

"We could not find you, sir. I went all over the house, except into Mr. Garton's room, and the door of that was locked."

"True," answered the master, remembering that it had never been unlocked since he turned the key upon his wife. When they left the room, it had been by the private stairway, and by the same he returned again, later.

Dismissing the boy, he went up to Geraldine's room, but she was not there. Mrs. Prince had caused her to be carried to her own. On his way thither he met the housekeeper, who was going below to get something for the doctor. He stopped her to ask a question.

"Is the child dangerously ill?"

"I am afraid so. You see the poor little thing was so still, and everybody was so confused, no notice was taken at all of her, and she probably sat alone in that room after Miss Eldridge went to bed, until she had one of her bad fainting fits. I woke up feeling uneasy, and went over there to see how the young lady was; and I found Geraldine on the floor. Jim was in the hall down stairs, so I called him to help me, and when we got her into Mrs. Prince's room, I sent for the doctor."

"That was right," he answered calmly, and went on. The housekeeper had expected a great show of anxiety, and was surprised to see how quietly he took the alarming intelligence. There was no time for reflections, however, and she hastened on to do her errand, while Mr. Prince entered his wife's chamber.

A low couch had been drawn up before the east window, and upon that lay the child, raging in a high fever. The doctor sat gravely upon one side

17*

of the couch, and the young step-mother bent weepingly over the other. Instantly, when he entered, she sprang to her husband's side and took his hand.

"Oh, dearest, we have searched for you everywhere."

"Well, I am here now," he said, putting her away from him with his prisoned hand. His answer was low, and the doctor, who was delicately absorbed with his patient, neither saw nor heard. A moment later the lady glided into an adjoining room, and the father sat down in the chair she had vacated.

"Is she dangerously ill, doctor?" was the question he repeated without any previous sign of recognition or a word of greeting.

The doctor hesitated.

"I do not like to say yet," was his cautious reply at length.

"I desire that you will speak plainly."

"Then I fear she is. The housekeeper tells me that she is easily startled, and has had several fainting fits, that I do not like. And now this blow has been too much for her. Had I seen her yesterday, so quiet and tearless as I am told she appeared, this evil might have been averted. She ought to have been made to weep freely. I wonder you did not see the danger yourself."

"I do remember now that she was unnaturally calm and strange; but the calamity that had fallen upon me rendered me blind to the extent of her danger. Poor little suffering daughter! She loved

Mr. Garton with all her heart. No wonder it is breaking now."

"If we can only break this fever a little and restore her consciousness, perhaps we can make her cry. But if that cannot be done, I will not promise that I can save her."

CHAPTER XVI.

HE CONQUERS WHO CONQUERS HIMSELF.

MRS. PRINCE did not return again after being dismissed by her husband. His manner and look had set her blood on fire with fear, doubt, suspense! What could have changed him in so short a time? Where had he been all night, and how occupied, to come to her with such a face as that which had shone upon her with terrible sternness for a moment?

For a time she stood still in the middle of the floor, with her hands pressing against her temples, a wild tumult in her heart. Had he come back to her with the look and smile and touch of last night but faintly repeated, she could have waited in peace. Now it was impossible. Those who risk all upon a single throw, after a desperate game, are rarely more cool than when the first loss tempted them to try again and retrieve themselves. And she, while feeling that one step more might ruin her forever in her husband's opinion, could not wait longer to assure herself of safety in a last venture. Soon as the key had been turned between her and the gentlemen, she took the hidden treasure from her jewel-case and

stole softly out through another door. This led her
into a corridor branching off from the main upper
hall, and favored her journey down the private stairway leading to Mr. Garton's room. There she
paused and listened, then tried the door. It was
not locked, and she went in upon tiptoe, with the
awed face and hushed breath one cannot avoid in the
presence of death. Cold and dark and dismal, with
the faint odor of flowers stealing from the pillows
where some friendly hand had placed them. Objects
became more distinct when her eyes grew accustomed to the darkness; and the intense desire to see
those flowers conquered her reluctance to draw near
the couch. She approached it, lifted the sheet with
shaking fingers, and saw a bed of beautiful bloom
about the still face. Flowers that spoke of delicacy,
of purity, of love, of remorse! Could the hand
that placed them there have been moved by a consciousness of their worth? She knew that they had
been clipped from her own conservatory, and her
heart throbbed yet faster as she questioned within
herself who had been here to heap them round the
murdered one.

"It must have been my husband," was the final
conclusion; but while she suffered the whisper to
escape her lips, the weakness of her frame forced
her to lean against the couch for support. "And if
it was, he has—"

What! No other words were fashioned by the
white lips, and her explanation was in action alone.
Rousing herself, as to a desperate deed, she crept
softly to the bureau, took from the drawer the box

that was there, and bore it to the window where a brighter light shone through the blinds. Here a sudden terror seized her. With chattering teeth, and limbs that almost defied control, she hid the box upon the floor in the deep shadows beneath the desk, while she went to the door and cautiously turned the key. Then she listened at the other to assure herself no one was near before stealthily unlocking the box to discover if the contents could touch her destiny with a record of ill.

She did not know that he kept a journal, but thought it possible that a man of his strict habits might be constrained to do so. His wonderful memory of the details of small events even, had led her to question whether this might not account for the ability he had shown in stating things long past with an accuracy that was almost marvelous. To learn the truth had brought her here on a previous night; but she had only secured the key, and her courage failed her before her design could be carried out. A step had frightened her, and, as we have seen, brought her face to face with her husband. Now she was wrought up to that point from which no backward step can be taken. To go forward was the only path by which she could hope to gain an advantage; and yet, how horrible it was to stand in that room, with the cold stillness of death pervading it, the odor of flowers steeping her senses with their sickening perfume, and the fear of discovery beating in every pulse. The beautiful lips were drawn in, and the pearly teeth pressed closely upon them. She struck her hand against her heart with a passionate " be still" on the hushed breath. And then when her determination was at its height, a reaction came which steadied her nerves. She opened the box, looked swiftly through the contents, and smiled with exulting joy to find nothing there which could harm her. If anything ever had been there, had not the key been in her own possession, and lain near her while her husband's loving care enshrined her? The hot tides of blood went down, and she was cool, clear, light-hearted. Even the disgust and fear of death seemed to vanish. She put away the box, came back and stood over what remained of the man who had once loved her fondly. Slow memories flowed back that made her heart very soft and piti-ful. She could bend down and look at his face, even touch his white brow with her fingers, murmuring : " Poor Nathaniel ! "

> " Oh, woman, most beautiful of all created things,
> And yet the most unfathomable and strange."

When she reached her room again, the doctor was still with her husband, and she could hear them talking in subdued tones. Still more reassured, she quietly returned the key in the lock, dashed some cologne upon her head and face, and threw herself into an easy chair.

Until now, not one moment had been given her to think calmly over all that had passed since roused to learn Geraldine's illness. It was a comparatively easy task now to arrive at a more satisfactory con-clusion with regard to his conduct. He had been sadly overtaxed for several days, and the child's danger following so swiftly upon all other ills, had been more than he could sustain. Perhaps he attached some blame to her for giving way to her distress, and so wholly neglecting the child he loved so deeply. He had confided to her the nurture of his daughter, the need for more than ordinary care and tender handling ; and to do her justice, she had fully meant to do what she fairly set herself to accomplish. She could not foresee this catastrophe, and was not prepared to meet it ; therefore her husband had seen cause to feel hurt and angered. There was another thought, sweet in the midst of all storms. His love for herself had won him from his child so far that he could put her first before Geraldine. Remembering this, the first pain of the shock might waken a sense of remorse, and it would be a natural thing for him to show it while the feeling lasted. No matter now. At peace with herself, and secure in the knowledge of her power, she gave up all thoughts that could disturb her mind, and ere long fell into a quiet slumber.

When she awoke, her husband stood before her chair, looking down upon her with unfathomable eyes, his arms folded across his breast in an attitude of sad contemplation. It was not sadness alone his eyes expressed, nor pity, nor anger ; but a mingling of all, and a questioning.

"Have I been asleep?" she cried, starting up. "Ah, how selfish—and you have wanted me, perhaps."

"No," he answered gently. "It is well if you can sleep. I think it must be sweet to be able to close one's eyes and forget everything in this weary world."

He walked to the window, and looking out sighed very heavily. She followed him and laid her hand upon his arm.

"My husband, I wish that I could comfort you."

"Do you?" and again that strange, deep, questioning look was turned upon her.

"Can you doubt it for one moment? Oh, I thought all doubts had been dissipated, and no more should come between us."

He turned his head quickly that she might not see the frown which knit his brow. His next words were wholly unexpected and startling.

"Do you know that my daughter will die?"

"Die? Oh, no! It cannot be so bad as that. I was aware of danger, but not sudden or positive; and I hoped the tender care I am prepared to give might restore her. Do not despair so soon. Everything shall be done—everything skill and love can devise. Oh, dearest, can you ever forgive me for having neglected her so sadly yesterday? I never shall be able to forgive myself."

"Yet you could sleep peacefully while she lies dying in the other room."

The rebuke was so keen and so well-deserved, she could not but quail under it. Womanly wit came to her aid with a ready answer, however. She spoke sharply, like one in pain.

"You sent me away with a manner and a look that forbade resistance. I would gladly have remained."

"How I acted or looked was of little moment, since it could not disturb your rest."

18

"I see you will be wounded with what I have done. Weariness I will not plead when I recall that you have taken no rest for two days and nights. But I will accept all your chidings, and never cherish a word as unkind against you. To have wounded you is sufficient punishment for my lack of strength."

Not now could such seemingly generous words move him; and the sweet, sad, self-accusing voice had lost its power. Yet he preserved his gentleness in speaking to her, and studiously kept guard over himself lest his strength of endurance should fail.

"To chide you was not my intention; and to punish you for lack of strength would not be just. What I came to say is that Mrs. Garton will be here to-night, and that I must go back with her to lay the remains of her son in the family burying-ground. It would not be seemly to let her return alone, after all that she must hear at—at—I must go! Meantime my own child may die, and—but no matter! Better now than later. I can give her up while this awful blow is still smarting and lacerating my heart. Only tell me before I go what shall be done to aid you till my return? Are any of the servants competent to the task? or shall I find some one outside to assist in nursing her?"

"Do nothing, but leave all to me, if you must go. I will care for her as never mother cared for her child; and if care can save her she shall not die."

"Nay, I hope and pray that she may find rest. This world is no place for such a tender plant as my little daughter. God in his goodness will not leave her here to suffer as—I must till the end comes!"

"Alas, what can I say to you! I know, dear husband, how dark the world must seem to you now; but it will pass after awhile. Have you never seen a storm in the mountains, when the clouds hung blackly over them and the rains beat in torrents— when the winds whistled in the trees, and writhed their limbs with the force of an awful fury? And yet a day brings a change—the clouds pass, the winds are still, and the sun shines as brightly as ever over the hoary brow of Nature."

"Storms may pass, and the sunshine will come again as bright as ever. But the tree uprooted by the storm no more can rise to its place. A little while its leaves will keep their green; a little while life will refuse to leave the hardy trunk; yet death must come at last, and the thing that stood so proudly with heaven-reaching boughs, lies in the dust."

" We will not talk more of this now; you are too sad. When the worst is over, hope will return again, and my love shall comfort you."

He groaned.

" Oh, God, my burthen is heavier than I can bear."

She laid her cheek against his arm, and kissed his hand as the tears rolled over her cheeks, but said no more. Words were too tame for a woe like his. The tremor that ran through his frame at her touch, seemed but a stronger proof of the agony that finds no outlet, and must spend itself within the helpless heart.

While they stood thus, a tap came upon the door

and she sped to it quickly, deeming it a summons to Geraldine. The housekeeper stood there anxiously.

"Is Mr. Prince with you?"

"Yes," answered he, coming forward, "what is it?"

"James has been up to say that somebody is inquiring for you down stairs. Shall I tell him to send the person away?"

"No, I will go down."

He first went to Geraldine, and kissed her with a passionate tenderness that brought tears to the good woman's eyes. Then he hurried away, as if trying to escape his anguish.

"Ah, madam, you have need to love him much," she said to Mrs. Prince, wiping her eyes as she sat down by the couch. "The best devotion of woman's heart will be little in compensation for what he has now to suffer."

Mrs. Prince ventured no reply to this. Her feelings were too much moved, and her tears that were flowing before now fell afresh as she leaned over the child and took her little hot hand. If tears can wash away a multitude of sins, hers should have been effaced then. They came from her heart, penitential, sorrowful, womanly tears—such as the Peri bore, a welcome gift, to the gate of Paradise.

Geraldine was sleeping now, a heavy, feverish sleep that rendered her condition far more painful to witness.

"If she wakes from this unnatural sleep, and we can make her remember and cry, we may save her life. Oh, we must make her cry away this killing grief! Poor little lamb—the knife of that bad boy has killed his two best friends at one blow. It is awful to think of the depravity of such a child."

"You condemn hastily," said Mrs. Prince, raising her head. "That poor boy was never guilty of such a deed."

"Who was it then? Ah, it could be no other."

"I cannot think so. Some day we shall know better."

The housekeeper could not be convinced, but would not venture to argue the matter with the young mistress, whose disposition she had yet to learn. Further remarks, had they been intruded, would have been cut off by the entrance of Miss Eldridge, who had glided in like a shadow. Mrs. Prince started at seeing her, and colored violently.

"Katie! is it you, dear! Poor child, how stricken you look; but we are all stricken sorely."

"Yes, very sorely," answered the young girl, without any attempt to conceal her feelings. "Few enough real hopes and promises of happiness come to us in this life. To see the brightest and only that one has ever possessed, swept away at a blow, as mine were, requires all the strength we have."

"He loved you, Katie."

"I know it."

"And you reciprocated—"

"Beyond the power of words to express! But do not talk of it. The struggle is past now, and I am resigned. Once I thought I never could be, but this poor little sufferer taught me better, by reminding me of what I had said to him of faith that could

18*

sustain us under all afflictions. Oh, Geraldine, faithful little heart! She did not leave me more than a few moments all day yesterday."

"If she had, it would have been better for her," said the housekeeper bluntly, forgetting caution. "No one could love Mr. Garton better than she did, as any one may know by looking at her now. She will prove it by dying, if what the doctor says comes true, and then you will both suffer the remorse of having given way so entirely to your own grief as to be unable to see how others were afflicted."

Miss Eldridge took the reproof as just, making no reply, while Mrs. Prince turned quickly to her.

"Whatever our faults may be, it is not pleasant, under present circumstances, to be criticised in such a way as you have chosen," she said, with some asperity. "My nerves could not bear the shock; and if it rendered me helpless, how much more must Miss Eldridge have felt—his promised wife."

"I did not know she was to marry him," answered the housekeeper. "Pardon me, Miss, for speaking so plainly. You *have* enough to bear."

The same apology was not extended to her mistress. Shocking as the event was, in reality, she could not see why it should render her oblivious of everything but herself. Now that Geraldine hovered on the confines of her grave, from want of care and tender treatment, her sore heart must give vent to its pent-up grief, which had discovered, in reproaching itself, that she was not alone in fault, to answer for her life. An awkward silence followed, broken by Mrs. Prince, who remarked that as she was not needed just then, she had better look to other things; and if any assistance was required, she would send for her.

The housekeeper made no reply, but rose with a bow, and retired, looking grieved and indignant.

CHAPTER XVII.

COURAGE SURVIVES THE GRAVE.

ACROSS the hills from Princeton, where the gorges were deep and wild, and the rugged cliffs added grandeur to the stately lines of giant trees, a narrow road led to a small cabin, whose surroundings indicated not only poverty, but the primitive habits of an earlier date by full a quarter of a century. The cabin stood upon a hill-side, a small enclosure serving for garden, corn-patch, and poultry-yard. At one corner of the enclosure stood the hen-house; in the other was built a pen of rails, where a fine pig wallowed lazily, or lay snugly curled up on a bed of straw. Below the cabin, stretched a long, narrow valley, a portion of which had been fenced in, and devoted to the cultivation of flax.

The cabin itself was of rough, unhewn logs, into which two small windows had been let. The chimney was built on the outside, a frame-work of logs carefully filled up with chinks and mortar, and lined with stones, after the fashion of many chimneys still to be seen in portions of the South. A glance inside will show us as quaint a habitation as ever graced the country in its earliest settlement, when women sat trembling by the hearth, and men kept their weapons loaded, and their knives sharp, against the attack of the stealthy red man.

There was but a single apartment, serving as sleeping-room, kitchen, dining-room, and parlor; and the walls had been covered all around with old newspapers. Two small beds occupied the further end of the room, and on the wall, back of the house, were hung the wardrobes of the inmates, plain home-spun dresses, with one or two of calico, which served as Sunday finery. For ornament, a small looking-glass hung upon one side of the wide chimney-place, and a picture, torn from an old magazine, framed in pasteboard, and trimmed with little knots of red ribbon at the corners, upon the other. The floor was of broad, heavy puncheons, hewn smooth, and worn glossy by frequent scrubbings. Overhead, the beams, that were of rough logs, the frame-work of the cabin, bore a floor of loose planks, forming a " loft " in the roof, to which access was gained by a ladder standing in one corner. An old chest, one or two stools, an arm-chair, quaintly fashioned, of hickory, and a rough table, composed of pine boards, completed the furniture, unless we add the cooking utensils that stood upon the hearth.

The inmates and owners of this simple dwelling were a mother and two daughters. The eldest of the daughters was a blooming, modest girl of sixteen. The youngest, slight and pale, with a beautiful eye, and a wealth of golden hair, never left her little bed in the corner, where the light from one of the windows fell on her, winter and summer, in cold gray or rosy warmth.

We present this trio to our readers on the morning following the murder of the young schoolmaster. And in strange contrast was the quiet of this habitation, the harmony and peace pervading it, with the wild tumult of consternation at Prince Hill. The invalid lay toying with the leaves of an open book, intently watching the movements of her sister, who sat on a low stool by the fire, paring apples. The heat had flushed her round cheeks, and her red lips were pouted in earnest forgetfulness of everything except her occupation.

"How pretty you look, Angie," said the low, child-like voice of the sister from the bed.

Angie answered by a quick look and smile:

"I'm glad you think so; it's such a pleasure to look at handsome people."

"I did not say you were handsome—only pretty, Miss Vanity!" laughed the invalid, childishly.

"Where's the difference? I can't see any."

"Oh, but there is, a great deal."

"At *any rate*, it's all the same to me. I'd as lief be pretty as handsome, if it's as agreeable to you."

"Either way I should love you," answered the sister affectionately, "because you are so good, and that is better than beauty. I wonder if everybody is happy and contented as we are. Wouldn't you like to see the great, busy world, Angie? I should very much, just to find out how other people look, and think, and feel about life. It seems as if they can't be so different as we are led to believe."

"But you know they must, though. No two people can be alike, and it's just as well they can't."

"Why?"

"O, because it'd be so stupid, you know. How'd you like to be just like somebody else, and not your own sweet self, that nobody can't help loving?"

"There it is again! Bad grammar, Miss Angie. What *shall* I do to make you speak properly. I declare it's quite discouraging."

"Oh, bother, with your grammar! Grammar won't never do me any particular good."

"So I should judge from present indications," answered the sister, laughing again, her sweet, gleeful laugh. "But seriously, Angie, you ought to pay more attention to putting into practice what you have learned. Who knows what changes may come? I am a frail girl, and cannot last very long, perhaps; and then mother is very old, and old people may die any time. You are the only one who has a prospect for a happy future. After we are gone, you can't live here all alone; and if you must go into the great world, you ought to be able to go with the best, without being ashamed. I'm sure no girl can be smarter or prettier than you."

Angie's lip trembled, and her eyes filled.

"I wish you wouldn't' talk so! It's foolish. Whatever happens, I never mean to live anywhere but here."

"Ah, Angie, you don't know yourself now. If the time comes, as it must, you'll feel very differently. A little, lonely, out-of-the-way place like this would soon become unendurable, and you'd have to go. Besides, you don't think Rufus would ever consent to stay here, do you?"

"Rufus! What's Rufus to me, Rose?" cried Angie, blushing prettily. "I declare you are too bad. Nobody ever thinks of him in this way but you."

Rose regarded her sister with roguish eyes, forgetful of the momentary seriousness that had shaded her tones but a moment since.

"I wonder why you blush so, then, if he is nothing to you. Why, what a silly little thing you are! You are not going to get angry with me?"

Angie had risen hastily, and was thrusting the apples, which she pared and cut fine, into the pan of hot fat with more spirit than the occasion required. Instead of answering, a sharp cry broke from her lips, and she lifted herself up to examine her arm, now tinged with a long line of fiery red. Rose started up from her pillow anxiously.

"Oh, dear, you have splashed your arm with the hot grease, haven't you? Get some flour and bind on it as quick as you can. Don't wipe off the grease."

Angie ran to the flour barrel and dusted her arm freely, her pretty face painfully expressive of suffering. Rose tossed her own handkerchief from the bed, and the injured member was soon bound up. In turning round from this occupation, Angie caught her sister's eye and burst into a laugh.

"You look as doleful as if I'd killed myself. Why, sis, it is nothing much, and won't hurt long."

"It would not have happened if I had not teased you about that ugly Rufus. I wish—"

"Hush!" cried Angie, with a finger on her lip, "you must not talk so loud. I wonder if mother ain't getting hungry. It's high time breakfast was over, and that flax got down from the shed loft. I'm going to break it to-day. By Christmas it's got to be in a web of linen, ready for bleaching in the spring."

"I wish I could help you; but oh, dear! I'm worth nothing, and can only make you trouble."

"Now you just stop talking that way, or I'll tell Mr. Garton."

"Oh, my! that reminds me that I have not half got my lesson, and he will be here to-day. Hurry breakfast, Angie, and then we can be quiet when it's all over."

"Yes, very quiet; with mother poundin' away at the loom, and me breakin' the flax, and only a thin wall between us. I guess you won't hear that, though, when he comes."

"No, indeed, I shall not mind it a bit; for he always contrives to make me forget everything but my lessons. How good he is, Angie! I wonder if the time will ever come when we can show him how grateful we are."

"Perhaps so."

Both were thoughtful for several minutes, and Angie bustled about busy with breakfast, while Rose lay quite still looking at her, but evidently thinking of something else.

"Do you ever dream bad dreams, Angie? I had a horrid dream last night."

"What was it?"

19

"I thought I was lying here waiting for Mr. Garton to come, when somebody came and stood outside the window at the head of the bed. It seemed as if the sun was shining, and I was trying to read, but could not. Whatever or whoever it was, it cast a strange shadow on my book, and I could not see the lines. But when I looked out, I could see nothing except the slope, the brook, and the autumn-tinted trees on the other hill. I wondered what it could mean, turned again and again to my book, yet could not get rid of the feeling. At last, when I was beginning to feel nervous and unhappy, I looked once more, and there stood Mr. Garton, his face very pale, and his eyes half shut, as if he was dreadfully sick. In alarm I asked him what was the matter; but he only smiled, without answering, a slow, sad smile, and then he seemed to float away. When I woke and found it was all a dream, I was so glad I could have clapped my hands for very joy. That's what put me into such good spirits all the morning. That's what made me tease you about Rufus."

"An excellent reason, indeed!" said a manly voice, apparently over their heads, which made both girls start and blush vividly. The moment after, a handsome, laughing face was thrust through the square aperture of the corner where the ladder stood, and a pair of mischievous eyes glanced around the little room merrily.

"I say, Rose, you have quite a genius for dreaming. I never used to believe in dreams, but shall after this, doubtless. Is breakfast most ready, Angie? I am as hungry as a wolf."

"You don't deserve to have any at all, because you wouldn't cut up that wood for me when I wanted you to last night. I guess somebody'll have to go without the apple fritters somebody likes so well, just for that piece of contrariness."

"Now you wouldn't be so cruel, I know, as to ·deny me those delicious fritters nobody can make as you can. Consider, my little beauty, that I had promised to go and see a pretty girl, and I was in honor bound to keep my promise. You wouldn't have me do anything dishonorable, I hope."

Angie turned very red at this, and pouted visibly, to the delight of the tormenting spirit above.

"Oh, of course not! You can go and see your pretty girls, and leave me to chop wood as much as ever you please, but you won't get any apple fritters for your breakfast."

"Come, now, don't be hard on a fellow! As for my going to see the girls, you don't care for that. What am I to you? And wood-chopping has been a common amusement for nearly all your life. You don't mind it half so much as you pretend, but only want to tease me. Isn't that it, Rose?"

With the question he suddenly let himself down through the loft by his hands, and dropped to the floor like a cat, upright and unruffled. Without ceremony he marched up to Angie, and catching her round the waist, kissed her heartily.

"There, now, let us be friends, my pretty Angie."

For response she dealt him a stinging blow upon the cheek, and turned away angrily.

"You mind how you take liberties, sir! If you

want kisses, go to your pretty girl! *I* don't mean to let you take such liberties with me!"

Mr. Rufus sat down upon a stool, leaned his head back against the wall and laughed, twirling his moustache saucily.

"Why, Rose, look at her! I do believe she is jealous!"

"Jealous, and of you! I hope I've got better sense!"

"I declare," he continued, still addressing her, "it makes her really handsome to be in a bad humor. I'm afraid, Angie, if you were to invite me to come over and sit down beside you, I should be fool enough to do it."

"Then you may place it beyond my power to tempt you so near me, as it is against my principles to make fools of people. Nature has done enough of that already."

"Bravo! You are as sharp this morning as a newly filed crosscut-saw! Did you have any remarkable dreams to put you into such a glorious humor, *ma petite?*"

"Yes, I dreamed that you came in, and I mistook you for a gentleman," answered Angie, with more readiness than truth. Rose looked anxious, but the good-nature of the young man was proof against all such assaults. The sharper the retort the better he was pleased and the greater his enjoyment. Still leaning back, he laughed more merrily than before, and pursued her tormentingly.

"So you mistook me for a gentleman! What a pity to have been so disappointed when that com-

modity is so scarce in this part of the country.   Did
you ever see a lady, Angie?"

"A few times."

"When?"

"When I looked into the glass."

"Whew?   How modest you are!   Did you ever
see an ape?"

"Yes, there is one present at this moment, and his
tricks are far from agreeable.   Rose, will you look
out and see if mother is milking the cow?   I don't
hear the loom any more."

Rose raised herself upon one arm and looked out
through the window.

"She has finished and gone to put the milk into
the spring-house.   Peter Jenks is talking with her."

"He's out early.   Which way is he goin', Rose?"

"Home, I think.   I guess he has been over to
Princeton.   Yes, he is going home, and now mother
will want her breakfast."

The young man sprang up, set the homely table
into the middle of the floor, and spread the cloth
upon it before Angie had time to intercept his movements.   Next, he ran to the little square cupboard
and brought out plates, knives and forks, and a stock
of cups and saucers.

"There! wouldn't I make a splendid husband for
a rustic lassie?   You'd better reconsider your bad
opinion of me, Angie, for I shall probably be a candidate for that honor some of these fine days.   Hallo!
Mother Ritter, how are you this morning?   What's
the news from Princeton?"

Mrs. Ritter came in and set her empty tin pail

upon a bench before answering. Her face was very grave and troubled. She glanced first at Rose, then at Angie; then turned to the young man, who had stepped into one corner, and with his hands thrust into his pockets, quietly waited her answer.

"There's been a great deal of trouble and sorrow in the world since Adam was a boy," was the somewhat unexpected reply. And then she sat down and took a pipe from her pocket.

"Don't smoke now, mother; breakfast is ready. I'll have it on the table in a minute." Mrs. Ritter paid no attention, but deliberately filled her pipe and lighted it.

"It's strange, but I suppose it must be so. Some families is born'd for misfortune, and all the good things that comes to them is took away as fast as they begin to feel 'em. I'm about ready to give up the hope of ever gettin' much good out'n anything any more. It just seems as if a cuss had allus hung over my family, and I can't withstand it. I never done anything to bring it on me and mine, I know."

"Why, mother, what has gone wrong now?" asked Angie, without any anxiety, however, for they were used to hearing their mother's complaints.

"What's gone wrong? Everything. It allus does go wrong where we're concerned, don't it?"

"O, I think not You are out of spirits a little this morning," said Rose cheerily from the bed. "Never mind, mother; if things do not go just as we want them here, they will sometime, when we are all angels."

Mrs. Ritter grunted, and the young man laughed, looking over at Rose.

"I doubt it, little Rosy. Some folks never will be contented, even as angels. Only a little while ago, I heard a preacher speaking of this class of people, and his remark was to the point, I assure you. He said even as angels, they would fuss and fume, and say 'their legs were too long, or their wings were too short.' I'm inclined to think your mother'l put her name on that list."

These remarks called a savage frown to the old dame's face. She looked up angrily.

"I'd like to know, young sir, where you learnt politeness? When I was young, I never would 'a' demeaned myself by speakin' in such a way of my elders, and to their own children."

"I beg your pardon, Mother Ritter. On my honor I did not intend to give offense. But what is the bad news Peter Jenks has been retailing at this early hour?"

Mrs. Ritter turned round and looked at Rose.

"Poor little thing!" she muttered, "your only comfort's gone now. Nobody'l ever be good to you like he was. But it's the way of the world, and the poor must suffer in more ways than one. You may shut up your book. Mr. Garton won't come to-day, nor never any more."

Rose half sprang from her pillow, her lips suddenly blanched white. Angie paused in her task of dishing up the fried apples, and Mr. Rufus regarded the mother intently.

"Oh, mother, what do you mean?" gasped poor

Rose, trembling violently. "Surely nothing has happened to that good man—my kind, kind teacher? Do speak quickly."

"Bad news comes quick enough," was the stolid answer. "Maybe he's forgot that he promised to make a scholar of you, so you could teach Angie to be a school-mistress. Maybe he's gone away and won't come back any more."

"Mother," cried Angie piteously, "Don't be cruel to poor Rose. Don't you see you are nearly killin' her? What has happened to Mr. Garton?"

"He's been murdered!"

Rose dropped back upon her pillow, and Angie flew to her side to fold her within her arms. Then both broke into wails and sobs of distress, while the old woman puffed at her pipe vigorously, and Mr. Rufus, after giving vent to a prolonged whistle, sat down and began to eat his breakfast.

CHAPTER XVIII.

A STRANGE VISITOR—SUSPICION AND TERROR.

WHEN Mr. Prince reached the hall after leaving Geraldine, he found awaiting him an old woman to whom a servant was speaking insolently, ordering her to go away and not trouble people who had enough to annoy them without the help of strangers at such a time as this. On his master's approach he ceased to scold, and remarked that she had better state her business at once and be off.

"What are you saying, James?" demanded Mr. Prince severely, catching his tone and detecting his insolence. "What does the woman want?"

At this she pressed forward eagerly, before the boy could reply.

"I come to see for myself whether poor Mr. Garton has been murdered, as they say. I want to see his dead body!"

"Why, my good woman, this is somewhat extraordinary. It is too true that he has been murdered; but I can not understand your interest in the affair. Who are you, and where do you come from?"

"Humph! pity your memory's so short. I live

on your own land, Mr. Prince, not half a dozen miles from your own house. Don't you remember Joe Ritter, that'd become a common drunkard, an' ye let him settle over yonder if he'd stop drink? He built a cabin an' cleared a flax patch, an' then died an' left me to take care of my poor girls, an' one a helpless cripple. We're poor, mis'able critters, but *he* didn't think us so fur beneath him he couldn't find out where we lived an' give us a helpin' hand."

"Do you mean Mr. Garton?".

"Aye! who else should I mean? Didn't him and Miss Geraldine come to my house many's the time together when they went walkin'. An' didn't he insist on teaching Rose, days—that's the cripple—so's she could teach Angie o'nights when the work was done? He said if Angie'd be smart like Rose, maybe he'd find a little school fur her some day in the country, where she could make a decent livin'."

"All this is new to me, I assure you," said Mr. Prince. "The good works of my friend were done so unostentatiously, I was not aware of these actions at all. Poor Nathaniel!"

He ended with a deep sigh, but suddenly touched his forehead, as if a new thought had flashed into his brain.

"A. and R. I wondered whom he could mean. Ah, I understand now, dear, good Nathaniel. Poor children! They no longer have a teacher, consequently no hopes for the future."

The old woman began to cry.

"None in the world! An' what'll become of them, poor girls, when I'm gone? I can't last long, an' they'll be left alone an' helpless. Oh, if I could know who killed him! Who did they say it was that done it?"

"Never mind now. It is a doubtful case, and I think it will be hard to fix the crime upon the right person. But if it can be done, I will—"

He stopped appalled and wiped his face with his handkerchief.

"What am I saying?" he gasped hurriedly. "Mrs. Ritter, I am deeply sorry, believe me, and I will see that your children shall not be left destitute. Would you like Angie to be sent to school?   I will send her if you will let me.   And Rose—what shall be done for her?"

Mrs. Ritter regarded him cunningly, and burst into a short laugh.

"You think I can believe you, but I've learnt better. In two hours after I'm gone.you won't think a word more about it. Besides, I can't spare Angie from home. She breaks the flax, an' spins while I weave, an' I couldn't get along without her to help me, an' wait on Rose."

"Then tell me what you would have me do for you. Do you want money?"

"Money? No! What could I do with money, unless I had enough to buy a town-house and send Angie to school? Keep your money, Mr. Prince, until I'm gone. Then if you want to help the children with it, you may. What I want now, is to see the corpse ; an' what I'm going to do, is to find out who killed him. I'll do it, as sure as there's a God that is just!"

The pallor of Mr. Prince's face was so extreme as to cause alarm. James hastily poured a goblet of water and presented it to his master.

"Let me drive her off, sir! She is an impudent old piece."

"No, no," answered Mr. Prince, hastily. "Take her into the room and let her see what she wants—it can do no harm. Go."

James scowled and obeyed, preceding Mrs. Ritter unwillingly enough to the door. Mr. Prince remained where he had stood all the while, his hand resting heavily against the balustrade, his eyes bent upon the floor. He did not move until the old woman returned and laid her hand on his arm, causing him to start as if a serpent had stung him. In turning his eyes he met an almost diabolical glance as the old woman hissed through her broken teeth:

"The devil's own child could do a deed like that! I'll be sworn that a woman is at the bottom of it, an' I'll find out who it is before I die, mind if I don't."

"What do you mean?" he cried fiercely, shaking off her hand. "Tell me this minute. *Whom* do you suspect? What right have you to suspect anybody without proof, woman? Why do you come here to torment me?"

"Softly, softly, good sir. There ain't no use in gettin' excited. I come here because I wanted to. The poor don't have so many friends that they can afford to lose 'em without knowin' how they've been lost. I say that a woman's at the bottom of it, because there never was a black deed like that done yet, when one of 'em wasn't in some way mixed up with it."

"Remember that you are a woman, and that you have daughters," said Mr. Prince, rebukingly, with a deep breath of relief. "It is horrible to hear such sentiments as those you have just expressed from a woman's lips."

"It's all the same if it's the truth," was the curt answer, while her cunning eyes never left his face. "If it wasn't so true as it is, there'd be no sense in the way you take it. You know as well as I do, that it will all come out some day."

"God knows I hope—"

Again he checked himself with a bitter groan, and waved her off, tossing his purse as he did so.

"Take it and go," he cried desperately. "I am not fit to talk on this subject any more. Go!"

"Go! is it? Well, I will; but when I come again, maybe I'll be more welcome."

Notwithstanding her previous refusal of the money, she took the purse and hobbled off stiffly, thrusting it deep into her capacious pocket as she went. She chuckled to herself—a dry, mirthless chuckle that sent the blood chilling through the veins of the man, who stood looking after her as if he had escaped a plague.

"It won't be the last he'll give me," he heard her mutter. "No, indeed, not the last by a good deal."

Mr. Prince turned into the library quickly, again passing his trembling hand across his forehead, where the cold drops gathered constantly.

"One night's misery made a coward of me. Oh, anything else but this I could have borne like a
20

man! But now, how shall I ever be able to hold up my face again among my fellow-men?"

Any one who had known Mr. Prince previous to the misfortunes which had overtaken him, would have thought him changed indeed to have seen him now, pacing the floor in his agitation. The clear, frank, manly glance was drooping, the open brow contracted, the once smiling lips pale and compressed. At every sound he started and trembled like a guilty man, wrapped in the tormenting folds of a sleepless fear.

Throughout the interval between the interview with Mrs. Ritter and the coming of Mrs. Garton, he avoided every one. A message from Mrs. Prince, saying that Geraldine was worse, failed to bring him from his dark retreat in the closed library. The sounds of confusion fell upon seemingly deaf ears. Not once would he stir outside the door until time to go to the cars for Mrs. Garton. When the hour came, he donned his hat and cloak, and was leaving the house without a sign, when Miss Eldridge came feebly down stairs.

"Oh, Mr. Prince, you will not leave the house now. Send the carriage, and come up to your child!"

"Katie, I can not see her suffer! Go back, dear, and say that I can not come."

"But you must, you must!" she said, clinging to his arm. "Come and help us to save her. We may save her yet if we can bring tears. Oh, can you think of nothing to do for your only child? Come, do come! It is cruel in you to keep away."

"Let her alone, Katie, for it is too late. Better that she should die now than to live on through years of suffering, perhaps shame. Can you doubt that I love my child? And yet dearly as I love her, had you come and said to me, 'She is dead,' I would have wept more readily for joy than sorrow."

"Is it then true, as Mrs. Prince feared? Has all this misery touched your brain?"

He laughed bitterly.

"Does she think I am going crazy, Katie. There is no such blessing in store for me. There are times when even madness might be welcomed as a boon beyond price, and this time has come to me. I wish that I could think it madness which has conjured up all the horrors which surround me."

"You will not come up stairs?" she repeated timidly, retreating.

"No. Say that I am gone for Mr. Garton's mother. And, Katie, you come down to meet her— you take charge of her, will you? Mrs. Prince is so occupied with Geraldine, there will be no other to come if you do not, and it would be hard to confide her to servants only."

"I will come," answered Miss Eldridge quietly. "Nathaniel's mother shall not want proper care while I am under the same roof with her."

"Thank you! I am relieved and grateful." And he looked so indeed as he pressed her hand.

Hurrying away, he sprang into the carriage and drove rapidly down the hill, his white face pressed to the window, his eyes uplifted to that part of the house where his child lay. Hot and bitter tears rolled over his cheeks. He might never see her living face again. But he would not turn back—would not venture into the presence of a mortal anguish which could wholly unstring his nerves, while such heavy duties lay on his hands as those that were yet to be performed.

On reaching the depot, he had to wait a short time, and occupied himself in walking up and down the platform. The station stood in the midst of a heavy belt of woods, and along a foot-path from an opposite direction to that by which he had come, a young man walked briskly toward him, a cane in his right hand, and a carpet-bag swung over his left shoulder.

When he reached the platform, he flung the carpet-bag down with a careless movement, dropped upon the step, and taking a match from a little box, lit a cigar.

"Happy man," thought Mr. Prince, looking into his handsome face. "No care weighs him to the earth. Young, free, joyous! What is it that makes the difference in the fate of men?"

His walk brought him close to the stranger, and their eyes met. Nothing in the serene, quiet eyes could warrant the sensation, but with that look a sickening, shuddering chill ran through his whole frame. He withdrew his eyes, then looked again, but the young man seemed to take no notice, and smoked his cigar with apparent enjoyment.

Ten minutes passed, and still the train did not come. Mr. Prince looked at his watch, and the station master remarked that the train had not started on time from Eastbrook. It would be in soon. Was he expecting anybody?

"Yes."

He did not say whom, but he saw that the question had wakened an interest in the stranger, who gave one quick, searching glance in his direction, then relapsed into dreamy contemplation of the landscape.

"Perhaps you expect some of Mr. Garton's friends?" pursued the man.

"Yes, his poor mother;" and again a quick glance flashed from the stranger's eyes. Mr. Prince sauntered over to where he sat, and surveyed him from head to foot with a keen, searching eye. In a moment the stranger looked up and remarked coolly:

"I hope, sir, you will remember me, should you have the fortune to meet me again."

"That is my desire."

"May I ask the cause of your very surprising interest?"

Mr. Prince drew still nearer.

"*You* are the murderer of Nathaniel Garton!" he answered lowly.

In an instant the man's face was as white as ashes, and his eyes flashed dangerously. But he did not lose his self-control for a moment.

"I think, sir, though I have not the honor of knowing you or the man of whom you speak, that the best place for you would be a lunatic asylum. No sane man could wantonly insult a stranger with such a charge."

Mr. Prince pointed to the carpet sack lying upon
20*

the platform, on which were distinctly marked the initials R. K.

"Do not be too hasty," he said, still in a low tone. "You are the man who call yourself Rufus Knight. In reality you are Richard Kelton."

"You seem to be well informed," answered the man accused, with a tremor he could not repress. "I must be allowed to say, however, that you are wholly mistaken. Neither of these names are known to me," and he deliberately drew a case from his pocket, took out a card, and with a half smile presented it to Mr. Prince.

"Ralph Kendrick," repeated Mr. Prince, reading the name on the highly embossed card. "Really, sir, if I have been mistaken, I beg to apologize. But the description of person and initials wholly misled me."

Mr. Kendrick bowed, touched his hat and walked away, indicating that he would accept the apology, but no more. Mr. Prince hesitated a moment, then went into the station and spoke to the agent.

"That man to whom I was just now speaking, has not bought his ticket?"

"No."

"Keep a memorandum of the place, and telegraph the description of his person to the Chief of Police. I want detectives kept upon his track until further notice from me. The expenses I will defray, of course. Speak to the conductor about him."

The agent nodded.

"All right. There's the whistle."

Mr. Prince hastened out, and the train whirled up

to the station. For a few moments there was confusion and bustling about, during which one gray-haired man stepped from the cars and looked anxiously around him. Mr. Prince grasped his hand.

"Mr. Graves, is it you, and alone? I thought she would have come also."

"She is not able. This blow has well-nigh killed her, and I have volunteered to do all she would have done. For heaven's sake tell me, has the murderer been caught?"

"Ask me nothing here. When we reach home I will endeavor to tell you all I know. The carriage is waiting."

The old gentleman, a lawyer, and an early friend of the Garton family, sadly followed Mr. Prince to the vehicle and entered it. As the gentleman sprang in after him, he cast a sharp glance round for Mr. Kendrick. That worthy was standing apart from the crowd, and lighting another cigar. He caught a glimpse of Mr. Prince, and mockingly touched his hat, at least the gesture seemed to convey that impression to Mr. Prince.

"Look well at that man, Mr. Graves," he said hurriedly, pointing him out; "do you think you can remember him?"

"Very well; but why?"

"No matter. I only want to attract your attention to him now. Nothing may come of it but I suspect there may. Drive on, Charles."

Very little passed between the gentlemen on their way to Prince Hill. On reaching that place, they descended, and Mr. Prince remarked sadly:

"A sorrowful welcome I have to offer you. Death and sorrow have taken possession of my home."

The housekeeper stood inside the door, with Miss Eldridge near her. Both were weeping bitterly. The latter slightly retreated when she saw Mr. Prince was accompanied by a gentleman instead of the bereaved mother she expected.

"This is Mr. Graves, Katie, and he comes to tell us that Mrs. Garton is unable to make such a journey. Miss Eldridge, Mr. Graves, and the dearest friend our poor Nathaniel had."

His meaning glance was sufficient, and the old lawyer took the young girl's hand, tears in his gentle eyes as he scanned her drooping, tearful face. The housekeeper seized the moment to speak with Mr. Prince.

"It is all over, sir."

"All what?"

"Oh, sir, our blessed little darling, our sweet Geraldine. She was taken with spasms, and she is—" Her sobs choked her, and she could not finish the sentence.

"Do you mean that she is dead?"

The housekeeper pointed to another streamer of crape that had been bound to the door with a long white ribbon. The father's eyes half closed, and his hands clutched at the back of a chair convulsively, but his deep voice uttered an unfaltering "Thank God!"

"Mr. Prince!" cried Mr. Graves, while the others stood horrified, "do you know what you are saying?"

"Yes, too well. Be patient, man. In time you will understand me. Now forgive me if I commend you for awhile to the care of my housekeeper. She will make you comfortable, and as soon as I can, I will see you to settle this sad business."

He went up stairs, sought the room where his child lay, and locked himself in.

All was peaceful now. The fever had died out. The sorrow that had charged her little heart, was felt no more. To join him she loved she had—

> "Gone in her childish purity
>   Out from the golden day;
>   Fading away to a light so sweet,
>   Where the silver stars and sunbeams **meet,**
>   Paving the way for her angel feet,
>   Over the silent way."

CHAPTER XIX.

THE DIE IS CAST.

SOME time had elapsed ere Mr. Prince again made his appearance. Mr. Graves had been shown to a room where a fire burned cheerfully, and a warm dinner was served immediately. After things had been taken away, his host came down.

"If you are prepared to hear me, I will now say what I have to say."

He spoke with the abruptness of a man who had made up his mind to do a disagreeable thing. The lawyer read in his face sorrowful determination and self-sacrifice, but no indication of insanity.

"Go on," he said, kindly.

"You must remember that I am not only speaking to you as a friend of my own, and of the Garton family, but as a lawyer. This interview must be a professional one."

"A moment, my dear sir. Have you no counselor nearer home to whom you could go more properly than myself? If what you are about to say should require any action on my part, it may be awkward for both of us. You will not act hastily?"

"I am acting hastily, but not unwisely, I am sure. You are the staunch friend of my friend, and for that reason I prefer to take you into my confidence, and ask your aid. This day I have been made childless, and I have nothing left on earth, but to do my duty to the dead and the living, made desolate by his death. When that is done, death cannot come too soon to me."

"My dear sir, you do not forget your young wife?" remonstrated the old gentleman, and he was puzzled by the expression that immediately changed Mr. Prince's features. It was hard, bitter, merciless for a moment, but softened presently into pity and pain.

"I do not forget," he answered briefly. "Let us understand each other, fully, however. I may depend upon your services?"

"Yes, as far as I may be useful to you."

"Very good. Now to business. First, these papers must be examined," and he thrust a package into the lawyer's hands, his own trembling violently. "When you came, the thought crossed my mind that there was a fatality in it. All the way home I could not get rid of the idea, and now the die is cast. Let worse come to worst, I must meet it."

The lawyer undid the package, adjusted his spectacles, and began the examination of the papers. Minutes slipped into hours, and the old man read on. Mr. Prince paced softly back and forth, a ceaseless beat of hardly curbed suspense. Finally he stopped as the lawyer laid the last paper on the table and wiped his glasses.

"I understand now why you could thank God that your child has died. This is terrible."

"Then you do think——"

"The worst that one can think from such evidence. There is scarcely ground left for the shadow of a doubt."

Again Mr. Prince strode up and down the room in great agitation, his lips working convulsively.

"What is to be done?" he rather gasped than asked, at length.

"That must be decided after due reflection. The boy must not die."

"No, no! the boy must not die," was answered vehemently. "Nor should the innocent be suffered to lie in prison through the long, dreary winter, waiting for the spring term to get cleared from a deed he never was guilty of."

"This boy is poor?"

"Yes, very poor."

"What are his parents?"

"The father is a worthless drunkard, the mother, a whining, complaining, foolish woman, who doubles her troubles, though the real ones are enough, heaven knows."

"What was the boy's character?"

"Bad as it could be. He has for years been the scape-grace of the place, a convenient tool for the unscrupulous, and a ready escape for all who chose to lay their sins to his charge. As a natural consequence, he was a hardened, reckless fellow, despised by all, pitied by few indeed. Geraldine's mother insisted that there was good in him, and the child religiously believed it also. Then Mr. Garton became interested in him, and hoped to make something of him as a man. One trait of his character is remarkable. He will not lie, and if I am a judge, will be faithful to a trust, even unto death."

"Noble and redeeming traits, surely," said Mr. Graves. "From these memoranda, I see the evidence is not remarkably strong. The knife may have belonged to him, and he may have threatened Mr. Garton's life. But these are not proofs that can do him serious injury, if he is able to prove his whereabouts at the time of the murder."

"That will not be so easy. His mother claims that he was home by eleven o'clock, while the murder must have taken place later. But her evidence will not go for much, and popular opinion is greatly against him. The knife he acknowledged readily as having been a gift from a man who for sometime has been about the neighborhood. The threat against Mr. Garton's life he has denied from the beginning."

"Who is this man—the one who gave him the knife?"

"I suspect the one I pointed out at the station to be the identical villain, but I am not sure. You already have his history there," pointing with white lips to the papers.

"You think this the same then who broke off the marriage years ago, with Garton and—"

"My wife," he finished grimly. "Yes, it can be no other, of course. The similarity of names, the stolen interviews, the flowers—there can be no doubt."

"I think there can be no doubt. We are investigating this matter, however, and it is not a time to reach conclusions. Would it be possible for us to see the boy to-night?"

"I fear not. See, it is nearly twelve o'clock."

"Then I must come back to finish my investigations. Meantime, I see but one endurable way for you, and I can conscientiously point it out."

"Well."

"Let things take their course. You must see to the family, that they are not in want; and you can provide all the comforts needed for the boy. As for his reputation, it can be no worse for his imprisonment. There he may be cared for, kept out of mischief, and learn a life-long lesson of wisdom. I repeat it will not hurt him. Meantime you will have a duty here, I one abroad, to keep us busy. When the trial comes on, see that the boy has proper counsel, and try to prove an alibi. If it cannot be done, and he should be found guilty, there will be but one course to pursue."

Mr. Prince dropped into a seat and covered his face with his hands.

"Come, come, my friend, this is vain. It is just possible that this deed may have been committed without the instigation of another party. We dare not judge until proofs stamp guilt upon the heads of the guilty. When we examine the boy, something may be gained; and I must find that man besides. To do more than keep him in sight will not be possible; but if things go wrong at the trial, our course must be shaped accordingly."

"You will take every precaution to guard against exposure? Oh, think of my horrible, horrible position!"

"I do think of it, and from my soul I pity you with a pity that cannot humble, for it is born of honor. Rouse yourself to bear manfully the terrible load laid upon you. God never deserts the good and true."

"But he hides his face unaccountably from us. Is it a sin for a man to love, that such a punishment should follow him as that which has pursued and found me? Oh, my little daughter! How much wiser was she than I? And yet, even she was lured from her better judgment, and has lost her life in consequence. My God, my God! The enormity of sin I see, is enough to strangle all pity, that untrameled justice may have full sway."

"Nay, nay, you are losing yourself again. Suppose you should be wrong? Is it not bad enough anyway?"

"Heaven knows it is! Ah, you do well to check me, for I am well-nigh beside myself."

"With good reason, I admit. Still, human life cannot be trifled with lightly, and you must wait. Leave these papers with me for the present. I must examine them again, and in the course of a week you may expect me back again."

"As you will."

"And now," continued the lawyer, kindly, "take my advice and go to bed. You must have some rest."

"Rest, rest? It is impossible!"

"No, it is possible. Do you want to get ill, or go

crazy? I see you are not yourself now. Before you leave me, one more word. Is Miss Eldridge a permanent resident here?"

"No, only a visitor. Garton loved her, and she had promised to marry him!"

"How long have they been engaged?"

"A very short time. In fact, their acquaintance was short, and I presume the engagement was hastened by the quarrel that took place between us the night before the murder. No one but my wife knew of that quarrel, and I remember hearing Nathaniel go into the parlor shortly after I left him in the conservatory. I know, too, that Miss Eldridge was there, and that they went together upon the terrace. From what followed, I infer the engagement was then made with the idea before him of his departure from my house."

"Did Miss Eldridge inform you of her engagement herself?"

"No; she betrayed it to my little daughter in her anguish on hearing of his death, and the child repeated it to me soon after."

"You were very jealous of Mr. Garton," queried the old man, with a scrutinizing glance.

"Madly, but I would not have harmed one hair of his head for worlds. In the midst of that quarrel I broke off and left him, because I could not trust myself to say in my passion that which never could be unsaid in cooler moments. Do you wonder at my jealousy?"

"No; I only wonder that you have been blind so long."

"Ah, you were not in love as I was," answered the wretched man, with a bitter laugh. "And I would have trusted Nathaniel with my life, before those strange meetings and evident disagreements woke my suspicions. Once having suspicions, I could no more quell them than I could have changed the course of the clouds. Now, when I think of what he bore to spare me, it almost drives me mad. He loved me, he pitied and strove to protect and to spare me; and yet my last words were angry and bitter!"

"You blame yourself too severely. Let all that go, and try to become master of yourself. Does Mrs. Prince suspect your thoughts on this subject?"

"No, for I have put an iron rule over my actions, while I felt ready to crush her! She knows I act strangely, but not exactly why, unless she judges from her own premises."

"It is well. Come now and lie down. I shall make you sleep with me."

Mr. Prince regarded the old gentleman for a moment fixedly, then smiling sadly, submitted, and lay down without undressing, while the lawyer sat before the fire pondering upon the papers beside him.

21*

CHAPTER XX.

THROUGH RIGHT AND WRONG.

"KATIE, Mr. Graves has returned to spend a few days with me, and he has brought a letter for you from Nathaniel's mother."

"A letter for me?"

Poor Katie looked up quickly at Mr. Prince, a faint color staining her transparent cheek. In answer he put the missive into her hand, saying in a low tone as he bent nearer to her:

"You will not lightly regard what she asks of you, my dear girl. Remember that she is old, and left very desolate now."

Mrs. Prince who was lying upon a sofa on the opposite side of the hearth, spoke quickly:

"What is it, Kate? Your face looks ominous of evil to me. Bear in mind that, whoever wants you, I cannot spare you yet."

For a moment Miss Eldridge was too absorbed to answer. When it was finished, she dropped her head upon her hand, and with the letter lying upon her lap, tearfully gazed into the fire.

"What is it?" again demanded Mrs. Prince, with some impatience.

"Mrs. Garton begs me to come to her for awhile —she is so lonely and heart-broken," answered the young girl, smothering back a sob. "Read the letter—it is very touching."

Mrs. Prince took it; her beautiful brow knitted as she read.

"Of course you will not think of going to that out-of-the-way, desolate place, with no other companion than a sad old woman for society? It is quite bad enough here, but there it would be horrible."

"She is very wretched, and I know how much she must need some one," answered Katie, gently. "You have still your husband, and at home I am not at all needed. What better can I do than to go and comfort his poor mother?"

"Take care of yourself; or rather stay here and let me take care of you."

An involuntary glance went from Mrs. Prince's eyes to her husband's face. Katie's rested there also, and she was startled at the strange expression it wore. A warning sign from Mrs. Prince followed, and she kept silent until asked what she meant to do. It was Mr. Prince who asked the question.

"I will go—I could not refuse," she said appealingly. "It is hard to leave you, Celia, when you are so unwilling for me to go. But you can do without me better than she."

"Very well, if that is your decision I must submit," was answered icily.

"Then," said Mr. Prince, "you will be ready to go back with Mr. Graves when he returns. Understand me, I am not trying to get rid of you. It will be a pain to see you go; but we owe to that bereaved mother more than we can ever repay, and must make sacrifices for her sake. I will write that you are coming."

He went out, and Mrs. Prince put her handkerchief over her face. Katie flew to her side instantly.

"Oh, Celia, do not think me unkind to leave you now. What could you do in such a case? She has no one?"

"And I have no one," answered the lady, bitterly. "Must you choose like this between a friend and a stranger?"

"Celia, you have your husband to comfort you."

Mrs. Prince took the handkerchief from her eyes, and looked into Katie's face. For a moment neither spoke; then she said in a slow whisper:

"Katie, my husband will never forgive me for that day of helplessness. I feel that he lays the death of his idolized child at my door. Oh, it is dreadful, and it will break my heart."

Again the eyes were covered.

"It cannot be possible," said Miss Eldridge, soothingly. "All that has happened has changed him, as I can plainly see, but he will get over it, and will not be unjust to you. How could you help sinking under the shock? Was I not crushed?—and I thought I could bear anything."

"Ah, but he was your lover, and he could think such weakness natural in you. But what excuse had I, apart from my poor nerves? No, no, he will never forgive me."

"In time he will. Only be patient and try to make him-forget the past in your love. Remember that he needs it now more than ever; and—forgive me, Celia,—I have noticed that you seem rather to shun than to seek him. Why don't you try to cheer him out of this dreadful gloom?"

"It is not a one-sided question, I think. A wife has a right.to expect some consideration in sorrow, some tenderness and care. In his own troubles, he has forgotten that I have feelings, and can suffer."

"Oh, Celia, I beseech you, do not let such thoughts divide you. Hard enough the trial will be for both when borne together. But apart, it will be like death to each. It is a woman's place and privilege to make the first advances if an estrangement has risen between her and her heart's choice, and her pride should never stand in the way. Had he lived to make me his wife, my poor Nathaniel should never have had one reason to feel or speak coldly. I would have given up everything for him."

"You think so, poor foolish girl, now that he is gone. But if he had lived, experience might have taught you a wiser lesson than to suffer the man to whom you had given yourself to be loved and cared for, to make a slave of you—to kill you with jealous exactions."

"Nay, the man I love, could not exact too much from me. But we think differently on this subject, and had better drop it. You and I are very unlike. I am not so proud. But then I never have been petted and made much of as you have. Until I loved Nathaniel, I had no love that could give me joy. He became my world, and I could have lived a blessed life with him, had God permitted it."

A very heavy sigh escaped the lips of her companion. Something in her heart had been touched by the words she heard. She put up her hand and stroked back the fair hair from the young girl's face.

"Poor Katie, poor Katie. It is awful to lose all one has. I pity you, sweet; and if it will comfort you to go to his mother, go without a thought of me. I will try to be brave and bear my cross till relief comes. Time is the great healer, as you say, and I will hope my wounds may not smart always."

Katie stooped quickly to kiss the beautiful lips.

"Dear, generous Celia! Some day I will come back to you again, if you wish it."

"There is no necessity for repeating my wishes, Katie. When you will come, I shall be only too thankful."

The conversation of the morning made a deep impression upon the mind of Katie Eldridge. Looks and tones as well as words, seemed to forebode a deeper trouble than had before been apparent, and she began to cast about in her mind for a means of bringing harmony between these people. So sad it seemed to her, that they should bear their heavy burthen apart, uncheered by loving sympathy and self-abnegation, each for the other's sake. But how to carry out her yearning desires, was a more difficult and delicate matter than she knew how to cope with, and it was not until a late hour in the evening that she decided to speak to Mr. Prince. To talk to the wife she knew would be vain. The opposition which

arose from the stubborn pride of Mrs. Prince, was
not an easy barrier to break down, and she who
shrank from contention as from a pestilence, dreaded
the trial that would end, perhaps, in a deeper determination to hold her ground against her husband.
Besides, was not Mr. Prince unjust? and was it not
his place to deal more tenderly with a woman whose
nerves could not, like his, withstand the shocks she
had been compelled to sustain?   Thinking over the
matter so earnestly, Katie succeeded in creating a
little excitement for herself, which had the effect of
bracing her with sufficient courage for the attempt;
so it was with quite a show of purpose and self-possession that she detained Mr. Prince after Mr.
Graves retired.   Under the plea of illness, Mrs.
Prince had not been down at all, and the burthen
of the entertainment had fallen entirely upon her.

"Give me just a few moments, please," she said,
looking at him, her sweet eyes full of solemn sadness and gentle pity. "I want to talk to you about
yourself."

"A wretched subject," he answered, a forced
smile upon his lips as he spoke. "Cannot you
choose a better?"

"No, I can think only of you and Celia. She
suffers terribly."

"How do you know? Has she told you she suffers?"

"Could you imagine it could possibly be otherwise, after all that has happened? But what is
breaking her heart, is the thought that you charge
her with neglect toward Geraldine. She thinks you

never will forgive her, and she is grieving bitterly.
Oh, dear Mr. Prince, she needs comfort! Do not
blame her; try to forget it, and make, her cease to
remember such miserable things. You cannot go on
living in this way."

His face was turned from her when she said this,
and she could not see his expression as he answered:

"No, we cannot go on living in this way. So you
think me unkind to my wife, Katie?"

"I surely cannot think you kind, if you let such
things make her so very unhappy," she answered
boldly, but she was amazed at her own temerity,
and waited breathlessly for the angry words she expected to follow. His voice had not sounded very
conciliatory.

"Better so, better so," he muttered.

"What are you saying? I did not understand
you."

"Well, never mind."

Now he turned to her and spoke with an effort at
cheerfulness. "Content yourself. You have done
your duty and shown me what a bear I am, and it
only remains for me to do my duty. Are you satisfied?"

"If I have not offended you by this meddlesome
spirit of mine, you must think me bold and lacking
in respect to you to speak so freely."

"On the contrary, I take it as a proof of your
kind regard for our happiness, and thank you for it."

She put her hand in the one he held out, frankly,
a glow of satisfaction on her lovely face, unlike any
that had rested there since the death of her lover.

" How glad I shall feel to think of you now," she said softly. " When my thoughts wander back to this place, as they must, daily, I shall not grieve in feeling you estranged, and suffering alone."

An exquisiteness of sympathy in her tone, a nobleness and strength in her candid words, touched him, and moved him very deeply. He could not keep back the tears in thanking her, and she went to sleep that night with the memory of his tearful look haunting her. She thought the discordant string had been touched and strung to harmony, and was happier in the belief; he knew how far she was from the truth, and sighed bitterly, but felt thankful for her mistake.

The next day but one, under the charge of Mr. Graves, she set out for the home of Mrs. Garton, and the miserable pair at Prince Hill found themselves alone in their home for the first time.

But never had he felt a keener pang than at the moment when his foot passed the door of his chamber after returning from the depot, where he had gone to see his friends off. Snows lay white on the hills, and the sky was wintry, cheerless and threatening. The fire burned dimly in the grate ; the room was worse than desolated. Was this the realization of his cherished dream? No bright face was there to smile on him ; no round arm to glide lovingly around his neck ; no sweet lips to murmur words for which his heart hungered and thirsted so madly. He had never pictured this hopelessly dreary scene as the first he should realize with her whom he had so fondly called wife, when their guests should all have departed, and left them to themselves. He thought of her now, lying upon her sofa in the next room, brooding over her own thoughts, forgetful, perhaps, of him—careless of him. Of what was she thinking? Oh, for a moment to look into the workings of the busy brain and see if there was one trait left for a softening impulse to build upon. His yearning made him pitiful. Hardly as he had condemned her in his own mind, if he could see one trace of real suffering, one sign of remorse or repentance, he could have found excuses for her —he would have tried to palliate the enormity of her sin. But no; she had deceived him, she had wronged him, she had lost the one object for which she had striven, and now gave herself up to stubborn pride and icy coldness of manner. More, she knew, that others must see that a trouble existed, and had taken pains to give a false impression of the cause. Well, he could bear that the blame should all be laid on him. Nay, he would not have it otherwise. Safety lay in this alone, and he must continue to make this impression, for her sake. For her sake? Oh, it was once a bliss to utter the words that pressed to his lips when he could find an opportunity to serve and give her pleasure! And now!— now he must serve her in humiliation of spirit, in bitterness of soul, and suffer in the serving!

"God, my God, why do I live to curse my life?" was his cry as he dropped upon the sofa, face downward, and strove to smother the dry sob swelling in his throat. "Oh, my dead wife! Oh, my little daughter, how gladly would I sleep beside you!"

She had come in unperceived and stood beside him now, the pale, proud, beautiful woman. She heard his cry, and turned again to leave, her dark eyes flashing, her lips compressed. A second thought checked the impulse, however, and she glided close to the couch, slipping her white fingers caressingly into his hair as she knelt upon a cushion.

"My husband, why do you shut me from your heart to grieve alone! Am I never to be forgiven?"

He sprang up as if a serpent had stung him, his pale face suddenly stained with two deep crimson spots. Unconsciously his hands were clenched as if he would strike her to the dust, and his eyes glared upon her. She remained in the position his sudden movement had caused her to assume, her eyes uplifted, her lips parted in affright.

"Woman, what would you? The farce ends here! The curtain has fallen; the guests are departed. Do not longer mock me by acting a part."

She rose up haughtily, and stood face to face.

"If you have a right to treat your wife so rudely and cruelly, explain the cause. *What* have I done?"

For a moment he regarded her with a fixed and searching stare. Was this beautiful, imperious creature the guilty thing his honor and his manhood urged him to despise? A crisis had come. There was no escape now. The farce had been played out.

"Oh for one hour more of unclouded and unbiased reason," was his silent prayer, "and God help me to be just."

"Let me ask you one question," he said aloud, still keeping her fixed with his glance.

"Speak!" she demanded.

"*Do you intend to let John Truslow die for the murder of Nathaniel Garton?*"

Her beautiful eyes dilated, and her compressed lips parted in a bewildered expression of surprise.

"*I* let him die! what have I to do with him? Guilty I do not believe him, but how can I prove his innocence?"

"By declaring who the guilty one is," he answered sharply and angrily. "I warn you, if you seal your lips, mine shall not be sealed. Another murder shall not steep my hearthstone with innocent blood, though the whole world rise up to hoot at me as an unnatural monster."

"What do you expect or wish of me?" she asked, her voice sinking.

"You know who murdered my friend. Expose the murderer!"

She crimsoned, then turned pale, her head drooping like a broken flower. The agony of that moment was a season of unspeakable torture to him. Cold drops gathered and shone like dew on his brow. Presently she raised her head with a gesture of desperation, and cried out passionately:

"Believe me, believe me! I do not know! That I have suspected I will not deny, but that suspicion was an unworthy one, and I have crushed it."

"Whom did you suspect?"

She would not answer.

"Tell me!" he demanded fiercely. "I *will* know. Speak this moment!"

"Oh, forgive me, but I cannot."

"You can and must, if you do not desire to be abandoned to your fate utterly. I can bear much, but there is a limit to my endurance. Take heed what you do now, for this may be the last time a chance for mercy may be allowed. For the last time, I ask, whom do you suspect?"

"Then if you will know—you quarreled that day —and you know you did not come to me until very late! Forgive me if I thought—if I sometimes feared—if—if—Oh, God, I cannot say it!"

"Say *what*? You shall speak " He seized her arm and held it so tightly as to force her to shrink with pain. Anger helped her to fashion the words he demanded to hear. She lifted her face again and fixed her eyes upon his steadily.

"I thought *you* did it, if you will know!"

"I? Woman, you—"

What he would have said we cannot record. He checked himself on the instant; but if a shell had exploded at his feet, he could not have been more astonished. Wholly unprepared for this answer, he had no fitting reply, and could only gaze speech-lessly into the beautiful, defiant face. Her gaze softened.

"I told you that I had killed that unworthy sus-picion," she said in addition. "Forgive me that I harbored it for a moment."

"Did you never suspect any other?" he found voice to ask. Now his expression was unfathom-able, but she answered boldly:

"Whom could I suspect? I did not know he had an enemy."

"Then you did not believe the boy to be guilty?"

"I did not at first, but now I have come to judge differently. If he is not the guilty one I am sure I cannot imagine who is. Don't look at me that way. Why do you doubt my words?"

"Because falsehood seems a component part of your nature. Cease these efforts to deceive me, madam. You are only plunging yourself deeper into sin, and God knows you have no need to do that!"

"What do you mean? Are you still jealous of Nathaniel Garton—and he in his grave?" she retorted with a curling lip, stung by his answer beyond the limits of prudence.

"Oh, no. A less worthy object has wrecked me. There would be less shame in the thought that you betrayed me for him. Alas, we were both betrayed—poor Nathaniel. Loving him you would not have murdered him."

She had turned from him while he spoke, but now her face turned slowly back, mantled by an expression of bewilderment.

"What an actress you are! How like you are to that soulless woman, Catherine De Medici! The child was right! It should be written upon your forehead, *Corpus sine pectore*."

"For God's sake tell me what you mean! I cannot comprehend you."

He laughed icily, and walked to the window. She followed him, grasping his arm with trembling hands.

"Tell me, tell me! Oh, do let us understand each other. Speak out plainly."

" Can I speak more plainly than I have spoken. I say that you could not have loved Garton. Loving him you would not have murdered him."

"You believe I killed him!" she gasped in a horror-stricken whisper.

" Or caused him to be."

" Just Heaven, it can not be possible! I, your wife? Why, what do you take me for? You would make me worse than any demon. As there is a living God—"

" Hold, you shall not steep your soul deeper in sin ! I know everything. Do you think that I would act as I have acted if I had not known how vilely treacherous you are? On that night when I found you stealing from his room, I accused you; you swore that you did not love him, and I was determined to place your word above my own jealous doubts. I went to his room; I found a key amongst my own that fitted his private box, and opened it. In that box I found a journal, and that journal contained a history of the past. Can you imagine what my feelings were when I read it? Dear heart, he dealt gently with you, and you had wrecked his life—you who had been little better than a pauper! You who had been reared upon charity, and kept as a lure to the rich and unwary. I can understand how Nathaniel came to love you—so beautiful, so seemingly guileless. And he would have married you, and worshiped you, had not his good angel stood between. Before it was too late, he discovered your arts, and cast you off, as you deserved. You could descend to love the low, ignorant, debased companion of your beggared childhood, and plot to deceive good and true men for his sake. More than this, you could entrap me without a pang of pity. I found you with those I deemed honorable, and was easily duped—poor fool. And then you could let him follow you, and feed upon my possessions like a leech, too greedy to be filled. Poor Natty thought to save me, but it cost him his life. You got rid of him, and thought me powerless, no doubt. But you have overreached yourself. Shall I tell you now what is to become of Richard Kelton."

She did not answer.

"Listen," he continued; "he is the murderer, and it was you who instigated the deed, hoping to screen yourself from exposure—to carry out your nefarious system of deceit. But detectives are on his track, and when Richard Kelton comes before a public tribunal to be tried for his life, you cannot hope to escape. Rather than see the innocent suffer for your crime, I, your husband, will denounce you !"

"Wretch, monster!" she gasped. "Do your worst, if you wish to ruin yourself in your madness. I am not guilty, and am not afraid to prove it. If Richard Kelton is the guilty one, I do not know it. From me he never had a word that could indicate such a wish as you declare against me. I did not desire his death, and I had nothing to do with it."

Mr. Prince stood immovable, his arms folded stoically. Desperation had rendered him proof against outward signs of emotion.

"You will not believe me," she cried appealingly.

"No. It is impossible."

"You hate me—you will try to destroy me?"

"All the papers I found—all the evidence against you, are in the hands of a lawyer."

This produced the effect he desired. A look of genuine fear shot from her beautiful eyes. She paled and trembled in helpless terror.

"You can not—oh, you can not want to kill me," she cried, falling at his feet and clasping his knees with her arms. "My husband, oh, my husband, spare me, pity me! I have been wicked—I have deserved to be censured where I have been loved, but I am not the horribly guilty thing you think me."

He stooped to lift her up and place her in a large chair. The action was silent, and seemed gentle while his hands clasped her; but one look into the cold, resolute face, chilled her. To her it seemed pitiless and cruel. She felt as if she had gone beyond the limits of his mercy. Yet who will not struggle for the dear life imperiled? She clung to hers the more wildly now, as she began to see her danger; and fear strangled the insolent, defiant pride that had risen against him. She addressed him humbly, and in a tone that went to his heart.

"Will you listen to me for a little while?—and I will tell you all the truth without reserve. Nothing else can avail me, if you believe me a murderer, and are bent upon my destruction. I know how much reason you have to doubt me, having become possessed of my history. Still, if you will listen, I believe you can no longer charge me with a greater guilt than I have ever taken upon my soul. Oh, I did not, I did not harm Nathaniel by word or deed, nor wilfully cause him to be injured."

He drew up a chair and sat down before her.

"If you can justify yourself in any way, I will listen. But remember that as I know you guilty of many falsehoods, you cannot expect credulity. Plausible stories will not move me."

Anguish and despair convulsed her face for a moment. Each tone of his once loving voice, now so icy and cutting, seemed to leave a leaden weight upon her heart. She bent her head to the arm of her chair and wept hysterically. He did not move, but sat patiently waiting. When the storm of tears had passed, he remarked quietly:

"I am ready to hear you. Proceed."

With a struggle for self-control, she sat erect, keeping her eyes upon the borders of the handkerchief with which her trembling fingers toyed.

"You found a journal?" she began tremulously.

"Yes."

"You say it gave you the history of my past life?"

"Yes."

"A part it may have given, but not all the details. You know that I was orphaned when young?"

"No, abandoned to the charity of strangers. Go on."

"I beg your pardon. My parents, who were of gentle blood, died when I was a child, and very poor. Their marriage was against opposition on both sides, and they were abandoned in consequence.

All parties were proud, and a reconciliation never was effected; so when the little money my father possessed was gone, there were none to help him, and he had not been reared to any trade or profession. Under the difficulties that arose, he fell ill and shortly died. My mother was left widowed and desolate before I was born, and it was under the roof of a miserable hovel that I first saw the light—that roof afforded by the charity of the poor. Want of care and proper treatment brought on a fever, and when I was three weeks old my mother died, leaving me in the care of people who had kindly sheltered her. They gave me away to others, a childless pair who wished to adopt me for their own. It was by them I was abandoned when only six years old. Why I never knew; but some trouble arose, and they fled the country, leaving me behind. After that another woman took me, a good, kind-hearted soul. She had one little boy, and we became attached. Then he was a bright, sturdy little fellow, planning always for means to support his widowed mother, until we one day lighted upon what appeared to be a splendid scheme. We were sitting by the window shelling peas for dinner, when a man paused with a flute and began to play. A little girl accompanied him and joined her sweet voice in a pretty ballad. I was enchanted, and Dick dropped his pan to lean out and look at the little vocalist.

"'How I wish I had a penny to throw to her,' I said regretfully. 'Come away, Dick, and don't seem to listen, or they will be disappointed.'

"He came reluctantly, and when they had gone, sat a long time in silent thought. Finally he said with abrupt confidence:

"'Tid, you and me can make a great deal of money, if we try.'

"'How?' I asked, amazed.

"'Why, very easy. I can play the flute most as well as that man, and you've got a real sweet voice. If we were to practice some ballads together, I know we could make money. And then wouldn't it be nice! Mother wouldn't have to kill herself over that horrid old sewing.'

"I clapped my hands with delight, but a sudden thought damped my enthusiasm.

"'You haven't got a flute, Dick, and where's the money to come from to get it?'

"'O, you never mind that. I'll find a way to get a flute. Will you go with me if I do?'

"'Yes, indeed,' I answered heartily. I thought it would be the greatest delight life could afford, to see all the fine people looking out at the windows, and listening to us. Then to see the bright coin fall upon the sidewalk and to run and pick it up, appeared the most interesting prospect possible for a poor little pair of half-starved children for whom a sick woman toiled, and to whom a dish of green peas late in the spring was a holiday luxury. We could think of nothing else, and talked of it incessantly when out of Mother Kelton's hearing, till finally Dick came home with an excited glow on his face, and drew me aside to whisper his good fortune. He had got a flute, and we must take our chances to practice when mother was out. She was to know nothing about it until our first earnings were thrown into her lap.

"All that week we practiced every opportunity, and the following, when she sent us upon an errand, we concluded it to be the best time to begin, and accordingly turned into the more aristocratic streets of the city. Dick had slipped his flute into his pocket; but when we were safely out of hearing, he took it out, screwed it together, and had it all in readiness.

"By and by we came into a beautiful, shady street, and paused in front of a large house. I was awfully frightened, but Dick looked so brave and confident, I was ashamed, and determined to rally my courage. We began and got through the first nicely, so it was easier to commence the next, and a sweet little girl came to the window to listen. Presently I saw her turn her head, and her lips moved. Then a lady came, and the child ran away. In a moment she came back, a servant raised the window, and she threw out a gold coin that looked like a fortune to us, though it was only a sovereign.

"'Come every day,' she said in a sweet voice, and I nodded, my heart throbbing with a great happiness, as she withdrew, and watched us with her lovely eyes.

"That day we carried home ten dollars, the proceeds of our first day's labor; and we were happy, happy children when we saw Mother Kelton's glad tears dropping upon the coin in her lap. She knew that her strength could not last long, and was glad to think we would have even this means of support, were she to be taken away from us.

"After our first successful effort, you can easily imagine what followed. Poor, obscure, without a thought of the degraded position we occupied, we went out, day after day, pursuing the avocation we had chosen, and returning at night with varied success. Sometimes, we made what to us seemed a fortune, though rarely exceeding ten dollars. At others, a few pence were our sole reward. Only the little fairy who claimed us every day, seemed faithful to us and our interests. She was always at the window, and never failed to throw something to us, saying as we turned to leave: 'Be sure to come to-morrow.' So it happened that never a day passed, for months, that we did not stand with our flute and tambourine before the window of that house, with her sweet eyes fixed earnestly upon us.

"At length a change came, just as the summer was closing. We went one day, as usual, to find the windows shut, and after a long deliberation, when we concluded to play, a servant came out and told us the child was very ill, and we must wait till she got better before we played again. The day was a sorrowful one to us. We wandered all over the city, but without thought except of the dear little child we had learned to love very much; and the next morning I stole away early, and went to the house, which was still closed, to ask the servant how she was. I could not rest, thinking her ill; and when the lady heard I was at the door asking for the child, she sent for me to come into the room where the little one lay.

"I never shall forget the feelings I experienced as

I passed through the luxurious rooms into that lovely little chamber. The mother sat by the child alone, looking pale and weary, but kind. The child was propped up by pillows and looked at me with large, bright eyes as I entered. In a moment she put out a little hot hand, and I took it shyly.

"'How kind of you to come and ask for me. Mamma, isn't the little girl kind?'

"But the mother was weeping, and did not answer.

"'Poor little girl,' said the child again. 'Are you very poor, that you go singing about the streets for a living?'

"'Yes, very poor,' I answered.

"'Where do you live?'

"I told her.

"'And have you no mother,' she continued pitifully.

"'No, my mother is dead. She was a lady,' I added with a sense of pride in the thought. 'If she had lived, I should have had some one to take care of me, as you have.'

"At this the mother raised her head and looked at me earnestly. After that she asked me a great many questions, and sent me away. Four days later, when I went to the door there was crape on it, and the grief that seized upon me was so deep, I fell sobbing upon the steps, and remained there until some one took me away. At first, I did not know what had happened to me, but when I could calm myself to look around me, I was surprised to find myself in a beautiful room, with luxurious things all around me. After awhile a lady came in whom I recognized to be the child's mother, and she told me to lie still where I was till she came again. She took my hand softly, and bending down kissed my forehead. Then she went away and I remained alone for many hours. I closed my eyes and thought of the lady's kiss; and I fell asleep dreaming of it. When I awoke, it was by the opening of the door, and she came to sit down by me, sobbing bitterly.

"'My little darling begged that I should take you,' she said at length, when she had grown calm, 'and this is to be your home in future. Do not worry about the Kelton's, I have seen Mrs. Kelton, and she has given you wholly to me. Now you must forget all the old associations, and remember only, that you are my daughter.'

"I was happy indeed. Elegance and luxury I loved dearly, and the thought of filling that sweet child's place, was an unspeakable delight. I seized her hand and covered it with tears and kisses, and from that hour I never left my new home.

"Years passed, and I was sent to school, cared for in every way, as a child, by the wealthy people who had adopted me. Old associations I never forgot, but I felt glad to be lifted above them. They had always been poor and lowly. With me it was different. I felt the throbbing of prouder blood in my veins, and rejoiced in the good fortune that had lifted me to my proper sphere. So it happened that I had reached womanhood before fate threw Richard Kelton in my way again.

"Gradually, as time passed on and I became more

observing, the character of my new mother was developed to my understanding. She was a beautiful woman, and had been much petted before her marriage. Mr. Osbret was much older than she, and less fond of society, naturally. But to please her, after the loss of her child, he went out with her more. Before I had grown up, however, he fell into his old habits of seclusion, and she was forced to relinquish what she could not well live without. It seemed a necessity of her nature to be cared for and admired. Probably the thought of what I would one day be to her, made her more tender of me as I grew nearer womanhood. I knew that she bestowed infinite pains upon me, seeking to make me as attractive as possible ; and that she counted much upon the time when I should enter society.

"Finally that time came. I made my debut, and was lucky enough to please my mother thoroughly. I was called handsome, brilliant, intelligent, and was pleased with the homage that was offered me from all sides. Our house was often thrown open to guests, and we drew many people constantly around us. Papa Osbret was proud of me, and mamma Osbret adored me. Ah, I was a very happy girl in those days ! and I thought they would last always, poor little fool ! "

She paused, but Mr. Prince would allow her no time to indulge regrets. His eyes never left her face.

"Go on," he demanded abruptly. " When was it you again saw this Kelton ? "

" It was at the end of my first season. We met

accidentally on the street, and he recognized me at once, though he had been from the city so long, and had grown so much, I never should have known him again. He looked handsome, was well dressed, and appeared gentlemanly. Fortune, he said, had been kinder to him than formerly in all respects save one. He had lost his mother soon after I had left them for my new home. Then he went into the world alone, and had conquered it. He had made some money, had been to college, and had traveled extensively. All this he told me as we walked home, and I was delighted. When we reached the door, I urged him to come in, and after a little hesitation he did so. I introduced him to Mrs. Osbret, and told her who he was, but was pained to find that she treated him coldly, and, after he was gone, scolded me heartily for speaking to him. She forbade my receiving him again in her house, saying she had raised me above such associations, and would not permit me to take up those that had been dropped years ago. A good match she had always intended I should make, and she would put herself between me and all dangers of thoughtlessness and folly.

" ' What do you mean ? ' I asked, half crying with vexation for having been lectured. ' I can see no danger in receiving him. He was a kind friend to me when a child, and his mother gave me a home when I had none. It seems heartless to treat him so.'

" ' Pooh ! I suppose you would like to get up a romance straightway, and fall in love with your old playfellow ! '

" I laughed at the idea.

"'You are not afraid, I see, but let me tell you, Celia, that I gave you more credit for discretion. Even if you are in no danger yourself, he is a young man, and I dare say not proof against such charms as yours. You have no right to risk his happiness, and there would be great risk in associating with him, were it at all allowable on other grounds.'

"I had not thought of it before ; and it was not unnatural that I should feel a secret sense of pleasure in the possibility of such an event as his falling in love with me. He did not come to the house again, for he knew he was not welcome, but I saw him several times ; and in some way it came about that I could not resist his influence. If he asked me to meet him I could not refuse, it was done in such an earnest manner, though I knew all the time how wrong it was, and how madly I was rushing into trouble. When I walked he joined me, and sometimes he would come to my favorite arbor in the garden, and entertain me with stories of his travels. He taught me to converse with flowers, and often sent beautiful messages through them to me. I would find them in the arbor when I went there to read in the morning, and at night upon my dressing-table, left by some unknown messenger. Never was a passage in woman's life so strangely sweet, so full of an excitement that was blissful without a foundation of love. That he loved me madly, I knew only too well, and I enjoyed it while fearful of the result. But love him I did not. The thought of being his wife gave me no pleasure. I never could imagine myself in such a relation with him. Such thoughts were always dismissed at once from my mind, if they crossed it, and I gave myself up to the singular fascination of his society, stolen though it was, and worse than foolish.

"At length, among others who came to us was Nathaniel Garton. He loved me from the first, and he sought my hand. I will not deny that I learned to love him. He was noble, handsome and intelligent, and I could respect him. He pleased my friends, and I became his betrothed. At this time more than a year had passed since Richard first made his appearance, and in the interval, though I had received attentions from many gentlemen, I had accepted no especial attention from any one. I thought, however, that Richard fully understood how impossible it was that we could ever be married, and would never ask me to marry him. But it proved different. He became madly jealous of Nathaniel when he saw him so much with me, and grew to hate him with a deep, fierce bitterness that frightened me. I was afraid to let him know that I loved Nathaniel, lest he should be driven to do him some secret injury. So I laughed about him, and sported madly with my own best feelings, lest some harm should come to my betrothed. Oh, how gladly would I have rid myself of him forever then. Once he did go away, and I began to think he would not come back. Nathaniel and I were very happy then in that brief season. We walked, rode, strolled through the gardens and sat in the arbor. There, in my thoughtless heedlessness, I taught Nathaniel to read the language of flowers as it had been taught to me. By that means I armed him against me. Richard returned, and his messages came to me in the old way. They were passionate protestations and jealous threats which made me miserable. If I could only have summoned courage to tell Nathaniel frankly how matters stood, it might have been well. I think he would have forgiven me and passed over my folly. But I never could bring myself to do it. I thought only of keeping the truth from Richard until after my marriage, and then we would be away, far beyond his reach for some time, after which we would settle where he would not be likely to follow us. It seemed as if it must all be right then. Once married, Richard would see how utterly hopeless pursuit must be, and would leave me in peace."

"Mrs. Osbret must have reared you with a very remarkable love for truth," remarked Mr. Prince, sarcastically.

"No, I was not taught to consider truth a great virtue," she answered quietly, lifting her eyes to his. "The lesson has come to me in bitter experiences which have served to show me its value. Then I cared only for safety."

"So it seems. But how did your plans end?"

"You must know something of it. I was one day in the arbor with Nathaniel, and we were in excellent spirits, happy and joyous as two children. I remember his breaking off a sprig of arbor vitæ and presenting it to me laughingly, asking me if I could read its language. I instantly pointed to my engagement ring and asked if that was not a satisfactory answer. Then he threw his arms around me, fondly kissing my forehead and cheek, until my heart was full. I caught his hand, drew it to my lips with an impulsive caress, and he smiled down at me with an expression. I never can forget.

"'Proud little Celia,' he said, 'I know you love me, or you would not do that.'

"Ah, I could have died to prove how much I loved him then!"

"Do you remember what you swore to me that night over his dead body?" demanded Mr. Prince, huskily.

"Be patient. What I spoke there was truth, as you shall see.   The day after that of which I have been speaking, Mr. Garton went away from the city, and I did not expect him back for some time. Almost immediately after his departure Richard appeared more furiously infatuated than ever. He implored me to fly with him, and so alarmed me by his threats if I refused, I did not know what to do. It required all my tact to calm him, and I never was so kind to him as on that day, when every throb of my heart was heavy with fear. He kissed me, and I dared not resent it. I was even weak and foolish enough to return his caresses, and to crown my folly, laughed at the suitors of whom he had been and was still jealous. Yes, I laughed at Nathaniel also, while my heart seemed breaking for his sake, and made sport over having duped him to the blinding of my friends as well. All the mad folly I was guilty of in that interview should have sent me to an insane asylum. But I had my punishment. Nathaniel came in the midst of it and heard what we were saying, saw him kiss me and had a right to despise me ever after, as he did.

"The moment Mr. Garton was discovered, Richard made his escape, coward that he was, and left me face to face with my enraged lover. All that he said I cannot repeat. Bitter, burning words, such as I had never heard from mortal lips, were showered upon me. He cast me off utterly, and I had no excuses to offer. It was too late then. I saw how despicable my course had been, and could utter nothing in extenuation.

"What passed between Nathaniel and my adopted parents, I do not know. But it was given out by them, that Mr. Garton had lost all his property, and they considered it their duty to break off the match. After that we went traveling, and I never again saw Nathaniel till I came here. It is needless to go over that period when you met and became interested in me. All of this you know. I thought I should be happy at last, when I became your wife. Such stormy years had rolled between me and the last interview with the only man I had ever loved. I did not love him when I married you. His bitter words and all the after sufferings I endured, had the effect of curing me of my passion. I think I hated him; and when he came here, I was overwhelmed with fear and anxiety."

"I told you that Mr. Garton made my house his home. Did you not then suspect it might be he?"

"Not once. Nathaniel Garton as a school-master seemed an incredible idea. I never had believed the story of his failure. That, I supposed to be a fabrication of my friends to shield me, so I had reason to be surprised when I discovered the truth. Our meeting was not pleasant, you may be assured. I seemed to see myself upon the verge of ruin. To deny what had passed, would have been impossible. To explain it satisfactorily to you, was also impossible, to all appearance, and I found myself in a strait. With a due knowledge of my danger, came a due sense of my regard for you. Let me be truthful here, though I pain you. When we were married I did not love you. There was a quiet calm regard, deep as I thought it possible for me to feel for any one after what I had experienced. But I learned to love you more and more, day after day, as I had to struggle to maintain my place. Nathaniel thought himself bound to protect you, and I saw that I had it in my power to wound and make him miserable. To him I denied any tender regard for you, and while using all the art of which I was mistress to keep him silent, I goaded him with fears that were only in part reasonable. To crown my distresses, Richard had traced and followed me here. He sent me flowers by that poor boy, and in my terror of a new danger I was compelled to meet him, that I might induce him to leave me in peace. Nathaniel saw me when those flowers were brought, as you will remember. It was the evening he came back, and his keen glance detected my emotion. The day following he requested me to show them to him, and I was compelled to do so, seeing that he was suspicious. I did not know that he would remember the language as I did, or that he really suspected Rich-

ard to be as conversant with it as we were.   Now I
think he must have guessed it was he who taught me.
And I remember he told me in a rather stormy quarrel
we had, that he once met Richard when he and Geraldine were walking on the river-bank, and he did
not recognize him then.   Afterwards he was haunted
with the thought that he had somewhere seen him.
It was only for a moment that he did see him, and
Richard had changed greatly in the time that elapsed
ere he saw him again.   I scarcely knew him myself.

"Although he would not go away, Richard did
not trouble me often, as I had feared.   He managed
to get such an influence over John Truslow as to
make him the medium of communication between
us, and two or three times insisted upon seeing me.
Then it was to demand money, and I gave it to him.
I never listened to a word of love from him.   If he
began to speak, I hushed him.   Desperation gave me
courage for that, and though I am well aware that he
still loves me, I have never wronged you by suffering
him to speak.   The wrong I did was in purchasing,
or trying to purchase, his silence.   I was in hopes
he would go away, and that I might then be allowed
to take rest and comfort in your undisturbed trust.
Oh, you do not know how I dreaded the thought
that you should learn all my sinful folly—you, my
husband, irrevocably bound to me, and who had
made me love you as my own soul.   I would have
risked my life to spare you pain and shame, such as
I knew would fall upon you in such revelations as it
was in their power to make.

"Thus the time has passed here.   You must see
24

how I have suffered, and what excuses I have had
for every unworthy deed. The errors of the past
were renewed and multiplied. I was forced into
them. They closed around me like serpents, and I
could not escape. If I had not loved you, I could
have yielded all. Only my love gave me still a motive for struggling against my fate."

"What took you to see the corpse that night I
met you coming from the chamber where it lay?"
he asked tremulously.

"I did not go to see the corpse. Fully impressed
with the necessity of self-protection, I went to discover if among his effects there were any things that
could do me injury in your estimation. I had time
only to get the key to his private box, when a noise
frightened me. The back stairway door was locked
on the outside, and I was forced to go through the
library. There I met you."

"Did you go again?"

"Yes, the next day. I found the box and opened
it, but there was nothing there to alarm me. Reassured, I went back to my room. Yet after that
you acted so strangely, I often wondered if you had
not made some discovery. To ask you I did not
dare, and after perplexing myself with all kinds of
conjectures, I at length came to the conclusion that
the disasters which had followed in quick succession,
must have confused your brain. It never occurred
to me that you could suspect me of having a hand in
the murder of Mr. Garton."

"But you suspect that Richard Kelton did the
deed."

"Yes, I will acknowledge the fact now, though I have no proof. I never heard him utter a threat, though I all the time feared injury to one or both of you. One thing alone, apart from what you know, would seem to make it most probable that he did it. You remember coming upon us in the conservatory, and we were quarreling. Mr. Garton had detected me receiving a note through the hands of John Truslow, and threatened to expose me. When I left you, you were quarreling, and I hovered outside the door until you turned to come out. Then I fled to my room, wrote a line and slipped it in a purse with all I had, and ran again down stairs. In the kitchen I found John, and gave him the purse for Richard, saying that he must go away. On the paper I had written that it was impossible to see him. As I returned, I heard Katie and Mr. Garton on the terrace. She had on my shawl, and we know that it was on that night that they were betrothed. Richard was perhaps near enough to see them, without being able to distinguish who she was, and suspecting it to be myself, got into one of his mad fits of jealousy. It was Richard who gave John the knife, and that knife was used to murder Nathaniel. This is all the grounds I have had for my suspicions. You must think as you choose. All my faults, sins, errors, I have admitted fully. More I cannot do. You, too, have a right to despise me, and I can now ask no more than that God will take me away—miserable, wretched creature that I am!"

Mr. Prince was looking at her with pale, trembling lips, and heaving breast. As she concluded, he got up and walked the floor once or twice rapidly, pausing at her side to say, through half-stifled sobs:

"Celia, I know now that you have told me all the truth. By the history he has left behind, and which you never saw, I have proved you, and—and, deeply as you have sinned, I—I forgive you!"

She sprang up, lifting a wet, white face to his gaze.

"Oh, do you mean it? can you, can you really forgive me? I do not deserve it. I am unworthy of anything but contempt. Why, even to this last hour I persisted in my sinful deceptions! And yet you forgive me—fully—freely!"

For answer, he took her in his arms, and held her beautiful head against his breast, great tears dropping down upon her hair.

"In confession, you have won pardon. A persistence in trying to deceive, after I told you I knew the truth, would have hardened me against you forever. I have made you do what I wished, and now I know that you are guiltless of his death. Now I may pursue the murderer without a fear that his exposure will prove the guilt of my own wife. Oh, this alone is joy enough to purchase your pardon. You are not guilty of that—I can forgive all else!"

Here let us close the scene upon the noble, generous man, and the humbled, penitent wife. Sin always brings its punishment, and she *had* suffered. If he, knowing the whole extent of her folly, could forgive her, what right have we to cavil at his actions, or longer invade the sacredness of the restoration and reunion by our presence?

CHAPTER XXI.

A DEATH-BED CONFESSION—CONCLUSION.

A FEW days later, Mr. Graves suddenly made his appearance at Prince Hill, having been summoned by Mr. Prince.   For some hours they were closeted together, to the evident satisfaction of both.

"Thank God, I can work now without fear," said Mr. Prince as the conference was concluded.   My dear friend shall be avenged."

"Yes, since the exposure will be so comparatively slight, you can give yourself to the duty without a scruple.   A man can submit to make some sacrifices for such a friend."

"Feeling her innocent of crime, I can bear anything else," was the earnest response.

By this the reader will see that they had made up their minds to bring Richard Kelton to justice, whatever the consequences might be.   Some exposure of the part Mrs. Prince had unwillingly played in the tragedy, they fully expected; but a man like Mr. Prince, loving justice as life, and above all selfishness, would not shrink from the lesser evil, the greater having disappeared.   It is not to be supposed that all the trouble was gone.   His trust had

21*

received a shock, his love a humiliation, and he could not rise above it at once. In his nobleness he could forgive her, but he never could feel the unbounded happiness again, that had been his in the first days of his married life. His implicit confidence in her truth was gone, and with confidence respect. Pride stood eternally over passion, and strove to shame him from the course he was taking, but Charity and Goodness said: "If you abandon her she is lost," and he could not send her adrift upon the world, unguarded and uncared for. Besides, he saw with a growing clearness that she had not only done but suffered wrong, and that, too, at the hands that were truest and dearest. The wounded feeling of Mr. Garton had betrayed him into unconscious injustice; he had judged her harshly from the moment when he learned that she could be guilty of falsehood, and thus when he again met her as Mrs. Prince, instead of aiding her efforts towards a truer life, he had goaded her proud spirit almost to desperation. Geraldine, too, the gifted, keen-eyed child, had carried her marvelous penetration farther than the truth would warrant. Whatever else she might have been, this erring, struggling woman was not a body without a soul. He had sought her in spite of doubts and warnings; his own hand had placed her in a difficult position, and she had a claim upon his aid in striving to fill it as she might. The conflict ended with a resolve to guard her, to deal tenderly with her, and by doing his duty faithfully, to make her the good wife his love had deemed her before the terrible awakening.

Having reached this point he was ready to do anything that was right and just. The first duty was to release the innocent and bring forward the guilty for trial. The evidence they deemed sufficient, after a careful investigation of all they had gathered, and they were about to act upon it, when a startling dispatch reached them. Richard Kelton, alias Rufus Knight had escaped, and the closest vigilance had failed to detect his hiding-place.

This was destined to be followed by a still more important event in the little village of Princeton. John Truslow, doubtless assisted by some person or persons unknown, had broken jail and disappeared also.

"Kelton had done it, you may be assured," said Mr. Graves to his friends in the midst of the confusion. "The fellow has some good in him after all."

"Evidently, since he provides against the boy's chances on trial. But we must have him yet."

It was a hot chase that followed, the authorities assisted heartily by Mr. Prince and his friends. But the fugitives probably took to the mountains, in the caves of which they hid themselves too effectually for detection. After the lapse of two weeks of fruitless search, it was given up, and it was nearly a year ere a trace was gained of them. Then the man Richard Kelton, was stabbed in a drunken broil, and on his death-bed confessed to the crime of murdering Nathaniel Garton, at Prince Hill.

On receiving this intelligence, Mr. Prince at once started in search of John Truslow, whose mother and brother had been objects of special care. He found him in very bad company, becoming more and more reckless, but finally prevailed upon him to leave them and put himself under his guardianship. In a short time he placed him under private tutors to prepare for college, at the same time giving Mr. Truslow a tenancy on his own lands, on condition that he would abandon intoxicating liquors. Thus a whole family were redeemed from poverty, and its attendant evils.

Soon after Mother Ritter's ominous visit to the Hill, she fell sick and never recovered. After her death, Angie came to live at the Hill as maid to the mistress, while the cripple was comfortably provided for. Mr. Prince felt that he could not do too much for those who had been objects of interest to his lost friend.

Miss Eldridge never married. Her time was divided between her own home and Mrs. Garton's during the life of the latter, and all the offers that were made her to change her condition firmly rejected. Mr. Bruce renewed his suit more than once, but failing signally, at a late period in his life married Mrs. Darby, who was widowed about a year after her visit at Princeton.

Woman in the War;

or,

A Hunt for a Husband.

At Paducah, Kentucky, I first realized what it required to be a soldier's wife. I had seen much before, and borne a great deal, yet it seemed but little, comparatively, when I came to take leave of my husband, and turned back to my lonely room to await his return.

True, I had expected this—was prepared for it in a measure ; yet a strange and overpowering sense of my position came over me that I had not felt before, when I stood by the window to catch a last glimpse of the beloved form. He was standing upon the deck of a large boat, with hundreds of others around him ; yet I seemed to see him only, his sad face turned to me in a mute farewell as the bell clanged and the ponderous vessel swept slowly out into the stream, and turned her prow toward the mouth of the Tennessee. It was but a moment, during which I leaned against the casement, breathless, agonized. There the waters lay cold and glittering under the spring sunbeams, and the sadness of utter desolation seemed to have fallen upon my spirits.

I am ashamed to say that I shut every ray of the bright, beautiful sun from my room, feeling as if it was a mockery too bitter to endure in that hour; that I threw myself upon my couch and wept as if my heart would break, for the time forgetful that there were any in the world more sorrowful and with deeper cause for sorrow than I. But it is true, and here I confess my selfish weakness repentantly, glad to be able to say that I have since that time learned to think less of myself and more of others—on whom the hand of affliction has fallen heavily, while, I am still unscathed.

After the first burst of grief I roused myself with the question, "What shall I do?" and the answer came so quickly that my cheek was dyed with shame. What should I do, with three hospitals in sight of my window? No need to ponder the question long. The call of duty was loud and strong, and I obeyed it without delay.

It was about two o'clock in the afternoon when I first entered the Presbyterian Church, which had been converted into a hospital, and walked up its aisle under the gaze of a hundred eyes. The very remembrance of that time thrills me again with the same sensation of pity and pain that rose in my heart as I looked upon the pale, emaciated faces around me. Near the pulpit two men were standing, whom I rightly supposed to be the doctor and steward. Toward them I went directly, and addressed the tallest of the two.

"Is this the attending physician of the hospital?"

"It is, madam. Dr. L—, at your service. What can I do for you?"

"Tell me, sir, how I can make myself useful to others. My husband has gone to Pittsburg Landing, to be away for several weeks, perhaps, during which time I shall have nothing to do, unless you make me useful here. Can I be of service?"

"Look about you and see. There has not been a lady within these walls since I came, nearly five weeks ago. Your voice is soft, your hand light and skillful—all women's are—and I have no doubt but your eyes will be quick to see what should be done. I shall be glad to have you come."

"Thank you. I may come to you for advice when I want it?" I asked.

"Certainly. I shall be happy to assist you at all times."

I bowed and turned away, feeling as if about to realize, indeed, some of the terrible consequences of war. In a few moments I had laid aside my hat and cloak, rolled my sleeves away from my wrists, and constructed an impromptu apron of an old sheet which I found among the bandages in the linen room. Thus prepared for the work which I saw before me, I went out to the kitchen and obtained warm water a tin wash-basin, and some towels. For combs and brushes I was compelled to send out before I could do any thing.

Then the work began in earnest. Commencing with the lower berth, I went up the entire length of the aisle, taking each patient in his turn until I got through. Grimed faces and hands were to be bathed, hair and beard trimmed and brushed—a long and distressing task. But I had undertaken it with a will, and, though my arms and neck ached, I would not yield until the last sufferer had been relieved.

It was half-past eight o'clock in the evening before I had done, and when I reached the hotel I could scarcely stand for very weariness. Such duties were new to me then, and the excitement helped to wear away my strength. But the memory of grateful thanks, tearful eyes, and broken, trembling exclamations of relief more than repaid me. Even as I sat beside them, passing the cool sponge over their faces or brushing the tangled hair, many of the sufferers had fallen asleep.

I slept little that night. It was vain to attempt sleep after such an experience. Moreover, an idea came to me that filled me with unrest. I had observed when tea was brought in how coarse and unpalatable the food was, and that many turned from it with loathing. There was hard, brown bread crisped to a blackened toast; some fat bacon, and black tea without milk served to the men on that evening. The tea was sweetened with very coarse brown sugar, stirred into it with large iron spoons. They drank from tin cups and ate from tin plates. This would have made little difference had the food been nice and palatable, which it certainly was not. Some of the men told me, in answer to my questions, that they could not have swallowed a mouthful to save their lives.

I rose very early the following morning, filled with the idea that many of those brave sufferers were actually starving, and determined to look into the matter more closely. But few of the nurses were astir in the hospital, and I went to the kitchen, where the cook had just commenced the preparation of the morning meal, and was greeted with a surly "Good-morgen" in mixed German-English. In a moment I saw that I should not have a very pleasant time in my examinations. After a few careless remarks, to set the man in a good humor, I asked him to show me the hospital stores for the day's consumption, which he did ungraciously enough. A moment's observation filled me with horror and indignation.

"Do you tell me that you are going to cook all this stuff for those men in the other room?" I said, indignantly. "Look at this tea, black and mouldy as it can be, and this bacon is one living mass! Here are salt fish laid upon boards over the sugar-barrel, the brine dripping through into the sugar? I hope you have not been using this for their tea."

"It is not my fault. I am not ze prowider fur ze hospital," growled the cook in response. "I does my duty so fur as I can. I cooks ze rations zat is bring to me, and zat is all so fur as I go."

"Well, that is farther than you will go in less than a week from now!" I answered, quickly. "If you had the soul of a man in you, you would refuse to have any thing to do with such horrible things as those! Poor boys? No wonder they turned away from such food in disgust. Some of those men are starving to death. Do you know it?"

He stared at me aghast and made no reply.

"It is really true, and I know it. How can they eat such bread and meat—drink such tea as this?

They are weakened by illness, and require delicacies. It would be utterly impossible for many of those men to swallow coarse food, even if clean and palatable. How then can they eat this?" I repeated, looking at him steadily till his head drooped, and I began to suspect that he was even more guilty than at first appeared. Afterward I found that he had carefully put aside all the delicacies that found their way to the hospital, and feasted upon them, while those for whom they were intended, faded and pined day by day under his eyes.

When Dr. L—— came, I went to him at once and told him how I had been engaged, and what I had found in my researches. He looked so much surprised that indignation was redoubled, and I could not forbear expressing it in plain words.

"Can it be possible that you, the physician in charge of a hospital, do not know, after five weeks' service, what your patients have to eat?"

"I am not here when the meals are served. I give orders for such diet as my patients must have, and my steward's business is to carry out my instructions."

"Do you never inquire into the condition of the stores? Have you never examined to see if they were as they should be? It seems to me you ought to know all about what is going on here. If three hundred lives were in my hands as they are in yours I should not dare to trifle with them thus!"

"You are severe, madam!"

"Ask yourself if I am unjustly so, sir. I do not desire to appear rude or assuming; but indeed I won't look upon this unmoved. What I saw last night and this morning has opened my eyes to a condition that is a shame to any hospital. See the confusion all around us! Remember how helpless men have lain without even a face bath or a wound dressed for three days, to say nothing of the more dreadful, slow starvation to which they are subjected! If all hospitals are kept like this, God pity the poor soldiers!"

"Since you see the evils so plainly, perhaps you can suggest a remedy," remarked Dr. L—— sarcastically.

"I will try, if you will act upon the suggestion," I answered quickly.

"Well?"

"In the first place, then, what do you do when a man fails to draw his regular rations?"

"He is entitled to its value in money, if he wishes it."

"Then why not refuse to draw such rations as those, and with the money buy food that can be eaten?"

"It might be done, if there was anything to buy. I am afraid it will be hard work, if you attempt it."

"No matter; it must be done. If you will furnish me with a boy to do errands, I will see if I can not get fresh butter, eggs and chickens, at least—perhaps milk also. These would prove invaluable just now. To-day I intend to send to a society for some sheets and mattresses; and, if you have no decided objection, will try to bring order out of chaos, if possible."

"I see you are one of the working kind," said the doctor. "Do all you wish, and call upon me when I can render any assistance."

"That will be very frequently, I assure you." And with that I turned away, still too much incensed to treat him civilly. He was willing enough to let other people take his work off his hands, since he would come in for a full share of the credit in the end. At least that was my uncharitable thought at the moment; and I am not sure now that I was far wrong, as I know his character better.

The same day I went to him again about the boy, but he had forgotten all about the matter; so I went to the quartermaster instead. He furnished a horse, and I sent my own waiting-man out to the country for supplies, making him take a receipt for every penny he paid in his purchases. This was for the purpose of ascertaining precisely how much was spent, as I desired to render a faithful account of my stewardship. I was fully aware that the ground I was taking might easily prove a dangerous one, should I fail to keep precise accounts of my expenditures, and resolved to give no chances for misrepresentation. Every receipt and bill of sale, after being duly copied in my own account-book, was carefully filed in the quartermaster's office, subject to the inspection of any who chose to examine them.

Mr. P——, the quartermaster, was a kind, gentlemanly man, in whom I found an ever-ready assistant. He had received a donation in money, for the benefit of the wounded, from some one in Illinois, which he begged me to use as designed, and I did so gladly. Even with that I had not enough, and was often compelled to draw from my own purse the means wherewith to supply the many wants of the patients.

It took me a week to get fairly started in my vocation as hospital nurse. There was such an entire absence of system in the establishment, that it seemed almost impossible to bring it into anything like order. The nurses were detailed each day from the convalescent corps—weak, spiritless men, who thought more of themselves than of the charges placed in their hands. I had seen them lounging about and sleeping while the sicker men, failing to make them hear, would try to struggle into a sitting posture to get at the medicines to be taken from time to time.

All this had to be changed, and strong, able men detailed for duty. The ward-master drank fearfully, and I was compelled to report him and get another man put into his place. With the assistance of these, however, after the changes were made I got along very well. Every morning we had the floor nicely washed, and when the sun shone the windows were opened to let in the fresh, balmy air, the effect of which was almost magical; eyes would brighten, and lips wreathe in pleasant hopeful smiles, beautiful to behold.

It was with more joy than words can express that I observed the rapid improvement of the men under careful attention. When the new sheets and comforters, with pillows and mattresses came, we were able to keep the place perfectly fresh and comfortable. But it required the most constant attention.

25*

I went to my hotel only for my meals, devoting the day, from half-past five in the morning to nine in the evening, to the care of the sick. I must be there at every meal, or many would go without anything at all. Some of the feeblest had to be fed like children, and what they ate could be prepared by myself only. I must toast the bread and make the tea; then I must sit down and support their heads with my left hand, while with the right I conveyed the food to their lips. Such constant care was very wearing, and I was often tempted to steal away for an hour's rest, trusting to some one to take my place for a time; but when I gave it a second thought the temptation faded. Suppose the man should die, could I feel that I had done all in my power to save him? Not if I should yield to the inclination I felt to abandon my post; so I remained, and tried to be patient.

Two hours each day were devoted to letter-writing for those who were unable to correspond with their friends. And sometimes, after tea, I would send for my guitar and sing for them, at the request of the music-loving ones under my charge. So the days sped, and all things began to run smoothly—for a time, at least. Death was not banished from our midst, however. Sometimes it was my fate to walk up the aisle in the morning and find some berth empty in which a favorite patient had lain. I might here go into particulars, and detail some of the most touching scenes in life; but I will speak of only one case:

One evening I was sitting by a dying man, reading

a favorite chapter in the Bible, to which he listened eagerly, even while his eyes drooped under the shades of death. One clammy hand groped for mine, and clasped it with a feeble, tremulous touch, and as I finished, his lips moved painfully: "Write to my wife and children. Tell them I can not come to them, but they may soon follow me to that place of which the Saviour said, 'In my Father's house are many mansions: I go to prepare a place for you.' Oh, how sweet and comforting! 'Let not your heart be troubled: ye believe in God; believe also in me.' Jesus, Saviour, I do believe in Thee. Receive Thou my spirit!" And the voice sank softly. A few moments later the last fluttering breath went out, and the mysteries of the unknown world were mysteries to him no longer.

Tears fell fast as I pressed the white lids over the blue eyes, thinking of those who were far away, and denied the sad privilege of paying the last tender rites to the dead. Poor children! Poor mother! How my heart ached to think that mine must be the task to tell them the story of death, of which, perhaps, they were not dreaming now!

Before I had finished, a boy came in hurriedly and said something to the steward, of which I caught only the words, "been fighting all day . . . rebels attacked them this morning . . . had a very hard time of it."

I grew for a moment sick with a terrible fear. A battle had taken place, and who should say how many lives in a few short hours had been crowned with the thorny wreath of affliction? It might be that I, too, was destined to feel the force of an awful blow. If so, God help me!

I could gain no particulars at the hospital, and was forced to wait until I reached home. There I learned that an attack had been made upon our forces Sunday morning, and the Confederates had occupied our camps for some time. Afterward they were driven out again, but we had lost many lives. They were still fighting an hour before nightfall. Further than this nothing was known.

All night I walked the floor in an agony of suspense and dread. Would the morning's dawn come to me with a message of gladness, or should I rank among the doomed, who henceforth must walk the earth in the darkness and gloom of utter desolation?

Ah, how I prayed that night! How I wrestled with my own fearful heart, and chided myself for the lack of faith which should have borne me up in that hour!

Monday came, freighted with death to thousands! All day the battle raged, and at night it was said that the federals had achieved a great victory. A victory it was; but oh! at what a fearful cost! How many hundreds of young heads were that day laid low in the dust, never to rise again! How many hopeful hearts throbbed their last impulses of human aspiration and ambition!

Tuesday and Wednesday brought hundreds from the field of action. Some of the wounded were transported to Paducah, and I was called upon to dress their wounds and to assist in amputations, which required all the strength I possessed. The duty was a terrible one; but I nerved myself resolutely to perform it, hoping that, if need be, some one would as willingly attend to one of whose fate I had as yet learned nothing.

On Thursday morning the St. Francis Hotel was alive with officers from Shiloh, but still I was left in ignorance of my husband's fate, and the suspense was becoming insupportable. Every excuse that could be made for a delay of tidings had been utterly exhausted, and I felt now that he was either killed or wounded.

In the hope of hearing something definite I went out to the table for the first time since the battle, and took my usual seat, near which sat two wounded officers. One had his head bandaged; the other's arm was in a sling; and both were pale and weary-looking. But they were talking of the late contest, and after listening for a few moments I yielded to an uncontrollable impulse and asked the one nearest me if he knew anything of the fate of the —— Regiment.

He turned politely, with a look of interest I could but remark, and answered :

"I am sorry to say, madam, that it fared very badly. Some other regiments of the same division showed the white feather, and, perfectly panic-stricken, broke ranks and fled. That gallant regiment alone stood its ground, and was literally cut to pieces. Those who were not killed were taken prisoners, only a few escaping."

"And the officers—were they all—?" I could not finish the sentence for the deathly sickness that was choking my utterance, and he answered it gently:

"I believe every one was killed. Did you have any friends among them, may I ask?"

"My husband," I gasped. "Captain S——"

I saw them exchange glances; and then, as if in a dream, a voice seemed to murmur afar off amidst the rushing of waters.

"Poor thing! He fell in the first onset. But see! She is falling!"

A strong hand grasped my arm, and a glass of water was pressed to my lips; but the shock of that deadly blow was too heavy, and I sank slowly into utter oblivion, conscious of a wish, as sight and sound faded, that I might never waken again!

It was an hour before they brought me back to a sense of my bereavement, and then I turned from the kind faces clustered about the couch to which I had been borne, and gave vent to a bitter cry.

"Ah! why did you not let me die? The world is so cold and desolate!"

Two firm, soft hands clasped mine, and drew them away from my face, and I saw the mild, reproachful eyes of a stranger gazing into mine. He was an old man, with hair as white as the snows of winter, and a voice soft and gentle as a tender mother's.

"My child, you are rebellious! Rouse yourself, and learn to say, 'Not my will, but thine, O Lord, be done!'"

"I can not!—I can not bring myself to feel that there is any mercy or love in the power that could

deal such a blow. God knew that he was all I had
on earth, and he has taken him from me. It was
cruel!"

"Hush! Resignation will come when you have
time to think. Perhaps, after all, it is a mistake.
There has been no official report of your husband's death, and he may only be wounded or a
prisoner."

I started up, wild with the hope his words
awakened.

"Nay, be not too hasty! I only say it may be
possible."

I was silenced, but the hope was not crushed. It
stung me to life again, and made every idle moment
seem like an eternity of agony.

In a few moments they began to leave the room,
and only one or two ladies remained in conversation
with the old gentleman, who was a physician, and
had been summoned hastily when I fainted. Seeing
them thus engaged, I formed a sudden resolution,
and raised myself from the pillows.

"What are you going to do?" asked the doctor,
turning his face toward me.

"Find my husband—dead or alive," I answered,
getting off the bed.

"My dear child you are mad!" he expostulated.
"You can not do anything. Look at your face—it
is as pallid as marble, and your eyes would frighten
any one."

"That is because I have not slept or eaten scarcely
since last Saturday night," I said, in reply. "Besides, I have been half mad with suspense. Only

for the sick at the hospital, who claimed my care, I don't think I could have borne it all."

" Go back and lie down on the bed," pleaded one of the ladies. ": It makes my heart ache to look at you."

" How dreadfully you must have suffered!"

" God and my own heart only know how much," I answered, forcing down a sob. Her tone of womanly sympathy shook my strong self-control till I trembled. Then I broke down entirely, and with a bitter cry fell upon my knees by a chair.

" Oh Charley, Charley! my heart is breaking!"

Instantly her kind arms were twined around me— her soft lips pressed to my forehead. She held me to her heart, and suffered me to weep until the fountain of my tears was exhausted.

" There! you feel better now, don't you?" said the doctor, kindly. " You must lie down and keep quiet awhile, or you will be ill. Your hands are like two burning coals now, while only a moment since they were like ice. You must not fall ill."

" Oh no! I can not afford to be ill. I must search for my husband," I answered, rising. " There—it is over now! I am done with tears for the present, and am ready to work. If I do not, I shall soon lose my reason. Don't talk to me, any of you!" I cried, as I saw them about to remonstrate. " I am determined to go up the river, and if I should never return, try to remember me kindly."

" The authorities will not permit you to go," said the doctor. " An order has been issued to allow no lady to pass up the river, and Colonel N——— has locked himself up to escape the importunities of the people."

"I shall go, nevertheless," was my reply.

"How will you manage it?" asked the old man, curiously.

"I don't know yet. But I shall go. Before night I shall be on my way to Pittsburg Landing."

They looked at me pityingly; but I paid no attention further, and when they left the room I began to pack some articles in a small trunk which I could easily take with me.

About noon a boat, chartered at Cincinnati and sent after the wounded, touched at Paducah, and I obtained passage. Fortune seemed to favor me here, for I not only found myself able to carry out my design, but came into the midst of sympathizing friends, who received me cordially, and did all in their power to make me comfortable.

There were a number of surgeons and their assistants on board. Three Sisters of Charity and two ladies from Cincinnati completed the list, and in about an hour we entered the mouth of the river and proceeded on our sorrowful errand.

I will not dwell upon the tediousness of the trip. To me it seemed like an eternity of misery. On Thursday, about one o'clock, we left Paducah, and did not arrive at Pittsburg Landing until Saturday night, near eight o'clock.

I shall never forget that night or a single incident connected with it. As we made fast to the shore I was standing upon the hurricane deck, looking abroad, with my heart full of a wild and bitter

26

fear. Here was Shiloh! There were the black, forbidding bluffs directly over my head, the banks of the river lined with boats from which profane and noisy men were unloading Government stores. Across the river two or three gun-boats stretched their black, snake-like lengths along the waters, and from them only a fiery gleam was now and then discernible. Above, the sky was clear and blue, and studded with myriads of stars that looked—oh so calmly!—down upon that terrible spot. There, where rivers of blood had flowed, lay the silvery white moonbeams, and on the death-laden air floated the rich perfume of spring flowers.

Even while I stood looking around me the *Continental* swung loose from her fastenings, and rounded out into the stream followed by half a dozen others. Now the lights blazed from every vessel, and a band struck up "Dixie" in the most spirited manner.

General Halleck was going up the river to destroy a bridge, and, convoyed by two of the gun-boats, they started two and two abreast, keeping in this order until a sudden turn hid them from sight.

Turning my face once more toward the shore, some dark objects became visible lying some distance up the side of the hill; but I could not discern precisely what they were, and the next moment my attention was absorbed in a painful scene taking place on the deck of a boat just along side of the *Lancaster*.

There were a number of men lying upon berths in the open air, and around one of them was a surgeon and his group of assistants. The wounded man had his arm bared to the shoulder, and had I not seen the glittering of instruments in the light of the numerous lamps held around him I should still have divined his fate. Poor fellow! I heard him sob and plead piteously, " Oh, doctor, don't take my arm off! If I lose it my little sister will have no one to work for her. I'd rather die !"

" Die you will if it does not come off, and that very soon," was the response. " No help for it, boy, so be a man and bear it bravely."

The next moment a handkerchief was held to his face, and after a brief struggle he yielded to the powerful influence of chloroform. I hear the deep, quick gasping so painful to the listener, and the tears ran down my cheeks unrestrainedly.

Captain V—— came up to me.

" Mrs. S——, I have been making inquiries for you, and can gain no intelligence whatever concerning your husband. I see no way but to wait until daylight, and then I will find a conveyance and send some one with you."

" Can not I go to-night? It seems as if it is impossible to wait."

" No, it is out of the question. The mud is two foot deep on shore, and it is quite dark in the woods. I am sorry for you, but it will be only a little while longer. Try to be as patient as you can."

" Thank you, I will. But it is very, very hard."

" I am sure of it. But let me say a word to you here, Mrs. S——. I fear you are hoping too much. Remember he fell early on Sunday, and the chances are that he was hastily buried with many others in the trenches."

"For heaven's sake, go no further!" I implored. "My husband buried in a trench! Oh, God forbid!"

He took my hand, and drawing it within his arm, led me to the ladies' cabin, which now presented a singular appearance, converted as it was into a hospital, and peopled by the wounded which the men were carrying on board.

There were three rows of mattresses spread upon the floor, the one in the middle capable of accommodating two patients, and one on each side a single man.

All these were filled already, and the clamor was terrible. Some called for food, others for water, and a few lay moaning piteously, their hunger and thirst forgotten in the sharp pain of undressed wounds.

One boy near the stern of the boat seemed to be in such distress that I hastened to his side and bent over him.

"Where are you wounded?" I asked.

"In the shoulder. I got it Monday, and it's never been dressed. I can not get at it myself."

Hastily getting a basin of water, sponge and bandages, I exposed the inflamed and swollen shoulder, and began to bathe it carefully. He regarded me for a moment with wide, fearful eyes, then, as he felt the gentle touch and cooling sponge, his eyes closed, and he heaved a great sigh of relief.

"Ah, that is so nice!" he murmured, presently. "I tell you it's hard enough to be shot down like a dog; but when it comes to lying out for a whole week in the open air, with only a blanket, a cracker, and a slice of dried beef, with an occasional drink of water, it's harder still. I thought I should starve to death before they could get a boat to take us off, and if I could only have had my shoulder dressed! Oh, how good that feels!"

I had just laid a folded napkin wet with ice-water over the wound, and it was this which called forth such an expression of delight.

"I am glad you feel better. Now I am going to bring you a cup of tea, with some bread and butter. If you are so nearly starved, it is time you should have something to eat."

"Oh, thank you!"

I hastened away, and in a few moments came back with the tea and bread, which he ate like a man who was indeed starving. The glare of his large, dark eyes was perfectly terrible.

"More, more!" he gasped pantingly, swallowing the last drop of tea at a draught.

"Not now. In half an hour you shall have more. To give it you now will do you more harm than good. We must try to keep down fever. Now, shall I bathe your face and hands for you?"

"If you please," with an eager, wistful look at the empty cup and plate that made my eyes grow humid.

While I was engaged in the operation, Doctor P——, from Cincinnati, passed me.

"Who taught you to nurse?" he asked. "I wish all women would take right hold of the boys as you do. There would be less suffering."

"They have surely earned this much at our hands, at least," I said, in reply.

"Ay, to be sure. But I know of plenty who would never get down on their knees on the floor as you are doing, and take hold of an object like that."

"I hope not. I believe there are few who would not do it if in such circumstances. There is not one who has a father, brother, or husband in the service, who would refuse to do it, I am sure."

He passed on, with some careless reply, and I continued attending the soldiers until it grew late. After three o'clock I threw myself upon a sofa in the chambermaid's room, and slept until half-past five. Then I rose and went again among the wounded until such an hour as I could set out upon my journey over the field.

I will here mention a case that may seem incredible to many; but if so, it will not surprise me, for I could scarcely believe the evidence of my own senses, when one of the surgeons came to me directly after I entered the cabin the night before, and asked me to come and "see a sight." I told him I would as soon as I finished "feeding my patient;" and did so, he meeting me half way when he saw me coming.

About midway of the cabin lay a rebel prisoner, badly wounded in the head. A ball had passed behind his eyes, forcing both upon the cheeks, where they lay in a most horrible and swollen condition. From the wounds in each temple a portion of the brains was slowly oozing, and the doctor pointed to it, saying:

"In all my life I have seen nothing like that. He

has been lying here for the last ten minutes in that condition, quarreling with this federal soldier just opposite."

"Surely he can not know what he is saying!" I ejaculated.

"Yes, he does, perfectly. You should hear him."

I had an opportunity soon, for in a moment he called out:

"Say! look here, Yank! I want a drink of water!"

"All right! You shall have it in a moment," answered one of the men in waiting. "I'm tending to a feller, and shall be done in a minute."

"Oh yes, I'll be bound you'll tend to your Yanks before you do to me! But when a man's on his last legs you might stop a moment to give him a drop of water. I sha'n't ask it of you more than an hour or so longer. Then I'm going straight to ——!"

I shuddered and retreated from the spot. Such profanity and recklessness upon the very brink of eternity! It was awful!

"Poor wretch! God pity and have mercy upon you!" said the doctor. "You have none for yourself!"

"I don't want any of your cant, sir," said the man, in reply. "My soul is not yours, and you need not trouble yourself about it in the least."

When I came again into the cabin the following morning he was just breathing his last—going home to his Creator hardened, reckless—utterly careless of the fate that awaited him.

An hour later Captain V—— sent for a conveyance, but could get none, to carry me over the field in search of the camp from which I hoped to gain some intelligence that should end suspense. While striving to devise some means the medical director of the —— Division came on board, and offered me one of his horses, proposing himself to guide me to the place where the —— Regiment was camped. There were but few left he said, but what there were had pitched their tents about five miles distant, and he thought he could take me to the place without difficulty.

Thanking him warmly I accepted the offer, and ere long found myself mounted and laboring through the mud up the side of the bluff.

The path led round it, ascending gradually to the top; and once upon the shore, I discovered the dark objects that had puzzled me the night previous were human bodies lying under the broiling sun waiting for burial.

Through the mud, over fallen trees, broken artillery, and pieces of shells, the carcasses of horses and mules, and by strips of woodland cut down like grass by the rains of iron and lead! How strange and solemn and fearful it seemed! Giant trees pierced by balls and shorn of their bark till the trunks showed a hundred grinning scars; boughs severed and hanging by a single fibre, or lying prone upon the ground, trampled and blood-stained!

Our progress was slow. It was long past noon ere we reached the little hollow in which the tents I sought had been pitched; and then, as we came in sight of the little blue wreaths of smoke, and saw a few solitary men moving about, I began to tremble.

I knew that I was about to meet my fate, and the thought of what it might be almost deprived me of the necessary strength to go on to the end.

Presently, after passing through several encampments, we descended into the hollow and alighted before the officers' quarters, which seemed almost deserted. There the doctor bade me go in and wait while he made inquiries of those around outside.

On first entering I saw nothing but a berth, on which lay a man with his face turned from me; but in a moment I discovered that another was seated beyond, his head resting against the side of the berth, fast asleep. A pillow supported the right arm of the invalid, and by the bandages I knew he had been wounded. My heart swelled with pity, and stealing softly toward the bed, I leaned over to catch a glimpse of his face.

Pale—oh, so pale and wan!—with the rich brown hair pushed back from the broad brow, pure and white as marble. The blue eyes were half closed, and the lips parted with such an expression of suffering that a loving woman's heart might almost break in looking upon it. Yet I did not moan, nor faint, nor cry out. I only fell upon my knees, and taking the white, clammy fingers of the left hand in my own, covered it with warm tears and gentle kisses—for it was my own dear husband, whom God had spared to me, and I had found him at last!

"I thank Thee, O my Father!" was the cry of my soul in that hour, and my lips breathed it audibly. With the sound Charley opened his eyes and looked into my face with a bewildered stare. Then a light broke all over his pale face, and his glad smile sent happy tears raining over my cheeks.

"Is it you, darling? I thought you would never come!" he breathed faintly. "But you are here now, and you will not leave me again, will you?"

"No, indeed. I will take care of you, and get you well again. Ah, how you must have missed me!"

"Missed you! It has been an eternity of misery since I fell, and I have called your name vainly a thousand times."

"They told me you were killed!" I said, chokingly. "I waited for tidings from you till I thought I should go mad, and then they said you were dead, and when I declared my intention of finding you, tried to keep me from coming. But I would not be stayed, and, thank God! I have found you alive."

"Ay, thank God from your soul, for it is one of His greatest blessings that he is here now!" said the doctor, who had entered and laid his hand upon my head.

"Tell her all about it," whispered my husband's faint voice, and as his fingers clasped mine closer, the old man sat down upon a camp-stool and began:

"I have just heard the story from one of the boys, and it is a wonder to me how he lived through that long time without the least care. He must have crept into the thicket where they found him very soon after falling, and there remained for four days. There was a dead soldier near him, and from his canteen and haversack he managed to obtain water and food; but his wound bled terribly. They say, to judge by the stains around and where they came across him, he had just a spark of life left. He will need you now to nurse him back to life again, and it will take nice nursing too."

"Will he lose his arm, doctor?" I asked, in a suppressed voice, lest Charley should hear.

"I will tell you after awhile," was the answer; and accordingly "after awhile" he examined it closely. As he left the tent I followed him out.

"Well, doctor?"

"All right, my little anxious woman! The Captain can carry that arm through several campaigns yet, I hope," he said, heartily; and I went back to my boy, my eyes wet with glad tears.

Three weeks later we were within our own quiet home, where I was nursing him back to strength to be ready for the fall campaign.

THE PRISONER'S CHILD.

CHAPTER I.

"Ollie, my daughter, what are you doing?"

"Looking out of the window, papa," answered the sweet, clear voice of a child, as she turned and came toward her father's cot. A pale, suffering man, was that father; very much emaciated, and, as he lay stretched upon the rude mattress in his prison cell, resembling a corpse more than a living being. Only the large restless eyes, full of a troubled light, saved his face from an appearance of utter ghastliness.

"And why were you looking from the window?" he asked again, as he clasped one frail, little hand, and gently stroked the brown curls falling over the child's forehead.

"I was trying to think how I should feel and act, were I to go out there among the green trees and fresh grass, and could hear the birds singing among the pretty leaves," returned the little one gravely.

A spasm of agony contracted the prisoner's brow, which was beaded over with large drops of perspiration. For one moment the restless eyes closed, and his lips moved; then he looked up, and drew the child closer to his side, with wistful tenderness upon every feature.

"And would my little Ollie love to go out there on the green grass to play?"

"I don't know, papa; I think so. It seems very nice. I can just see the tops of the trees over the walls beyond; and if all the grass looks as fresh as the little patches that grow here and there in the yard, I think it must be delicious. I can see the cage hanging from the matron's window, where the little birds sing all day; and I imagine I can see those trees full of them, and hear them twittering everywhere. Would it not be very nice to go out there, papa?"

A sad smile parted the father's lips. "Yes, dear little Ollie, and it will not be long ere you can go forth among green fields and flowers. God grant this prison odor may not taint their fragrance with its bitterness for you, when that time shall come. Ollie, these walls are very dark and dreary. I am weary of them. Will not you be glad when I, too, can go forth and know their gloom no more?"

"O, yes, yes, dear papa! Are you going! When? Ah, how nice it will be!"

"Yes, my child, and the time is drawing very nigh. My deliverer is close at hand, and soon his merciful hand will fling wide these ponderous doors, and I shall pass out to return no more."

The little girl's face was radiant, and both hands came together joyously. Her voice was intensely tremulous with feeling, as she exclaimed:

"Oh, how happy we shall be. We will go away

into the beautiful forests that you have told me about so often; where there are clear, sparkling streams, and the loveliest flowers and plants! Ah! how happy we will be!"

What a hard thing to check the poor child's joy, and force upon her mind the painful truth! How could loving lips speak such sickening words! Yet it must be done.

" Yes, Ollie, we shall be very happy, no doubt. Freedom is the sweetest earthly blessing, and after we go forth, we shall both be like different beings. How do you think you could enjoy it, if you went without me?"

" Oh, not at all. I should not know what to do without you, and would not want to be there."

" Ollie," asked the prisoner painfully, " do you remember what I have told you of the great world beyond these walls?"

" Yes, sir," was the ready response. " You told me it was a very beautiful world, where there are a great many good, lovable people; and that there are a great many, also, who are cold and cruel. You said there were those who, for lack of charity, would watch every word and action, to construe them into evil; and through selfish motives, would not hesitate to trample us down to utter ruin, if by it they might themselves rise to power and greatness."

" Ah! you are an apt scholar, my little daughter, and have learned the sad lessons taught you but too well! You remember, too, how I have told you the cold world will look upon *you*, at some future time. My poor baby, this is a sad dower I leave you—an insight into the heart of the world, with a dark cloud upon your young life as you start in it! But remember this in all time—never forget for a moment: God has endowed us all with intellects, from which judgment of good and evil must spring. We must use them. If one person tells us that one thing is right, or that another thing is wrong, we must not take it for granted that it *is* right or wrong because they think it so. We must consider it, use our own powers of thought, pray to God for guidance, and act upon what we ourselves are finally led to believe right. When we reach that point where we conscientiously feel that we are right, let nothing turn us from our purpose. If we let the world sway us, and listen to the varied opinions of the many, upon things important only to ourselves, we become weak and characterless—unfit for decided and righteous action. I tell you these things to make you self-reliant, for you will have need of it, and it is not without purpose that I have tried to show you the necessity of firmness, in whatever you may undertake. Do not accept conclusions hastily. Take time, and let your own heart be the judge of your actions. When you have thought well and *prayerfully* over anything, then act without fear. You may find hundreds to condemn, where there will be one to commend. Yet the commendation of that one is worth more than all else, and is an adequate reward, for that one will understand your nature and motives. Never violate your own self-respect by an unworthy thought or action, and you may hold up your head and *command* honor. Do not be hasty to condemn others yourself. Be charitable. Many actions *appear* what they are not, and many long years of suffering spring from misconstruction. Give people all the credit for good motives and generous feelings you can, and do not believe them guilty of evil, unless you *know* them so. You will see enough. Let the rest pass. I scarcely know how to make you understand what I wish. My feelings are conflicting. I want you to be generous and charitable toward mankind, and still watchful and wary. You must trust the world but little. It is full of deceit and cruelty. I shudder to send you into it, in your helpless innocence and ignorance.

"Oh! my God," he groaned, covering his thin face passionately with trembling hands. "It is a bitter cup to drink in my last hour. Help me to drink it humbly, and in faith of Thy mercy toward my little, lonely lamb!"

Ollie stood terrified beside him, now listening with strained glances and parted lips to this burst of agony.

"Oh, papa! papa! what is it?" she pleaded, striving to uncover his face in her fright and distress.

He looked up at her through blinding tears, but the old, troubled light was fading from his eyes, and his voice was very sweet and tender as he answered:

"Nothing now, my child. The spasm is past. I am reconciled, I trust, to God's will. My little one, you remember, among other things, what I have said to you about death?"

A shadow fell upon the child's face.

"Yes, but papa—"

" What, love ? "

" You do not mean—oh—you do not mean that it is coming here ? "

The poor little girl's lips had grown very white, and her voice husky, while the slight frame shook convulsively.

" Yes, my precious. I must tell you the truth, and not let it come upon you unawares. It is painful, yet it ought not to be. Stop crying, Ollie, and listen to me. You know that death only can deliver me from these stone walls, where the best part of my life has been dragged out in expiation of another's crime. Were I to go out among men, I should be scorned and shunned for another's deed, and no action of my life could wipe away the stigma that rests upon it, and sets me up as a mark before my kind. I could not bear it. Death holds out to me a far more pleasant asylum than the world can give. By his hand and through his gates I shall enter into eternal rest, where music, flowers, and all things fair and beautiful are perpetual. When we go forth, as we were speaking of doing a little while since, one of us will be borne to the resting-place of the dead. The other will be led by the living into the busy haunts of life, to meet its duties and difficulties. You love me, my child, and, I am sure, will be glad to know that I shall suffer no more. Think of me in the world, meeting cold words and harsh looks, scorned and despised—turned from by those who are in every respect my inferiors. Could you bear that ? Then picture me in another world, where the redeemed of God are washed white in the blood of Christ, and where trouble, sorrow, or pain can never come. A few years of patient toiling and struggling, and you can come to me. Then we shall never part again. Ollie, look up, my child, and tell me which you would choose for me—life, miserable, agonizing, and full of shame—or death, through which I pass to rest, peace, love, and life eternal in the glorious Heavens."

A white, still face the child lifted to the prisoner's gaze, and a strained, unnaturally calm voice answered very sadly and gravely:

" Death, papa—and—life."

" Right, my own darling. I see you understand. Now, Ollie, kneel beside me, my love, and pray that God will give you strength and judgment, and make this affliction to you endurable. He is merciful, and though you will feel my loss very much, He can give you a cheerful, contented spirit, and reconcile you to His will."

With the same unnatural, calm, pervading voice and manner, little Ollie knelt beside the cot, folding her hands reverently over the rude covering. Thus, for ten years, had she knelt, morning, noon and night, and repeated with her father the simple prayers she learned first to lisp unmeaningly, then with the faint dawning and final upward growth of thought and feeling. Her little eyes had first seen the light within the self-same walls, and the ten winters that threw their white mantles and gloom over the earth, were followed by summers fresh, fair and beautiful, which this child of misfortune had never seen, except from grated windows, and little flights into the prison garden, where she was permitted to wander, at times, when she could be induced to leave her father's side.

James Winfred had been tried for murder and robbery, and upon circumstantial evidence, imprisoned for life. His position had ever been one of the utmost respectability previous to his trial, and everything in his nature and bearing, had gone to substantiate his denial of the crime. Still, proofs were so strong against him, as to seem beyond dispute. Any other man might have been hung. He was imprisoned for life.

And to prison he went in the bloom and freshness of his manhood, followed by his young wife whose heart broke under the burthen he could ill sustain, and live. Better far, had both young lives gone out together. But God willed it otherwise. The devoted creature stayed with him day after day, refusing every effort or entreaty to leave his side, until little Ollie first opened her brown eyes to the light. Then as the first pulses of a new existence throbbed upon earth, the life that had created it, slowly ebbed away. Mrs. Winfred died two hours after her child's birth, and was buried from the cell of her husband's prison-house.

Ollie was, for the first few months, the charge of the kind-hearted matron. But the yearning heart of the sorrowing father refused to give her up to strangers. He would beg her for a few hours, and fondle her with such tenderness, that the woman could not bear to keep her from him. Soon he was suffered to keep her all day. By-and-by, she slept

upon his bosom—became his idol. Day and night
he clung closer and closer to this last earthly tie.
She was everything to him. The glance of her
pure eyes, was his sole light; the sound of her
baby voice, his only music. She combined everything that he had lost—love, honor, freedom—all, all
of earth! What wonder that he worshiped her.
And yet, though he taught her little feet their first
steps, and guided her child-tones in the sweet lisp-
ing of his name—though as weeks, months and
years rolled on, and she was his companion, receiving all that she could know of the outer world,
through his experience, and was moulded in mind
and manner after his ideal—though she became
more than the life pulsing at his heart—the only
thing he could leave behind him, for her, was a
memory of his shame. She would carry that into
the world, and the world would fan the sparks she
could scarcely comprehend, into an undying flame.
Perhaps the fire would burn up and extinguish all
else in her heart. The sufferings that the unfortunate entail upon their innocent children, often
crush the remembrances of love and gentleness, and
they are made to see and remember only the evil,
cursing the hour that brought them into an existence blackened by shame. Would it be so with
James Winfred's helpless daughter? A pang of
inexpressible agony shot through the long-tried
heart of the dying man, as he asked himself the
question. Would his child ever be driven from a
remembrance of his love, and made to remember
the sin the world had charged upon him, and which

he had been made to expiate through years that had traced through his soul like waves of consuming fire? God forbid!

"Oh," he breathed, as the dash of the waves broke louder and louder upon the ear, stilling to earthly sounds, and waking to the throbbings of eternity. "Father, take away this last cloud from my life. Let me die with the hope that my memory may not in after years be despised by my innocent child when I shall have passed from the sufferings Thou hast been pleased to make me endure! Thou seest me innocent—let her not suffer the consequences of guilt. Or, if it please Thee to order it otherwise, give her strength to bear. But, oh God, let not my child, whom I so love, ever grow to hate the memory of her father."

The last sentence was breathed audibly, and fell upon the child's ears. She lifted her face from where it rested beside him, and said in clear, thrilling tones:

"My father, be not afraid. I feel that you have suffered·unjustly. You have a thousand times told me so. Through my whole life you have impressed me with truth as the one great and beautiful principle of life. In your death-hour, could I believe you capable of falsehood! You say you are innocent, and no trial, however great, could make me think you guilty, or ashamed to call you father. I shall never forget you. I shall always love you. Should I live an hundred years, you will live in my heart as the very embodiment of all you have taught me to believe—noble, generous, pure and good."

Even to James Winfred's ears, the tones of his child's voice seemed unnatural in their grave earnestness. Old-fashioned and unchild-like she must naturally be, with none but a sorrowing, embittered man for a life-long companion. Still, such words were strange to come from her lips. Was it a divine influence that prompted it to set the soul of the dying man at rest? He accepted it as such, and folded his hands while a peaceful smile crept around his lips.

Slowly, slowly the shadows crept over the wan face. The troubled eyes were calm, at last; the purple lips smiling. A great, sublime faith stilled the tempest of grief that had arisen for the helpless child he was leaving behind him. God, the Father, would watch over her. Through all his suffering, he had not lost his trust in divine mercy, though in hours of intense agony, he had sometimes rebelled. Had not Jesus suffered more? Why should he refuse to taste of a cup the Saviour had been compelled to drink to the dregs?

An hour passed without a word having been spoken, after Ollie's voice had uttered the answer to his prayer. She clasped his cold hands in hers, and stood with her little white face bent above him —her brown eyes gathering the shadows that passed from his.

Ah, it was a sorrowful picture—that little child watching alone over a dying father, from a morbid sense of duty crushing down the sorrows of her bursting heart, and no voice to soothe and comfort her with words of sympathy.

Who shall describe the darkness and misery of the hours that followed? She never once moved, or took her eyes from his face. She saw the eyes fix at last in the glazed stare that heralds death, and felt that the struggle was nearly over. Colder and colder grew the hands in her clasp. Whiter and whiter became the face. She heard the faint breathings dying to still greater faintness, and then it was hushed. At last she put one little hand into his bosom, feeling for his heart. The pulse was still. Not a throb fed the spark of hope struggling in the child's breast. Then she knew he was dead. This was what he had described to her many a time, and it had come. She did not shrink away in fear and awe as most children would have done. But she felt that a great change had come, and that a wide gulf separated her from her dear father. It was as if a light, guiding her steps through the vastness and unexplored depths of an unknown wilderness, had suddenly been extinguished, and she was left to grope helplessly on alone, amid dangers that might rise on every side. In all its bitter fullness, she felt her deep loss, and with all the strength of a strong, wild nature, she sorrowed. No need, now, to hush the moans of agony. She knew, poor child, that they could no longer pain him. He had passed beyond the sound of her distress. With her white, wet face pressed upon the still heart, she moaned in the bitterness of her bereavement—wept, till strength gave way. And when the turnkey came, he found her cold and senseless, upon the bosom of her dead father.

CHAPTER II.

A DEEP undercurrent of excitement was running through the great body of Madam Lansing's fashionable seminary. Groups of girls were gathered everywhere, talking in subdued tones. Something unusual had occurred. They were busily preparing for examination, and, as is usually the case, became earnest, eager, and fearful as to the result, when a new stimulant was added to their energies. An unknown gentleman had appeared, and offered a splendid diamond bracelet as a prize for the young lady who should prove herself the most perfect mistress of music. She must play piano, harp, and guitar. The thing was unusual, and very exciting. Madam Lansing boasted a few very good musicians, and had given permission to her pupils to compete for the prize. It would be something for her school to turn out so accomplished a scholar as must win such a prize, and she was eager and anxious as well as they. She was too wise, however, to let her anxiety be seen, and forbade the discussion of the subject after having given her approval, and enjoined them to make good use of the time allowed for their preparation. But she could not still the strong tide of excitement that ran through the school. Some were wild with hope ; others, less fortunate in their acquirements, were in despair. Every moment they dared give the subject, was seized for its discussion, under cover. There was little promise of study for a few days to come, after such an event as that.

In a far corner of the recitation-room sat a tall, pale girl of seventeen or eighteen years. She held a book in her hand ; but her eyes were fixed upon the clouds which she could see from the window, and there was a thought in their depths beyond the light babble of the many tongues chattering around her. Something remarkable there was in her whole appearance. It was a very girlish face, taking it in a casual light. A fair, high brow shaded by soft, brown curls, that fell in a wealth of rich beauty over her shoulders ; a cheek full and rounded, with regular, ivory-white teeth, and a general contour of feature very pleasant to behold. But in the deep brown eyes, fringed by their long lashes, lay the chief beauty of the girl's face. Their expression was enhanced and deepened to a great degree by the full, rosy lips ; and in both combined you read firmness, deep, earnest feeling, and high resolve. There was that in both eyes and mouth that spoke of suffering—suffering too intense for expression. The wells of those eyes carried unutterable sadness. The lines drawn about the mouth traced deep weariness, but sweet patience.

She was very slender, and the black dress fitting closely to her rounded form, contrasting with the pearly whiteness of her skin, gave her an elegant appearance few young girls possess. There was

stately dignity and girlish grace in every movement.
This fair young girl was called the "prodigy" by
less favored ladies of the school; but it was in bitter
mockery that stung, and petty envy that gave birth
to contempt. She was undoubtedly the best scholar
there. Her intellectual powers were beyond medi-
ocrity. By some she had been already dubbed
"blue," because no one was so perfect in every
branch of her studies as she. No mind grasped,
analyzed and absorbed ideas, putting them to use,
as did hers. And yet she was despised by all, or
almost all around her—despised for her beauty, her
talents, her acquirements. Poor and obscure, she
had still steadily mounted the ladder, and, in spite
of every barrier, had attained a point they might
not hope to reach. What wonder if ire was excited?
It is human nature. Do any of us like to see others,
struggling and toiling through difficulties, outstrip
us in an object, when we have every advantage they
lack, and still can not attain it? No. And it brings
us very, very bitter and unholy feelings, sometimes,
to see ourselves defeated under such circumstances.

Still, absorbed in her own thoughts, the girl sat at
the desk, when a rude voice broke in upon her rev-
erie:

"I say, Olive, are you deaf? I have spoken to
you three times. Why do you not answer me?"

The young lady turned with a stare and a shiver,
but said politely:

"I beg your pardon. I did not hear you. What
is it?"

"None are so deaf as those who do not want to

hear," was the insolent response. "Some people take airs upon themselves with precious little grounds. I asked you if you meant to compete for the prize?"

"The prize? What prize?"

"Tush! What an actress you are! To pretend you don't know what 'prize,' when the whole school's gone mad over it! Of course you will, though. You've got too high an opinion of your abilities, not to show them off on such an occasion."

"I am sure I do not understand your meaning," she replied gravely. "You are talking riddles!"

"I know better! you do know. Why, it is impossible not to have heard about the splendid diamond bracelet that has been offered as a prize, by some old, eccentric nabob, who chooses to throw away his money for the small pleasure of seeing who can drum the hardest upon the piano."

Her listener sat passive and dignified. She did not know anything of the offer before, and cared little for gossip. She knew too well how excitable school girls are over trifles, and had deemed the present stir of no importance. The haughty girl addressing her now, fired up at her look and became more insolent.

"You are provoking beyond measure! I hate self-importance and deceit above everything; and you are the quintessence of both."

A flush mounted to the fair forehead, but faded instantly. A slight, gentle, blue-eyed girl close by, spoke up stoutly now in her defense:

"Miss Ollie, why do you permit such insolence?

I could not hear myself called deceitful and self-important, openly, and not openly resent it."

Olive turned her large eyes gravely upon the speaker, and answered with quiet gravity:

"Nay, Miss Giles; if people forget to be ladylike, we need not make ourselves their equals by like actions. A *lady* will not insult me without reason. With others I have nothing to do."

A passionate outburst followed this speech, and the girl who had first spoken came up close to her, and clasped a hand tightly over her arm, hissing out in her hot passion:

"Olive Winfred, if you dare to use such words again in reference to me, a *gentleman's* daughter, I'll have you turned from this school, as sure as my name is Agnes Ives. *You* to speak thus! *You!* What are you, pray, that you set yourself up for riding on such high horses! The daughter of a *felon!* A prison child all your life, with its taint still around you! I will never bear more from you after this, let me warn you. I have borne enough in times past. Now you must look out for yourself."

Olive rose from her seat, white and quivering. It was not the first time she had been stabbed in a like manner. For five years she had borne it from every little, petty-minded thing who chose to make her misery their amusement. But feeling was not dead. The stings grew keener as the wounds were probed, and were becoming unbearable.

"Oh, for shame, Agnes!" cried Helen Giles, her heart full of pity and indignation, as Olive crossed the room. "How can she help what her father did?"

"If she can not help it, she should still remember her place. A more hateful thing does not breathe than she; but she has the air of a queen. One would think her the finest lady of the land, judging from her own actions."

"A neat compliment," replied Helen significantly. "It is not all persons who can. be judged ladies 'by their actions.' But you have expressed it precisely. I never saw Olive Winfred otherwise than perfectly ladylike in my life, and yet no girl in the school has been so tried as she. Her notions of right exceed the standard of the masses, and she carries out every principle she holds, most beautifully."

Agnes stood before her school-mate, her angry eyes flashing wondering glances on the fair face, now lighted by a lovely impulse. She was struck dumb by this unexpected defense.

"I think you have taken leave of your senses!" she said, at length. "You have, or you'd never take up for that girl—insolent thing! But I am served rightly for noticing her at all. When people stoop to their inferiors, the consequences are sure to prove mortifying. It shall be a lesson to me. Henceforth I do not notice her, and those who value my friendship will not. More than this, Madame will send her from this place soon, or the best scholars she has will be withdrawn. I shall take care to mention what kind of people we have to associate with."

She turned and joined another group, where the topic was discussed excitably till called to order and study by. the bell. Then Olive again made her appearance, and, more than usually quiet, took her place at her desk. There were tears still on the calm cheek, and for a long time they hung silently upon the lashes. Helen's sympathizing glance and the angry looks bent upon her from resentful eyes, were alike unheeded. She was busy with her own thoughts.

How hard a task it was, with her proud, sensitive nature, to bear patiently that to which she had been subjected so long. Sometimes she felt as if she should go mad. Would it ever be thus? Must she go on through life thus scourged daily—scoffed at, despised, scorned? What were her gifts or acquirements, if they must ever prove useless to win love and happiness? The past was bitter; the future looked dark. She could hope for nothing better. It was her dower—her only dower from childhood up. And yet, just so must life go on, till the sands run out, and she was left in peace beyond the reach of human stings.

Something like despair bowed the young head when the duties of the day were past, and she could sit down in her own room to think over the bitterness of her lot. Tears were spent. Only moans came faintly over the white lips now. She felt as if life was no longer worth the struggle to maintain it, and wished she might die and be at rest.

A light tap upon the door roused her at length, and to her faint "come in" one of the teachers entered. She was a grave, pleasant-faced woman. Kind to all, she won especially upon the feelings of the lonely and desolate who longed for sympathy. Now with gentle mien, she came and sat down beside her grieving pupil, and took the bright head on her knee.

"Do not despair, my child. Helen Giles has told me what passed to-day, and I feel deeply grieved and indignant that it should have occurred. Yet be patient, dear. All will grow brighter after awhile. I have come to comfort you, and to tell you that I am proud of your behavior under the trials put upon you by the more fortunate of your school-mates. Not one of them can boast such acquirements, such native talent, or wondrous self-control as yours. You are a noble girl, and carry out most beautifully the great principles of life you have adopted. Again I say that I feel proud of you. So does the lady principal. She appreciates fully your character, and she bade me say as much, and also to tell you that it is her wish that you enter the lists as competitor for the prize."

Ollie lifted her pale face quickly, her breath coming in short, quick gasps.

"She bade you tell me that? Why?" she asked tremblingly.

"Because she has confidence in your power, and wishes you to be appreciated by those whose opinions are of value. You are here for the education of a teacher, my dear; and such a success would prove a card of inestimable value. It will prove good for the school, also, and there is not one in it to whom we could wish success so heartily as to yourself."

The girl's tears came now, thick and fast. She clasped the teacher's hand to her lips gratefully.

"Oh, it is worth something to hear this from

you !" she murmured. "My patience has not all been vain, my struggles useless!"

"No. Far from it. They have won our esteem and love, as no others have. Your trials, borne so meekly, must have won admiration and respect anywhere. It is only those who sink in the scale beside you, who could dislike or injure."

"Thank you for this sweet comfort," said Ollie gratefully. "Yet, should I do this, I will make enemies of the whole school," she continued thoughtfully. "If I entered the lists, I should do my best to win—not for the sake of the gift, but my reputation. If I succeeded, they would all hate me for having dared to rival them. Oh, I had better not!"

"Nonsense, child. What will it matter? You leave the school this vacation, and could not feel annoyed by them in future. They would soon forget it. If people hate us without just cause, there is no need for us to crush or retard our own interests. You have equal right to this advantage. Use it."

"Suppose I fail?"

"When did you ever fail in an undertaking you entered into with your whole heart? Is it not your repeated success which has made you so many enemies?"

"Not altogether, I think, ma'am. My poor father's misfortune and my poverty have had much to do with it. How can they bear that a child of charity, on whom rests the stains of a dishonored parent, should meet with them on equal ground? To them, I am inferior. They think I should be kept back, and allowed fewer advantages than themselves."

"Well, it does not matter, so long as you are innocent, good and noble in yourself. You are more than their equals, and you have no right to abuse God-given power by self-depreciation. Ollie, you *will* do your best to win this prize?"

"Yes," she responded slowly, after a moment's thought. "I will try, for your sake and my dear lady principal's. You have encouraged me so kindly through these long years, I owe you a debt I would fain repay. I will gratify you in this. It is for your sake I shall strive and pray for success—not my own."

The teacher stooped and kissed her, and then left the room.

———

Time sped away, and the grand examination drew nigh. The general excitement had spread far and near. Relatives and friends of the pupils, drawn by the peculiar interest of the occasion, came flocking in, and on the evening in which the trial was to be made, the house was filled to overflowing. Wreaths of flowers twined every pillar, festooned every arch in the long room devoted to the exhibition. A raised platform at one end bore the various instruments, around which the teachers were ranged in a semicircle. A little to the right of this platform, and communicating with it, another platform was raised for the accommodation of the lady principal and her distinguished guest. The audience gathered beneath, were packed as tightly as seats could be placed for their accommodation, while over the whole, many colored lights broke gorgeously, and the spirit of excitement stirred like the vast waves of the mighty deep.

One by one the pupils were led forth, dressed in light, flowing robes, looped up with ribbons and flowers. Six comprised the whole number announced for competition, and Agnes Ives, reserving her strength for the effort, declared her purpose of waiting until the last. She was buoyant and confident. She knew she played well, and depended upon the last impression to win the prize.

All, however, acquitted themselves well. The principal's lips were wreathed in smiles of triumphant pleasure, as they retired amid bursts of applause.

And now a flush of proud consciousness was on the cheek of the brilliant beauty as she was led forth. More regal in her person and tastes, her dress differed as well from the simple robes of her mates. She had assumed a rich dress of white silk, over which a fine robe of lace floated, looped up with sprays of pearl. Her white arms were banded with shining jewels, while a tiara of the same beautiful and chaste ornaments she had chosen for her dress, rose above the midnight blackness of her hair. Applause greeted her appearance. Applause broke forth at each effort she made to prove herself the queen of song. She left the stage amid thunders of delight—delight wakened as much by her personal beauty as her skillful performances.

It was so arranged that each pupil, as she retired,

could take a seat just in the rear of the teacher's, and as Agnes assumed hers in full view of the audience, her heart throbbed with expectation. She looked for the old white-haired man, seated by the principal, to rise, and coming forward in full view of that great, enthusiastic crowd, clasp her arm with the sparkling diamonds she could almost see flashing beneath the closed lid of the case beside him.

There was a hush, sudden and profound. A light figure was led forward. No one recognized it in the first moment of bewildered surprise. The soft folds of pure white muslin were confined at the waist with a shining belt of gold, while loose sleeves of the same, open from the shoulder and flowing from the arms, gave it the appearance of angelic beauty. Soft, lustrous brown curls swept back from the broad, white brow, fell away to her waist in free, luxuriant masses; and the pale face, with its calm yet soul-lit eyes, beamed full upon the waiting assembly—an embodiment of perfect beauty.

A ballad first, accompanied by the guitar, sitting with child-like grace at the feet of the music-master. Then followed a grand instrumental piece, written for the piano. It was very difficult, exceedingly sweet and powerful. Agnes had chosen the sublime, and bewildered her hearers with that grandeur. Her rival had chosen the grand also, lifting her hearers gradually to the most elevated point of interest, and then held them thrilled by tones of such heavenly sweetness and power as seldom wake the sparks of *divine* appreciation within us. Then she brought them back slowly, sadly, out of the great world of sound, fading upon their senses, in light, rippling waves, dying at length in soft, purling murmurs.

Her success might have been complete here, without addition; but the grand finale was reserved for the harp, before which she at last sat, flushing and quivering with excitement. The soul of music was stirred within her. At that moment everything else was forgotten. The brilliant lights and assembled faces faded from sight as her light hand swept the trembling chords, and her voice rose solemnly in a song of praise beneath whose power every heart thrilled. Now the large eyes grew deep and humid, lifting upward their intense glance as if to pierce and penetrate the throne with their profound adoration of the divine. The little pearl-white finger stealing softly over, yet drawing full, rich notes from the chords; the flowing hair and airy drapery—all combined, rendered her a creature of more than earthly beauty. Not a sound arose to jar upon the waves of melody that flowed from her lips. Entranced, subdued, enthralled, they listened till she had finished, and then a roll of applause as of reverberating thunder, shook the building to its center.

Agnes Ives covered her face with her handkerchief and groaned. The gentleman was at Ollie's side, the sparkling jewels glittering in his hand. He led the young lady before the audience again ere she had time to seat herself, and in clear, distinct tones, awarded to her the prize put up that night for competition. His judgment was applauded spontaneously by the audience as one voice, and turning his face to her, he clasped the bracelet on her arm.

Congratulations followed. Teachers and pupils, with some exceptions of the latter, crowded around her, and in the confusion that succeeded, Agnes Ives made her escape, burning with rage and mortification.

CHAPTER III.

MONTHS had passed away. A great change had
come over Ollie Winfred. The unnatural gravity
and dignity of manner, had given way to a more
girlish lightness and gaiety of manner. Clouds
were slowly rolling from the sky of her young life,
and the dawn of love was brightening it to rosy
light. She had found one who could look upon her
in full appreciation of her merit, who standing beside a pillar of the school-room on that night, had
witnessed her approach with feelings akin to bewilderment. Her voice carried him away with its
matchless power and beauty, and he could not rest
until he had sought an interview with the lady
principal, and learned something of the young
songstress.

She told him her painful history frankly and fully,
urged to it by Ollie, who, learning his motive, refused to be sought except through a full knowledge
of that history. She told him of the father's unhappy death, and the child's removal to her school,
where a charitable association had educated her for
a teacher.

Yet what did all this signify to him who sought
her? Brilliant, beautiful and good, she was fitted

to adorn society as no other he had ever met. He would take her to distant climes where, safe from old prejudices, he could proudly call her his, and claim for her the homage which was her due.

Ollie found him generous, manly and noble. He won upon her regard by his manner, almost imperceptibly. His respectful tenderness of manner was as if he addressed a beloved queen. Shut out from elevated associations on equal grounds, and all her life starved for true unselfish affection, what wonder if she yielded herself to the entrancing sweetness of this new existence, and forget past sorrow in present joy?

We will not dwell upon the few bright weeks that preceded the wedding of Ollie Winfred—the poor prisoner's only child. Suffice it to say that in happiness and joy the ceremony was performed in the church where she had heard the word of God preached for five years. Solemnly and with deep reverence she took upon herself the vows that bound her to another, her whole soul elate and profoundly happy with the knowledge of the great duties that were to crown her future life and fix her in woman's destined sphere of usefulness.

Immediately after the ceremony, they entered a carriage and were driven away. Four days later, they embarked for Europe, and set sail under the happiest auspices.

Dear reader, would that I might here let fall the curtain and leave to your imagination the coloring of the picture I have drawn but faintly. Yet I may not do it, for the most important period of life does

not pass with one's girlhood. We do not close the
gates of interest on the boundaries. of wedded life.
It is then that the real and solemn interests of life
begin. For a little time we must still trace our her-
oine through the mazes of an eventful existence.

29*

CHAPTER IV.

A WILD, tempestuous night! Winds wailed around the building, windows rattled, trees writhed beneath the fury of a beating blast.

Seated before the glowing grate in her own luxurious chamber, Olive Alban listened to the saddening sounds with starting tears. Four years a wife, yet little changed, except it be that she was thinner and paler than when we last saw her at the marriage altar. Happy she had been, yet changes had come. A little girl, with a fair face and sunny temper, she had laid to rest in the church-yard, and to-night the beloved father of that child slept upon the field of battle, exposed to the wind and rains.

Many another wife and mother had sat as did she, with tear-wet cheeks and sorrowing hearts. Yet few bore the trial with more strength and cheerfulness generally. She felt that he had done right thus to leave her side and home for freedom's sake, and though her yearning heart bowed sadly under the need of his absence, she would not murmur nor repine.

Presently she rose and went to the piano. Sad notes only could come from her lips on a night like this. She remembered when her voice had won her

her dearest earthly treasure, and wished now that he might hear the cry welling up from her heart, to tell him of her love—to breathe to him encouragement.

> "How sadly and coldly the wind wails to-night,
> How heavy the passage of him in his flight!
> My heart's reft of sadness, my voice of its cheer,
> For one who hath blessed me with love is not here.
> The damp earth receives him—the earth, bare and cold,
> While dark clouds their mantle will over him fold,
> And the wild winds will whistle a drear lullaby
> While I sit me here sadly to weep and to sigh.

> "Yet, while hundreds are sleeping the slumber of death,
> And others are resting the heavens beneath,
> While the lashes of many lie wet on the cheek
> With the sorrows that tears and prayers only can speak,
> While hearthstones grow cold, and music is hushed,
> And cheeks with the tint of the rose no more flushed,
> While sad hearts must break 'neath the woes of this war,
> I rejoice, my darling, to know you are there.

> "My dearest one, rest thee, God help thee to rest,
> Though to-night with no kiss will thy slumber be blest,
> Though my bosom may pillow no more thy dear head,
> And to-morrow thou sleepest 'mid thousands of dead.
> Thou hast left me, thy home and the pleasures of youth,
> And offered thy strength in defense of the truth;
> And God, who is strong in the cause of the just
> And the right, will shield and protect thee, I trust."

Tears still hung upon her lashes when she left the piano, but the light of a trustful heart shone from the depths of her eyes. Ah! why should such light ever be doomed to fade!

Wailing winds continued. Mournful as a funeral anthem, they swept around her. Lifting the curtain and throwing back the shutters, she looked forth upon the night with pitying eyes, thinking of the hundreds who were stretched for scant repose upon the storm-drenched earth.

Her eyes fell in their wanderings, upon the gate leading into the road beyond the lawn. For one moment the clouds drifted from the face of the moon, and by her obscure light, she saw a form pass through and come toward her. He wore the uniform of a brigadier-general, and it needed no second glance to tell her who it was. With trembling eagerness, she dropped the curtain, and flew down stairs to the hall to welcome her husband home; words of joy and thankfulness upon her lips, ready to pour forth as soon as he should reach her side.

One minute. He did not ring. She could not wait. Unfastening the bolts with her own trembling fingers, she flung wide the .door, suffering the wind to sweep with a hiss and gust into the hall.

Again the moon was hidden. Black darkness was beyond. She was glad the light streamed brightly from the hall chandelier to guide her darling's step to the loved shelter awaiting him, yet she strained her eyes vainly to catch a glimpse of his form. He seemed long in coming. Growing impatient for the sound of his voice, she called his name.

"Horace! Horace! Ah, how glad I am to bid you welcome to your home this stormy night! Hasten, dearest!" but no manly voice with its hearty ring of cheer responded. A nameless chill

"With an exclamation of mingled joy, grief and love, she sprang from the couch."—*Page* 345.

crept over her, and she called again, but almost fearfully.

" Horace, where are you ?"

Still no response. She waited a minute, shivering in the chilly air, but no steps were heard upon the marble porch of the dwelling, and feeling convinced of having been deceived, she turned once more to her lonely chamber; a nameless fear and dread deepening the sadness that weighed upon her heart.

Hours passed ere sleep visited her tear-wet pillow that night. She could not banish the painful illusion. She had seemed to see her husband so plainly, she could not give up the hope that he might have returned and would still come to her yet. But when hours had sped, and still he came not, she knew that fancy had deceived her, and at length calmed herself to slumber.

The little clock upon her mantle striking four, awakened her. A light from the grate glowed and flickered over every object, showing them distinctly, and there, in his large easy chair, sat her husband, his arm on the arm of the chair, his cheek resting upon his hand. He seemed regarding her with ineffable tenderness, a sad and mournful smile hovering about his lips. The first rapid glance showed her all this; also that a broad, red scar crossed the high, white brow in an oblique line.

With an exclamation of mingled joy, grief and love, she sprang from the couch, and with extended arms approached him, throwing herself at his side, the better to clasp him in her arms. But instead of folding him in a loving embrace, a cold wind swep⁺

over her, and her frame felt a jar as of an electric shock. A sudden blindness seized her, as if a mist had gathered over her eyes. When it passed away, she was kneeling by an empty chair!

"Missis Ollie, Mrs. Pearly has sent up to ask will you please come down to her house a little while. Her baby died last night."

Olive lifted her white face from the cushion by which she knelt, and asked sadly:

"Dead, you say, Mandy? Poor babe! poor mother! Yes, tell her I will come at once."

"Oh, you are ill yourself," cried the girl, as her mistress rose from the carpet. "Don't go, Missis Ollie. You are as white as a sheet. Let me tell her you are sick."

"No, say that I am coming," returned the lady steadily. "Never mind me, Mandy. I am not ill; only a little nervous and disturbed."

The girl turned away reluctantly, and Mrs. Alban, going to her wardrobe, took from it a dark street dress, and calling her maid, arrayed herself for a walk.

She had not far to go, and soon reached the house of mourning. There she found the mother wild with grief, while the little form of her babe, white and still, reposed in death, free from its sufferings.

Shedding tears of genuine sympathy, she took the poor mother's head upon her gentle breast, and strove to soothe and comfort her. No touch than hers could have been softer, no voice more sweet and tender. With a heavy weight upon her own heart, she took up another's grief and tried to lighten it.

All day she remained near her, with busy fingers smoothing the difficulties that lay in the path of the mourners. They were poor, though of the best parentage. Reverses had come, and she had on many previous occasions found means of helping them in a manner that had won their deepest gratitude and love.

Now she sat near the bereaved mother who lay upon a sofa, and while breathing words of sympathy and kindness, cut and fashioned the little garments for the dead. A sweet earnestness was in her face; a tender light in her eye, while the dark velvet of her bodice, made her pale face appear more pale. The father sat near, and regarded her through his tears. Every look and tone touched his heart strangely. He noted the soft bands of brown hair, the sweet, grave mouth, the little white fingers so steadily plying the needle; and a reminiscence of some one whom he had met years ago, seemed slowly rising. He nearly forgot his sorrow in the effort to recall the features so strikingly like those before him. Almost bewildered, he sat for hours watching her as one entranced, until she rose and went into the room where the dead child lay.

She had finished what she had been working upon, and now arrayed the babe in the little white dress that was to take the place of a shroud. Almost like life the little creature looked, and she felt pleased with the effect. She thought it cruel to have the last impression of a lost one engraved upon the mind, arrayed in long robes that speak only of the grave. As nearly as possible, she preferred to see them look as when in life, wearing some dress familiar to sight. Thus might it seem the more true that "they are not dead, but sleep."

A mist gathered over her eyes as she gazed at the beautiful little face. Slowly it seemed to fade from her sight, and in its place her husband lay, every outline of form and feature distinct.

With a half smothered cry, she clasped her hands over her eyes to shut out the sight. When she removed them again, the vision had fled, and the child lay in its calm beauty before her !

Who shall tell what a sad and troubled heart she carried in her bosom after these strange events! Several days passed as in a dream. She attended the funeral, afterward selecting and arranging mourning for the lady, busying herself forcibly to drown the sad thoughts and fears that haunted her.

On the fifth night from that on which she had seen her husband approach the house, a letter was brought her, penned in a strange hand.

Premonitory fear told her the contents. When her trembling fingers broke the seal, she expected to read the death-knell to every hope, and she was not mistaken. In a late battle, amid the bravest of the brave, he had fallen, surviving his wounds but a few hours. A few lines penned by his hand in his death hours, fell from the missive, in which he bade her farewell. The date was five days back—the hour of his death the same in which she saw him seated in her chamber. He wrote :

"My wife : I have received my death wound. I

have only a moment to breath undying love, a prayer for you, and a farewell. I am with you in spirit, dearest. I see you as you sit thinking of me, and my soul yearns in tenderness over your tenderness, and pity for your grief when news shall reach you of my fall. Good and blessed angel wife, we shall meet again. I grow faint! In God's care I leave you, commending you to His mercy for comfort in your affliction."

The trembling hand had essayed more, but failed. No more should she listen to the dear voice; no more gaze upon the loved features. Widowed and childless, once more alone, the long maintained struggle against sorrow gave way, and for a time oblivion wrapped her in a merciful unconsciousness.

The remains of the beloved lost one came home, and the sad funeral rites were performed. Heavily affliction had laid her hand upon this child of sorrow. She had fondly dreamed a different fate—had dared to picture a future of pride and joy the good and brave only may hope to win from noble deeds. Her husband in his true patriotism and strong manhood, was sufficient to call up visions of this glorious future we all love to dream of and hope to enjoy; and yet where do often these visions end? Alas! the grave covers many a hope as fair, and death cuts down relentlessly every aspiration that springs in the human heart.

Wearily she took up the burden of life, now lonely and desolate. The only pure joy her life had known was in the years of her happy wifehood.
30

Now the future, stripped of that blessing, looked blank and joyless. Had Olive Alban been less noble in her nature, and content to live without a purpose, she could not have endured the long prospective future blank that stretched out before her. But she was not of that cast, and straightway began to look about her for greater means of usefulness, that she might the more readily learn to bear her lot in patience.

Useful she had ever been, and beloved by all who came within the circle of her influence. But now, fired by noble impulses, it spread wider. A pleasant circle of friends she had about her, whose esteem and gratitude were very dear to her in her bereavement. There was something to live for in their affection; and as she grew more accustomed to her loss, she appreciated this kindly feeling the more as extending her sphere of usefulness.

Wealth, gentle manners and sympathetic feeling, paved her a free way into all classes, giving her power none used so wisely. And thus for years it must have gone on, had not an old enemy, sprung from some unknown quarter, once more crossed her path and sowed the seeds of bitterness which were to yield sorrowful fruits for the last years of her unhappy life.

One morning a friend called some time after Mr. Alban's death, and imparted a piece of news. All news connected with those around us, have more or less interest, and Ollie was not free from this strange feeling when her friend mentioned names known to her.

"Young Gerald Marcy has brought home a bride," she said pleasantly. "A most beautiful, sparkling creature, though I confess there is a fierce independence in her dark eyes that rather repels me. I have just been to call upon her, and cannot imagine where that harum scarum fellow could have found her. She is, as I say, beautiful, and very accomplished, with a winning fascination of manner very peculiar."

"Do you know who she was," asked Ollie.

"No. A Miss Ivers, Kivers, or something of that sort. I can't remember the name. I think he met her first at a fashionable watering-place, where she was a great belle—afterward visited and married her, though I hardly remember where. Her reception was splendid."

"Will they reside here?"

"O yes. Mr. Marcy will be one of our nearest neighbors. They have taken the Bower cottage."

"Indeed? That will be pleasant for you!"

The conversation changed to other topics, and after awhile Ollie thought but little more about it, except the usual interest of giving a pleasing addition to their circle of society, until they met. Then in Mrs. Marcy, she at once recognized her old tormenter, Agnes Ives. The recognition was mutual. One who had so mortally offended her as Ollie Winfred, never could be forgiven by the haughty girl, and she hated her too much to strive to conceal it.

Those who witnessed the meeting were surprised beyond measure. Agnes drew herself up haughtily while Ollie's paling and flushing face told painfully her remembrance of past wrongs. When questioned, generous Olive was silent on the subjects most painful to her enemy, quietly answering that she was a pupil in the same school, and that they did not get on together very well. Not so lenient was Agnes. She proclaimed in haughty confidence her sovereign contempt for the " charity child, the felon's daughter, whom all the girls at school had despised." Everybody was dumbfounded. Curiosity and excitement were rife and Agnes gloried in giving her own version of their old school life.

Ollie's friends were numerous, and many refused indignantly to believe, others generously defended, but as she held herself aloof, forbearing to make good her own part by exposing Agnes, the latter soon gained ground, especially amongst the younger classes, and in a very little time, her enemy had shattered and scattered her adherents as the autumn blasts shake the many colored leaves from a tree, leaving her nearly stripped and bare of a single friend, while they, faithless, turned their worthless allegiance to her destroyer.

Strange how soon evil can eclipse good influences, and public opinion change! All the great kindness she had shown, and the good done them, seemed forgotten in a little while, or regarded more as a condescension to accept than a favor received. What the lady of wealth and spotless character gave was forgotten when a felon's daughter became the almoner. All the old bitterness of life came back with redoubled intensity, and at a time when grief and affliction rendered her less fit to cope with it. Day after day, Ollie Alban faded and pined away beneath her unshared burden. Agnes standing proudly aloof and witnessing the fruits of her labor, gloried in the downfall from the hight of respect, love and power! It were a bitter thing to have seen Ollie maintaining her place at the head of a circle where she was ambitious to move its queen, and all the fibres of her nature had risen against it. The complete success was satisfying even to her.

At last the suffering woman sank under her afflictions. She could not leave her room, and the rumor went abroad that she was dying. A few, firm in the end, though moving at the first onset against her, remorsefully came back to comfort her last hours. But for her, one comfort only remained for earth to afford; and that was a strange fulfillment of a life-long desire.

One day Mr. Pearly came and begged to be allowed to see her. He had them raise her up with pillows, and at his urgent entreaty leave them alone. His manner was painfully agitated, and his hands shook as he nervously brushed the hair from his brow ere he began.

"Mrs. Alban, you see before you a miserable man. I dared not let you die without easing my heart of some of the pain which is fast killing me. Of late I have heard your name mentioned often, and the discussion led to a knowledge of your history. I learned your maiden name, and then it was that I remembered whose features yours resembled. On the day my boy died and your kindness aided us to bury him, I was strangely troubled by something in your face, which seemed to recall some one, and until a short time since, remained in doubt. It was your mother," he went on, growing more and more agitated. " I saw her once or twice, and never forgot the sweetness of her fair young features. Your father was once my friend. But I wronged him, and we parted. After that I fell into bad habits, got into trouble, and in a desperate moment, was guilty of a crime. The story is too long to relate now, but by strange circumstances, I escaped suspicion, and they fixed upon Mr. Winfred. Glad to see this loop-hole through which I might pass, and elated at my power of gratifying a grudge, I left him to suffer for my crime. But no peace has been mine since that day. Wealth, power, friends, everything, have melted and faded away. From place to place I have wandered, burying one after another of my children, until my last now lies beneath the sod. His grave-clothes *you* prepared, his funeral expenses, *your* bounty defrayed. You, the daughter of my victim, have been our kindest friend! Innocent, good and pure you have suffered the wrong of my doing, even unto death, as did your father before you, while I, in my cowardice, have never dared till now, when you are near the grave, attempt to repair the wrong. I do not ask forgiveness. Too great has been my crime. But God has punished me terribly, and His justice I acknowledge. Too late I come to you with my confession except to render your dying hour sweeter with the knowledge of his—your father's innocence."

He ceased, his white face convulsed with remorse. Hers was lifted with grateful thanks, and a breath of thrilling sweetness bore a prayer to the throne of God:

"Father, thy innocence I knew, but now, that innocence proved, I come to thee rejoicing that my faith in thee has wavered not! Oh, God! receive my thanks. I die in peace!"

Four days later, Olive Alban was laid beside her husband and her child. In her will, all her wealth had been assigned to benevolent purposes, among others a handsome legacy for Mrs. Pearly, whose position she had often thought upon with compassion. Strange how mysterious powers work out Divine vengeance on evil-doers! The wretched man could not bear this last unconscious act of retribution. Driven wild by remorse and fear, he wrote a full confession of his crime, sent it to proper authorities, and then deliberately put an end to his miserable existence.

Presentiments,

AND

HOW THEY WERE FULFILLED.

———

I SHALL never forget that night upon the broad, shining waters of the Mississippi! The weary day had gone by, and with the evening shades, revived our drooping spirits, luring us to the pilot-house for social chat and music, spite of the danger lurking among the green leaves and blooming flowers upon the banks.

I well remember the picture as I took it then in my eye. The pilot stood at his wheel, apparently engaged in the management of the *Imperial* as she steamed royally over the flashing waves ; but there was a half smile upon his lips, which betrayed a hearty enjoyment of the gay sallies of wit shooting around him. Below us, the water glowed with ruddy gleams of light, such as can only light up the beauties of the Mississippi to sunset radiance. Purple shades crept in with the gold and crimson along the green banks, and the monotonous, yet musical splashing of the waves under the vessel, helped to kindle the romance of our natures beyond the limits of total reticence.

We were a large party, and the little pilot-house was full. The captain sat at my side, holding the guitar which he had brought up from the cabin, with exemplary patience, while the first clerk finished a story he was relating to an officer's pretty young wife opposite. The others listened in amazement, or looked out upon the scene, as best pleased them. When it was ended, a song was called for unanimously.

I did not feel like singing, yet the sweetness of the hour made me obliging. I took the guitar and accompanied myself in a gay little song from "La Traviata," which met with such signal success as to seal my doom for the remainder of the evening. Duets, trios and quartets followed, and we entered into the spirit of what we sang, after a while, most heartily. The sun was gone; the night deepened, and the moon rose calm and white over the still earth. Out upon the night, mingled with the rush of the waves, floated the voices, and the woods caught the echoes to send them back faintly, when we swept by a hill in our steady stateliness. By and by, I played only, while others sang, listening with all my soul alive and reveling in sweet sounds —listened till my arms wearied and my fingers fell limp among the strings of the instrument.

"Thank you, Miss," came from the pilot with a deep breath of satisfaction, as the music ceased. "I have passed many a night on this river, and have seen beautiful scenes; but no night has ever been happier and more beautiful than this. If I never see another, I shall not forget the pleasure this gives me."

Something in his last words struck me as sad, almost prophetic. As we made a curve round a bend in the stream, the moonlight fell full upon his face, and I saw that it was earnest, his dark eyes dreamy and sad. Yet as his glance met mine he smiled cheerily, and again glanced at the guitar.

"It is a little thing to give so much pleasure."

"Our chief pleasures come from little things often," I said.

"Yes. After all, though, it only speaks through some kindly hand—not of itself. A moment since, it almost brought tears to my eyes. Now it lies mute and lifeless," and he sighed.

Here a merry laugh rang out, and the captain's blue eyes turned roguishly upon the bronzed pilot.

"Romantic and sentimental, as I live. Why, Powell, what has come over you, man? You are not often guilty of such weakness."

"I guess it's the influence of the company I'm in," answered Mr. Powell, with a laugh.

"To be sure," broke in the pretty little creature opposite, whose soldier husband waited her at Memphis. "You forgot, captain, that the lady by your side is a 'story writer.' Oh, my! we must all look out, or the first thing we know, we shall all be in print."

I laughed,—perhaps was guilty of a slight blush, but thought to myself that they need not be afraid. Alas! that fair young creature little thought how soon the public prints would take her name and bear it far and wide over the country, or under what mournful circumstances.

"Can you tell stories as well as write them?" asked the captain, turning to me.

"I do not know. The little ones at home used to think so, when they gathered about me in the twilight."

"They are good critics, and I have a childish fondness for stories myself. Ladies and gentlemen, I vote for a story. What say you? Something impromptu and original."

"Yes, 'a story' 'a story,'" ran through the group, and I was helpless. It did not please me wholly, to be set up as 'entertainer general' to the party, but I had nothing better to do, and the next moment smiled at the momentary feeling of annoyance the request had called up.

"I will gratify you on one condition," I said. "You are to believe what I shall tell you religiously, and at the same time acquit me of any element of superstition in my nature. I shall tell you a very marvelous story, if any at all."

"Oh, of course we will believe you, and not think you a bit superstitious. Marvelous stories are exciting. Pray let us have it at once."

The captain's tone was playfully mocking, but I leaned back in sober earnestness against the glass of the window, and began without preface, as the little incident drifted to my mind :

"I was quite a young girl when the event occurred which I am going to relate—perhaps not more than ten years of age. Timid I had never been. On the contrary, I was rather rash and fearless than timid. Old stories of 'ghosts' and 'hobgoblins' only made me laugh, while the faintest whispers of a mysterious thing, set me into a search for an *exposé*. I generally inferred that there was a natural cause for everything, which a practical person might easily get at, with a little patience, and it was my delight to unravel mysteries and have a good laugh at the expense of others.

"One night our house was crowded with guests from the country, who had come into our little town to attend a 'protracted meeting,' as it was called there. These 'meetings' generally lasted a week,—two, and sometimes three, were added, if the excitement could be kept up—and now every available chamber was brought into use for the guests, until this interesting time should be over.

"I had been promoted from the nursery to a dear little white chamber of my own, but had to give it up to two young girls on this occasion, and share my sister's lower down the corridor. The door to it opened from the first landing above the main hall, and the light from the hall lamps lighted it brightly, so I was in no hurry to get up-stairs on account of the gas being extinguished above.

"The family, save my mother, were all at church that night. She remained at home to tend a little baby brother who was ill, and as my father was absent, my thoughts constantly turned to her until the excitement in the church completely absorbed my childish interest.

"When it was over I stole away from the others, and as it was but a little distance, ran home and hid myself in the recess of a window, where I sat think-

ing over the scene and trying to get rid of the doleful sounds of weeping and lamentation which still
rang in my ears.

"No one found me out. After awhile they went
up-stairs, and I could hear the merry little peals of
laughter peculiar to young girls when three or four
get together, floating down-stairs now and then.
Gradually all grew still. A servant came and put
the lights out in the parlor. Still I sat where I was
for some time—till every one except mamma was
asleep, indeed; then I stole softly up to sister Lillie's
room.

"As I opened the door a long line of light fell
across the carpet. As hers was extinguished, I left
the door open in order to see where to put my dress
when I disrobed, and sprang thoughtlessly into bed
without closing it. Lillie was tired and slept well.
She had not heard me, as I moved about softly, and
just as I was going to lay my head upon the pillow
I bethought me of the door.

"'Pshaw,' I said, and a little flash of annoyance
came over me. 'I have left the door open and
must get up again to close it. What a silly little
girl!'

"One more moment and I should have been upon
the floor had not an object attracted my attention
which prevented the quick movement I contemplated. A large cat came upon the threshold,
crossed the bar of light and stood out in the darkness of the room. I then perceived that the creature had innumerable eyes, at which I gazed steadily
in wonder, but with no thought of fear. I even

laughed a little hushed, amused laugh at the 'funny Tommy' which had so suddenly made its appearance. I could remember no cat in the neighborhood so large as this one; certainly none with so many eyes; and while I was puzzling myself over it the thing disappeared as quick as it came, though it did not go out at the door.

"As I went to the door to close it, I heard the sharp cry of my little pet brother from mamma's chamber on the first floor. She had let the nurse go home that night, and with the thought that she might want assistance with the sick child I went below. I found her sitting in a large chair hushing Neddie to sleep again when I entered. I told her what I came for, and sat down beside the grate, in which a pleasant little fire glowed brightly. Pretty soon Neddie was deposited upon his bed, and mamma drew her chair near the grate. She seemed wearied and sad, scarcely noticing my presence as she rocked herself back and forth gently.

"While I sat watching the flickering light upon her pale, sweet face, the soft, distinct pat of little feet fell upon my ears. I turned my head involuntarily and saw the great cat spring from the lower stair through the open door, and walk directly toward me. As it passed, I noticed that the color was gray, barred with black stripes around the body. Brushing against my side as it passed, the creature walked up to the wall, turned around, and, lifting itself upon its feet rabbit fashion, seemed to brace its back against the marble most determinedly.

"Filled with wonder and amazement, I took up

the poker and touched it. To my astonishment it
resisted me like a stuffed figure, without life or mo-
tion. A cry of surprise and consternation burst
from my lips!

"'Mamma! see what a strange cat! I saw it up
stairs awhile ago. Now it is here. Just take the
poker and see what an odd thing it is.'

"Mechanically she took the poker into her hand
and touched it, an amused smile upon her lips. But
the same instant a shade of surprise passed over her
features, and she bent an earnest look upon it which
doubly excited my wonder. My mother was no
timid visionary woman, but earnest, sound and
practical. I could trust her face as I trusted God's
beautiful sunshine, as an indication of genial Nature's
blessings and good-will to man; therefore her swiftly
changing features told me of alarm as well as surprise.

"In a moment she checked herself suddenly and
leaned back in her chair.

"'Child, go to bed! Why do you sit up so late?
I ought at once to have sent you back, for you ought
to have been asleep two hours ago.'

"'But the cat?' I said persistently. 'Isn't it
queer?'

"'Queer! what can there be in a cat that can be
called queer? My child, go to bed, and trouble
yourself no more about such silly things.'

"I obeyed her from a habit never to hesitate in
this—always to me pleasant—duty. I loved my
mother fondly, and her word was law. But as I
went up stairs it occurred to me that she sent me off

merely to prevent my growing excited over a really mysterious thing. She had always taken pains to root all fear and superstition from our natures. I had often heard her say that nothing could pain her more than to see a child of hers growing up a coward, either morally or physically.

"I had not more than reached the chamber before that strange thing—cat, or whatever it might be— was beside me. I heard it pat, pat, pat up the stairway, and then it touched my garments as it passed. You may not believe me, but I closed the door and went to bed, absorbed in thought of my strange visitor, but not at all frightened. Once or twice I looked out of my nest to catch the gleam of those kindling eyes, but it was gone-—at least it was not visible to me.

"On the following morning, I, of course, told the story to the others of the family, and got well laughed at for my pains. A vivid imagination had always been imputed to me, and in the face of all my fearlessness and freedom from superstition, they would insist upon it that I had been 'deep in some of my wild legends from the German, and that my imagination had played a trick upon the strength of them.' Expostulations were vain; they only laughed the more. In despair I appealed to mamma, but she only shook her head and smiled. Thus beset, I became proudly silent, till on the succeeding night, when the same 'vision' appeared to me. At the first glance I started up in bed and called out to Lillie. I had not expected to see it again, and the sight rejoiced me, as I thought it would prove that all was not attributable to my ' legends ' and my 'imagination.'

"Sister half rose upon her elbow, eager and trembling, but saw nothing, and fell back laughingly. I continued to talk fast, and try to point it out, until I grew excited and angry. She would not look, but only laughed the more, while I sat there in bed, looked at the strange, twinkling, perplexing eyes, and wept with vexation.

"From that time forth my 'ghost' was the pet joke of the household. I heard nothing else. They twitted me about it from morning till night, and usually my greeting upon leaving the bed was, 'Well, how's your ghost? Are his lordship's eyes as numerous and bright as ever?' Whereupon I would close my lips in proud disdain, and keep my own counsel. It came every night, invariably. No matter if the doors were shut or not. If I fell asleep without a glance from the bright eyes, I was sure to wake before morning and see them some- where in the room. But what was strangest of all, those eyes disappeared one by one, till only a single orb remained. Suddenly, while I gazed at that, sparks seemed to fly from the outer circle of the fiery globe, and continued until it was gone, and there was no more to be seen. That was the last visit I ever received from the mysterious cat, and ends my story."

A little storm of applause followed the effort I had made, mingled with merry laughter and jesting. Only the pilot was serious enough to ask if anything strange happened after that in the family.

"Neddie died," I answered with a great sob swelling suddenly in my throat at the pain recalled by his loss. "After that, my beautiful mother, whom we laid to sleep beside him ere the grass covered the little grave that held so much of our hope and joy. But if I talk this way you will think I *am* superstitious; so we will have something pleasanter. Though I acknowledge myself powerless to solve the mystery of my cat's visits, I still insist that there must have been a natural cause for this singular occurrence, and will not think of it, save to amuse myself and others. Suppose, friends, we go down to the cabin, and have a game of whist or chess."

The proposition was accepted readily, and the party descended the stairs merrily. In leaving, Mr. Powell detained me to say good-bye, and express his thanks. A depth and earnestness in his voice thrilled me as he held my hand for an instant in his hard, rough palm.

"Thank you for your music and your story, miss. When you are sleeping, I shall remember as I drift along the stream, how kindly you have tried to amuse us, and it will help me to pass the lonely night. It will be lonely, for I am very unaccountably depressed this evening. I am not often sad— seldom foreboding."

"But are both to-night, I see. I dare say it arises only from the sweet soft beauty of the night, and the dangers that lurk among those fragrant thickets we may pass. There are many dangerous places."

" Yes, we can't tell when a pack of those soulless guerillas may pour a volley of shot and shell into us. But I am used to that now, and scarcely think it troubles me. Don't let me detain you longer. Good-night, and God bless you."

A smile was upon my lips as I went below, for I was really amused at what seemed mere sentiment. Still, when I had time to think of it more, it impressed me to a restlessness I could not overcome. We played a game of whist after going to the cabin, then separated for the night, and it may have been only fancy, but I thought that there was more of earnestness than usual in our leave-takings, more of kindly interest and feeling expressed than on any other occasion. The gentlemen each shook hands with us, and the ladies left kisses upon each other's lips before entering their state-rooms. The pretty little wife of the young officer waiting at Memphis came up to me with a sweet, child-like manner that won my heart at once, putting her arms round my neck, and leaning a bright little head with a wealth of glossy tresses against my bosom.

" It makes me sorry to say good-night," she said, with a soft little laugh. " I'm sure I don't know why. Perhaps it's only because I've been so happy this evening, and am not sleepy now. Besides, you know we shall get to Memphis to-morrow, and I may never see any of you again. This is the curse of travel. All the nice friends we meet, drift away from us, and that is the last we know of them, nine cases out of ten."

" You will find a good substitute for all you have

met on this trip," I smilingly said, looking down at her till the quick blood leaped to her cheeks in crimson spots, and a glad light beamed from the blue eyes.

"Yes," softly and tenderly. "I shall find my own dear husband." Tone and words said: "All my world," in the frank utterance.

When she was sweetly sleeping hours later, I still sat inside of my state-room door, but looking through it and out into the calm night. I could not sleep, and my restless wakefulness made me inexpressibly sad. The thousands of stars beaming from a clear sky, were but as pitying eyes bent upon the earth, now the scene of contention and war such as history had never recorded. I was thinking of the many desolated homes; the many crushed hearts whose hopes had gone out with the red tide of warm young blood upon many battle-fields. Even that river, could it yield up its secrets, would tell tales of sorrow and bereavement almost surpassing credulity.

A sudden grating sound made me look out towards the shore. The Imperial had landed for wood, and in a moment more, the crew had planted a blazing torch upon the lower deck, by the light of which they worked sturdily till the huge pile of dry hickory had diminished.

Leaning over the guards, I watched the rough, uncouth figures as they passed between me and the ruddy light, thoughts of that strange, wild scene in the "Fire-worshipers" passing through my mind. While I looked, a splash in the water just beneath me, called my attention to the spot, and I saw the figure of a man lift itself from the water to the deck. It might have been one of the crew, who had taken an impromptu bath; but it did not seem quite likely. There was a cautiousness and silence in his movements suspicious, to say the least, and he had glided from sight too quickly to satisfy me that all was right. All my restlessness had gone in a moment. Ideas and visions floated away. There was necessity for immediate action, and I went straight to the stewardess to waken and send her to the captain.

Contrary to my expectation, she was sleepy and cross, uttering a prompt refusal to be "bothered with timid white folks' whims." So I went away, resolved to find the captain myself, and tell him what I had seen.

The Imperial was under way again, when I went out upon the guards. With steady clang the ponderous wheels began to move, propelling us swiftly down the stream. In a few moments the captain passed up the guards to ascend to his room in the Texas, and as he neared me I accosted him with my brief story. He listened with attention, and went immediately below to institute a search; but nothing being found, he soon came, back, smiled a little at what he evidently considered my womanly timidity, and bidding me good-night a second time, bowed himself into obscurity.

The prescience of coming evil grew strong upon me—so strong that I was angry at the seeming indifference displayed by the captain. The sentinel still paced upon the lower deck, and the whole crew was there. Still I was dissatisfied and sat down upon the side of my berth in thought. That evil was near, I *felt* rather than feared. But the shape did not define itself in my mind. Speculation did not avail me in rendering the matter any clearer, as the hours sped by, and I should at length have retired, endeavoring to forget my restlessness, had not a singular odor penetrated my state-room just as I rose to disrobe.

Softly unclosing my door, I looked out and saw a thick cloud of smoke rising along the side of the Imperial from the lower deck. That instant I knew that the vessel was on fire, but even then, paused to assure myself. By leaning over the guards, I could faintly see through the smoke, a red glare, and a line of flame leaping along a quantity of hay which was stowed away in large bales on deck. Near these were some barrels of oil which I remembered to have seen when visiting the machinery below, and this had taken fire. Though I had not paused the space of a minute, the terrible element was making rapid leaps toward the cabin, while the confusion on deck had become awful. The men shouted hoarsely, while the horses plunged in mad fright, screaming with almost human voices in their agony.

I have always thanked God for presence of mind during moments of danger, and it was not denied me in that awful time. In less than a minute I had thrust my purse into my bosom, dropped all superfluous portions of dress, and taken off my shoes. The next thing was to tie on a life preserver which hung by my berth. and then to run to the other state-rooms. I knew by the commotion that the inmates had been awakened, and it was now my purpose, having prepared myself, to aid them all in my power.

The scene which met my gaze in the next moment beggars description. The state-rooms were vacated, the inmates rushing out into the cabin, pallid with fright, and giving vent to such screams as never before greeted my ears. The fatal truth had spread already, and the word "fire" quivered upon every lip. The gentlemen had rushed out also, without dressing, save in their pantaloons; and many were as feeble and helpless in their fright as the ladies. I saw at once that little help could be expected from them.

"Friends," I cried earnestly, "try to calm yourselves for a moment and act. Let each lady tie about herself the life preserver in their rooms. Do not try to save any baggage or articles of dress. Life is worth more than all these, and we must take to the water. Be quick, and do it without confusion. I will help you."

Some obeyed readily; others fell helpless to the floor, while a few rushed about wildly, screaming, not knowing which way to go. Amidst the clamor and confusion, I made myself understood sufficiently to give directions to their movements.

"Go to the stern of the boat and stand still. The fire is nearer the bow, and you cannot escape forward, even if they succeeded in running in to the shore. Those who cannot swim will have to be taken off in the boats. But for your lives do not rush about so confusedly. You expose yourselves to the danger you would avoid."

All now burst through the door, and I hastened to find Mrs. Nelson, the officer's wife, whom I had missed in the excitement. She was lying upon the floor of her room in a deep swoon. To seize a life preserver, tie it around her waist, and then dash water from a basin in her face, was the work of a minute. She gasped, started up and looked at me wildly.

"Be quiet," I said as assuredly as I could. "We are in danger, but a little care may save us all. I can swim, and with this life preserver on, you cannot sink, so if we get into the water, as we must, I will help you to the shore. Only be calm, and do not let fright unnerve you."

She clung to me like a child, while I half carried, half led her out. But what folly to hope for reason in a moment like that! With all their efforts, they could not run the ponderous vessel ashore, before the whole of the lower deck was enveloped in flames, now leaping in great red tongues along the guards, till the heat scorched us. The boats had been cast to the water, and one man, braver and steadier than the others, seemed to have taken into his hands the management of them. The captain, in despair of saving us by other means, had by this time made his way back to the stern of the vessel, and began to lower the ladies into the boats.

The first two loads went ashore safely, but as the fire roared nearer, the people grew more mad and rash, leaping into the water headlong. Holding Mrs. Nelson by the hand to keep her back, I saw them go down—rise, sink again, and rise struggling. Some struck out for the shore; others went down to rise not again, swallowed up by the waves, now lashed into billows by the rocking of the vessel. Suddenly, with a wild plunge, Mrs. Nelson escaped my grasp, and leaped down to the water. I saw the flutter of her white night-robe for a moment, then followed her. My heart was in it. I thought of the waiting husband at Memphis, and for his sake resolved to save her if it was in human power. Yet as I rose to the surface of the water, I could scarcely buffet the strength of the troubled waves, and it was a minute before I saw her. She had risen a second time, and quite near me. The force of the water drove her under, but could not keep her there with the life-preserver on, and I took courage. By a few strokes I reached the little white form, and bore her up with one hand.

A glad cry burst from her white lips, now vividly lighted up by the burning steamer. Her eager, wild eyes were fixed upon me with a look I can never forget. Both little hands grasped me like a vice.

"Don't do that!" I gasped. "Let go, and trust yourself to me. We are near the shore, and the current is not strong. You must lie still—I will swim out with you. But if you do not obey I must let you go, or both will be drowned."

With a still more frightened look, she released me, resigning herself to my care. I would have died to save her then, in her child-like beauty and helplessness. With one hand I kept hold of her, bearing her along as I swam, and slowly neared the

bank. It was laborious work, but the glimpses I
caught of her sweet, white face, nerved me afresh,
and gave new impetus to my motions. Six yards
more would have landed me safely, when a long
black object drifted directly across us. I could see
that it was ponderous, but could not tell what it was.
The end struck Mrs. Nelson's temple with a dull,
heavy sound, driving her against me forcibly, but,
with the quick instinct of self-preservation, I dived
beneath, bearing her down with me. We rose beyond by a little more than a yard, and a few more
strokes brought me to the land.

Fortunately the steep bank at that point had been
worn down in ruts, and afforded me a species of
steps by which I endeavored to mount to the level
earth. Mrs. Nelson was a dead weight, and, wearied
with the double effort of swimming and taking care
of her, it was a minute before I could recover
strength to proceed, and rested myself upon the
end of a log lying on the edge of the water. I
thought my charge had fainted, and just there a
shadow concealed her face from me. But as soon
as I could get breath fairly, I took her arms, and
placing them round my neck, clambered up the
bank. Then I was so intent upon success, I scarcely
heeded the weight of the tiny figure which I held
with one hand while assisting myself with the other.

A moment's hard labor brought me to a place of
safety, and I laid my burden down upon a little
grass-plot. The flames rose high and fiercely now,
and the water was still full of the struggling pas-
sengers. The captain had leaped from the guards,

and I saw him swimming toward me, a figure held
above water by one arm. But all seemed to have
been rescued from the steamer. Not even one of
the crew was left. All had leaped to the water and
made for the shore. With a great sigh of relief, I
bent down over Mrs. Nelson.

There was no sign of life. The pale face was uplifted, every feature lighted up by the glare from the
fated Imperial. A second glance showed me an ugly
black mark upon the temple, where that thing had
struck her, extending back under the hair. On close
examination, a deep dent in the skull struck a chill
to my heart. I felt her pulse—her heart. They
were still. In my very arms, so near to safety that
my heart had beat with grateful thanks, she had
been smitten dead in an instant!

I could not help it then. All the pent up feeling
which I had resolutely locked within my own bosom
burst forth now, and on my knees beside her I sobbed bitterly. I had done all I could—exhausted my
strength to save this one, and in the last moment
failed. Now with bowed head I heard as in a confused dream the roar of the flames—the cries of the
people—the lashing and hissing of the water as the
flaming objects fell into it. I only raised my head
when a more fearful excitement broke forth, and a
look at the burning steamer revealed to my startled
gaze the pilot, Mr. Powell, standing still at his post,
now powerless to help himself. He had labored to
the last vainly trying to land the steamer, but, deserted by all the others, found it impossible to accomplish his purpose. Now he stood with wistful eyes,

looking down from his perch, while the smoke and
flame curled around him.

"Jump into the river, Powell!" shouted the captain, who had just landed, pantingly. But the advice was vain. There was no path left by which he
could reach the side of the boat without rushing
into the fire itself, and the next moment he was hidden from sight.

At this moment the steamer trembled violently—
gave a great leap forward, and scattered thousands
of burning fragments into the air. The boilers had
exploded, and poor Mr. Powell was in eternity!

I can not dwell upon the horrors of that night
longer. Just at day dawn, those left of us, were
taken on board another steamer bound for Memphis,
and I had Mrs. Nelson conveyed to my room that I
might take her to her husband. An hour or two
would bring us to that point, and I knew that I was
able to do this much for him at least.

Others of the dead formed the complete list on
that sad passage. A dozen or more lay sheeted upon
the deck—the stiff outlines of their figures showing
through the white folds chillingly.

When we landed at Memphis there was a rush on
board from the wharf, and then—oh! what a scene!
I could not bear to witness it. In my room, with
that little figure laid out upon the berth where I
had composed her in that last sleep, I sat down and
waited until a hand fell on the door, and a pallid
face shone in upon me. I knew whose it was. He
was searching for her, and with one fearful groan
fell upon his knees at her side as I pointed to the

bed. I had heard her describe him, and his captain's uniform confirmed the impression, the moment he came, of his identity as her husband.

Gently I drew the sheet from her face, then slipped from the room through the door opening upon the guards. I heard his sobs, deep, fearful, heart-breaking—as I stood outside, and the tears ran down my cheeks like rain. It seemed then as if my heart must break.

Later, he came to thank me for what I had done; but it only added to the pain I suffered. I am afraid I felt rebellious, and ill-disposed to acknowledge the blessing of the life spared to myself.

Those that followed were sad days at Memphis. Some were buried in a strange land, others embalmed and taken home. Some were so badly burned that they died soon after, while others suffered for weeks ere they recovered. Mrs. Nelson was one that was buried there, and I thought with agony, as I saw the loving husband bending speechlessly over her grave, of the different meeting she had anticipated. Poor little wife! Poor husband!

When, a few months later, I heard that Captain Nelson had fallen before Vicksburg I was glad of it. It seemed a merciful shot which reunited them in eternity, and I knew that it was best. What happiness is there in life when the heart is utterly bereaved?

It was, doubtless, a guerilla who had succeeded in secreting himself on board the Imperial and destroyed her. But the truth has never been ascertained fully.

The Coquette's Fate.

"Oh! Nellie, Nellie! Oh! Nellie, Nellie!"

A tiny pair of white hands raised deprecatingly, and a pair of large, violet eyes sought her face, bearing in their depths an expression of entreaty beautiful to behold; but the proud face of Nellie Raymond turned away, perhaps to shut out that beautiful vision, and a low, trilling laugh ran over her red lips.

"Oh! Nellie, how can you be so heartless? How can you lead a man on to believe you love him, and then, when his heart is yours, with all its great, deep font of manly love and tenderness, laugh in his face and bid him go from your presence—hopeless, despairing. I tell you, Nellie Raymond, you will some day have to account for the misery you have wrought."

"Do you think so?" lightly. "Ah, well!"

"But it will *not* be 'well.' You will see it in a different light some day. I could not close my eyes an hour in peaceful slumber were my life so weighed down with evil deeds such as yours."

"Evil deeds! Really, Alice, you are harsh!" exclaimed Nellie, a flush of momentary mortification and anger staining her white forehead.

"Dear Nellie, what is the use of calling things by other than the right names? If I seem severe, I only tell you the truth, and you know that I have ever been your best friend—candid and frank."

"Well, Allie, you might have a little more regard for one's feelings."

"Have *you* regard for the feelings of others, Nellie? There is a good old book in which a glorious teacher said: 'Do unto others as you would have them do unto you.' Now, how far do you carry out this rule?"

"Oh, Allie, spare me, for pity's sake — don't preach to me now; I'm not in a mood for it."

But Allie was relentless.

"You did not spare poor Horace Morton, whom you so cruelly deceived, and then drove him from you with despair in his heart, and the burden of a hopeless life. The green sod of an Italian vale to-day covers two hearts that loved you but too wildly, and whose reward was a pistol-shot after weeks of weary wandering, and a hopeless, pining life, which soon sank beneath its weight of sorrow. Then there is another—a widow's only son and pride— who frets his life away in a mad-house—a *mad-house*, Nellie, to which your cruelty consigned him. Oh! Nellie Raymond, better a thousand times despoil your rare face of its dangerous beauty than bear the load of sin it brings upon you, for it *is* fearful."

A slight quiver in the erect frame of the beautiful girl was the sole response, and Alice continued sadly—

"Poor Walter Mayfield! Sometimes I pass the window of the cell in which he is confined, and catch a glimpse of his haggard face, and he always smiles like a pleased child when he catches sight of me. Then I contrast him now with what he once was, and weep in spite of myself over the wreck of a strong, great life. He used to be so pleasant and gay always, yet he was strong and self-reliant when anything occurred to call forth energy or action. Oh! he was a noble, handsome man, and now he is a frail, helpless, feeble man—a hopeless maniac! God help him!"

Nellie's face wore an expression of mingled grief, defiance, and mortification; but she remained silent for a few moments, watching the tears as they rolled slowly over Alice May's cheeks. In a little while Alice looked up and said mournfully:

"And my own dear, only brother will be your next victim. Oh, Nellie, he is all I have—I am alone in the world with him only to love me—spare him to me, for the love of mercy!"

Nellie rose with a hotly flushed cheek and flashing eye.

"Allie, how can you talk thus? But I tell you, Allie May, if art or beauty can bring your proud, cold brother to the feet of woman, he shall come to mine. He *shall* love me."

"And if he does, and you turn him from you, you will murder him. Once unbend his proud nature, and unlock the founts of tenderness in his heart, and then cast him from you, and see the consequences. Oh! Nellie Raymond, there are enough murders on your soul already. Spare yourself, if you spare no other."

The last words were unheeded, for Nellie had swept from the room, and then poor little Allie May bowed her head upon the sofa cushion and sobbed piteously. She had warned her brother repeatedly, but he seemed heedless, and with an aching heart the gentle little sister looked forth to a hopeless, desolate life for him who had ever been her all on earth.

Several weeks passed away, and little Allie May stood before the altar. The man she had chosen was noble, true, and good, and for *her* feet a bright path lay before her; but there was another to whom her eyes wandered uneasily—Clarence May—and who hovered incessantly round the gay butterfly form of the proud syren, Nellie Raymond. Her dark eyes flashed with triumph, and a low laugh bubbled continually over her lips, as the proud man bent his handsome, stately head with such devotion. Allie's sweet lips quivered when she saw him bend down and whisper in her ear, and hear the request that she would walk with him upon the piazza, and the two wandered off.

The moon shone brightly, and Clarence May, drawing Nellie's arm within his own, walked slowly down the broad gravel walk, his face upturned towards the calm stars, and a smile of infinite happiness softly wreathing his sweet mouth.

"Nellie;" he spoke very low and softly. "Nellie, I am very happy to-night—happier than I had ever hoped to be, and I want some one to sympathize with me in it. Allie has another just now to occupy her attention. May I tell it you?"

"Yes," she whispered softly. "None can share your happiness and sympathize with you more freely. Tell me all."

For a moment he was silent, only stretching out his hand to draw her down upon a seat beside him. After awhile he began half dreamily and very softly:

"I once believed that I could never find a woman whom I could love fully and truly—with such a love as I *must* cherish for the woman whom I would call my wife; but I have found her, Nellie—why do you tremble so—a sweet, pure-faced little thing, fresh and fragrant as a budding rose, gentle as the summer breezes, and gay and glad as the lark whose song she trills the whole day long. Tell me that you rejoice in my happiness. Tell me that you will love my little wife that is to be, sweet Lilly Walton?"

But Nellie's lips were rigid and ashen, and she rose up, quivering like an aspen.

"Oh, I am ill!" she gasped. "Take me in the house."

Clarence May rose hastily and supported her with his arm, but she nearly repulsed him as she planted her foot fiercely upon the gravel. She had learned to love the man with all the hidden passion and fire of her strong nature, and now he told her he had won another, and that other was only a poor, but beautiful seamstress, in a rich man's family. Oh, it was too much! He knew Nellie Raymond's weakness, and he had punished her fearfully, though he believed in his heart that she was incapable of deep feeling.

Alice went to her in answer to her brother's call, and, when every one was gone from the room, she held out her arms to her, white and stricken, with an anguished moan—

" Oh, Allie, I gave him my whole heart, and he *loves another !*"

Then she sank down white and lifeless, and it was many weeks ere Nellie Raymond woke to life and consciousness. Then she was a changed, repentant woman; but it was hard to feel the soft touch of a little hand, and see the light form of *his* wife bending so pityingly. Oh, the punishment of her "evil deeds" *had* come, and it was heavy and bitter!

Nellie Raymond is Nellie Raymond still, but she has grown into a calm, dignified, but lovely woman. She can sympathize with the suffering, because she has suffered; and strives, by tenderness and love to her fellow-men, in a measure to atone for the misery she wrought while yet in the noon of her pride and selfish love for admiration.